PENG

THE WOMAN WHO FLEW

Nasreen Jahan is a novelist, short story writer and literary editor of the fortnightly *Anyadin*. Her short stories began appearing in the early eighties, and after publishing five collections she published her first novel, *Urukkoo* (*The Woman Who Flew*), in 1993. It won the Philips Literary Prize. She received the Alaol Literary Award in 1995 for children's fiction. She also received the prestigious Bangla Academy Award in 2000. Jahan is prolific, with fifty titles to her credit to date, and has recently started writing for the stage as well. She lives in Dhaka.

Kaiser Haq was educated at the universities of Dhaka and Warwick and is professor of English at Dhaka University currently on a visiting appointment at the University of Liberal Arts Bangladesh. He is a poet, essayist and translator and has published seven poetry collections and edited two poetry anthologies. Haq has been a Commonwealth Scholar, Senior Fulbright Scholar, Vilas Fellow, Royal Literary Fund Fellow and Café Poet at the UK Poetry Society's Poetry Café. He is a veteran of the Bangladesh independence war and lives in Dhaka.

the WOMAN WHO FLEW

NASREEN JAHAN

TRANSLATED FROM THE BENGALI BY
KAISER HAQ

PENGUIN BOOKS

PENGUIN BOOKS

Published by the Penguin Group

Penguin Books India Pvt. Ltd, 11 Community Centre, Panchsheel Park, New Delhi 110 017, India

Penguin Group (USA) Inc., 375 Hudson Street, New York, New York 10014, USA

Penguin Group (Canada), 90 Eglinton Avenue East, Suite 700, Toronto, Ontario, M4P 2Y3, Canada (a division of Pearson Penguin Canada Inc.)

Penguin Books Ltd, 80 Strand, London WC2R 0RL, England

Penguin Ireland, 25 St Stephen's Green, Dublin 2, Ireland (a division of Penguin Books Ltd)

Penguin Group (Australia), 250 Camberwell Road, Camberwell, Victoria 3124, Australia (a division of Pearson Australia Group Pty Ltd)

Penguin Group (NZ), 67 Apollo Drive, Rosedale, Auckland 0632, New Zealand (a division of Pearson New Zealand Ltd)

Penguin Group (South Africa) (Pty) Ltd, 24 Sturdee Avenue, Rosebank, Johannesburg 2196, South Africa

Penguin Books Ltd, Registered Offices: 80 Strand, London WC2R 0RL, England

First published in Bengali as *Urukkoo* by Mowla Brothers, Bangladesh 1993

First published by Penguin Books India 2012

Copyright © Nasreen Jahan 1993

Translation copyright © Syeda Zinath Haq 2012

All rights reserved

10 9 8 7 6 5 4 3 2 1

ISBN 9780143065142

Typeset in Minion by Guru Typograph Technology, New Delhi
Printed at Chaman Offset Printers, Delhi

To Amma

Translator's Preface

Modern Bangladeshi women's writing can be traced back to Begum Rokeya Sakhawat Hossain (1880–1932), who was a pioneer feminist in a subcontinental as well as a global context. A string of distinguished names followed over the decades. Even if we limit ourselves to Bengali fiction, Razia Khan, Dilara Hashem, Rizia Rahman and Selina Hossain will feature prominently in accounts of post-Partition literature. They are the seniors in the field. They have scrupulously addressed 'feminine' as well as 'feminist' issues, but generally without breaching the conventions of literary decorum that have been in place since the nineteenth century.

A younger generation, imbued with the spirit of the new feminism that evolved out of the radical sixties, began to make itself heard from the late seventies onward. I daresay the first name likely to occur to the reader is Taslima Nasreen, although she is seriously flawed as a novelist. Her poetry is more successful, but it is as an essayist and columnist that she has made her most significant contribution. Her unabashed exposé of the unmentionable was vivid frontline reportage on the gender war, and her exile has deprived Bangladesh of a vibrant presence. More significant as fiction writers are some of her internationally little-known peers, among whom Nasreen Jahan stands out, alongside, say, Shaheen Akhter, Audity Falguni, Monira Kayes.

Nasreen was born in 1964 into a middle-class family in a remote village in Haluaghat in the greater Mymensingh district of Bangladesh—on the face of it hardly the most propitious beginning for one with a literary ambition. Fortunately, her parents valued literature, and she did not lack encouragement. Her father revered Rabindranath Tagore, declaring that he was a prophet. He was also drawn to the occult and set great store by horoscopes. Nasreen's predicted a literary career and her family waited expectantly for the talent to show. Her earliest productions were simple rhymes, but when in high school and no more than sixteen, she had a short story accepted for the prestigious literary page of a national daily.

She moved to Dhaka and at nineteen married the poet Ashraf Ahmed, who after publishing three volumes of verse swapped the lyric muse for corporate prosperity and has been an exemplarily supportive husband. Nasreen's output has been prolific—about fifty titles to date. She had a half-dozen well-received short story collections behind her when she published *Urukkoo* (*The Woman Who Flew*) in 1993, the first and still the best known of her novels. It won the Philips Literary Award in Bangladesh. Critics duly noted the appearance of a landmark text in Bangladeshi fiction. Uniquely, it gave utterance to a lone, embattled young woman facing the pressures of a fractured life amidst the brick-and-bamboo jungle of the Third World conurbation that Dhaka had turned into since the eighties. It's a nervy, unrestrained, first-person narrative, with straining syntax, verging at times on stream of consciousness, and it is unlike anything else in Bangladeshi writing.

Among admired writers Nasreen lists Edgar Allan Poe, Franz Kafka, Fyodor Dostoevsky and Gabriel Garcia Márquez—all read in Bengali translations (she reads little English, less than most Bangladeshi writers). And in Bengali literature, Manik Bandopadhyaya, Bibhutibhusan Bandopadhyaya and Jagadish Gupta, who dealt with taboo subjects like incest a hundred years ago, but gave up writing in the face of Tagore's virulent criticism. All these writers inspired Nasreen rather than influencing her. Nasreen's writerly voice is distinctive, unmistakably so, down to the emotional turbulence and neurotic logorrhoea.

A first-person narrative like *Urukkoo* is bound to raise questions regarding its possible autobiographical roots. Certain connections between the text and its author are obvious. The novel's female protagonist and the author share the same initial; both come from the mofussil middle class; the fathers of both are interested in the occult. With a bit of research, I daresay, one could find many more parallels; and yet the novel is not disguised autobiography. The narrative is set in motion by Nina's failed marriage, a situation diametrically opposite to that of the author. Like so many other novelists, Nasreen has created a persona through whom she can project her grimly realistic and disturbingly candid vision of contemporary Bangladesh.

It is a sign of the times that she identifies female sexuality as a new area to explore. As she told an interviewer,

There are very few writers who have dealt with feminine sexuality. Women especially are very hesitant to bring this aspect into their works. And I am sorry to say that our male writers have little idea about female sexuality. As you may have noticed, in my works sex is often presented as a painful experience. In fact, most women are unaware of sexual pleasure. I have talked to many women about this. And most of them, especially from the lower strata of society, consider sex as something akin to other household chores and derive no pleasure from it. I have dealt with homosexuality and adolescent sexuality too and I am not hesitant about the subject, as sex is always present in our psyche.*

At the same time Nasreen firmly distances herself from feminist activists, though out of scepticism and not lack of sympathy for their struggle.

Like many modern novels *Urukkoo* is constructed around a simple plot, with the focus on psychological and sociological points of moment. The narrative seesaws between the past and present, between Nina's mofussil hometown and metropolitan domicile. Nina lives alone in a room sublet from another young couple, Shanu and Kamal; they bicker often and Shanu seems to resent Nina's independence. Nina's weekdays are divided between the subtle and the not-so-subtle harassments faced by a single woman, a divorcee at that: in the workplace; groping hands on crowded buses; and lonely hours in her damp, poky room. What little she earns has to be shared with her family and her younger brother Arefin, who is often on the run for his political activities.

A central character in the novel is Abdul Ali Majumdar, a moneylender in Nina's hometown who practises a bizarre mix of Islamic mysticism and Tantric occultism. He could have come straight out of an Orientalist fantasy, but the fantastic here is all too real. This explains why some critics place Nasreen in the magic realist camp. Majumdar's mesmeric hold on Nina's beautiful younger sister is disturbing yet psychologically convincing.

Urukkoo is defined by the *Samsad Bengali–English Dictionary* as 'flying; capable of or given to flying; very restless or

*Translated from Bengali by Kaiser Haq.

impatient'. It is a well-chosen title. Nina and Rezaul's friend Satyajit at one point lauds her for having taken off. In so far as she has asserted her individual freedom, she is indeed urukkoo.

Both in the context of Bangladeshi literature and of world literature, *Urukkoo* is an interesting example of the new post-feminist woman speaking out. In an engaging comparative study, Professor Mostain Billah of Chittagong University, Bangladesh, has pointed out a series of parallels between *Urukkoo* and Arundhati Roy's *The God of Small Things* (1997), both, incidentally, written by women born in the early sixties and to Bengali fathers. Although the novels are stylistically very different—Roy's being more controlled, while Nasreen's is often like a demented monologue—Billah finds a profound similarity between the protagonists of the novels, Nina and Ammu. Both have weak and unsuccessful men as fathers; both contract unhappy marriages that break up; both earn the opprobrium of immorality. Such incidental similarities serve to underscore the fact that both novels respond to the continuing conflict between modernity and the tenacious traditional patriarchy that dominates the subcontinent. And that is why they are valuable existential documents of our times.

To Parvez Hossein, short story writer

By the time I'd found the house, daylight was fast running out. All this time, despite the many twists and turns in the lane, the open drains, decomposing coconut husks, insufferable drift of thick dust, there was an enthusiasm at work—the house had to be located somehow! I had got off the rickshaw at a bend on the main road. There was sunlight still, albeit wan. The scribbled house number in my hand, I was about to start looking, when the air grew hazy with rain. I dashed through the lazy drizzle to seek shelter on a narrow roadside veranda. As I took a deep breath and positioned myself, I noticed a man right behind me, rolling up his wet trouser legs. There were others too—a couple of beggars swaddled in a tattered quilt, fast asleep. Parts of their bodies showed embarrassingly through holes in the quilt. I began to feel very uneasy in the presence of the man with the rolled-up trousers.

The streetlights came on though it was still afternoon. The rain was a steady drizzle and the lamplight seemed to drip. The pitted, broken lane grew hazy. Opposite it loomed the indistinct white shape of a huge house. Looking at that blank whiteness I felt dizzy, my throat felt parched. My limbs trembled. I remembered I hadn't eaten anything since noon. Instead of going to work I had spent the whole day just romping around. I was experiencing such unrestricted liberty after many days. I had let myself loose after many days.

The rain draped the surroundings in a widow's white garb. A man in the building in front picked up a flowerpot by its rim and carried it indoors; his expression made it obvious that he might be a gardener, but he could never be a father to his plants.

I felt stifled. There was no way I could shake off the spell of that pale, liquid emanation of nature. It held me with magnetic force. What a vulnerable state to be in! I stared at the white spray and willed myself to move forward, defying the magnetic attraction. Suddenly, involuntarily, my tongue stuck out. I projected it further into space. I was nearly drenched by the spray when someone almost bellowed from behind, 'Hey, what are you doing? You're getting wet!'

When I withdrew till I had my back to the wall—literally— I discovered myself in a perilous vacuum. Strange, the man who had been rolling up his trousers in preparation for a dash through the rain now stood at ease. Even stranger was the fact that the two beggars had vanished from the veranda. But even if they left, one would expect the foul smell of the tattered, soiled quilt in which they had wrapped themselves to linger. I peered through the thick vaporous screen and saw that they had indeed gone, without leaving a trace. I had no inkling when they went off into the rain. Now there was only that man and me. He had unrolled his trousers and was staring at the street. But why had he revised his decision all of a sudden? I glanced anxiously at his impassive face. Cold waves of apprehension flowed down my body. A flock of crows crowded on the water reservoir on top of a high-rise building. The rain kept getting heavier, drowning me in billows of spray. It grew misty all around. In the vacant, grassy plot by the road a few frogs

2

engaged in full-throated croaking. What if the man grabbed me from behind? My cold skin broke out in goosebumps. In this rain, by this deserted lane, would I be able to defend myself?

Damn! It was turning into a melodramatic Bengali film. I had almost shaken off my fears when I heard the sound of breathing right behind me.

I was fidgeting inside when I noticed that the man, standing still at a respectable distance, had shifted his gaze from the road towards me. There was profound perplexity in his eyes. At once I realized that it wasn't breathing I had heard but the squally wind. O timid soul! In order to cover up for my weakness I drew myself up straight as a steel rod.

I dredged myself up from the depths, put on a silly, wooden smile and approached the man.

'Excuse me,' I stammered, 'I've been looking for this house, number –. Do you know where it is?'

I could now scrutinize the man in his blue trousers and white shirt from head to foot. His shirt looked like it hadn't been washed in a week. The collar was begrimed. Probably he hadn't shaved in three days or so. Wrinkles showed through the bristle. The eyes looked watery. His entire countenance was utterly grotesque. His attitude and bearing did not appear reassuring, but I overcame my hidden fears, especially when he said he could help me find the house when the rain let up. Then he added, 'Where are you from?'

There you go! Now he would ask: What did I do, how many brothers and sisters did I have, what did my husband do—the questions would go on till they scraped the bottom of things.

So I replied quickly, 'Rayer Bazar,' and stared at the road.

By then the rain had begun to move away. Mild light spread all around. I overcame my inhibition and stretched out a hand towards the light. Soon the man and I came out on to the street. He led me into alleys to the right and left, asking various people about the address I'd given him. I followed him in silence. At some point, when we were supposed to be close to the desired address, he suddenly consulted his watch and became agitated. He told me hurriedly, 'If you go right, then left you'll probably come upon the house.' I thanked him profusely. He left in precipitate haste and I was alone again.

Then I had to spend even more time looking. The simple right and left that the man had explained to me turned out to be inaccurate, for houses in Dhaka are not arranged in an ordered manner. My nerves were getting frayed because of hunger and weariness. I came upon a huge construction site where many labourers were at work. Bricks and other construction materials were piled up in front. It was disconcerting to have my feet slip between the long iron rods laid end to end. Just then an irascible-looking fellow came removing the rods one by one and stopped in front of me, but in reply to my query said flatly that he didn't know the house whose number I'd mentioned. Now I felt really helpless. Dusk was sucking away the last remnants of daylight. Deep shadows were spreading all around. Muddy water had collected in the potholes in the road and I could feel the wet sand clinging to the lower border of my sari. If I tried to shake it off my entire body tingled with an unpleasant sensation. I began to skip on my toes in the hope of saving myself somewhat from the badly damaged road. Most of the buildings in the locality were unplastered and some of the red bricks protruded like buck teeth. Maybe the house-owners had rented them out in a half-completed state after taking a fat advance from the tenants with a false promise to finish the construction. There was a power outage. The faces of people in the darkened windows looked queer.

4

It had been over two years and a half since I'd set up home. I doubt if anyone else has had such a varied experience of life in rented accommodation within such a brief period. In that dark, perilous road, my feet seemed to slip, plunging me into my past, but I drew back. Which way would I go now?

The question upset me no end. And then—splash! I stepped into a small hole. Ouch! The big toe had broken probably. Gritting my teeth, I tried to retrieve my foot. It didn't do much good, for the slipper was stuck fast in the mud. I lost my patience. Everything in front of my eyes seemed to sway a little. I was overwhelmed by the profound darkness, I was seized with nausea. On top of that I felt terribly hungry.

Should I turn back and return home? A mysterious fear induced dire thoughts in my head. Better die under a truck on this dark road than go back there. In an instant I shook off all qualms and with near-desperation approached a ruffianly young man. 'Please, Bhaiya—'

My entreaty seemed to provide him an opportunity to display his abilities. He almost took me by the hand and escorted me to the gate of the house, where he asked abruptly, 'Are you related to Irfan Sahib?' Even at this impertinent question from his bidi-smoking mouth I maintained my equanimity. Relaxing in the abundant breeze, I replied in staccato tones, 'Oh yes, he is my uncle.'

'Go right in,' he said, and disappeared.

But after all the hassle the pleasure of finding the object of my search began to subside at a steady rate. My entire existence seemed to become shrouded in a thick fog. Irfanul Kabir! I was at last standing at his front door. All our lives we hadn't got anything from him; no sympathy, pity, affection— no, no hatred either. We didn't even see him, such was his indifference towards us, and yet I had become so anxious to find his house.

5

I felt my heart knock against my ribcage. In the calm shade of evening I stood transfixed by despair and irresolution.

The house was an old one. Its architecture belonged to the feudal age of zamindars. The plaster had peeled off in patches. The house had a front yard with unkempt grass. A luxuriant neem tree obscured a part of the front wall. A flock of crows perched on the top branches, cawing loudly. The darkness deepened, and the light from the lamp post grew in intensity. Amber light trickled out of the house through chinks in the doors and windows. The house and its grounds were encircled by a boundary wall. My feet felt heavy as I stepped up to the door. I was there, then. My steps were ungainly. There would be no turning back today.

I knocked and held my breath. I was devastated by wariness and anxiety. The sudden onset of intolerable self-consciousness had induced such sweating that I looked as if I had taken a shower. Just then the door opened. In front of me stood a middle-aged lady, her hair untied, dressed in a Jessore-stitch sari. I was at a loss for words, but she ushered me in. I walked in very self-consciously and settled into a sofa. 'Well,' I began. 'Mother had given me the address. I, I mean, you probably don't know me. My father is Sobhan Tarafdar. Irfan Uncle is his cousin.'

I saw the lady give a start. But the next moment she had recovered her aristocratic poise. 'I recognized you,' she said. 'I suppose you live in Dhaka—at least that's what I had heard.' Her curiosity satisfied, she sat down calmly in another sofa.

'You must be Auntie,' I began, but then, as always happened in such circumstances, I grew flustered and said, 'So you know that I live in Dhaka? I mean, you know me? How extraordinary! But how?' As soon as I had asked the question I got up, like someone slow on the uptake, and stepped closer with the intention of touching her feet as a token of respect, but

I couldn't go through the motion in the face of her protests. She stood to stop me from diving for her feet. As we stood facing each other she said, 'Someone said that one of Tarafdar Sahib's daughters lived in Dhaka. Anyway, make yourself comfortable, I'll be back in a moment. You see, this is what happens when people don't keep in touch, even blood relations don't know each other.'

I was about to stand up again when she almost expostulated with me to sit down. Then she went in with slow, soft steps. Now, as was my wont, I looked around the room.

The interior, like the façade, reflected the taste of the age of zamindars. The white wall in the niches had become discoloured. Even though the room was huge, a single 100-watt bulb was the only source of light. As a result my eyes felt strained in the jaundice-yellow atmosphere. The two massive sofa sets were upholstered in velvet. Geckos roamed the walls. Their free and easy movements suggested they were pampered pets. In one corner on the eastern side the stump of a tea plant held a vase in which a bunch of plastic flowers were gathering dust. A stuffed falcon hung on the wall, heightening the impression of antiquity. The rug on the floor seemed to be a tiger skin spread in the centre of the room. It was so stuffy it seemed the doors and windows hadn't been opened in ages. The air that seeped in through the ventilators beneath the ceiling wasn't enough to breathe easily.

As I stood in the centre of the room, observing these details, the humiliation of my position as a supplicant began to slowly dawn on me. I had come for sanctuary to the very person I had hated every day of my life. A wave of chill shot through the sole of my foot and rose right up to my head. I felt like running away. At the same time a sense of unease and dejection kept my feet riveted to the floor. I was entranced by the waves of pale light. Besides, it was in this house. It belonged to the person who was at the root of my parents' unseemly cat-and-dog fights. I remembered that all her life my sickly mother had been plagued by poverty. Between her and Father I had never seen any sign of love, affection or tenderness. Even their anguish lacked depth. It was on the basis of such a relationship that we were brought into this world—the whole thing seems absurd to me. In her early years of course the main reason behind her agony was this Irfan Uncle. Because of this relationship she had suffered such unspeakable physical and verbal abuse that eventually she just became inured to all suffering. Mother's relationship with Irfan Uncle had in fact turned into a disgusting scandal. And yet I had shamelessly told Auntie that Mother had given me their address! Why did I drag Mother into this? Did I think referring to her would give my visit added significance?

I couldn't think any more. Hunger, thirst and my embarrassment began to make everything look dark. I was overcome with nausea. Would I faint under the spell cast by the weak light? Why did I get the smell of Savlon from all around? Was it a home or a hospital? Was I standing amidst ancient ruins? When I had been reduced to a state of unearthly confusion, a woman appeared in the doorway and asked me to go in. Then she led me in, like I was in a trance, with the bag I had been carrying all day still slung from my shoulder.

When, after all the courtesies food was served and my hunger assuaged, I was shown into the room where I could sleep. I put my bag down on the floor and lay down on the handloom cotton sheet spread on the bed and rediscovered my existence in a new void.

This room was as stuffy as the drawing room, so relaxed breathing was impossible. Not that I was used to light and air. I had never had the chance to grow like a tree with its branches and leaves reaching towards the freedom of the sky.

Now the darkness all around had grown really thick. Obscuring everything else, Rezaul surfaced in my consciousness. When we split up, everything around me seemed covered in smoke, in gathering darkness. After being together for so long! Habit was a deadly thing. In marriage, life's struggle took one form. Now that it was over the struggle had to take another shape. I was floundering. I passed my nights alone in a dark room. The slightest noise sent me into a panic. A factory whistle resounded continuously in my head. My condition had almost become pathological. A tiny room, the bathroom next to it in a state of terrible disrepair. The bricks of the walls stuck out like blackened teeth. The hole in the middle of the toilet seat looked as if its flesh—so to speak—had been clawed away.

All the intense fears of those lonely nights were centred on this bathroom. And on the noise of bolts bearing down. If someone in the next flat bolted or unbolted a door or a window, or if the wind unbolted one of mine, I would get up in a flurry. Then I would sit up in a night-long vigil. I had never got used to sleeping by myself. In my parents' home we'd grown up clinging to each other. It was strange to recall that even in such dire straits, without any encouragement from anybody I cultivated an astonishing hobby—painting and drawing. It was as if I had developed the passion as a means of escape.

In those lonely days that old passion was rekindled. I dragged my paints and brushes and rickety easel from under the bed. The paints had become dry, the brushes were covered in dust and cobwebs. I just sat and looked at these things. The night deepened.

By then I had sold off some of my belongings. The landlord would drop in to ask if I would like to leave. I really was in a state of extreme uncertainty.

When Rezaul had been there, this room had seemed to me like a dark cave—utterly damp and stuffy, affording not even a glimpse of the sky, the window opening to show another building with the plaster peeling off. The worst thing was the absence of a balcony. You stepped out on to the landing of the stairs. You could either go down or climb up.

Then there was the torment of an ancient ceiling fan. It made a horrendous noise that would frequently disrupt sleep. It made me apprehensive for another reason. After two days of rattling service it would suddenly stop with a loud bang on the third day. For the next two and a half days there would be no fan, no breeze, only steamy air. I was slowly being roasted. Like a madwoman I would leap to part the window curtain. Then the neighbour's wall seemed to rush at me.

Yet that fan was the centre of Rezaul's attention. When it came to fulfilling domestic responsibilities, spending hours trying to mend that fan was his idea of doing his bit.

He used to work in a private firm. As soon as he got back from work, right in that sweaty state he would get the fan down from the ceiling, lay it on the floor and begin an endless process with the screwdriver. Looking at all this made my blood boil, because he'd be so absorbed in his tinkering that I had nothing to do but sit on the bed and watch. Often we'd have a big fight over this. The most self-destructive thing in my system was my rage. At times I would feel like doing something that would drive him to distraction. Of course I was also a past master at mastering that rage: I would baulk at the naïve attitude of paying him in the same coin. Why should something that was unacceptable in him be okay for me? Doing something wrong would merely lower me to his level. Still, my suppressed rage found expression—I wouldn't talk to him for days. I would walk brazenly past him, hurling the bunch of household keys on the floor. The outcome: he would come home late and fall asleep straightaway.

All this gradually diminished the attraction I felt towards him. Making up with him translated into animal sex. Horrid, sour kisses. Cold war therefore became a more preferable state for me. Eventually at night Rezaul would himself melt and make up. I saw him as a wage slave with no scope for entertainment except crude physical excitement. I would pity him, and so, without excitement, without any spasms, I would make up with him out of sheer force of habit.

Like my father's household, my husband's too had one big problem—money. The struggle to make ends meet during all those years at my parents' had left me exhausted. After marriage it was the same. Often in our flat we had no water, and power outages were a regular feature in our locality. The sun seemed to hover over our roof. I would be in a sour mood all the time. When he got home from work Rezaul would start a rumpus. 'Couldn't you save a little water?' he'd shout.

'There is only one bucket,' I'd shout back. 'How much water can I save in it? And then, don't I have to cook? How would I know that the water would suddenly be turned off?'

Rezaul was at that moment covered in soap suds from head to toe. Like a fool he'd be turning the tap this way and that. At one point he'd wipe off the suds and come out to resume the braying. 'How would you know anything about the water supply? All day you just sit like a nawab. If you had to work like me and came home to find there was no water, you'd see . . .' Muttering angrily, he'd empty the talcum powder container on himself. The white powder on his sticky body turned him into a clown. But instead of making me feel any sympathy, it only increased my disgust. Besides, his allegation that I lived like an idle nawab made me venomous with rage.

We had to ration water and food. And then the toilet would overflow and flood the bathroom with excrement.

I would throw up all over the floor. But that wouldn't solve the problem, would it? In that tiny rented flat in that estate what could one do about nature's imperious calls? I would go to the landlord to ask for a solution, sometimes in a huff, other times in helpless, beseeching tones. Every time the landlord's reply was simple: You can't expect a modern bathroom with foreign fittings at this rent. I'd plead further. But the overflowing filth . . . my husband might be able to finish the main thing at work, but how can a woman go from house to house asking if she might use the loo?

Even to this argument his lukewarm answer was, Let me see. Two or three more days would go by. In that time the stench of urine and excrement would reduce me to lifelessness.

So much for this problem. As soon as we overcame it we would be harried by the household expenses on food. Even careful budgeting wouldn't enable us to balance the budget. Chapatti and bhaji for breakfast, a simple rice-and-curry lunch, rice and a mashed vegetable at dinner. Of course both of us scrupulously followed one rule. The quantity of rice consumed at dinner was strictly controlled. If anyone had come to know about it they would've thought we were on a diet. Nothing could be further from the truth. We were anxious. Let this come to light: even in such a situation I managed to put away a taka or two in an earthen pot. But around the twenty-first day of the month we would have to dip into it. The last few days of the month were the worst. If we bought a new bed sheet to replace the tattered old one, we would find that we'd run out of rice. We would somehow buy half a kilo, but the spices, sugar, biscuits, vegetables were also nearly exhausted. If we somehow managed to borrow a few takas to tide over the crisis, no sooner did we heave a sigh of relief than our lone electric bulb would give out. Then laughter would well up from within. The truly destitute had nothing to worry about, the sky is their father, the moon is their uncle. I would just sit and stare at the candle flame. It was melting down, just like me, on to the saucer on which it had been stuck. O dying candle flame— I'd mumble an invocation—burst into a conflagration, unleash an obedient demon.

And then? What else but keep the door open and make do for another couple of days with the light that seeped in? I would chant the children's rhyme inviting the moon—*O Uncle Moon*—to come in. And some more rhymes thrown in for good measure. I would sit still, then jump up and down in the dark. On one of these days, as he lay in bed, sunk in despair, Rezaul said, 'Just lie quietly on your back or go to sleep. How can we buy a bulb when we can't even afford another candle? Half a kilo of rice won't last more than a day. That's the top priority item. First of all one has to put something in the belly. But how can one live like this, in such dismal surroundings? It is disgusting. Even a dog's life is a lot better.'

If life in such a household was called living like a nawab, it was too painful to gulp down. The outcome of course would be another battle royal. But before we could come to blows I would lock myself inside the kitchen and spend a long time crying loudly. At some point both of us would calm down, and the battle with our circumstances would resume. Every single day I thought of leaving. I wanted to escape to a faraway place. Perhaps everyone dreams of such a place but never gets there. Eventually I would just bow to this harsh reality and try to get on with life. I'd spread my hair before Rezaul's face and ask, 'Tell me what it smells of.'

'Soap.'

'And my body?' I'd ask, bending over him.

He'd laugh and say, 'Sweat and talcum powder.'

But someone used to say I smelt of wild flowers. It would seem that I had never taken any care of myself and had grown up in close intimacy with nature. The clean breeze of memory blowing through the rude reality of that stuffy room would bring tears to my eyes. Because of such experiences, that room remained an essential part of my existence even when I came to live alone. Leaving its protection meant turning into meat for vultures and dogs to rend and gobble. Alongside the terrors of the night was the fear of losing the flat. Selling off what little I had—my gold chain, chair, table—it wouldn't be long before I had absolutely nothing left. Where would I turn then?

I was almost crazed with anxiety and apprehension. My weightless body whirled round and round and thrashed about a circle of emptiness. Days passed. I remember that one night I was like one possessed and threw away my paints and brushes. Just then groans and a loud scream reached my ears. I was suddenly alert. Then came the grotesque sound of someone being beaten up with sticks.

Behind the flat, to one side, there was an open field. But if the back door was opened, as there was no balcony, one had the feeling one might slip and drop into limitless space. As a result the door was never opened. But the intensity of the screams drew me like death. I was like an actor in a horror film, and just as such an actor would do, I put my hand on the bolt. It was rusty, encrusted with dust. It wouldn't slide open. I pulled with all my strength and fell over backwards. When I stood my eyes seemed to take in a bottomless pit, while for the first time I felt a strong breeze enter from this direction. My chest felt cool. Then the screams again. Fearfully I looked at the vast emptiness, lit up in patches by the light from lamp posts, and saw a couple of half-naked men being roughed up. Snatches of conversation suggested that they were thieves. Their bodies twisted and turned as the blows fell. There were clusters of men all over the field.

There were groans and screams, I didn't do it, O help me, and so on. One of the thieves was carried spreadeagled by some men and tossed on the ground on the other side of the field.

I shut the door and lay down, burying my face in the pillow. I had a bad headache and felt feverish. Just then the power went out. Even now if I remember that terrible, lonely night, I get the shivers. I had become unbearably thirsty. To get to the kitchen one had to go past that stinking bathroom. There was a pitcher of water in the kitchen. I felt my way towards it. The groans had stopped. Were they dead? I wondered. Suddenly I felt something cold underfoot. A sliver of ice pricked my breast. Could it be a snake? Then I reasoned that a snake couldn't have climbed the drainpipe to the first floor. I bent over and picked it up. A bottle. Breathing deeply once again, I reached the pitcher. I took a glass from the top of the meat safe. After I had drunk my fill I stood in the narrow passage in the middle. When there was a whispering in my ear. I scrammed to my room. Again there was a whistling sound. I felt suffocated. I shook my head. It dawned on me that an ant or some such creature had got into my ear. Then began mortal agony. It didn't seem like an insect, more like a whole cobra.

I stood in the middle of the room and shook my head, lay on my back, then on one side, but there was no relief. The insect seemed to bite even harder. The pain grew from bad to worse. No, it wasn't an insect or even a snake; it was death itself that had got into me. Azrael had inserted a long needle into my dark ear. I felt so helpless I started wailing and running crazily around the room. What could I do? Arefin, you son of a bitch. I started abusing my brother. He had asked me to wait patiently for a few days. He knew someone in some office or the other. He had promised to get me a job there. But I had no confidence in his assurances. He was involved in student politics. Every now and then he would be hiding from the police and seek refuge with me. It often created bitterness between Rezaul and me. And now he had abandoned his sister. Every bugger was self-centred. I groped for the matches and lit one. If I could even find a stump of a candle. Again I made my way to the kitchen. As soon as I pulled the broken meat safe drawer I was surrounded by a horde of cockroaches. My skin prickled all over. After lights out the cockroaches took over the whole flat. They held sway over the floor, the meat safe, even the bed. Under such circumstances I couldn't find even a tiny remnant of a candle.

Suddenly the commotion in my ear seemed to diminish. I stood still in the middle of the kitchen, utterly petrified. I was scared to move, lest it began again. I stood holding my breath, but that did not prevent the turmoil from starting again. I sank to the floor with a groan. The electricity came back just then. I was close to complete exhaustion. With wobbling hands I poured some water into my ear, then tilting my head thumped hard on my skull. It worked. In a few moments a larger than average red ant came out—dead. Though the ear still ached, I was free of the tension as I lay down in bed. Hungry and worn out, I dozed the rest of the night.

The next morning I decided not to spend another day in that flat. I would go straight to Father's house. But the very next moment the thought of going there made me feel even more hopeless. That was probably because I had married out of my own choice. My parents might be relieved at the turn of events but they wouldn't accept any share of the responsibility for what had happened. The thought of the bitterness that would be manifested when we met after the divorce was enough to slow down my thoughts. One day Arefin came in with urgent news. His political activities had taken him close to a powerful man who had more or less given his word that there would be a job for me. I would only have to face an interview.

It was like the biscuit races in childhood. A biscuit dangled from a string above the head. Yes, jump! A little higher!

But even after the firm commitment the job evaded me. I remember I was very tense and self-conscious when I presented myself for the interview. The job was that of an office assistant in a small private firm. The ambience there struck me as very strange. Girls in skirts and sleeveless blouses lounged about, gossiping. There were very few men. I almost held my breath as I made my way down a long passage to the boss's office. The girls gave me such looks, as if I were a freak. I straightened the folds of my sari hurriedly as I entered. I remember the smell of coffee and, vaguely, the boss's face. I was the sister of so-and-so and so-and-so (the honcho) had sent me. After I had introduced myself thus I was asked to sit down. And without any preamble I was told that I did not appear to be smart.

The faint noise of typewriters came from other rooms. The door was ajar, the boss wore a frown, and he directed a cold gaze at me. He was completely bald. My nervousness left me when he started talking. Naïvely I asked, 'What do you mean?'

'Your blouse isn't ironed properly, and you haven't pinned your sari at the shoulder. There is something called a smart look.'

At this comment I pulled myself up, straightened the sari and composing myself said, 'Please take my interview.'

'That is precisely what I am doing,' he said, as a malicious smile lit up his eyes. 'Do you think I am exchanging pleasantries?'

I began to relax. I said, 'I will be able to shape up when I start working.'

He took a long drag on his cigarette. 'Then let me test you with a question. What will you do if a man bumps into you while you are working?'

I asked a question in return: 'Does he bump into me on purpose?'

'Perhaps.' Between sips of coffee he said, 'Let's say he does it on purpose.'

'Then I'll push him back so hard he falls.'

He gave a weird smile. 'If he feels you up?'

'I'll give him a tight slap.'

'Very well, you can inquire after a week.'

I was desperate for a job. Did I have the patience to wait out a week? After three days I was back there. But the gentleman did not even recognize me. After many irrelevant things, he said, 'Oh yes, a job! We'll let you know if you get the job. You can inquire a week from now.'

Another week! I felt dizzy. Arefin used his contacts to lobby for me again. I went back after a week. The boss was too busy to see me. I sat stunned among the girls lounging in suggestive postures. Then I simply barged into the boss's office. On seeing me he grimaced and shouted, 'Who asked you to come in?'

'Well, you had asked me to come today,' I said hesitantly.

'Come back later,' he said, and went back to his files. What to do but leave? Later I came to know that Arefin's Big Shot contact had fallen out with the firm's boss. Besides, the ambience in the office was not pleasant. Hearing all this I could only sit in a daze. But Arefin did not give up hope. He kept after the party Big Shot, ran errands for him. Meanwhile I looked up newspaper ads and braving the hot sun ran desperately from office to office. This is the dominant image I have of life—its true face is revealed in struggle and agony. When I was sunk in such thoughts, like a ray of light, a fresh wind, Arefin came to tell me I had got a job.

As I was thinking about these things I turned and got a sharp prick in the back. I sat up like a jack in the box. The light had not been turned off. I felt around the bed sheet and discovered a needle. How shocking! A needle lying on the bed, pricking me to remind me where I was passing the night. I couldn't deny I was spending the night in a house even whose vicinity I wouldn't have imagined I could pass through only one day ago. It was a humiliating thought, it made me feel hollow. Then at some point I fell asleep.

I woke up very early and didn't immediately realize where I was. And when I did the first object to come into focus was the desiccated deer's head with antlers hanging on the wall. Those antlers seemed to go right through my breast.

I would have to come face-to-face with the great personage now. When I had turned in the previous night he was still out. His wife had quickly extracted information from me about my parents. The collapse of my marriage and the place from where I had come that day. I cannot resort to pretence and subterfuge over anything so I answered her questions frankly. She seemed to listen with sympathy. But did she think that an extra burden had landed on her shoulders? To hell with her then! The main thing now was to meet the gentleman of the house. I stretched in bed and looked about me. The maidservant had also slept in the same room, but she wasn't there now. She had gone out, leaving the door ajar. Strange, this room also smelt of disinfectant. Another smell was mixed with it—that of the damp floor. There was hardly any furniture in the room. A bed in the centre, a clothes horse on one side. Last year's calendar hanging on the wall. Possibly they did not have children. Why possibly? No doubt they did not have any. I'd have seen them if they did. But then again. Anyway, what difference did it make? I had bunked work yesterday and felt uneasy about it. The situation in the office was delicate. There was a lot of office politics. And then I was absent—what would happen now? Who cared? It was Friday today. No point spoiling the holiday mood. But now that I had come running like a demented person to this place, what would be my decision? To stay on here indefinitely? What high hopes! The turmoil in my head again reduced me to a state of numbness.

Soon after I got the job Arefin had arranged a sublet for me with a couple. I had been staying with them for nearly seven months. Next to the bedroom of the couple was a passage in which a single cot was placed. On the other side of the passage was my room. The experience of my seven-month stay was strange, painful, bitter. It was as if I had been born to see conjugal life in all its hideousness. The couple had a wonderful rapport with me. Yet there were frequent clashes: I kept the light on till late, used too much water. This was despite my paying a share of the monthly bills. If the complaints came only from the woman it would not have mattered much. But her husband also added his two bits: prices were on the rise while income remained static; a decent life could only be a dream; in days ahead even skipping two meals a day wouldn't allow one to balance the budget. After such comments he would add: 'Of course, you have a job and pay a share of the bills, but your situation is a little different. You are single. Still, if you would be a little more careful . . .'

Staying up till late had become a habit. I would just lie down with a book. They didn't like that. After my marriage to Rezaul I had become friendly with a strange fellow called Satyajit and his pastime was chatting with friends and reading. He was a close friend of Rezaul's and had unrestricted access to our place. In that stuffy single room he brought a breath of fresh air. His first words would always be, 'How can human beings live here? You S.O.B., you'll turn your wife into a kebab. Let's go out.' Rezaul would be stiff with embarrassment. I knew he'd be calculating expenses. Going out meant the rickshaw fare, and the price of chapatti and *foochka*.

Thanks to Satyajit I got into the habit of reading good books. Of course my own taste in reading wasn't too bad to start with, because I had been involved with several cultural organizations since childhood. Later, many other things intermingled with my early interests. A wide window opened to the world at large. After a hard day's work and unsavoury chores, the only time to read was at night. So would I heed the nagging of those two?

My salary was modest. I had to help out Arefin. Then my parents and other siblings, who lived in a small town, had their expectations. After all the other expenses I did not fail to pay my share of the water and electricity bills. But if I had to give up the small luxury of reading in bed at night, what remained of life for me?

Eventually, however, I had to give it up. I cannot stand too much bickering. Even though I had stood my ground thus far, fresh dissension arose over something else. There was a basti right next to our building. A strange friendship developed between me and a woman who lived in that basti. Her husband used to drive a rickshaw, and they had a lovely little boy. He was the centre of attraction for me. There was something so engaging in his appearance that I felt drawn to him. His ungainly walk, the sound of the bell fastened round his waist, his tinkling laughter, and his plump, dust-powdered body simply wove a web of enchantment around me. The child was also drawn to me. He would walk down the dirt road running through the basti all by himself and quietly stand in front of my door. He would push it open slightly and peer inside comically. As I looked up he would snick his tongue in such an extraordinary way that I would run to catch him. It is because of him that his mother began to visit me regularly. She would do little things for me, put my room in order, sometimes she would wash my clothes. Then one day I came down with a vile fever. The couple in the next room had gone to Comilla on a visit. I lay alone tossing helplessly in my bed. The veins in my forehead turned bluish. I was too weak to get off the bed and pour myself a glass of water. I could only turn my weary eyes this way and that. I had come home early from work, collapsed on the bed and fallen into a deep sleep. I couldn't have imagined that when I awoke my body would become glued to the bed. I was also shivering uncontrollably. Every joint ached. My nostrils were blocked. I had to breathe through my mouth. At this point the woman from the basti came over. It was as if God had sent her to drag me out of a deep chasm.

At once she began admonishing me: 'Such fever and you did not even think of calling me? You could die.'

Everything was gradually receding and slowly fading from my vision by then. The woman stayed with me all night, applying cold compress to my head. She bought some Paracetamol tablets and made me have a couple of them with bread soaked in milk. She was by my side the whole night and had to suffer for it. Her husband had been out all night, drinking. When he got home in the morning and heard about what she had been doing he gave her a sound thrashing. After that she and her son took shelter with me.

The couple in the next room could not accept this. For some reason my fondness for the child was intolerable to the wife. One day she exploded in anger. 'Don't you care for social norms?' she asked me. 'I cannot allow these low-class characters in this house.'

I replied calmly, 'They come to visit me. That shouldn't cause you any inconvenience.'

'You don't understand,' she said in altered tones, 'they are petty criminals by nature. They will win your confidence and then stab you in the back.'

I couldn't help laughing. What precious belongings did I have that might tempt them? My sarcastic tone shut her up.

Of course I wasn't always at loggerheads with the couple. Since we shared the kitchen there naturally were disagreements over this and that, but the wife, Shanu, had the laudable quality of not bearing a grudge for long. After a falling out I would lock myself in my room. So she would come over with an offer of truce. She'd affectionately run her fingers through my hair and say: 'Try to control your temper. Don't you see, you have already lost everything on its account.'

In spite of this we couldn't stay together. One day such an ugly incident occurred that I had to leave at once, in a state of distraction. My hands and feet felt numb as I came to this point in memory. How could Shanu feel such hatred? It is as if she had appeared before me with a raised lance in her hand, and I stood helplessly with my back to the wall.

A loud clattering noise of something falling on the floor made me sit up in panic, the thread of my thoughts broken. The maidservant was standing in stunned silence. She was bringing tea for me, and when she pushed open the door, the tea tray balanced precariously on the other hand came crashing down. Shards of broken crockery lay scattered on the floor. So it was customary in this household to have the morning tea in bed. Anyway, the embarrassment of the whole thing moved me more than the maid. 'Who asked you to bring me tea?' I asked in mortified tones.

'Auntie,' she said, swallowing to overcome her nervousness. 'She wanted you to finish the tea and go and meet her.' The maid pulled herself together and began picking up the debris. Irfan Sahib must have come home late. I began to review in full consciousness everything I had done in a semi-trance since yesterday afternoon. Where had I landed myself? I was overcome with shame. My mother is his jilted lover, and her daughter was at his door as a humble supplicant! My whole being was repulsed at the thought. For the first time in my life I had foolishly done something that made me feel small.

I put all the blame on Satyajit. In the heat of the moment, when I decided to get out of that house I went straight to his confectionery. He was busy looking after customers. As soon as he saw me he shouted, 'What's up? What happened to your job? Have you thrown it away?'

I was feeling quite tetchy. I said, 'Yeah, it makes me throw up. Now will you tell your employees to mind the shop and come with me?'

In a second he was walking beside me, puffing on a bidi.

'You seem to be in a serious mood,' he said. 'What's the matter? You aren't in trouble, I hope.'

I broke down. 'Believe me, Satyajit, I can't carry on any more. I cannot live like this.'

He called a rickshaw. Soon we were travelling full tilt. A harsh sun hovered over our heads. I tried to protect my head with my handbag. Satyajit waggishly suggested: 'Let's get married.'

'Cut out the junk,' I said irritably. 'Marry an infidel Hindu like you and go to hell—no way.'

'You already have one foot in hell,' he said, blowing clouds of smoke skyward. 'You have divorced your husband, which is a reprehensible thing to do according to your religion. Now you can cap it by committing the sin of marrying me ... Come on, don't get so riled up; just tell me what you have to say. Are you in fresh trouble?'

'No, it is not that,' I said. I began to feel fatigued. A column of ants seemed to crawl across my brain. Our rickshaw nearly fell under a bus and our rickshaw-wallah swerved sharply, giving us a severe jolt. Satyajit angrily raised a hand to strike him. I begged Satyajit not to create a scene. After all, I was bunking office for the first time in days.

Once again we were pelting down the middle of a broad thoroughfare. Satyajit suggested we visit Salauddin. 'The S.O.B. has locked himself in for two days to work on his novel,' he said, 'and doesn't answer the door. Today I will get in even if I have to break down the door. Besides, you are with me. The plaintive tones of a woman can even rouse gods from slumber.'

It was noon when we got there. But contrary to expectations, Salauddin's door was wide open and he was engaged in lively chitchat with Shahtab and Ranjan.

The three of them greeted us noisily but in a moment became eerily quiet. They seemed rather a pitiful lot. Especially Ranjan. Around his thin beard, grey eyes and slim figure there circulated clouds of cigarette smoke.

'That is the end of my novel for today,' Salauddin said bluntly. And then he went on: 'There has been a big police raid on Gawsia Market and poor Ranju has been stripped to the bone.'

'Really? What were the goods worth?' asked Satyajit.

'A hundred and fifty thousand,' Ranju said with subdued bitterness.

'That's what we were talking about,' Shahtab said loudly. 'The buggers have even taken away many Bangladeshi saris, claiming they were Indian ones. When he got wind of the raid Ranju quickly hid some pricey ones beneath the discarded sacks or else he would've lost everything.'

'He could save just a few,' said Salauddin, his voice a growl of suppressed rage. 'The S.O.Bs can't stop the smugglers at the border, so when their wives and sisters-in-law ask for new saris they launch a raid on city markets. Poor Ranju had to beg his father for the money to start the business . . . the old man had little confidence in his business acumen . . . and now, just when the business was beginning to flourish, comes this. Well, back to your old life, Ranju.'

I found myself in a quandary. I wasn't prepared to deal with such a hard-luck story. Whenever I had visited Salauddin and his friends, our conversation would centre on things like literature, the complexities of personal relationships, the anomie affecting our society. Today it was veering towards the hollowness at the heart of Bangladeshi politics. Now, politics might hover around my mind, but it could never penetrate it to produce comprehension. I was reminded of Arefin, for I could never understand what he was madly chasing in his political activities. While his parents led a precarious existence, and his sister slaved from morning till evening to earn a few takas, he had become embroiled in ugly, violent, gangster-ridden politics! It was depressing. And these people were also behind a smokescreen, wrapped up in their own problems! I felt uneasy. God knows what Salauddin was rolling into a cigarette. Shahtab was sitting with his legs splayed out on the floor where the cement had started peeling off. Ranju and Satyajit sat close together on the narrow bed. 'There is a letter from home . . .' Salauddin began—it was the same story about letters from home with all young people. What a terrible decision I had taken when I left that house: now there was nowhere I could stay in the city. I had simply made my decision and gone to seek my friends in the hope that they would be able to help me think clearly. Instead, my thoughts had become even more confused.

The pendulum of the clock was immobile. A plump woman smiled in an ad for vanishing cream. Live flesh overflowed her blouse. Amidst the loud chatter of these sad, despairing young men, I felt immersed in ineffable loneliness. That loneliness seemed to have a yellowish hue, it was shapeless yet it had a form, though it was like fluffy cotton or smoke . . . Was I really awake? After a long time Satyajit languidly reached out to me and said, 'Want a drag?'

My lips swelled up in anger. I looked at the extended hand. Everything was quiet. But what was this jangling noise in my temples? Had the smoke begun to affect me? What a disgusting picture on the calendar! Bright whitewash on the walls, contrasting with red betel juice stains, hurt the eyes. There I was in a chair, like an uninvited guest. I stood up abruptly and ignoring their protests said something about urgent business and left. As the smoke cleared from my consciousness I took a sudden decision to go to Irfan Chacha's house. A relative encountered in New Market had given me the address, which, scribbled on a slip of paper, had been secreted into my handbag without entertaining the slightest possibility that I might one day look it up. Yet in my hapless state this was the first address that came to my mind. And then after so many twists and turns . . . But now it was a serious matter just to get out of this room. And then to face Chacha's steady gaze. What would I say when I would face the master of the house? And what would be my next step? The first thing to do would be to look up Arefin. The sooner I was out of the discomfiting stuffiness of this house the better. As I washed in the en suite bathroom I thought of Shanu. Her face, her expression of intense hate. Her venomous accusation. Just thinking of it made me squirm. I squinted at my averted face in the bathroom mirror. So pale and weary. 'Hi! How are you?' I said to the mirror.

A whirlwind seemed to be blowing through my chest, kicking up dust, dry leaves, leaving me denuded. I had forgotten to pack a toothbrush. I'd left it behind in the bathroom of that house. So I squeezed a little toothpaste on to my index finger and massaged my teeth and gums. Suddenly lost in thought, I saw only darkness all around—intense, deep.

∼

The house I had been living in, in a mossy building, had a deodar growing on one side. There was a front veranda, a grassy plot in front and the basti a little way off. From the veranda I could observe the ghastly life of the basti-dwellers—the revolting stench, the shouts and screams and constant hullabaloo, the sound of hammering.

I went over the details of that night's events, analysed them, tried to determine if I was at fault. I was just falling asleep when I was startled by a crashing noise. So, it had started in the next room. Shanu was in the habit of throwing things when in a rage. She had just given fresh evidence of this. There followed utter silence; everything was calm, as if nothing had happened. Then, suddenly, Shanu's hissing tones reached my ears '. . . Cur! Swine! . . .' Then the sound of uninterrupted moaning.

Such incidents took place every day. But tonight it seemed that Kamal Bhai had got her by the throat. I got out of bed quickly and started knocking desperately on their door. But the sound of my knocking was drowned in the tumult of their struggle. I was seized by terror. In his fit of anger Shanu's husband took on an appearance even more frightful than a murderer's.

Shanu's sobs reached my ears at last. At least something disastrous hadn't occurred. I went back to bed in a calm state. But as soon as I lay down a ghostly version of Rezaul seemed to appear out of nowhere. Without a word it lay down beside me, placed a hand on my throat, gripped my windpipe. His face was exactly like Shanu's husband's.

I began to sob. At one point, amidst all these strange goings-on, my usual nocturnal sleep began to weigh down my eyelids. Was Rezaul like this, I thought. Each individual is different from the other, so could there be any comparison?

Suddenly I was startled awake. I had been dreaming all sorts of terrible things. I was falling off the roof. When the body was dismembered by the fall I saw that it wasn't mine. As soon as I woke up I thought of my kid sister Ranu. It was so long since my last visit home. So many days since I last saw everyone. Now a month might go by without me thinking about them.

These thoughts drove away sleep. The window above my head was so rickety that it swung open with a slight wind. At once the sound of heavy breathing reached my ears. My first thought was that I was hallucinating. But the sound steadily grew louder. My eyes got used to the dark, which lightened to grey. I sat up. Was there a burglar outside the window? I was instantly covered in goosebumps. I didn't have the nerve to part the curtain and have a look. Silently and swiftly, I moved to the door. Gingerly releasing the bolt, I went out and walked down the passage. I rapped frantically on Shanu's door—once, twice. My legs were unsteady. A light came on. Overcoming her sleepiness, Shanu opened the door and noticed with wide-eyed surprise that her husband wasn't in bed. The back door was lightly closed. They had gone to bed together, but why was it empty now? Shanu's voice was moist but fuzzy. 'Why did you get up?' she asked. Her words lent me courage, I don't know why. Though I couldn't make head or tail of what was going on, I led her to my room. Then things happened very fast. Dragging her to my window, I asked her in suppressed excitement: 'Do you hear anything?' Shanu pricked her ears. The sound had altered. It sounded like someone panting after a tremendous struggle. At one point Shanu's hand opened the door of my room with a swift movement and then she nearly sprinted across the veranda and then round to the space outside my window. I followed her, bewildered. In the pale light two shadowy figures were clearly visible as they sprang apart. One of them was a male figure that sprinted across the narrow grassy yard and vanished down the road, but the other—

a dishevelled, cringing woman—made no attempt to flee. By then Shanu had grabbed her. My ice-cold eyes discerned the rickshaw-wallah's wife from the basti. She stood like a statue. Shanu dragged her by the hair. My distressed voice came out in a screech, shaking up the woman's docile body, 'Kallur Ma, you!' But out of fear of the embarrassment it would cause if people came to know, Shanu couldn't rail at Kallur Ma for long. So turning her out by the scruff of her neck she pounced on me.

I was trembling, overcome with conflicting emotions. The gist of Kallur Ma's tearful testimony set off a turmoil in my heart. Why hadn't she said anything all these days? What we gathered from her words was that her husband led his own life, crashing out where he pleased, contributing not even a penny to his family's upkeep. She had to bear the burden of running the family, doing odd jobs, piling debt upon debt. There was no way she could make ends meet. She was floundering in debt. Her creditors were in relentless pursuit. Meanwhile, Shanu's husband had been trying for long to seduce her, indirectly making tempting offers. Tonight was the first time ... etc., etc. I didn't feel like listening any more. I was growing numb. After many days I was desolated once again by a scene coming alive in memory. It was nothing fanciful. It was real enough to crush me to pulp. This was the event that triggered off the process of loosening our marital ties.

A lively young girl appeared before me, her hair plaited with red ribbons. She used to live near our stuffy old flat. Dressed in a frock, she would often come traipsing along to our flat. Terribly restless, she used to scream her head off calling out to me: 'Mami, Mami!' Her spontaneous laughter, her gentle, innocent face, her impetuous behaviour was like a breath of fresh air in that confined space. A charming intimacy developed between her and Rezaul. He was full of affection for her. Our bed occupied the middle of the room. Round and round the two of them would run. I'd sit on the bed and delightedly watch their childlike games. Often on his way home Rezaul would buy some titbits for her, and she would sit on the floor with her feet splayed out and eat them. Rezaul would playfully tug at her pigtails or tickle her. She'd burst into giggles and roll on the floor.

It was when their relationship was so close that the event occurred. As usual they were chasing each other round and round the bed. I was busy in the kitchen. The crackle of frying fish mingled promiscuously with their laughter and high-pitched screams. While playing with the girl Rezaul also became a little child. It pleased me that he no longer got down to futile repair jobs when he came home from work. That day the gas cooker suddenly gave out and I was about to enter the room to look for the matches in Rezaul's pocket when I was stopped short in the doorway by the sight of the girl thrashing about in desperation while Rezaul had her pinned down and kept shouting, 'Got it, got it!' He was oblivious to my presence. 'Tell me where it is,' he said as he groped the girl's thighs, breasts and other intimate parts. I was looking on wide-eyed when I felt as if someone had in an instant drained me of all my blood, leaving me inert. This was not innocent play, I thought, as the darkness reeled drunkenly; but what was it?

I didn't realize at once what was really going on. Rezaul was startled to see me standing there. Pulling himself together in haste, he swiftly dragged the girl off the bed and demanded, 'Where have you hidden my cigarettes? Come on, tell me.' The girl seemed utterly dumbfounded as he shook her roughly, sweaty-faced, voice filled with embarrassment. Overcome with disgust and rage I rushed to rescue the girl. Straightening her crumpled frock, she fled down the stairs. Then I faced Rezaul. His breath came thick and fast, his face was flushed.

The thought of what had happened brought tears to my eyes. I was shaking uncontrollably. I cast a distracted look at him.

'How shameful, Rezaul,' I said at last. He seemed to fall from the sky. There was twice as much astonishment in his voice as in mine when he said, 'What does that mean? What are you trying to say?' My breathing seemed to have stopped. Fixing him with a cold stare I could only say, 'Thank God we don't have a daughter.'

Later, we had long discussions about this. I could only mutter psychotically, 'You have ruined the girl's childhood—how could you do it? Do you realize what would have happened if I wasn't at home?' Rezaul was at pains to explain it away as sheer playfulness. Even then my attitude towards him kept seesawing so that I couldn't entirely overcome my distrust, and the disgust I felt for him deep in my heart alienated us further and further.

That night Shanu's bitter accusations were mingled with insinuations: I had pampered that slut, making her welcome at my place. Since my own marriage had broken up I had a hidden motive for engineering what had happened. I had planned the whole thing, or else why did I drag her out of bed in the middle of the night? Why did she have to witness such a horrible scene? Shanu went on like a delirious woman. Since that single episode of Rezaul's playfulness had poisoned every inch of my body, I could gauge Shanu's state of mind. So I remained calm even though I was inwardly seething with rage at her unfounded allegations. I didn't give her any inkling of the furious turmoil in my head.

While I struggled with my mental crisis Shanu gradually calmed down and began a desperate fight for survival. Her husband had disappeared in order to hide his shame—what if he did not return? Shanu broke into heavy sobs. Gradually, the sky lightened. I was sitting still with my back against the wall. I could see Shanu's limitless rage against her husband begin to ebb. She went distractedly from one room to another. All her anguish and fear were focused on one thought—surely her husband wouldn't come back. When lacerated by such emotional conflict Shanu again became aggressive towards me, I pulled myself together and stood up. Distractedly, I packed a bag. A horde of insects droned in my head. The scene rose clearly before my eyes. Why did it still render me numb? The bed in the middle, the careering round and round, the charming games . . . the tickling . . . the pounce . . . Rezaul had become a child . . . Got it, got it . . . the cry . . . O God!

In a flash I got out of there.

~

'So you have decided to go back to your place?'

At Chachi's cold query I raised a startled face. 'Yes,' I said uneasily. 'Actually, my coming here—it happened because I became too emotional.'

'That's ok.' There was neither disapproval nor support in Chachi's tone. 'It's only human to behave like that. Can human beings always act in a calculated manner?'

In fact I had reached my decision as I was coming out of the bathroom. The entire thing seemed to become totally confusing. Gradually Shanu's psychological crisis elicited my empathy. Anything ill-mannered in one's behaviour in such a state should not be taken to heart. Come to think of it, what if Shanu's husband really never turned up. Shame was a terrible thing. I would have to accept responsibility for causing it though I wasn't really to blame. The incident might have occurred even if I hadn't got to know Kallur Ma. True, the opportunity for its occurrence arose out of my acquaintance with her. But exactly such an incident could have occurred with anyone else. Who knew if the same thing hadn't occurred elsewhere? The other party involved was far from innocent. He had been trying to seduce Kallur Ma for many days. This indicated that what had happened was no accident. He had been mulling it over for a long time. What certainty was there that he did not harbour such desires about me as well? Perhaps he managed to exercise self-control. I was an educated woman, I worked in an office—it was too risky to try anything so he kept himself in check. Actually, it isn't possible for everyone to remain pure at heart because desire is enough to arouse one. But then, human civilization consists in the exercise of self-control. Did I not have any wayward desires of my own? I had become habituated to my conjugal relationship with Rezaul. And yet, sometimes in the small hours my physicality would shed its trappings and roam under the wide sky, naked, restless, and it quivered in excitement. But did that mean if Shanu's husband came prowling round I would make myself available? Wouldn't my good sense guide me?

The two of them had a tremendous row in the evening. The reason was money, nothing else. At one point Shanu broke into sobs and retired. In the middle of the night her husband got up from the bed and went out. It wasn't something he did on the spur of the moment, it was pre-planned. What was my fault in this business? That I had helped Shanu witness the scandalous scene involving her husband? The incident could have occurred in the silence of the night. Then there would have been no furore; no one would have known or suffered. It would not have been such a disaster. This line of thought made me see it in a new light. But then, did I know how things would turn out? Where exactly did I stand in this imbroglio? Anyway, now Shanu was more helpless than me. It was unconscionable of me to leave her like that in a moment of impetuousness. Mellowed by such thoughts I had entered Chachi's room. But my new decision renewed my disquiet. Besides, there had been another source of tension all along—what if Irfan Chacha came into the room? I had heard he was of the reserved, taciturn sort. The thought of coming face-to-face with him was enough to give me a fever. I tried to figure out a way to avoid meeting him. Finally I asked, 'Hasn't Chacha got up?'

'No,' placidly answered Chachi as she handed me a cup of tea. 'After an evening with his friends he doesn't wake up before ten.'

'But I have to leave right now.' I was fidgety with anxiety as I sipped the tea. It seemed to get stuck in my gullet.

'But why! Won't you wait to meet him?' Chachi's surprise was unconvincing. It gave me the latitude I needed to say, 'Not today. I feel a little uneasy. Maybe I'll come some other day.'

Did Chachi respect my feelings? Strange that she did not remonstrate. Why were they so polite, so excessively polite? Or was she glad to be rid of me? That would be irrational jealously in someone of her age. Of course I knew little about the psychology of the elderly. And anyway, how could I dismiss it as irrational? What was the extent of Mother's relationship with her husband? How deep was it? How much did she know about it? How much of physical contact could there be in a love affair in the older generation? What thoughts!

The bed in Chachi's room was so huge, so high! I had seen such beds in the museum. They had made me wonder at the strange fancies of kings. Imagine climbing steps to get into bed. Hadn't anyone in a tipsy state ever slipped and suffered a fall from those iron steps? Of course the queen would be at hand to keep him steady—an excellent maid . . . Of course this one wasn't high enough to necessitate the use of steps. The four posters were deep black and spiralled upward like snakes. The sheet was silken. The two bedside chairs were massive, aristocratic in design. The ambience was courtly. Two lovely oil paintings hung on the wall. They were really lovely.

Semi-abstract in form. A giant of a man amidst a storm, with seven arms raised in seven directions. Two hands grasped cloud clusters. Red and blue forms dominated the entire canvas. The other painting showed a ruin—that of an exquisite mansion. I had never before set eyes on bricks and stones of such vivid colours. Just looking at the works of art stirred my dormant longing to start painting again. My fingers itched, a painful sensation. Observing me gaze at the paintings, Chachi commented, 'I don't understand anything of these. Your Chacha used to collect them at one time.'

How could such a sophisticate have fallen in love with a simple, ordinary, rather dull person like my mother? It was amazing enough to leave me utterly confounded. It also filled me with secret pride. When I took my leave it was with a sense of lightness.

The fact that I had avoided meeting Irfan Chacha doubled my sense of well-being. I sailed down the fresh breeze and for the first time in days got on a rickshaw on the main road.

The first destination that occurred to me was Arefin's hostel. I needed to talk to him about the situation, because it was he who had introduced me to Shanu. But I also knew that my visit to Irfan Chacha's house wasn't something he would be able to take lightly. What would he think about me? That I was stupid? Spineless? Shameless?

How would he interpret my emotions? I was again floundering in a deep pit. Everything began to go blank.

Tall buildings seemed to walk past me, and with them went the freshly rounded sun, swift trucks and buses and undisciplined rickshaws and motor rickshaws. I pushed back the rickshaw's hood and bathed my face in the sunlight. Through the sunlight, the broad road, the traffic jam, the flicking amber and red of traffic lights, the rickshaw reached Meherunnessa

Market, with rows of shoe stores on the right, shoes of varied designs. Then it turned left and presently came to a sudden halt with a sense of relief.

I settled the fare and almost ran across the wide road, walking along the damaged boundary wall behind the Bangabandhu Hall. I soon found myself at the main gate. My name, name of the person I wished to visit, estimated duration of visit—after answering the list of questions, as I walked along the long corridor, a crowd of curious boys lined up at the windows on both sides to devour me. Studying in a co-educational institution hadn't quenched their desire to ogle at women. My discomfiture clung to my body as I made my way upstairs. I avoided coming to the hall as far as possible—this was my second visit. The other occasion was when the divorce proceedings were under way. One of Arefin's friends came along as a witness.

Anyway, another sort of discomfiture awaited me in Arefin's room. Though it was now unbearably hot, one of the occupants was busy doing push-ups on the floor. Another had abbreviated his lungi into a loincloth and sat on the bed, rocking back and forth. My entry seemed to give them an electric shock. They hurriedly pulled down shirts over their glistening bodies. I overcame my embarrassment to say despondently, 'Arefin seems to be out.'

Straightening his lungi and assuming a normal posture, one of the two boys informed me that Arefin had not returned to the hall last night.

Where could he have spent the night, I was wondering, when the boys began bustling about to make me welcome, offering me a seat, and one of them shot out of the room to fetch tea and biscuits or a Coke or something for me.

As soon as I realized this I protested I didn't have time for refreshments. I had to leave straightaway. I used the familiar form of address with the boys, but didn't know if it was proper. On the other hand, they were my younger brother's friends, and the formal mode did not come naturally. I was pondering this dilemma and taking in the details of the interior—three scattered desks, two creaky beds, numerous cut-out portraits: Marilyn Monroe, Sheikh Mujib, Maradona, Rekha . . . a really mixed-up taste. Arefin's wall was bare, though. I stepped over to his desk. On it lay Tagore's head, woven out of rice stalks—a reassuring sight. I thought of hanging it on the wall, but at once I was seized with tremendous unease. I picked up a book from the table, and immediately a few nude photographs tumbled out.

My discomfort was infectious and spread to the two boys. Right in front of them my earlobes turned red with embarrassment. The boys busied themselves in putting them aside and then as they tried to regain normality asked if I had any message to leave for Arefin.

'Yes, listen, as soon as he comes in, will you take the trouble of telling him to come straight to my place?'

After leaving the hall there was the familiar wait for a bus; I stood roasting in the sun at Nilkhet. Sweat ran down my face. It rankled that the money on the rickshaw ride had gone to waste. It was the nineteenth of the month. At the start of the month, after paying the rent and the bills and doing the monthly shopping, I had only a quarter of my salary left. Spending that money in dribs and drabs involved subtle calculations. Spending an extra five taka could upset the budget. Just buying a pair of sandals, for which provision had not been made, nearly ruined me. And yet it could not be avoided. Repairing the sandals with pins for two months had reduced them to such a sorry state that one day a pin penetrated my sole in its entirety. I applied Savlon as soon as I got home. Shanu had warned me that the prick might turn septic, and I had spent three–four days in nervous apprehension. It was eventually at Shanu's urging that I had bought the new sandals.

As a result I was now down to a hundred and fifty taka, on which I would have to live for the rest of the month. Since yesterday my life had deviated completely from my usual routine. I had not had such a long rickshaw ride in ages. I had become so conditioned to a carefully regulated budget that the slightest deviation brought on limitless anxiety. But my innate nature— and this had been particularly evident before marriage—had in it bohemianism, rootlessness . . . I was a wild bird. Yet I had learned to fold my wings, teach patience to my wild self. How well I had learned!

A bus ground to a halt. The waiting passengers in a swirl of body odour rushed at the door, preventing those who wanted to get off. Obscenities flew thick and fast. I had become used to dealing with such situations. As the bus was pulling out I squeezed in with an 'Excuse me'. In a crowd my body lost its squeamishness, it became a ball or a spring or some such thing.

Squashed by men on all sides, amidst darkness and body odour, I stood with eyes nearly shut, stifling in the muggy heat. Worry clustered inside me—what if Shanu's husband did not return? The thought oppressed me like a boulder on the chest. Silent amidst the noise, I simply let go . . . What more could happen? Life must go on . . .

But no matter how readily I let go mentally, when I reached the door of the flat I found my feet resistant. God alone knew what new experiences awaited me. I thought of dragging a foot forward and placing it on the threshold, of knocking on the door with a finger that felt the weight of the whole world, of holding my breath awhile. I was standing at my own door like a criminal. Should I turn back?

I was struck dumb to see who had come to open the door. There in the doorway stood Shanu and her husband, both of them beaming. He said with casual cheerfulness, 'There you are! We've been dying of worry.' Even warmer was Shanu. She took both my hands and dragged me in. 'I am so relieved. I can't explain how guilty I have been feeling. I've been such a bitch.'

'No, no, no, what are you saying'—that's all I could muster. How I was maturing in experience with each passing day! I used to pride myself for knowing people, for my ability to interpret behaviour. Whatever happened, pleasant or nasty, I had thought I would be able to sense the outcome; how wrong I had been proved. But could I take the present situation with equanimity? After the mental turmoil I had been going through the reception should have set me at ease. Did not the reconciliation of husband and wife remove a profound worry from my mind? But how could a problem that had upset me so much find such an easy resolution? What would have happened if I had remained here?

It would seem that my marriage should not have ended in a divorce. Was it my fault, after all? Everything in my inner world became a confused tangle. If I took life easy, like this couple, would I have to tread such perilous pathways?

'Arefin was here,' Shanu told me in mysterious tones. 'He waited a long time.' I felt my insides turn cold. Overcoming my nervousness I asked, 'What did you tell him?'

Shanu began dusting my bed with the edge of her sari as she said, 'I told him you were at work.'

'You did the right thing, you are great,' I replied and pushed her gently towards her room. 'If he had come to know I had left this place he would have worried unnecessarily.'

'I am not as stupid as you,' Shanu riposted . . . Her open laughter was infectious. 'You have at last said something absolutely incontestable,' I said, laughing. 'Now give me something to eat, I'm dying of hunger.'

Her husband, who was in the bathroom, shouted out, 'Why, didn't swallowing the air fill your belly?'

∼

When I went to work the next day the lift was out of order. My heart sank. Barua Babu was there before me. Before starting the climb up the stairs he inserted a paan into his mouth with a leisurely movement of the left hand. He was almost totally bald and had grown a tuft of hair on the right side so as to spread it all over the bare space. His lips were always bright red from chewing paan with catechu. His massive stomach had to be seen to be believed. And in that heat he had slipped his grotesque torso into such a garish shirt that he was a sight! As soon as he saw me he asked, 'How are things, why didn't you come to work day before yesterday?'

Without replying to his question I asked, 'How are things in the office?'

'You will find out as soon as you walk in,' he said, stepping on to the stairs. 'Now let us start our exercise. After all, my figure is, how would you put it, something to see. If the lift went out of order occasionally . . .'

'What is the matter, why is the lift not working?' Without waiting for a reply, I started climbing the stairs alongside my colleague.

'You want to know why the lift isn't working? It is that old problem'—he paused—'demands.'

I started panting by the time we reached the second floor. Was I losing my strength and stamina? Even at work I had noticed I tired easily, I felt faint, everything around me became shadowy. And amidst all this, red, blue, pink balls tossed about. But I got a grip on myself and did not collapse.

'Did the boss tell you anything day before yesterday?' Barua Babu asked me casually.

41

I replied in surprise, 'What do you mean by "tell me anything day before yesterday"? I didn't come to work that day!'

'He didn't come to work either.' As he finished the sentence his foot stepped on the flight of stairs leading to the fifth floor. A current of rage flowed through me, depriving me of speech. I controlled myself and asked coolly, 'What do you mean by that?'

Both of us paused on the fifth floor landing. He looked into my eyes and asked, 'Why are you getting so worked up? You are an employee of this office, like the rest of us. If you can solve a complex problem on our behalf why should we look askance? After all, it is easier for a woman who works in an office to keep things going smoothly.'

Again, I could feel the blood throbbing in my temples. Only a day's absence and so much had already transpired. My feet were disinclined to trudge up to the sixth floor. There seemed to be a dizzying darkness around me. I asked innocently, 'Didn't the boss come to work day before yesterday?' But the very next moment it rang comically, even in my ear.

'Why, don't you know?' There was obvious disbelief in Barua Babu's voice.

'Believe me'—I felt helpless. I could sense I wasn't handling things right. I was only making myself more and more . . . but I couldn't control myself either. I felt tearful. 'Please believe me. Actually, day before yesterday, I had, you see, such a nasty fever, something went wrong, I kept throwing up . . . Couldn't sacrifice myself for my job, could I? I don't know how to explain it to you.' Trying to find the right words made me lose my breath.

'Why are you getting upset?' Now his attitude was that of someone trying to be reassuring. 'The situation in the office has not taken such a dire turn. It is just that he had also taken the day off. The atmosphere in offices is not very healthy, as you well know.'

I dragged my feet up the stairs. My spirits had sunk utterly. I wasn't the only one, and despite the admirable cordiality among everyone many were subjected to various innuendoes. Still, I couldn't help feeling a chill within me, a freezing sensation, while the blood rose to my head, it felt so intolerable. Just my luck—or else why did the boss have to take that particular day off?

To hell with everyone! In an attempt to lighten up I marched up to my desk. The first thing I did, by force of an old habit, was to spread open a newspaper in front of my face. At once my eyes fell on an announcement—there would be a twelve-hour hartal on the 27th. And just beneath that, under the headline 'BESTIALITY', the news of the rape and consequent death of a three-year-old girl. The ceaseless tapping of typewriters reached my ears. Just as I composed myself and buried my head in a file, Sultana's voice came across from the next desk: 'You were unwell, I suppose?' The faint yet unceasing click of computer keyboards kept breaking on my ears as I replied with a simple 'Yes' without raising my head. There was nobody on the other side of the glass partition; presumably the boss hadn't come today either. Normally he didn't come even a minute late. He had the reputation in the whole office of being as efficient as a computer. As soon as he pressed the bell to summon someone the person must be present before him. And how he would rebuke me if I made the slightest error in typing; rolling his eyes he would say, 'Be alert!' I mimicked him, and the entire staff had got wind of it somehow.

Meanwhile the situation among the office staff had become quite volatile on a number of occasions. The chief cause was the question of bonuses and increments. For long the Eid bonus had been given at the rate of an eighth of the monthly salary.

The employees complained this wasn't enough to even buy a sari for the housemaid. In the inflation-inflicted market, prices had been spiralling upward. Yet there had been a freeze on promotions and increments since long. The murmur of discontent had reached the boss's ears, but it hadn't led to any concerted protest until now. The boss had only one thing to say: the company was losing money. Yet, with every passing day the employees were growing increasingly apathetic towards work. If things continued like this, the owners would have no alternative but to close down the business.

Mutterings, sighs of hopelessness, expressions of anger or disgust, innuendoes—these were an everyday fare in the office. But while I was at work I kept my lips resolutely padlocked. Whatever happened, I had to hang on to the job. The employees' demands were my demands too; but I was plagued by the fear that I might lose my job if I went along with my crusading colleagues. The job guaranteed my survival, so I was anxious not to get embroiled in anything that could jeopardize it. Besides, the boss had so far been considerate in dealing with the situation. Instead of talking of the looming danger of a closure he could have threatened selective dismissals. After all, he himself was an employee of the company. The way everyone blamed him did not make sense to me.

Some had buried their noses in ledgers and files, others were busy chatting. I could make out that some of the gossip related to me. I felt vulnerable, my fingers froze stiff when I tried to write. The atmosphere had steadily become unhealthy. When I started on this job everyone was cordial and helpful and it was a pleasure to work. The same 'I' had slowly moved to a position opposed to everyone else's. But whether I had actually gone through such a transformation was not a question that had been examined; instead, there were these innuendoes and taunts. All this was a new phenomenon, and extremely distressing.

These goings-on centred on me yet again showed that life did not flow in a sweet and simple rhythm. My anxieties mingled with the black tea I drank, sending up confused swirls of vapour.

'Tell me truly, didn't you meet the boss that day?' Sultana had drawn up her chair to sit across my desk. Unconsciously, I folded the paper noisily and placed my extended hands on it. My gaze dropped. My heart was pounding. My veins and arteries seemed to swell to bursting point. My temples throbbed. A scraggly grey cat leapt out of the box of existence. I raised my face from dense shadows. Pen, writing pad and files lay haphazardly before me. Prepare yourself, I said to myself, prepare yourself to mouth an obscene clarification. But something was stuck in my throat. I couldn't say much. I had thought I would utter a string of obscenities; instead, my tone was lachrymose, it sounded strange to my own ears.

This is how I started: 'Sultana, do I have to play truant and date the boss for the sake of an ordinary job? You are a woman like me, I had hoped at least you would appreciate that I have some self-respect.' My words stopped, what I said next seemed to come involuntarily. A strange rage drove me on. 'Even prostitution is better than that. At least the money is better in that line of work.'

As soon as the words were out I realized that my anger had further revealed my vulnerability. Flushed with a sense of outrage, Sultana virtually leapt out of the chair. 'You have given a simple question such a twisted meaning! Have you gone mad?' In response to her sharp words I had to make no effort to turn myself into a shrew. With a malicious smile I said, 'The boss isn't here today either. Will you investigate and find out who he has an engagement with? Why don't you look around and see if anyone among the female staff is missing.'

Sultana was standing. She sat down again and said, 'I am senior to you, at least in length of service. You should learn to adapt. With such a temper, you won't last in any job. Impossible!'

Ah yes . . . Adapting oneself. Shanu and her husband . . . a happy couple in a framed studio portrait. Adapting oneself . . . how it simplified life . . . put the soul to sleep with a sedative injection. Live like a statue, a mummy.

Before leaving the office at the end of the day I went over to Sultana's desk. By then I had cooled down. Facing her squarely I said in contrite tones, 'I am terribly sorry, I misbehaved with you then. I am not really so ill-mannered.'

'No, no, that was nothing.' Her voice now was gentle, 'You didn't realize you were becoming a bit too excited. Let's forget it.'

Stepping out of the office I felt I was slipping again into my habitual hole. My self-analysis resumed. Actually, I had never liked a quiet life. On the other hand, travelling along a self-created uneven track also seemed terribly artificial. Whenever someone intimate, like a lover, tried to work on my love, I felt they were not close to my heart. Someone who could not be my antagonist would never qualify as a man after my heart.

But what if the antagonism wasn't mingled with any affection? Was the person with whom I had lived under the same roof as selfish as my colleagues? Were not my evenings ever lit up by his passionate kisses? Why then did I declare war on him and beat a retreat? Must an antagonist too be as fascinating as my longing? Mulling over such thoughts I paused on the broad stairs. What did I have of my own, apart from my weird pride? One day my friend had said bitterly, 'You are so proud of the passion that's in your blood, and that's why you are so discontented. You are dying of your own venom.' That was why I liked Satyajit so much. He had discovered my discontent, he had identified my agony. What did I really want then? A staunch friend or a bitter antagonist?

What had Rezaul been? He had been like an intolerable something that did not fit anywhere. As a result I could no longer live with him. If I were to spit at someone and he just laughed, I would find him to be spineless and irritating. Rezaul did not fall into that group either. I liked people who didn't fit in anywhere, outsiders, but if they had Rezaul's visage, to hell with their outsiderdom.

Suddenly, for no reason whatsoever, I remembered Mother. When I had grown up she explained the mystery of my birth in this manner: In the small hours she had dreamt that the sky was filled with light. A strong wind was rustling the jamrul tree close to the veranda. A pretty mynah had come from somewhere and perched on a branch of the tree. It was wearing a necklace. 'If only the mynah were mine,' Mother fervently prayed. At once the bird flew into her mouth and went straight down to her belly. Early in the morning she shook Father awake and told him that she would have a jewel of a son. That very day I was born. The agony of seeing her dream shatter was so intense that for several days she couldn't bring herself to look at me.

What if the golden mynah had been a son? Today my younger brother Arefin was able to walk upright thanks to my earnings. Meanwhile, Mother's anxiety over his involvement with a divorcee had no doubt increased. I would have liked very much to know what dreams she had for Arefin, her son, who lived off his sister, dabbled in student politics, failed his exams. Such thoughts kept weighing me down, until I managed to get a grip on myself. I was pondering life's chaotic form—whether I had seen it reflected in anybody. Had I found a friend who could be my affectionate antagonist? Satyajit? Ranju? Did any of them deserve that position? Who knows?

～

On my way down the stairs I ran into Arefin on the first floor landing. As it is, his complexion is very dark and his face is pitted with smallpox scars. Exposure to the sun had made him darker and more unattractive. Sweat dribbled down his dark face to drench his white shirt. As soon as I saw him I thought of the nude postcards, the embarrassment of his roommates. It was disconcerting. No doubt his friends had told him about the incident. Because of it I was annoyed to see him. But then I thought, this was the age for such things, though his personality didn't seem to go with collecting dirty postcards. And anyway, he had come to see me, so I smiled a welcome and almost shouted, 'Look who's here! What brings you here?'

'I have come to see you, I've got a heavy problem on my hands.' He looked at me strangely as he spoke.

'That's what I thought: you wouldn't come to see me if you didn't have a problem.' There was a hint of bitterness in my voice.

'Listen, I am not that selfish.' His tone acquired sudden pungency. 'You are a victim of money-related anxiety. Don't think I can't get along without taking money from you. Besides, I don't ask for it every month.' We continued to go lazily down the stairs as we carried on this exchange.

'What will you do then—thuggery?'

Around the giant lotus of the traffic island dense crowds swirled, rickshaws stood gridlocked.

'There are other things one can do,' said Arefin in a sober tone. 'Why do you think I am such a good-for-nothing? You have spoiled the pleasure of coming to see you.'

Now it was my turn to show sobriety. 'Let's forget all that. Tell me your problem.'

'The problem . . .' He stopped short, as if he had remembered something, then continued, 'Why did you go to the hall that day? I have been worrying myself sick about that, but on coming to see you I forgot it all.'

His face flushed with embarrassment, and through that a charming smile came to life.

'That's what put my back up. Instead of broaching the matter of my hostel visit you . . .' We walked the short distance to the bus stop. 'Now tell me what's your real problem. You haven't eloped with somebody, have you?'

'What an idea!' Arefin wiped the sweat off his brow with his palm. 'I am worried sick thinking about earning some money . . .' That gesture and his tone of voice took me back to our shared childhood. We had been born one after the other. I remembered hunching over to carry him on my back, while he laughingly hammered my neck and head with his tiny fists. Suddenly I lost control, he slipped and fell on the floor, and started wailing. My guilty fear sent me running. It was late evening when I came back.

'Tell me, why did you go to the hostel?'

'Why, don't I have the right to visit your hostel?' I began to bite a fingernail.

'But of course. It is only that you had never been there before.'

Suddenly the subject of Irfan Chacha surfaced in my consciousness. I wanted to talk to Arefin about it, but something made me desist: I knew he would kick up a fuss over it.

'I was going past your hostel and on the spur of the moment I decided to drop in to see you.' Then quickly changing the subject I asked, 'Can't I act on impulse just because I am a woman?'

Just then the bus arrived. Absolutely packed. Damn! I didn't feel like jostling my way in. I remained standing on the kerb. A procession went by, shouting slogans. We stepped back. Arefin's expression clearly showed that he hadn't taken my point. But he didn't want to argue either. 'I've got to go to Old Dhaka. I am looking for work, some sort of fly-by-night business. Waiting to finish my university studies will only land me in a desperate situation. Every day there is some political meeting or demonstration. Of course I will need some capital.' The colour drained from his face. 'Actually, you had sussed me out quite correctly.' He looked embarrassed now. 'You cannot finance the whole thing, but if you could manage a little . . .'

A violent flame came alive within me and tongues of fire seemed to singe me. Sweating because of the intense heat I hissed out, 'I cannot manage even a single paisa. It pains me that you could ask when you know how hard up I am.'

The procession turned left and disappeared.

My reply reduced Arefin to utter helplessness. 'I know,' he muttered. 'But this penniless state has become intolerable. Even that tutoring job I've lost today.'

His words drove me frantic. Dust swirled in the hot, humid breeze. People brushed past. I missed another bus which too was overcrowded. People had finished work and were rushing homeward. Had Arefin not been with me I would have joined the fray and fought my way into the bus. But my feet felt leaden. The conversation had left me weak and listless. If I wanted to take a step forward, somebody seemed to hold on to both my legs, so any forward movement was impossible. Seeing the expression on my face, Arefin said, 'Don't worry about me. I lost my tutoring job because the child's parents want to get him admitted into a better school. They have decided to hire a teacher in that school as a private tutor so that the child doesn't have any problem at the interview.' He kept talking without a pause: 'I am also looking out for fresh opportunities. I think I'll be able to find another private tutor's job. Of course getting to know where these bloody opportunities lie is one hell of a job. Life has become so difficult.' Just then another bus appeared and without waiting for Arefin to finish I grabbed the door handle and levering myself up said reassuringly, 'Don't give up hope. I'll see if I can manage some money.' He smiled as he waved goodbye. 'I'll come to your place tomorrow.'

I got home and, after a bath, began preparing a snack of *moori*, or puffed rice, mixed with sliced onions and green chillies. Shanu came in and sat down beside me; she exuded an air of mystery. I made myself comfortable by leaning against the wall with the bowl of moori in my lap. As I looked at her she seemed like a strange being. She sat without saying a word and kept twirling the end of her sari around a finger. But she was itching to say something. My guess proved right. Breaking the silence she unburdened her soul all at once: 'It seems I have news.'

'What do you mean?' I asked with feigned innocence.

'Strange! Can't you guess?' And then, as if I was her husband, pretending not to understand just to pull her leg, she continued, 'Stop play-acting and tell me how long you had taken to realize that it had happened.'

Suddenly, I began to tremble. How effortlessly I had forgotten everything. And whenever I did remember it the whole of my body seemed to become drenched in venom. I had meanwhile mastered the art of forgetting. So many thoughts had crowded my mind over the past two days, and yet not once . . . I cast a helpless glance at Shanu. The moment demanded the expression of great joy. But here I was with my moori turning soggy. My back seemed to be pasted to the wall. Though it was buried in the distant past, I had mulled over this episode repeatedly in anguish and I simply could not learn to accept it. A tiny wisp of a baby . . . its cry shook the very roof of the hospital . . . Savlon . . . nurses . . . spittle . . . clapping hands on my ears I ran while the piercing cries drove me frantic, mad. O Allah, stop the crying, stop the heart-rending sound. A huge hammer had been pounding my head to a pulp. From the cavity between my legs the doctor had pulled out this strange thing that would not stop crying even after two months. I rushed here and there like a locust. Off to the pharmacy for medicine. An endless stream of saliva dribbled from the child's bleeding lips. But the worst was the lack of money. What a strange power it had, controlling the life and death of human beings. All the rushing about was in search of money. We had borrowed right and left, till we were on the point of bankruptcy. Rezaul looked pale, haggard. There was nothing we could do. We were falling back, and behind us lay a gaping abyss. At one point all became still, quiet. The newborn child's cries stopped. I was then plunged into a witless state . . . At home, on the street, at work I would prick my ears in the hope that I would be able to hear those cries. At night I tossed and turned in bed. In my heart resounded the cries I had tried to run away from. And now, just to revive those cries my sleepless nights stretched endlessly . . .

Noticing my strangely altered expression Shanu controlled herself. Perhaps she had realized that it wasn't wise to bring up the subject of pregnancy before me. I too had learnt to control myself. Raising a fistful of moori to my mouth I nearly shouted, 'What? All this had happened and I have been totally in the dark! Does Kamal Bhai know?'

Shanu's excitement was something to see. 'I have been telling him for several days now. The date has come and gone and still there is no sign of the period. I have never had even a day's delay. Eight days after the due date, I ate *hilsa* fish and threw up . . .'

'The hilsa can induce vomiting even when one hasn't conceived.' But what was the point of putting doubts in her mind? I changed tack at once. 'Since you always have regular periods, it probably is pregnancy. Do one thing, go to the doctor and get a test done. It's best to be certain.'

~

That night stifled sobs reached my ears. I sat up in bed in the dark. I was just dozing off when in a moment this most tender of earthly sounds completely drove sleep away. I groped my way to turn on the light.

In the evening Kamal Bhai had brought a gift of apples and oranges for me. Shanu's expression revealed all. As it is, it didn't take much to make her feel inferior. She thought she was unattractive, even though her dark face was adorned by an exquisite pair of eyes. Her hair was ungroomed, yet I had seldom seen such silken glossiness as it had. Her nose might be a trifle broad, but it went very well with her thin lips. Her figure too wasn't bad at all. It was only because she had no dress sense that her beauty ultimately didn't quite blossom. Nor did Kamal Bhai have the eye to be of any help in this regard.

Be that as it may, Shanu was still attractive. Let her agonize over her dark skin, brand herself ugly, believe that without a fair and pinkish complexion there could be no beauty, it made no difference. She was attractive to my eyes. But strangely enough, Shanu's laments over her poor self-image influenced her husband's views. Of course right from the start he had a somewhat ambivalent attitude regarding her looks. They set eyes on each other for the first time on their wedding night. According to Shanu, her husband was terribly disappointed with her at first sight. 'You didn't look so dark in your photos,' he had said. And with that the subject of her complexion became an oppressive weight on her soul.

'What, you saw each other for the first time on your wedding night!' I said with feigned surprise just to needle her.

'What else,' she replied with a touch of offended pride. 'Do you think I would go for a love marriage like you?'

'My God! You went to bed with a stranger the very first night you met him.'

This annoyed her. 'Have you come from another planet? What is the matter with you; you are giving a twisted shape to what is proper and sanctified.'

'After calling you a darkie Kamal Bhai went ahead and did it!'

Shanu burst into laughter. 'That's the male for you. When he is excited by the scent what does complexion matter?'

'Why? Did you drench yourself in perfume?'

'Stop being naughty. As if you had whiled away the night doing nothing. Besides, marrying out of your own choice didn't help you keep your marriage intact.'

I was ready with a snide retort. 'The way you are keeping yours intact, if one uses your method even a shattered plate can be glued together.' I don't know what she made of this, but she was silenced. Actually, she wasn't one to relish the intricacies of a battle of wit, so instead of pursuing the subject she just commented, 'Women shouldn't be so hot-headed. It harms family life.'

After this noble sentiment there could be no more argument.

Anyway, her husband now felt free to taunt her endlessly about her appearance. 'Will a flower stuck in the hair improve your looks? Don't put on lipstick: your skin is so dark it will glow like Lalbagh Fort.' What a vulgar simile! As for Shanu's response, it made my blood boil: 'I didn't make myself this way. Allah did, so what can I do?'

The fact is Shanu is weak and cowardly—she could retort straight to his face with: 'Why don't you look at yourself in the mirror, you dried-up jute stalk. Look at your hollow cheeks, your weak little chin, the two elephant's ears flanking your undersized head.' That would have shut him up for all time. But does that mean I want a catastrophic battle between them? Nina, I said to myself, every day is a battle, every day is disastrous. You have severed all bonds and still you want more conflict? What strange addiction is this? Don't you know how to come to a compromise?

Well, after the gift of apples and oranges for me, there was some hilarity—unbecoming at their age—as they were turning in, then the obscene creaking of the bed, the trip to the bathroom to wash—no sign of discord in all this. Then why was Shanu sobbing like this now?

Of course everything about them was different. I just could not figure them out. Recently one night they broke out in a violent quarrel. Shanu was enraged enough to give as good as she got. 'Don't I know how characterless you are, you wild beast, you son of a bitch . . .' 'You bitch, you whore.' Kamal Bhai's words were an indistinct hiss.

The response was a loud crash. Glass shattered on the floor. In such a situation, a third person like me could only feel an ineffable unease, a strange apprehensiveness and fear. I lay flat in my bed. I tried to soothe myself with remembered snatches of songs and lullabies while Shanu's bitter tones resounded through the flat: 'Go and pimp for whores. You aren't worth even two paise . . .' Etc., etc.

Then Shanu's sudden scream: 'O my God, he will kill me!' At once I was on my feet. But when I tried to move I found that my feet were glued to the floor. Would it be wise to interfere in a domestic quarrel? I felt utterly helpless. I got back into bed. Everything fell silent. A cold fear gripped my heart: was she dead?

In the morning I was struck dumb with astonishment. Shanu after an early bath looked so serene. She was towelling her hair. She came over when she saw I had got up. 'You must have felt very . . . you know . . . last night,' she said casually. Droplets of water enhanced the softness of her face. I tried to be as normal as I could. 'Oh, don't worry about it. These things happen.' Shanu went back to their room, still towelling her hair. 'Come on, get up. What an addiction to sleep!' I was filled with loathing. Were these people human? Had their souls died? Was it possible to find happiness in habit? The next moment I tried to restrain my thoughts. After all, why should I want everyone to be like me? If the heat of two bodies could wipe away intolerable distress in a moment, who was I to complain?

But tonight the sobs were of a different sort. I couldn't hear Kamal Bhai's voice. What had induced such ceaseless sobbing in Shanu? I lay down with a book. Shibnarayan Ray's *Sroter Biruddhey* (*Against the Current*). It had an essay, '*Nastiker Dharma Jiggasha*' ('Religion of an Atheist'), which Satyajit had asked me to read long ago. For various reasons I hadn't gone beyond the first page. Again I entered the whirlpool of its ideas—well, did I believe in God? I did not know, because whenever I set forth to look for Him, there was no sign of Him.

Sometimes, when I used to walk along the railway track— this was before my marriage—I used to see a shadow somewhere in the distance. Rather like a hazy fog that had merged with the sky. But the days have rolled by since then; where in the depths of my faith was God to be found? Where were the railway tracks? I would hasten along them till I went really far. Would I then catch sight of that shadow standing in the distance like a hoary banyan tree? Or is it that there wasn't anything after all? And anyway, weren't they all lost to the march of time—those railway tracks, my hurried walks, that shadow? Who knows? Did I know everything about myself? Strange! I hadn't remembered it for some time. Then suddenly today my child came crawling across the pages of my book. The letters faded away, and in their place the baby took shape. The child's yellow body shook involuntarily. It gripped my nipple with toothless gums and let out an endless earth-shaking scream when I pushed it away.

I went back to my old life. Wringing me dry, scenes from those days came floating on the surface. The child buried its face in my breast, as if to forget the anguish of the whole world. In the depths of my breasts, in every cell there seemed to be poisoned blood instead of milk. But as soon as the child was pushed away it set off that wail again. Lying on one side made my body ache. In order to take his mind off these things, Rezaul's friends used to force him to go out with them. I remember how one night they got him sozzled on gin. What a pathetic state he was in when he got back. He staggered and fell upon the baby. 'It has come into my life like a curse, like death. Oh, I will suffocate to death.' And what about me? I didn't know what sort of intoxication would liberate me from this agony. I whispered to the child's soft body, 'Sleep, dearest, sleep . . .'

I dreamt whenever I fell asleep. In scientific language, it was shallow, REM sleep. Did a demon pursue me in sleep? Why else would I see my father dangling from a banyan tree like a langur with outstretched arms hanging in space? How he guffawed! I woke up. A ferocious beast seemed to entwine me like molten lava from a volcano. How varied was the world of dreams! But most of the time I would lie awake. Like Kajal Rekha I spent the whole night taking out the poisoned needles from the body of the fairy tale prince. When all but the two inserted into the eyes have been taken out, I go for a bath, lest the prince wake up to find me unkempt, unattractive. I return and see that another woman has removed the needles and is the prince's betrothed. The invisible sign in my heart remains unknown to him. My bones grow cold with the passage of the small hours. Memories come crowding in. The harsh realities of my present shroud my childhood, my youth, like a fog. I am so attached to memory that Satyajit says I relish sorrow. Relish! Such a sweet word. Could I taste sorrow with my tongue I would fall in love. A magical time seemed to descend on my life. The young man used to draw and paint . . . I wished he would be my companion. Intense desire brought venom to my lips. I wanted to strike without warning and inject my envenomed love. But was anyone robust enough to withstand it? I might have wanted him as a companion, but did he turn around even once to look at me? Did I get the opportunity to gather venom? No, I could draw close to him in dreams rather than in reality. And those dreams too were like mediocre verses. One night I dreamt that he was muttering, as if in a trance, 'Here, take my existence, sink your teeth in, lick my blood with your greedy witch's tongue. You'll never forget its taste. Its bright hue will never come off your tongue.' When I woke up my words were like poems or songs, spreading their shade around me. This is how in those days a man used to enter my life and stand beside me like a companion. I used to wield a knife, expecting blood, but he would only yield water . . . nothing but water. But how can I not acknowledge Mahim, for did he not arouse my youthful passion? His innumerable kisses amidst the library shelves . . . I couldn't breathe . . . as soon as my lips parted . . . amidst those stacks of books . . . how can I deny that excitement? The books stood witness around us as he declared, 'Your touch has awakened my dormant existence and made me a man. Nina, my debt to you is incalculable.' How can I dismiss that Mahim from memory? For that is how dream and reality would come together. I would toss and turn with these thoughts in the small hours. I would turn off the light and lie flat till I fell asleep.

I got up early. The light came crawling in through the window like a spotless white cat. A helicopter droned overhead. My whole body tingled: what a strangely exciting dream I'd had. Someone was caressing me with tremendous ardour; after a long time I felt the arousal of physical desire. My hand gripped the man's hair by its roots—who was he? I was sinking into a dense fog but came up again. The pale moonlight tirelessly played on the folds of my body. Obscuring the moonlight, Rezaul's grotesque naked body stood up straight. Like dew, I disappeared into the air.

I opened the door and stepped out on to the balcony. Clouds floated in the sky like the black hair of the dark fairy tale maiden. The moist air softly beckoned. Phosphorescent lights glimmered all around. A chill settled in my veins. On the roof of the next house a man was cleaning his teeth with a neem twig. Further off, a young girl practised scales to the accompaniment of a harmonium. From the basti came the sound of the watchman striking the tin walls to warn off criminals. Ignoring all this, other thoughts surged through my brain: in the folk tale of Behula and Lakshmindar, the serpent dispatched by the irate snake goddess entered their bridal chamber through a tiny chink. Did my bridal chamber too have such a chink? What strange thoughts!

I woke up very early. Why Shanu had cried at night for so long was still a mystery. She was in bed when Kamal Bhai left for work. Before long I had also got ready to go to office. Then the daily routine followed—typing, filing, the sombre countenance of the boss, the small talk of colleagues—'Know what, my niece missed the merit list by only a single mark,' 'What a marriage I have got into, my friend, the wife's unwell for twelve months a year,' 'Had to leave home without breakfast after a tremendous tiff with the wife,' 'I can never find the comb when I'm getting ready to come to work,' 'When is the hartal? Is it the 27th? Not bad, hee hee hee, a day of rest,' 'Paying the son's exam fees has left me broke: eating dry bread makes my tummy rumble all night,' 'You have said it, Brother, this is no way to live,' 'Who? Mrs Gupta? Well, I too have seen her with him once, in a Chinese restaurant,' 'There's no end to hartals and political agitation in this country,' 'Damn, not a single pen writes,' 'I went to my younger brother to ask for a loan, but the way his wife behaved! . . . It would have been less galling if she had beaten me with a shoe,' 'What a country! The price of something shoots up from 10 taka to 18 taka, yet there isn't a whimper of protest! Every son of a bitch is a dalal, a paid agent of the government.'

Amidst this chorus my ear pricked up at hearing something. Someone had lowered his voice to say, 'Our boss is the biggest dalal. He must be getting something extra from the owner. He has bought a plot of land in Basundhara.'

The words fell on highly receptive ears. Everyone piped in, 'Is that so?'

Now a loud voice proclaimed, 'Is he the only dalal? There are many dalals in this office, but you cannot tell who.'

But today even such spicy gossip had to give way to the topic of the newspaper headlines: 'Saddam Hussain Occupies Kuwait'.

The invasion had generated tremendous excitement in the office. News and views were being heatedly exchanged. Amidst all this my eyes calmly took in the reports. Iraqi troops had massed on the Kuwait border. The United States was gravely concerned. The significance of all this escaped me. Some were shouting, 'What business is this of the Americans?' Anyway, I am a very ordinary person, so I quietly weathered the chaos in the workplace and slipped out at the end of the day. I jostled my way into a bus and later walked through the dark, smelly lane to my door.

As soon as I got in I heard that Satyajit had come looking for me on some urgent business. I wondered what that could be as I changed my sari and entered the bathroom. Shanu's expression was grim. I glanced at her surreptitiously but did not say anything. Let her tell her story of her own accord. The shower had a copious supply of water. It had been many days since the last time the dark and narrow confines of the bathroom had witnessed such a surge of water. I drenched my entire body with exquisite abandon. The pungent sweat and dirt that had accumulated in the folds of my body began to dissolve and disappear. Such peace. My eyes grew heavy with drowsiness.

I came out and was towelling my hair when Shanu sobbed out the words, 'Last night I went to the bathroom and discovered I had started bleeding. I had deluded myself. Your Kamal Bhai feels terribly let down; tell me what I should do.' Her voice was choking.

I felt sorry for her. I made her sit down on my bed and consoled her. 'If it hasn't happened this month, it can happen next month. Why do you give in to despair so easily? I have seen many women conceive after fifteen years of marriage.'

Those who lack inner strength are quick to accept facile consolation. She asked eagerly, 'Is this true?'

'It happened with one of my aunts,' I said. 'She conceived after ten years.'

Shanu's eyes brightened. 'Please tell this to your Kamal Bhai.'

When she left I came back to my own world. Why was Satyajit looking for me? Arefin too had said he would come, but hadn't. Should have asked how much he actually needed. I had just borrowed 200 taka from Sultana. I wouldn't be able to pay any of it back out of my salary this month. Well, if I asked

Satyajit would he be able to lend me some money? If only Arefin would be able to get something going and stand on his own feet. Boys these days were streetwise. Maybe he would find a niche for himself even as he was buffeted by the wind.

Gradually my thoughts led me to the town I had left behind. I remembered Ranu's face. I would get news of her gradual degeneration. My limbs felt heavy. Sometimes I would seethe with rage. The youngest of my siblings, Montu, dozed over a book in the barred light of a hurricane lantern.

Even at the fag end of the twentieth century this house was the scene of the mysterious play of shadows cast by hurricane lanterns. The electricity had been disconnected three months ago for non-payment of bills. But why was I so bitter about my entire family? I tried to analyse myself, but it didn't help, for the bottom line was that I lacked the means to give them the assistance they required. Parallel to their bad luck ran my inadequacies. Was my loathing a defence mechanism to protect me from distress? No, I decided, I wouldn't worry about my family any more. Ranu was an unfortunate episode in my life, every detail of which I wanted to expunge from memory. Then, as I flicked open a magazine my eyes fell on a child's picture . . . Oh, where could I hide? Pressing the throbbing veins in my temples I tried to figure out why Satyajit was looking for me.

Another week dragged on like this. But at the start of the next week such an unexpected event took place that its impact left me in a state of limitless wonder. The tedious tenor of my life was suddenly replaced with a strange pulsation. My self-image was greatly enhanced, I felt I had extraordinary intrinsic worth.

Before this happened I had gone to see Satyajit. As soon as I reached his confectionery he said, 'Wait a minute, let me finish the work at hand.' I had gone there straight from work and the dusk was already gathering. Presently he came and joined me. In front stood a brand new Vespa scooter. He said with evident pleasure, 'Just bought this.' The western sky was growing inert as the night drew nearer. I couldn't help complaining, 'Did you go to my place just to tell me about your new scooter?'

'Do you think I am such a crass fellow?' he rejoined with some heat. The next moment he looked a little distraught as he ran his fingers through his tousled hair. 'Of course,' he said. 'I feel guilty about spending money on a scooter at a time when Ranju is facing a crunch.'

'Life does not stand still for anybody,' I said, reiterating a time-worn platitude. Then I asked, 'How is Ranju these days?'

'Getting a lot of flak from his father. Meanwhile, Salauddin has started hosting regular *ganja* sessions.'

'Your hypocrisy is really annoying. You all are worse than docile cats.'

Satyajit had pushed the scooter quite a distance. 'Will you ride behind me?' he asked. 'Or will you lose caste if you do so?'

'I don't have such cheap prejudices,' I said, laughing, but I had no clue where we would go on the bike.

'Don't begin to suspect that I am trying to take easy advantage. The way your life is kicking up a stink, the ride will give some fresh air that will do us both some good. Of course if you aren't comfortable . . .'

'Look here, Satyajit, I have already told you I have no problem, but this is a small city and people's mentality is correspondingly narrow.'

'Who do you have in this city? Do you care for anyone's opinion? Don't you trust your own soul? If you are honest before it, nothing else matters.'

Satyajit started the scooter. It revved up and went flying. The city had begun its nightlife. The whistling wind blew my sari edge backward. It made his voice quaver as he asked, 'What were you saying, hypocrisy? A guy suffers such a loss and you reduce it to insignificance? Don't you understand Ranju's plight?' The speeding Vespa narrowed the brightly lit world into a tunnel. It was a wonderful sensation. I had never felt such ecstasy. My nerves tingled. Still, I had to say something in reply, so I braced myself against the wind and said, 'Is smoking ganja a solution to the problem? You have all turned thirty. Does such a reaction to frustration do you any credit? Tell him to go to a whorehouse, that's the next step in this direction.'

The wind distorted my voice, making it sound strange in my own ears. At last Satyajit stopped near Crescent Lake. Bare steps stretched along it. Beyond them lay the silky hair of water. The current braided the hair in such mysterious ways. 'This is not a safe place,' I said. 'The police pick up young people and slap on them a charge of indecent behaviour, and then there are muggers and purse-snatchers.'

'It seems you are speaking from experience. Who did you come with?'

'I don't have to tell you that. Damn! I feel quite uneasy here.'

'You will never appreciate spontaneity, not in your lifetime. You felt uneasy coming with me and that's why you are nervous. We'll just stroll along this path.' Then he turned back to the previous subject. 'Why do you see ganja in such a bad light?'

'If one naturally enjoys it I have no objection, but to resort to it for solace when one has had bad luck in business . . . it is like being the hero in a sentimental Bengali film.' I was just rattling off the words because I had to say something, not because they arose out of deep feeling.

Trees lined the path which was broad and smooth. Sodium lights gave off tremulous radiance. The breeze whipped the water. I felt drowsy. I walked close to Satyajit, who was pushing the Vespa along. The nature of the light, the breeze, lent him an unfamiliar aspect, made him look quite splendid. His tousled hair played about his head. His eyes, the burnished cheeks beneath the slight bristle, his peculiar style of holding a cigarette between the fingers of his left hand . . . Did I really know this Satyajit? I looked ahead with sleepy eyes. The breeze rustling in the tamarisk trees was strangely intoxicating. What if he put his arm around me? A ripple of excitement ran through my body. If only he would touch my hand!

'Rezaul wants to meet you,' he suddenly blurted out. 'It seems he has something serious to say.'

Satyajit flung away a half-smoked cigarette. 'Where did you meet him?' I asked, dragging myself out of a chasm.

'Why, doesn't he know my confectionery?' Then in a tone of accusation, 'You are not treating the matter seriously.'

'Why, did he say anything that deserves serious attention?' I countered in an ironic tone.

'He seems to be going through a rough patch. He has lost the insurance job. He's got a job in a business house now but isn't happy there and has proposed a partnership with me. He is determined to do something profitable.'

'Where will he get the capital?' I asked foolishly.

'Didn't say anything about that. He did say he needs you, though. But that has no connection with his present state, of that I am sure.'

'Needs me? Why?' My bile rose as I spat out the questions. That bastard Satyajit, why did he have to bring me to such a lovely place to raise such a subject? It was clear I wouldn't find peace in this lifetime. I knew that we would now ruin the exquisite evening, sully it, for the subject was such that a conversation about it could never reach a happy conclusion. Bracing myself for that unsavoury resolution I asked, 'Have you told him anything?'

'I asked him to come to Salauddin's place tomorrow just after five. I said I would take you there.'

The skin on my body became taut. 'Does he know Salauddin's house?'

'Why are you conducting an interrogation? I gave him the address.'

'Satyajit, did you ask me before promising him anything?' My annoyance brimmed over. 'Am I a plaything that you can carry about?'

'Look here,' said Satyajit. 'I made the promise in good faith. I know you as a liberal person. After spending so many years together, just because you are divorced how can you refuse to listen to what he has to say?'

There was silence for a while. Bright lights all around had turned the night dazzling white. We had left behind the area lit up by sodium lights. I felt a creeping fear. My body trembled in apprehension. So long I had been in a trance that neutralized fear. Why did I blame Shanu—didn't I too become gratified at the slightest attention paid to me? Did I have any personality? If somebody uttered a few sweet and dreamy words to induce me to lie down in the moonlight, wouldn't I unfold myself at once? Such thoughts were too distressing, so willy-nilly I went back to the embarrassing subject of Rezaul.

'Has he concocted any new story about our divorce?'

'Yes, but I don't want to talk about it,' Satyajit said coldly. 'What he said didn't seem to be a concoction to me.'

'Why don't you come out with it?' I asked, laughing. 'I wouldn't be surprised by anything he says.'

'But this thing will disturb you,' Satyajit said in sombre tones. 'He had given hints earlier. Yesterday he told me the whole story. Of course he asked me not to tell you anything about it.'

'Then don't tell me,' I said.

The conversation stalled again. Of course I was inwardly bursting with curiosity. Satyajit fidgeted. Minutes passed. Satyajit couldn't hold himself back any longer. 'Rezaul said you had some sexual perversions, and that was the chief reason behind the break-up.'

I stopped dead in my tracks. I was shaking, and my desolate voice burst forth desperately, 'What are you saying? How could he give such an interpretation of what happened?'

Satyajit reacted angrily, 'I don't want to get involved in your intimate affairs. Get on the scooter. I'll drop you home. I don't understand all this. I had no inkling that something like this might lie behind the divorce. I had believed you. I used to blame him all the time. Damn, why did I have to tell you all this?'

I felt my heart would burst. I dragged myself somehow and mounted the Vespa. It started moving.

'Are you coming tomorrow?'

'Really, Satyajit, after all this! Do you think I am not human or what?'

My chest lightened. I could hear the child crying again. All night those cries would flood the universe. What was it in my ear, the whistling wind or an endless cry? Ranu, why did you turn yourself into a snuffed-out lamp-wick? Why had my life taken such a turn? I stood on the veranda to enjoy the steady breeze. Children played happily in the field. They hurled a dead rat into the air. Swollen-bellied and ant-infested, it landed with a thud on my feet. Ants swarmed over it. Why was there such a stench at all times? An enraged Rezaul slowly turned into a demon king and advanced on me. With a swift motion his hand had gripped a tuft of my hair at the root. Pale with fright I drew back. My head struck something . . . so dark . . . black, bestial blood! Horrid! Everything grew faint. I bumped into things . . . darkness . . . only darkness. That man at last put his arms around me and broke down in remorse! But why?

When I got home I collapsed into endless sobbing. I hugged a pillow and just cried and cried. So, that's how Rezaul presented me to Satyajit! When dropping me off Satyajit kept explaining to me Rezaul had told him repeatedly that I shouldn't hear about those things. He had confided in Satyajit because they were old friends. I should go to Salauddin's house. It ill behoved me to be so sentimental. I remained silent throughout, but when I came in I couldn't control myself any longer. I drifted in a torrent of tears till I gradually calmed down.

I asked myself why I had not explained my point of view to Satyajit. Who knows how Rezaul had expatiated on perversion in order to cover his own guilt? How angry Satyajit had been with me! When I got home I should have told him, detail by detail, everything that had happened. But then, what exactly would I have said? Is it possible to explain to another person the subtle forms of anguish one goes through? Especially to someone who had no first-hand experience of marital life? But why did Rezaul come after such a long time to say all that to Satyajit? Where had he got the gumption to say it? And after saying it all, why the desperate desire to see me? I was mad at Satyajit for being such a deceiver, for saying breezily to someone whose life had become a stinking mess, 'Come, let's go for a ride,' and then on reaching such a romantic spot saying all those things with an utterly uncalled-for theatricality. No, there was no point clarifying matters relating to that disgusting subject. Let people think as they liked. It did not matter if my fragile friendship was severed. I wasn't even going to see Rezaul to prove that I was different from the majority of women. I just did not care.

At half past nine that evening Arefin dropped in. Relaxing at once, I asked him why he had become such a rare bird.

'What's the matter, were you crying?' He became quite anxious on seeing me.

'I felt weepy, so I cried.' I spoke frankly, without any pretence. 'What about you? Have you decided what you will do?'

'Astonishing! Why don't you tell me why you were crying?' Arefin was upset. 'You know I don't consider you a weakling.'

'Does that mean I can't even cry a little? Do I have to prove my strength to myself? Have I cried in front of you?'

'There are lots of things you conceal from me.' He looked glum, as he often did during such exchanges—it touched me to the quick.

'Actually, nothing worth telling happens in my life. I don't feel like bringing up mundane matters.'

'Really, doesn't anything worth talking about happen?' There was a sharpness in his voice. 'Have you told me where you spent the night after you had a tiff and walked out?'

I was startled at these words. 'Who told you?'

'Whoever it was,' he said, suddenly becoming sombre. 'I went to your office that day to see if you would tell me of your own accord.'

I felt anger brewing inside me. This was certainly Shanu's doing. Yet what an innocent show she had put up that day. It wasn't an easy task to see through such people. How smoothly she had lied.

'Often, you don't stay in the hall either—do you tell me about that?' I looked into his eyes as I counter-attacked.

'Not often.' There was annoyance in his voice. 'Don't try a stab in the dark. A friend's entire family had gone to their village home, and I had to stay in their house to guard it. Anyway, do we have to regard each other with suspicion?

Can't we ask a simple question? Otherwise, what is the point of relationships? Everyone can live just as they please. No problems would arise then.'

'Let's forget all that. Tell me about yourself.'

'There was a gunfight on campus last night. It was nerve-racking.' As I turned on him an anxious stare, he changed the subject. 'Have you seen the news on TV? Five hundred Kuwaitis have died. American aircraft carriers are heading for the Gulf. There is tremendous excitement over this throughout Dhaka.'

'What have petty clerks like us to do with warships? *Che sâra sâra.* Now tell me about your fly-by-night business plans.'

'That sort of thing is not for me. A friend of mine tried it and landed in jail. His initial success had attracted me. He would go to Chittagong port, buy contraband cigarettes, cloth, cosmetics and sell them at a profit to shops in Dhaka. But the risk is great: if you get caught you've had it. Thank God I didn't get into the racket.'

'I am glad you have shown such good sense,' I said appreciatively.

Arefin fidgeted around a little. I couldn't tell if my words had pleased him. 'Actually,' he said wistfully, 'one needs a lot of money to do business—a lot of money.' Then suddenly his voice dropped to a whisper. 'There is some bad news.'

'What bad news?'

His voice almost broke as he said, 'Day before yesterday a pickpocket stole my money. The bus was crammed full and I could barely stay upright by holding on to the rail with both hands ... seizing the opportunity ... I didn't want to tell you about it.'

'How much money?'

'Nine hundred taka.'

'So much! How did you come by so much money?'

The blood drained from Arefin's face. 'I had just got paid for my tutoring job. I bought a shirt for Montu for a hundred taka. He had written to me asking for one. The next day I'd have gone home to see Father. I'd got a letter saying he was very ill. My wallet was in my left trouser pocket, but it was empty. I had kept all the money in the right pocket. The son-of-a-bitch pickpocket outfoxed me and didn't touch the wallet. I know it is making you feel awful, but I just couldn't keep such a big thing from you.'

'Splendid!' Anger and despair made me tearful. 'It happened day before yesterday, and you come and tell me only today. Clearly it didn't bother you all that much.' I was overwhelmed by a desire to discomfit him with a barrage of criticism, so I fixed him with a stare and let loose. 'I have always noticed that you are callous in handling money. You would learn to respect money if you had to work like me, put up with snide comments from colleagues, obscene insinuations involving the boss and yet hang in there just to get 2,000 taka each month and then half-starve in order to send money home, pay for a younger brother's education. Then you wouldn't be careless while travelling by bus with so much money in your pocket. Only an idiot would be such an easy target for a pickpocket.'

Unburdening myself, I leapt off the bed and, without giving Arefin a chance to respond, entered the bathroom and bolted the door. A bitter juice pushed its painful way up through my chest and reaching my throat brought tears to my eyes. I splashed my face with water. Actually, I had to admit that I buckled under very easily these days. Did it mean I had reached the end of my tether? The low-powered bulb made the air in the bathroom look pale yellow. The plaster was flaking off the walls. There was a single tiny ventilator and that too was obscured by cobwebs. The space was claustrophobic.

When I had composed myself I came out, only to be stunned to see that Arefin had left. 'Couldn't you stop him?' I demanded of Shanu. Now it was her turn to show surprise: 'How would I know what had transpired between you two? I shut the door after him, which he asked me to do.'

I felt like dying. Perhaps I had overstepped the limit. Wasn't want of money a cause of torment for Arefin as well? Maybe that's why he hadn't come earlier. I had to admit that at times I was blinded by all-consuming rage. I sat in a chair and rested my head on the tiny desk. Had I alienated myself from everybody? If that was the case, was it entirely my fault? Suddenly I recalled Arefin saying that Father had become very ill. Strange that the news hadn't struck me at the time. Arefin was right, wasn't he, when he accused me of having a perverse relationship with money? He must have noticed some changes in me.

Father lay paralysed in bed. Mother's eyes had grown weak. She could hardly be called old, yet as soon as it was dusk she had to feel her way inside the house like a blind person. But it wasn't just my parents; everyone in the family seemed to me now to be inhabitants of a distant isle. Father's chalk-white eyes and Mother's laboured breathing and continuous cursing of herself were enough to make me suffocate. In such a situation how could Father become very ill—what could be worse than the state he was in? Was he nearing the point then . . . ? No, if things were that bad why should Arefin be the only one to be informed? If I was such an outcast, then why those letters imploring me to send more money?

What a disgusting crowd of flies! Weren't they ashamed to lick up my leavings?

Meanwhile, there was intense excitement in the office. My colleagues had split into two factions over Saddam's Kuwait invasion. Some hailed him, others declared his action as uncalled-for aggression and supported the USA. The office frequently became as volatile a place as the Gulf. For a simple clerk like me who had been demoralized by the mundane struggles of life, such things were a matter of indifference, and it was out of mere curiosity that I scanned the headlines— 'IRAQ WARNS AMERICA AND HER ALLIES: WE WILL WREAK HAVOC IF ATTACKED'; 'IRAQ TELLS EUROPE— RESTRAIN AMERICA TO AVERT WORLD WAR', etc. . . . Slowly, sleep descended on my eyes . . .

∽

Within a few days of all this occurred the unthinkable event I have already mentioned. I lay sprawled in a chair. Since my room was nearest to the front door, the chore of opening it when anyone knocked usually fell on me. I had set Shibnarayan Ray's book aside and picked up *The Autobiography of Vincent Van Gogh*. The book was lying open yet asleep, so to speak, on the table before me. It was so readable that one could easily lose oneself in it. Van Gogh's early years, his prolific output of paintings, his failure to sell his work, his acute impecuniousness and utter desolation. And before all that, his sufferings when he shared the life of coal-miners. In that situation too he did not stop painting. As I read I was overcome with despair as I thought of my own life. I had given up everything at the slightest obstruction. Did Van Gogh too face defeat? I sat still with the book before me. I was torn within myself as I grappled with the question: why suicide? Even after that his art had triumphed. Extricating myself from this labyrinth of thoughts, I answered the door with my brows knit in annoyance. A middle-aged gentleman, tall, well-built, fair-complexioned. A clean-shaved face, broad forehead. Touch of grey at the temples. Good taste in clothes. I took in his appearance at a glance. Must be someone to see Shanu or her husband. I turned to go and call them when he cleared his throat and asked, 'Does anyone called Nina live here?' I stopped dead and replied incredulously, 'Yes, I am Nina.'

'Can I come in?'

'Yes, of course, just look at me,' I clucked, removing my hand from the door. 'Do come in.'

I pushed the chair towards him. His appearance in my poky little room seemed utterly incongruous. But such misgivings gave way before my overwhelming curiosity. I couldn't remember ever having seen him in this or any previous life. And yet he had come specifically to see me. I couldn't make head or tail of it. What he then said gave me such a surprise I almost had a heart attack.

'Can I address you in the familiar manner, using *tumi*?' Then, after a mysterious smile: 'It will make it easier for me to communicate.' In a state of great uneasiness I stammered: 'Yes, of course, but you ... I don't quite ...'

'You have never met me. My name is Irfanul Kabir ... I ...' He stopped.

I was speechless for a few moments; when I had regained my composure I spoke with suppressed excitement. 'Extraordinary! I could never have imagined! Where did you get my address?'

'My wife gave me the address. You had left it with her.' By now he had made himself comfortable in that chair. 'I still can't make out why you left that day without meeting me. Yet you had come to see me.'

'I, I mean—actually, the events of that day were all terribly embarrassing. I cannot tell you how ashamed I felt later. It is not like me, you know, to land up somewhere when we've been out of touch. I don't know what happened that day, it was as if my brain wasn't working properly. After I got to your

74

place I realized my mistake. I didn't meet you to save myself the embarrassment.'

'Since you did go there you should not have left without meeting me.' He spoke with great authority. 'Just think a little and judge for yourself if you acted consistently.'

I was racked by complex feelings. A lifetime had passed. Not even once had he looked up his cousin or his cousin's wife and children. And here he was today, in the role of a self-appointed guardian, picking faults in my behaviour. Strange was human character. By then I had overcome my discomfiture and relaxed a little. 'You know, my fundamental error was in going to your place. To be honest with you, turning up there without any warning wasn't really proper. I acted very immaturely.'

As soon as I had finished, an eerie stillness descended upon us. The sound of dal cooking reached my ears. The scent of condiments rushed into my room, distracting me. I had noticed Shanu come round to take a peep a couple of times. My visitor said calmly, 'It is not that I'm not aware why you regret going to my house. Perhaps you are thinking that a sudden visit to people with whom you have no contact, not to mention intimacy ... My visit too is rather dramatic, isn't it? Well, does life always have to follow a familiar pattern?'

Had he read my thoughts? Anyway, I sat quietly as he spoke. The dusk had thickened. As soon as I turned on the light the whole room looked amber. I would have to get a bulb with more wattage. My unironed green handloom sari hugged my body closely. A dark blister had grown on my fingertip. I touched it with the tip of my tongue.

With the arrival of my visitor my poverty showed up even more. The faded bed sheet had become frayed at the bottom. The bricks placed under the broken leg of the table looked like teeth bared in a grin. Unsightly stains showed clearly on the walls. The rough floor was even more damp than usual. And the rusty, rickety fan seemed to be making an exceedingly loud racket.

My visitor broke the silence. 'You are quite mature, you have seen much of life. Now, tell me, if I had kept up relations would it have been desirable all round?'

Splendid reasoning! My thoughts went in another direction. What was he trying to hint at? It was clear as day that his words carried allusions to his relationship with my mother. It wasn't possible to hint at the matter with greater delicacy. It wasn't that I hadn't given this matter any thought given the obscene manner in which it would surface in our poverty-stricken household whenever my parents had a tiff—what would have happened if my gentleman caller had kept in touch? But my ire towards him had another source. He had promised to marry Mother. The matter became common knowledge in the two families. Why did he change his mind at the last moment? Why did he lie low for some time, then come to Dhaka and at once get married? And Father, who had seen all this unfold in front of his eyes, decided to show that he could be noble. He offered to marry Mother. What shape that marriage took I had seen for myself in disgusting detail. Whom should I respect? Did I know what would have made life beautiful in all its aspects? I had seen life from the bottom of the gutter, like a wretched worm, and no, I did not feel any anger towards anyone. My only complaint was, why he had come today to stand in front of that gutter? But let the matter rest for now, I said to myself in an effort to calm myself. Quietly disengaging myself from the sensitive subject I said casually, 'Would you like some tea?'

'Are you trying to brush me off?'

I had begun to overcome my diffidence. I said with a laugh,

'How will I acquire the ability to avoid you? You are the protagonist in a legend.'

'You are insulting me.'

'No, no, not at all. I implore you to believe me. Actually, I haven't learnt any manners. It is entirely my fault. You might even call it bad breeding. But please continue with your account.'

'Since there is a complication at the very beginning, a knot, it is hard to say how far the story can proceed.'

'Can I unravel that thirty-year-old knot?' Again I was growing bitter inside. 'I know my own age. That's why I exaggerated the shame of my going to your house. Now that you have visited me today, I will not feel ashamed to visit you tomorrow.'

'You won't feel ashamed?' A fountain of merry chortles sprang from his face. 'Are you sure about that?'

'Yes, I can say that confidently. If I had met you even once I wouldn't have felt ashamed about visiting you, in spite of all that happened in the past.'

'Coming to see you has been a very pleasant experience.' After that frank declaration the gentleman ran his eyes over the entire room. Its filthy state again heightened my unease. Without thinking what I was doing I slipped my feet into my rubber flip-flop. I was about to enter the bathroom when I heard the gentleman's firm voice behind me. 'Who has done this painting?'

'Which painting?' I gave the impression of having fallen from the sky. I looked about me. 'Where is the painting?'

He was too big for the small chair and was obviously quite uncomfortable. And my famous clattering fan provided so little relief that he was soaked in perspiration; yet his face was relaxed, his attention fixed on the wall. 'That one, on the wall.'

Why, yes, there was a painting hanging on the wall, nearly hidden by a layer of dust. I had almost forgotten its existence.

Sheepishly I said, 'It is mine. I used to do a lot of painting at one time. You might say I was a regular pseudo artist.'

My visitor stood up, apparently startled by my words. He advanced towards the painting while a flush of embarrassment deepened on my face. Shit! If only the painting hadn't been hanging there. He took it down with great care and blew away the accumulated dust. 'You used to paint, but why have you stopped?'

The dense smoke of memory came spiralling up. Those days of chaos and confusion. What a tremendous desire to be an artist. Later I would die laughing at my own folly—were these works of art? Yet what hadn't I put up with in order to paint! Like an addict crazy for a fix I would desperately scrounge together the money for paints and brushes.

Father had of course categorically forbidden the creation of visual images. Orthodox in his faith, he thought it was a great sin—especially creating human images. But how could the free, self-willed brush find pleasure within the confined canvas of an unpeopled landscape? 'Concentrate on your studies,' Mother advised. 'Painting isn't respectable work.' Amidst such adverse currents I was stuck with a half-executed painting. I was out of paint. And I was penniless. I lay insomniac, with a single thought on my mind—how to buy paint. In the middle of the night little Montu, quivering with suppressed excitement, drew close to me and whispered, 'Listen, Apa, I found an earring on the courtyard of Selim's house. When I showed it to Mother she snatched it from me and hid it, and asked me not to tell anyone. I think it is gold.' I sat up straight, while caterpillars seemed to crawl on my skin. In the dim light Montu looked terrified. I asked him in the softest of whispers, 'Did you see where Mother kept it?'

'Wrapped in paper concealed inside the cloth bundle in the loft.'

'Does Father know?'

'No. I think it belongs to Selim's sister . . .' Montu was literally panting in his nervous fright.

'Who says it is Selim's sister's?' I asked angrily. 'Did you see her wearing it?' I shouldn't be humouring him, I thought, and went on in authoritative tones: 'Besides, who told you it is gold? Can Mother's eyes see properly? Don't pick up things like that ever again, do you hear? Now go to sleep.'

'Okay,' Montu said in a faint voice as he withdrew. Then, as I lay awake with bated breath I became filled with a strange loathing for my mother. This loathing infected everything around me. Where had I taken birth? Father, obscenely struggling to bring home some bread; the reeking filth of the household; the sluttish Ranu; the tin containers with holes in them and the cotton bursting out of tattered mattresses—towards all these I felt a disgust that made me feel like choking.

Should I run away from here? But where? Ahead I could only see a desolate road, an empty space. What a face Mother had revealed! Her eyes popping out at the sight of money! And Father? He hadn't an iota of faith in either wife or child. Lest someone dipped into his pocket while he slept, he hid his money like a miser in a folk tale, beneath a brick or in a chink in a wall. My adolescent sister, Ranu, who had assignations with the balding Majumdar in his half-complete building, was well on her way to being labelled a young fallen woman. Really, did my obsession with painting have a place in such a family? Yet this passion had consumed me. In the sordid, hateful situation in my family, it offered the only refuge to my soul. And I wanted to forget that terrible night, that intolerable night, the agonizing nocturnal operation. The next day the earring was no longer in the cloth bundle.

Mother frantically searched the bundle. She couldn't scream or shout, of course. Her hand searched everywhere, as if she

had gone crazy: drawer, food cupboard, under the mattress . . .
Two days later I brought home a cheap wooden easel, sheets
of drawing paper, paint and some brushes . . . Mother's face
showed feline aggressiveness, and Montu fixed me with a
steady stare. I felt small. With each day I seemed more and
more petty before those eyes.

～

Marriage did not change things for me. As if this sort of life
was my destiny. Half of it to be spent with my parents, the other
half with my husband. The strange youth whom my pre-nuptial
passion had endowed with elegance became careworn under
relentless worldly pressures. Within days of our marriage the
boy who used to feel self-conscious about taking off his
shirt in my presence lay stretched out in bed, breathing deeply,
while his lungi rode unabashedly up his legs, and he would
blow his nose thoughtlessly on the floor. He would hawk loudly
and talk to me with his mouth full of phlegm. Before my eyes
the shutters opened to reveal the elemental man. As for Rezaul,
the waves that used to dance in his eyes whenever he set eyes
on me were no longer to be seen.

I changed into a rather tepid personality. At twenty-seven
I was like an old woman. Painting, the only passion I had
brought with me from my mofussil days was now exorcised so
thoroughly from my life that it felt as if it wasn't just paint
and canvas that had been banished, but the only patch of
green grass had been wiped out of existence, the last ray
of light snuffed out. At the mention of painting after so many
years, I could only stare blankly at Irfan Chacha like one in
a trance.

'Why did you stop painting?' he asked again. 'Was it because
of lack of confidence?'

'Let's not go into that,' I said with a faint smile. 'I don't think I was cut out for it.'

'There is a lovely easel in my house,' he said as he replaced the painting on the wall and sat down again. 'You can have it if you want.' The next moment he seemed a little discomfited. 'Of course if you don't have any objection to accepting a gift from me.'

I didn't know what to say.

'If you like I will provide you with all the art materials you need.'

'Why do you want to do this for me?'

'Why, out of self-interest, of course,' he said, laughing. 'One day when you become famous my name will become attached to yours as your patron. That will be no small achievement.'

He was really taken with my work; it was an overwhelming realization and it rendered me speechless. He was a connoisseur—this had become clear to me when I went to his house, a grand mansion that housed a magnificent collection. He was truly sophisticated and indeed very handsome; I was struck by the incongruity of Mother beside him. After all these years even the thought of the contrast between them filled me with shame.

Damn, what rubbish I was thinking! Chiding myself, I pulled myself together, and said modestly, 'Actually, you have figured out the secret reason why I have given up painting, but you are too embarrassed to pity me on that account.' I felt the urge to start chattering again. 'That's why you are trying to put me at ease by talking about the satisfaction of being a patron.'

'My wife told me you are very intelligent,' Irfan Chacha said with a winsome smile. 'Or else our first meeting wouldn't have gone so smoothly.'

81

'You are avoiding the main issue,' I said, gasping in the heat, 'but by acknowledging my intelligence you are virtually admitting that I have figured out your true intention.'

The gentleman's greying temples were now dripping with sweat. He blew on his chest and ran his fingers through his hair. Behind a broad forehead, his hair had thinned. He was reserved, might even appear overly so. But my gentle argumentativeness had teased out a very different side of his personality; his affability, I had to admit, was utterly charming.

'Just as wealth cannot add to one's character,' he said, 'poverty—and here I speak from experience—can make one characterless. That's because poverty forces one to demean oneself, to make too many compromises. But there are some who attach ultimate value to their obsessions and then accept the humiliation. These things are relative, you see. You have read Van Gogh's autobiography. What wouldn't he do for art's sake? Didn't he accept help from an impoverished brother?'

'I don't understand how you can build such hopes for me on the basis of only one painting. Besides, the agony of such a humiliation is so terrible that someone who hasn't experienced it will not understand it.' I became excited and said firmly, 'It is not as easy for everyone to struggle as it is to encourage people to do so.'

'What I have seen in your painting is not the real issue. All I am pointing out is that you have abandoned an activity that used to be a passion. You have done this out of apathy or hurt pride arising from a sense of defeat or some sorrow. Whether the painting is good or bad is not for you to judge.' He wiped his face with his handkerchief and again looked straight at me. 'As for the anguish of having to demean yourself . . . if that is your reason for giving up art I have strong reservations about it. It pains me to see a possibility, even if it is a tiny spark, getting snuffed out. War is always an ordeal, for everyone. For us, it is best if we can take everything in our stride.'

'When I started painting it was like an addiction, I didn't philosophize about it. Besides, when there are so many people in this world why do you want to inspire me to be creative? Considering that our connection is on the basis of my brief visit to your house, isn't this a bit excessive?'

'My sudden visit and our prolonged conversation—these too might be described in the same way.'

'Yes, but why this drama? Does it have its rationale in the context of something that happened in the past?' With a childlike laugh I continued: 'Do you have any remorse, for which perhaps you wish to make amends in this manner?'

A sombre expression came over his face. It made me nervous. This man, who had come across as a hard-boiled rationalist, gradually turned pale. I left the room precipitately. Shanu rescued me from my embarrassment by asking if she should send some refreshments. She had surmised I had an important guest and sent a boy from the basti behind the house to get some snacks. Really, she was such a dear. I felt a fresh fondness for her.

Arranging the snacks on the table, I remarked, 'How terribly hot it is! I realize how intolerable it must be for you. Surely you have never before visited anyone in such a dingy alleyway?'

My embarrassment was now mingled with a strange excitement. I moved to the door, mainly to hide my embarrassment, and was opening the door wide in the hope of letting in a bit of breeze when I noticed the child from the basti, a vague figure standing quietly in the shadows. Nude, sucking a finger. For some days now, the infant who had been a source of daily joy to me had slipped out of my memory. Overcome by a sudden flood of affection I walked down the veranda. In an excited whisper, I called out to the child, 'Hey,

Kallu . . . ,' but he kept retreating. A little bell around his waist tinkled indistinctly. But how long would I conflate his existence with memories of my own child? How long would I be at odds with myself? Actually it was my child that I loved, it was another being who dwelt in him. Kallu was a mere husk, all that existed between us was pretence—still I advanced, towards the husk. I climbed down from the veranda, for the child's behaviour seemed abnormal; maybe Shanu had been rude to him.

'Hey, Kallu . . .' my voice a tremulous undertone in the hazy light, 'come here, come.' He ran off. His tiny body disappeared into the hideous damp and dark basti. I stood still for a few moments, overwhelmed with pity for the child's mother. That night she had to bear such limitless . . . ! For that I had forgiven her everything. Whatever had happened, I was only the third party in the matter. I would never be able to feel the greatest agony generated by that incident. Besides, when Shanu had generously accepted the protagonist in that drama, what was the point in turning this poor woman into a criminal?

I returned to my room, saddened by the sight of the boy disappearing into the gloom. I tried to blow away my inner unease with the breath of small talk. 'Chachi told me you had taken early retirement—five years before it was due. I found it surprising. You must be a strange man.'

But he was lost in thought. He had been devastated by a single salvo of words and had frankly revealed his weakness before me. Now I felt a little annoyed, and asked him, 'How do you occupy yourself all day? I can barely make time to breathe, life is so busy. You can't even imagine living in a room like this, can you?' I kept up a stream of chatter along these lines.

Silently he picked the teacup. This was the first time in my life that I'd had a chance to talk to someone his age, with the conversation ranging from serious to light to desultory. But I was pulled up short by the thought that the way I was talking to him might amount to bad manners. Gradually he became indistinct in my habitually befuddled consciousness. Had he really come to visit me, did I really have an argument with someone? Or was the whole thing a hallucination brought on by an addiction to books? I looked about me. Everything seemed hazy. I became a prey to mixed feelings. What a complicated delusion, it made me get everything mixed up! I started laughing silently, inwardly talking to myself . . . Why was the child standing there in the dark? Are children mind-readers or what? Did he see through my pretence? Had his mother built a wall of fear so high that he could never scale it? He had come drawn by habit, by the force of affection . . . then the sudden fear, and the sudden flight in the opposite direction.

'Listen, Nina,' his voice startlingly broke the silence. 'I don't know how you have taken my presence. But I cannot believe you are unreasonable enough to demand that my character traits correspond to your suppositions. A clear-sighted view will diminish many of the pressures of life. Regarding what you have hinted as the reason behind my interest in your painting, I can say very clearly that nothing necessitating remorse has happened in my life. I believe that sin resides in remorse . . .' He paused here to take a sip of the tea.

Silent moments went by. Looking me straight in the eye he started talking again. 'I believe that people try to compensate for an error by experiencing remorse—and that remorse, felt long enough, kills off the guilt associated with the error and shakes it out of the consciousness. But I don't have the mindset to belittle anything by compensating it in the currency of remorse. Besides, I have a healthy respect for every aspect of my life. That includes me at birth as well as the imbroglio I was once in. Subsequently wiping it from memory with the wet rag of remorse in order to settle into a smug life is a form of cheap trickery that any clear-headed person would detest—at least I do.'

He had finished his tea and was on his feet. My turn now. A surging current seemed to be pushing me from within . . . words, there was so much fanciful wordplay all around that I felt weary . . . Still, since I had started, there was no easy escape. I said, 'What are you saying? Every civilized human being feels remorse. How can someone who doesn't acknowledge their errors and doesn't feel any shame on their account be considered a healthy human being? Take the case of a murderer who has killed someone for money. Let us say he has gone unpunished—it wouldn't be anything new in our country. When he is alone in his room, he doesn't even answer to his own conscience—what will you say in this case? This person doesn't experience remorse, sleeps without a care in the world—but would he become a sinner if he had given in to remorse?' I grew excited as I spoke. 'Only those who arrogantly accord supreme value to their own decisions are immune to remorse. Hired assassins tend to be like that.'

How strange! Even after this barrage he stood still. After a few silent moments he sat down again. Picking up a magazine he used it as a hand fan and began speaking again in a calm tone, 'In this instance even a murderer is spotless before his own soul. If he had known it was wrong he wouldn't have committed the murder.'

I nearly screamed in reply to his reasoned statement. 'Strange! Are you supporting this? Maybe one doesn't break the law knowing it is wrong; at the moment he does it he may be spotless before his soul, but what about later? If he is incapable of realizing that what he might have done on the spur of the moment is actually a sin, would you call him a self-aware being?'

'To tell you the truth, remorse seems to be a hoax.' He was still steadfastly holding on to his view. 'People seek absolution for their worst misdeeds through remorse. The remorse lightens the burden that the deed places on the conscience.'

'You are wrong,' I retorted. 'This is how he begins the penance for the misdeed.'

'What remorse will be penance for the worst misdeeds?' he said calmly. 'Is this how he will escape from his inner world?'

'It seems you would prefer to have him face external punishment? Like the lynching of a burglar or the hanging of a murderer? But I want something more subtle—the punishment of the soul. It is through the punishment of the soul that human beings can purify themselves.'

The sultriness kept increasing as the evening deepened. The clamorous voices of the basti drifted on the air. They would go on, for no rhyme or reason, till late at night. Side by side there was a loudspeaker blaring Hindi film songs night and day. The scent of frying parathas came from the eatery across the street. My guest was sweating so copiously that the sight diminished my combativeness. Was he feeling any inward discomfiture at carrying on a conversation with me? Oddly enough, I no longer felt distant from this man. Though I had known him for only a little while, carrying on an argument with him was a bewildering mix of torment and joy. Now he nodded slowly as he resumed talking.

'I am not completely dismissing your reasoning. But in pursuing our arguments we have moved far from the real issue.' As he finished he carefully replaced the teacup on the table. Then he sat up straight and looked me in the eye. 'We were talking about remorse as atonement. Why do you lump together all crimes, sins and misdemeanours? Robbery, theft, rape, adultery, loss of faith in God . . . are they all sins in the same measure? Love is a virtue, but if a woman engages in it with someone other than her husband society deems it a sin. But to the two persons involved in the relationship it is a supreme virtue. It will not do to weigh everything on the same scales, even for the sake of argument. But let's leave all these matters aside and come to what concerns us, shall we?'

'Okay,' I said.

'I respect a particular episode in my life from deep within my heart, so why should I lower it in my esteem by feeling remorse? Atonement presupposes remorse, that is why I have described remorse as sin. People try to atone for grievous wrongs in crude ways. However, I don't claim my ideas have universal and eternal validity. Like you, I too value my time. But does time stay still, Nina? Climbing up is tiring business, and now I am a man with greying hair. You know about the Pandavas, don't you? What fierce battles, bloodshed, deaths . . . And such despair when it all ended! Why all the carnage, the bloodshed? Who had been killed? People close to the Pandavas, kinsmen. At last the Pandavas embarked on the great journey to the afterworld. Such a long journey! Across so many rivers, with turmoil in the heart. One by one they collapsed in exhaustion, only Yudhisthira carried on. His tremendous will power carried him along till the very end. But I have come this far for nothing, Nina. Once I had thought I would be like the sagacious Yudhisthira. But I have fallen face downward on the desolate road. Now if my modest encouragement induces you to start painting again, it will be really gratifying. The things you have hinted at are not present at all—there is no pretence, and I don't have any ulterior motive.'

Such fatigue! Everything blurry all around! It seemed my whole existence was trapped in a grey whirlpool. Round and round it went. Now my guest got up to really leave. Stepping out on to the veranda he paused to say a few words that thrilled my ears. 'This has been yet another experience to remember. I am glad I came. Or else I would have been deprived of something very significant.'

'I will come and see you,' I almost shouted as he was stepping out into the street 'I would of course like to have that easel of yours.'

He flashed a strange smile as he walked under the wan streetlight and gradually disappeared down the filthy, uneven, malodorous alley.

A dog had mounted a bitch. Someone in the basti began a theatrical lament that was punctuated by the noise of tin sheets being beaten flat. I stood there awhile. Dog and bitch had finished their business and were walking towards the basti. When I got tired of watching such scenes I went in. At once I began to be disturbed by images of Yudhisthira lying with an injured face on the road to eternity. No, this was the creation of his modesty. He hadn't fallen on his face. Every aspect of his behaviour reflected his firmness of attitude. As I thought about the events of the evening I was lost in a sense of wonder. What had happened seemed out of place in my life, an aberration. His sudden presence in my petty, harassed world, his appreciation of my painting, his urging me to take up art again—all these didn't go with my familiar everyday life.

Nothing was more valuable to me than to be able to lead my life just as I wanted. If Mother's shadow lay in its background, what did it matter? I had stood before him as a fully autonomous being. That could only enhance Mother's dignity. Her daughter had not bowed her head before anyone despite her distressing poverty. I was suddenly filled with pity and sympathy for Mother. My poor mother, who hadn't been able to hold her head high in this world, not even for a single day. She had been through a terrible time. Fighting destitution from day to day, bent under the pressure of domestic life, she had been gradually drained of love and affection. The struggle to feed her family on a shoestring budget had left her embittered and irritable. She had never got any respect from her husband either. She had had to learn various subtle tricks to plug the hundreds of leaks that her household had sprung. Words like honesty and frankness were gradually expunged from her consciousness. Take her behaviour one day—it was really extraordinary—when Ranu quietly began cooking a chicken stolen from a neighbour. Mother busied herself in other chores and pretended not to notice. When the neighbour came looking for the missing chicken she seemed to fall from the skies, and in wonderfully vibrant tones declaimed her commiseration: 'Oh, how aggravating such a thing must be, a big, healthy chicken vanishing like that! Really, the country has become infested with thieves and criminals.' I had also noticed that when she went to ask for a loan from one of my uncles she would cry more piteously than was called for. One could say of course that for our sake she had lowered her self-respect to such a level that she had lost all our sympathy and respect. Even if an utterly philistine personality like hers had once cast a shadow on my visitor's sense and sensibility, it wouldn't hurt my self-respect in any way.

Then my remembrance witnessed the entry of Majumdar the Bald. A wintry breath chilling my body, I was sitting on my bed, leaning against the wall, my brain seething with activity . . . Was it really the case that if I were induced to lie down under the moon I would automatically open all the folds of my sensuality? Had I become so desperate? Or was the moon a malignant deity that would render me passive, pliant? I had been as full of wifely devotion as Behula on my wedding night, but just when I had plugged every hole and was about to give myself wholeheartedly to Lakshmindar, Manasa mysteriously entered. Did she enter through the gateway to the

90

soul? Was Manasa my true beloved? My heart resounded with psalms of lamentation.

As a shadow-wall of such perennial conflicts in me grew ever more lofty, Ranu scaled it and walked past, Majumdar following, and once again I watched them like a spectator.

How many houses separated Majumdar's 'half-building' from ours? I began to count. Three, there were three houses in between. We had been born, we grew up, in front of this man's eyes. He lived alone. When we grew up we learnt that his wife and daughters lived in the country. He despised his wife because she hadn't borne him any son. Then why didn't he take another wife? There were a thousand such questions about him that no one could answer. His house was a half-built building. The strange tale behind this made Majumdar appear as a curious, mysterious figure from the days of our childhood. When the building was only half-complete he learnt in a dream that as soon as it was completed it would collapse and cause his death. So he stopped the construction work at that point. Majumdar had acquired a reputation for infallible oneiromancy and so believed that this time too the dream would come true.

Majumdar! The hateful face that is at once conjured up by the name defies adequate description. No eyebrows surmounted his eyes, which were a horrible red, like the flesh of the fig. A huge black mole squatted on a sunken cheek and through it grew a clump of hair: it looked like a frog. The feature that dominated his face was the nose. The nostrils were a pair of terrifying orifices. His figure was unusually tall. Nearly seven feet. His arms, though, were disproportionately short and thin. His habitual attire, too, was incongruous, novel. Loose pyjama trousers flapped beneath a black kurta.

He was famous in the town as a tantric. Everyone took note of what he said he dreamt. He had also earned notoriety as a usurer. As a matter of fact almost every lower-middle-class family in the neighbourhood was hostage to his money. One of these families was our own. And in childhood, whenever Mother would send me to get money from him my blood would curdle in fear. If I didn't go the simple fact is that we wouldn't be able to eat the next meal; so I had no choice. Each time I went, Majumdar's weird behaviour would increase my fear twofold. One evening I found his room completely filled with incense. Not a single light had been turned on. When he saw me he lit a lamp with a naked flame, then sat with closed eyes, mumbling 'In the name of genies and *pari*s, the seven heavens, etc., etc.' He didn't have two of his front teeth, so that his slimy tongue protruded through his thick black lips. This gave him an increasingly fearful look. It was so terrifying that I ran home, panting. Mother looked at me with eager eyes. 'Did he give it?' I was silent. Mother came closer. 'Did he scold you?' Nervously, I narrated what had happened. 'The man is a tantric,' Mother explained. 'He has occult powers. Your father says he wanders the streets all night, both Allah and Bhagawan on his lips.'

How terrible! How could Mother be so callous as to send me to him on an errand? Didn't she have any feelings for me?

Ranu's plight was worse. Though utterly fearless by nature about everything else, she was terrified of Majumdar. She would shrink at the sight of the man. Once when she was a sleeping three-month-old infant Majumdar had taken her up in his arms. She opened her eyes and let out such a scream of terror that Mother snatched her away and comforted her. It was so long ago, yet my memory of it is vivid. Majumdar was both embarrassed and offended. He held such sway over the neighbourhood that none dared express in his presence the fear he inspired. Everyone in that overcrowded locality had the same economic profile. In other words, prosperity was simply beyond their reach. So they had no choice but to suck up to Majumdar. His normal behaviour was polite and decorous. But I had seen many decent people who were defaulting on loan repayment fall tearfully at his feet to beg for mercy. He was in a business where heartlessness was the key to success, and he was fully aware of this.

Majumdar's rise to wealth and power took place right before our eyes. At the root of his success was his money-lending operation. Nobody had kept count of those who had mortgaged all they had to him, had lost all and vanished from the scene. I had heard of many such cases from neighbours and had personally witnessed others. They were the inevitable outcome of the mountain-tall accretion of usurious interest. Still, nobody could deny that he fulfilled a useful function.

Frozen with fear, I would ask Mother, 'Why do you borrow from him? What if we too lose our home?'

'We don't borrow that much,' she reassured me. 'Around the middle of the month we borrow some money, and when your father draws his salary the following month he pays it back with a little interest. How else can we survive?'

I was too young to check out her mathematics. But one thing was clear—Father's profound reverence for Majumdar. Father himself was a God-fearing soul. He had suddenly taken leave from work to go on *tabligh*. Sometimes he would pass the night in a mosque, praying.

He had to bear the additional burden of bringing up and educating the youngest two of his brothers. Unable to meet all household expenses, he'd often play truant. When things went from bad to worse he would seek Majumdar's counsel. He believed that thanks to Majumdar's advice he had overcome many crises in his life. When he had any free time he would visit Majumdar. Consequently, all the problems at home had to be faced by Mother.

Mother's family was from Murshidabad, where most of her kinsfolk still lived. Her parents had died long ago. That is one reason why she was always anxious and unsure of herself and lacked the spirit to complain about the burden of somehow running the household. And in her desperate efforts to do so Majumdar had an inalienable role. So the fact that Father had the most intimate relationship with this personage was a source of pride for her.

The events of one day still bring tears to my eyes. Father had handed over whatever little he could manage to Mother and departed for another tabligh trip. Mother somehow kept us fed for a few days, then one morning she gave me and Ranu one seer of wheat and asked us to go get it ground at a flour mill. The previous night we had swallowed dry chapattis. That morning Montu started wailing, he was so hungry. Ranu was bare-bodied, wearing only loose shorts that kept slipping down. I had the bag of wheat in one hand and with the other held her hand. The sun was fierce. My head swam. Our hungry eyes greedily devoured the sumptuously displayed food in the restaurants we passed by—Mughlai paratha, *Keema-puri*—I had to literally drag Ranu away and lead her towards the flour mill. Pushing through the crowd I held out the bag, only to be roughly told off by the man in charge: 'We don't handle such small amounts.' We waited, hoping he would relent. We waited a long time. Ranu's mouth was bone dry. She kept licking her dry lips. 'Come Ranu, let's be off again . . . Come, sweet Ranu.'

My eyes were overflowing with tears.

Another nearly aimless walk. Ranu's fair cheeks had turned ruddy under the sun, and she was soaked in sweat. The road seemed endless. Crossing many alleys jammed with rickshaws, negotiating the hullaballoo of schoolchildren, we reached another flour mill. The reception was another grimace of rejection. Ranu burst into loud wails. I begged and implored. The flour mill employees might have thought we were beggars. I looked at my clothes. My cousin's hand-me-down kameez hung loosely around my knees. I was completely encrusted in dust. My dry braided hair hung over the shoulder. That was the first time I felt really small and humiliated. I dragged Ranu outside. We walked dim alleys where butchers had their stalls. Past the red, pink, whitish meat hanging from hooks, then at the railway tracks I stopped and let Ranu sit down on the tracks to rest. The sun was directly overhead. Ranu's nose ran with muck. She also got a fit of hiccups. Sweat and dust had mingled to make her face look horribly sticky beneath the shock of curly hair. Even her sobs were weary. I too felt exhausted and drowsy. 'Hey, Ranu,' I asked. 'Do you know where these rail tracks end?' She just kept crying.

'Hey Ranu, do you know where we'll go when we die?' She kept on crying.

We started walking along the tracks, skipping from sleeper to sleeper. My feet ached, my head buzzed. 'Hey, Ranu, look at that red kite in the sky.' Ranu stopped crying to look up and gave a smile that I would now liken to Mona Lisa's mysterious one. Her face, her nose had grown puffy—and now her attention shifted from the kite and she began crying again. How to stop her? She seemed to have lost all control over herself. How would I get her home now? I started chatting to distract her. 'Ranu, when we grow up we'll work in offices, and we'll marry well, like Reshmi Apa. You are beautiful, your husband will keep you well fed—on *pulau*, meat, vegetables, ice cream and whatnot.' Ranu pulled her loose shorts up, and as she wiped her eyes her soul seemed to brighten up: 'Really?'

Then, wandering through the dying morning we eventually got home. Bitter sobs heaved up from my breast—what would we feed Ranu? Mother was probably waiting like a bird at a pilgrimage site. No, not at all. When we got home there was rice cooking in the pot. Mother had got some rice and dal from Uncle's house. What an aroma—strangely intoxicating, the fragrance of coarse red rice.

Father was supposed to have returned two days ago. He hadn't, of course. The problem of lunch had been solved, but what about dinner? Our reputation among our neighbours was seriously tarnished because we would borrow right and left and then on the question of repayment were either incapable or indifferent. Arefin used to live with Uncle, Father's eldest brother. And, as I have said already, Father had accepted responsibility for his two younger brothers. One of them was a final year MA student, the other had got his degree and was looking for a job. The elder uncle was quite wealthy. His daughter's, our Reshmi Apa's, wedding had been a grand affair. Still, our younger uncle's responsibility fell on Father's shoulders. I don't know why. But this I knew very well, that to our elder uncle we were objects of contempt. None of us, other than Mother, would visit his house if we could help it. Mother would go there frequently to see Arefin. And to share family gossip and burst into lamentation, something Uncle's family found extremely distasteful. Uncle would call Father a good-for-nothing, then throw something to Mother, saying, 'I haven't started a charity operation here. Tell my hopeless brother that he ought to try to keep his job. Only then can he think of serving Allah. All that's left for him to do is beg on the streets.'

Mother would bring the money carefully tied up in a knot in a corner of her sari. 'Your uncle is no ordinary human being,' she would say. 'He is an angel. He is educating my Arefin.' How little it took to make her feel gratified, and how extraordinarily dull was her sense of dignity. Our younger uncles were being supported by Father because Uncle, despite his wealth, had shirked the responsibility. Even a little girl like me realized this, but not Mother.

Anyway, we had hot rice for lunch, but what about the evening meal? 'Your father will definitely come back today,' Mother reassured us. The afternoon rolled by but he did not return. Mother sat in the yard, sobbing away. The ramparts of her patience were crumbling. Soon she began cursing her birth and the birth of her children. After a while I asked myself if there was anything I could do to arrange for the next meal. A weird plan came into my head. It made me tingle with excitement as I went indoors.

There were innumerable cockroaches in our house. Mother had kept a biscuit coated with insecticide on the broken food cupboard to see if the cockroaches would eat it. In spite of my intense hunger I forgot about my food-seeking mission and stood staring at the biscuit; it made my mouth water. Mother had got the poisonous biscuit from next door, for there were hundreds of thousands of cockroaches at our place, under the bed, in the kitchen, in the cupboard. When we slept at night they walked all over us. They had even started destroying the clothes on the clothes horse. But how would we pass the night, I wondered, coming back to the urgent question oppressing us. Should I go out to beg for food? Mother had just given up all hope and sat listlessly in the yard while Ranu groomed her hair. I was still standing in front of the food cupboard. Even at that age I was possessed by strange feelings and thoughts—of the end of the world, death, the hair-thin bridge leading to heaven . . .

I would hang around graveyards, my heart throbbing with fear. Father's religious discourses had instilled the fear of Allah. It was distressing to think that he had been cruel enough to exile us in this world. While such thoughts were playing in my head my eyes were fixed on the biscuit. Suddenly a cockroach advanced upon it; from the opposite direction came another. Afternoon shadows were lengthening outside. I stood stock-still. The biscuit was being nibbled. I stared, not batting an eyelid. The creature had relinquished its grip on life. Death was on its way. We were the killers . . . neat: lure it with a biscuit . . .

Steadily, both the cockroaches became drowsy, yet they wouldn't let go of the biscuit. Ranu suffered such hunger pangs . . . what if someone lured her with a *bakarkhani* or a *jalebee*, coated with poison . . . Ranu's face flowing with delight, her open mouth reaching forward. A cold current shot through my arteries. I couldn't even cry.

The two cockroaches had become drowsier and tipped over. A strange thought took shape in me. Mother suddenly seemed terribly cruel. What if one day she finished us off like this with poisoned biscuits? In such a world what hope of survival did we have without Majumdar's help? But his sight was enough to send Ranu scampering. There was no sign that she would change. He had tried many times to win her over with gifts, to no avail. Right after her birth Ranu screamed when he came near, and there was no change in her reaction over the years. Father scolded Ranu about this on a number of occasions; he even beat her. The reason is that he had noticed the hardening of Majumdar's features whenever Ranu acted like that. He was fearful Majumdar might be so offended that occult retribution would be visited upon Ranu. Father was totally enthralled by Majumdar.

Notwithstanding that I had once run away from Majumdar, scared by the dense incense and the murmured mantras, Mother sent me to him again. Again I dragged my unwilling feet along towards the 'half-building'. I was trembling all over. It was getting dark. The door had been left ajar and peering through I noticed that he was lying on the floor. On hearing my footsteps he looked about with ghost-like eyes. He gestured at me to draw closer. 'Hey, come here.' Nervously, I inched forward.

'How much?' he asked.

'Thirty taka,' I said. As if this was a very natural thing, he got up and opened a drawer. The unnatural atmosphere of the room had dispersed. In the well-lit surroundings I overcame my nervousness and relaxed enough to ask, 'Tell me, why do you sleep on the floor instead of the bed?' Without answering he simply held out the money, then asked in a stentorian voice, 'Hasn't your father come back yet?'

'No,' I replied softly.

Then silence. Fearfully, I began to walk out of there when the light suddenly went out. As opaque darkness filled the room I opened my mouth to scream, but no sound emanated from my benumbed lungs. My extended foot touched an obstacle and the next moment Majumdar had grabbed me from be ind with both arms. All windows were shut. In that dense darkness he hoisted my weightless body up in the air. It fe t as if someone had sucked out all the moisture from

my breast. There was no way I could beg for mercy for I had lost my power of speech. Before I knew what was happening he began whirling me around, with my hands held high above me. A deep chasm seemed to open beneath me. My body was precariously balanced on a demon king's forefinger. I would fall . . . there, I had nearly fallen . . . My body was knocking against the rough sides of a very tall mountain and falling apart. Majumdar put me down abruptly. My ears felt hot, they were ringing. I felt like throwing up. What next? Fear and excitement had driven me to the verge of death. The light came on suddenly. Majumdar was sweating profusely. The sticky sweat gave him a gruesome appearance. Everything looked vague, unfocused. The turmoil seemed to have completely shaken up my brain. Moments passed. Then began his manic laughter. What a dreadful sound it had. It seemed to make the entire half-building quake. His long red tongue forced its way out between the toothless gums, slid in again . . . out and in . . . At one point he seemed to be tickled and bending over with laughter asked, 'You were terribly frightened, weren't you?'

I stared at him like a deaf mute. Cold, wordless.

'You came in the evening once before, didn't you?' He giggled in a seemingly good-natured way. I nodded slowly.

'Why did you get scared—because of my appearance?'

'I don't know,' I said, quaking with fear.

'I look horrible, don't I?'

'No.'

'Lying again? Ranu is scared of my appearance, isn't she?' The question came so suddenly that I couldn't give a ready reply. He gave me a rude shake and asked again, 'Tell me if she is afraid of my appearance, will you?'

'Yes.'

Now he began pacing round the room in high dudgeon. When he had had enough of this he looked at me and, coolly, said, 'I will show you something.' He took out a cloth bundle, which he unfolded to reveal a dead cat. It had become swollen and had blood all over. He swung it before my nose and hissed, 'Scared?' Fear had in fact curdled my blood again. He kept on talking dementedly, 'I slaughter evil djinns by killing animals that harbour them. Ranu has been possessed by a djinn. I am looking high and low for that djinn by examining every animal I come across. I will find it no doubt. Majumdar thwarted? Fah!'

'If you kill a cat will an evil djinn die with it?' I asked naïvely and stood quietly.

'Not only cats, other animals as well, for instance, birds, rabbits, dogs . . . Evil djinns live in these creatures. Of course not all members of these species, but one look is enough for me to tell.'

'But what exactly contains Ranu's evil djinn?'

'She is a brilliant spark! She has a fire that I haven't seen anywhere else in this world. Her djinn will not live in just any creature!'

Such fantastic, bizarre goings-on! Had the fellow gone totally mad? Suddenly he closed his eyes and began muttering again. After a while he opened his eyes and swinging the cat before my nose began laughing again. This time I really burst into sobs: 'I want to go home. Why are you trying to scare me?'

'Ranu's djinn . . .,' he kept on muttering, 'I have told your father about it, and before going on tabligh he especially entrusted me with this task. That's why I am searching tirelessly for the bastard. I have a special affection for Ranu, do you understand? I will not let the evil djinn get away.'

'Father knows about these things?' I was at the height of astonishment.

'What do you think? I have a request from a venerable elder, otherwise affection alone wouldn't drive me to such hateful exertions. Animal after animal has to be slaughtered, so you can imagine what a tough job it is.'

Now I was really worried. The whole thing was no joke. Only, I was unable to appreciate its significance. Still I ventured a timid question. 'What if Ranu's evil djinn is in the belly of an elephant? In that case it is pointless to kill cats and dogs.'

He was annoyed. 'Do elephants live among humans? You are quite clever, but remember, I don't like smart alecks. You are only pretending to be scared. Listen, I dreamt at night that I was wandering with an empty bottle. It means that I will marry into an impoverished family. You should try to persuade Ranu. I am fond of her. I want her to be happy.'

'I want to go home,' I said plaintively, swallowing my sobs.

'Go, then. Am I stopping you?' he barked. I walked towards the door, dragging feet that seemed as heavy as the earth. I couldn't breathe. What if I was grabbed again and lifted straight off the floor?

As soon as I had stepped out on to the road, I just ran.

When I got home I handed over the money to Mother and burst into loud wails. Mother became very anxious. What had kept me so long? I lost all sense of time if I went anywhere. My wails steadily gained in intensity.

Mother seemed to get cold sweat. She dragged me to the kitchen and whispered in my ear, 'Why are you crying?'

Cockroaches leapt off the food cupboard. I remained wordless.

Mother's voice became even softer. 'Did he make any indecent proposal? Why aren't you saying anything?' As her words only made me cry more uncontrollably she pushed me towards the far corner; then in cautious, extremely serious tones asked me, 'Did he take off your clothes?'

I shook my head.

'Did he make any indecent suggestions?'

'No.'

Mother's sigh of relief gave way to anger. 'Then why are you crying like this?'

Now my words came in incoherent bursts. 'Ma, he killed a cat and then, O such . . . In the dark he lifted me into the air . . . He said Ranu had been possessed by some djinn or whatnot . . .'

'He has a hotline with the great pirs and aulias,' Mother said. 'He has strange ways of communing with God, that's all. But I haven't heard any rumours accusing him of immoral behaviour. Actually, your father told him about Ranu. He has extraordinary powers. He can make wishes come true.'

I lost my temper. 'He worships idols and also prays to Allah; how can Father be so devoted to him?'

Mother nonchalantly said, 'I don't know about these things. Your father says such people are above religion.'

I remember clearly that I protested loudly. 'Then Father also is a charlatan like him.' Mother rewarded me with a tight slap.

While we were growing up in such an atmosphere, Father kept building the walls of religion around him ever higher. He lectured us on the benefits accruing from prayers and fasts, and the ceaseless torment of infidels in the fires of hell. This was how he tried to create the holy climate of religiosity in our minds. By now our uncles had found jobs and left us to take them up. We had nothing to do all day except take care of household chores and just sit in utter boredom. How long can one go on like that? I had always been a bit of a tomboy. Dragging Ranu along, I used to go and gaze at cinema posters, play truant from school and wander along the riverbank, and when it was time for Kali Puja go to stare in fear and fascination at the goddess's protruding red tongue amidst the swirling incense. Of course when I got back Father would treat me to a sound thrashing. But that was the age when one grows wings: how could the manacles of religion restrain me? But Father kept a stern eye on us: how could I take off? So I would get into arguments with him instead. If there were such ghastly punishments awaiting sinners, how could God be called merciful? Why should only women be required to keep themselves covered from head to foot—why not men as well? At first Father would let us engage him in argument. He said that if women did not behave modestly men would be led astray. I boldly answered him back: what if women went astray on seeing bare-bodied men? My words fell like a thunderbolt. In response Father's hand fell on me in a mighty slap. 'Are women's and men's bodies the same?'

When describing the houris in paradise Father's eyes were a sight. I saw the shadow of incurable lust in those eyes. It was astonishing that a man with such eyes had spent his whole life with a physically unimpressive woman like my mother. On another occasion I risked yet another slap by asking if people of other religions would go to paradise? 'No,' Father sternly replied. 'Why?' I asked. 'Why didn't an infant become a Muslim at birth? A child would learn from its environment. It was possible that I had been born into the wrong faith. But would it have been possible for me to go beyond what my parents taught me?'

Rage drove Father to the verge of tears. He had arrived at the definite conclusion that I had gone to the dogs. Mother's indulgence was surely the cause of that. But how could I abandon the argument in that unresolved state? Ask no questions—what sort of a culture propounded such a dogma? I had by then seen enough of the world outside to learn about the nature of the man–woman relationship. Defying Father's staunch opposition we had joined an organization whose members were all boys. Ranu and I were the only girls to join. Events like poetry readings and public speaking were organized there. Alongside the misery and sheer poverty of our lives we had found a secret space of freedom. The office-bearers of the organization would carefully instruct me on how to recite a poem on stage. And when there would be a function the rows of eyes watching me would little suspect that the girl on stage reciting the poem had abjectly begged a flour mill employee to accept a seer of wheat for grinding. Or indeed that she lived in a tin cottage with a damp floor that had for furniture a pair of broken chairs, a clothes horse, a shaky bed on which the mattress had burst and the exposed cotton had turned black with dirt and the pillows had no pillowslips; or that cockroaches crawled over their bodies as they slept.

The nature of my arguments with Father led him to believe that I had become friendly with a communist who was leading me astray. It caused him great sorrow and made him inquisitorial.

On stage the pride and excitement I felt made me break out in a sweat. But Ranu lacked any enthusiasm for such activities. When quivering with excitement after a performance I'd ask her how I had done she would be busy distributing laddoos among the guests. Screwing up her lips she'd only say, 'These things make me want to laugh. I wouldn't have come at all if it weren't for the refreshments.' Cut to the quick, I would demand an explanation. 'What's so funny about it? What exactly makes you laugh?' Mouth full of laddoo, a mocking smile playing over her lips, she would say, 'Why, gesturing with your arms while reciting a poem . . .' She'd now really burst into laughter. 'Someone standing before so many people and waving the hands and putting on strange expressions. Really, it's a scream.'

It was heartbreaking. Why was something that gave me such joy so ludicrous to one so dear and close to me?

We used to go to school. Of course we hardly got any education there. The girls would just read aloud from their textbooks by turn. The teacher would be busy knitting a sweater from a ball of wool that lay on the floor, or else she would ask us to copy something out of a book and shut her eyes. What a lousy, tedious time we had. What to do but skulk on the back bench and doodle and draw in the exercise book? That was the origin of my passion for art. I played truant frequently, going off with my friends from the cultural organization to a football match, to a wedding of one of their relatives, or a political demonstration. Eventually, I was betrayed by Ranu. She wouldn't participate in any of those illicit activities because she just didn't see what was so enjoyable about them. Of course I tried to persuade her to come along. Then one day I lost my temper with her. 'All you care for is food and things you can get,' I screamed. 'You have become so greedy, so these things don't appeal to you. You'll do anything for some goodies.' Father was resting in the next room. Ranu said loudly so that he would hear, 'Don't I know what you do with the boys? I'll tell Father.'

My blood boiled. 'Am I like you?' I shouted and fell on her. 'The sight of good food makes your tongue hang out obscenely.' What followed was predictable enough. Father came in and let me have it, but worse than the beating was the final judgement. 'No more of those organizations as long as you live, do you hear? If you try to go there you'll see . . .' Thus, because of Ranu, walls went up all around me. In my rage at Ranu I didn't talk to her for days.

Life went back to its dreary routine. Day after day at the same boring pace. Then something unexpected happened. I had just finished primary school and started going to high school. One day Ranu didn't come back from school. Usually she didn't go anywhere after school and came straight home. We went to her school, looked everywhere in the neighbourhood, then inquired at the houses of relatives. No, she wasn't anywhere. As evening drew on we became deeply worried.

Father had gone to Sylhet to attend a huge *wag*, a religious gathering. It was the Durga Puja season. Pale with worry, Mother sent me round the various puja mandaps. Looking for Ranu gave me a chance to see all the ten-armed idols. I ran along the rail tracks. Moonlight was diffused through the misty air. Soaking myself in that light I skipped from one sleeper to the next. The mandap closest to our house was terribly crowded. The air was heady with incense. Songs were ear-splittingly broadcast over loudspeakers. I advanced into the crowd, squeezing through till I reached an altar

106

festooned with red and blue lights. My eyes desperately searched for Ranu. At one point I stood right in front of the altar, which was protected by a bamboo fence. On the other side lay an array of various fruit—apples, bananas, pineapples, watermelon—and beyond it was a celestial realm. A radical Durga spread out ten arms while other idols encircled her. For the first time I was plunged into thoughts about my appearance. I could gauge the inferiority of my looks compared to Ranu's. It was a distressing realization. Before the goddess I learnt what separated Ranu from me. I felt drowsy. Where was Ranu? I felt drawn by the otherworldly beauty in front of me. I had never known that the scent of clustered fruit could be so sweet. If only Ranu could see them. I was about to turn back when the drumming began. A hunchbacked drummer set the rhythm which others enthusiastically took up. Then a large number of men and women with bird feathers stuck in the hair started dancing in a circle. Smoke spiralled upward like a snake. In a moment I became utterly indifferent to my entire world.

I became suddenly aware that someone from behind was pulling my hand. I looked back in a trance-like state. It was a boy I had seen around the place. What was his name? The smoke confused me. Yes, I remembered, Ajay! He whispered in my ear. 'Come and watch the fun.' More fun? Like someone under a spell I pushed my way out through the crowd. He dragged me along to a corner and raised a pointing finger— a horrible-looking, dark, fat man with a blood-stained face sat laughing. There was ceaseless laughter, ha! ha! ha! It was a terrifying sight under the full moon. The blood of sacrificed he-goats was being poured down his throat. Blood dribbled down his face, chest, belly and on to the ground. I shut my eyes in terror.

Was this fun? I gave Ajay an interrogative look. He seemed terribly cruel now.

'Feeling scared?' he asked. I was quite overwhelmed by the attention he was giving me. He dragged along by my trembling hand. 'You haven't yet seen the real fun.' He manoeuvred through the crowd and took me to a secluded place behind the puja mandap. In that dimly lit place he placed his hands on my breasts. This was my first experience of this sort. Pre-pubertal breasts are terrible; it seems one is carrying two bundles of pain around. So the touch at first was so painful that I thought I would die, but the next moment an unearthly pleasure spread like flames over my whole body. His mouth descended on my tremulous lips. There was nothing but shadows in the world around. What a feeling, what a ripple! His mouth had a strange smell. I felt dizzy. At the same time a profound lassitude and weariness made me feel sleepy. The bestower of the kiss was not a little restless. Suddenly thrusting a half-taka coin in my hand he disappeared into the crowd.

What fun! It took a while for me to understand what had happened. A kiss, just a kiss, and nothing else? And a whole half-taka for that? I had just had a hint of the delights of physical contact. But the person burying his mouth in mine—didn't he feel repulsed? What sort of fun was this? All it meant was a mingling of abundant saliva. The ghostly, mist-shrouded moon had grown older. Now the half-taka meant joy. The moonlit rail tracks stretched away before me. Along them I went dancing home. My lips became moist at the touch of the mist-soaked light. But the next moment brought weariness. The stillness of night had descended. Had Ranu got back home?

As soon as I reached home Mother ran forward to meet me. 'Have you found her?' I froze in shame and a sense of guilt. This is how Mother was waiting for me!

So Ranu hadn't come back. The night deepened. Mother hadn't said anything to the neighbours, for fear of scandal.

The neighbourhood slept peacefully. Mother sobbed inconsolably. I could see Ranu's face as we had made our way carrying a bag of wheat on a hot, hot day. Ranu's face was flushed, she was crying.

I buried my head in my knees and sat crying till dawn. Mother really doted on Ranu. What if I went off somewhere? Somewhere really far? Would she cry like this? If Ajay married me, turning me into an otherworldly Durga?

Flat on the bed Mother lay. There was some leftover rice from last night. I sat carelessly slicing a green papaya for stir-frying. Suddenly an unsteady finger fell on the blade and was covered in blood. I was about to raise it to my mouth when Ranu appeared in the doorway. Her hair was dishevelled, her eyes sleepless. I dropped everything and almost shouted with joy. Mother sat up in bed. I put my arms around Ranu and led her indoors.

'Where did you go?'

Ranu didn't say anything, she just gave me a strange look. 'Where were you? We were sick with worry.' Ranu sat in silence. I took out the half-taka and slipped it into her hand. I became incoherent in my excitement. I was almost panting as the words poured out. 'How I looked for you! Everywhere at the puja, a lovely dance, Ajay . . . damn . . . Where were you? I was scared out of my wits. I was afraid I would never see you again in this life.'

Ranu seemed so tired and listless. She seemed to be a stranger as she went to lie down on the bed. She turned her back on us. Not a word out of her. Mother wept, so did I. 'Strange, why aren't you saying anything?' now it was Mother's turn. Vigorously shaking her she demanded: 'Tell me where you went. Aren't you growing up? Don't you have any sense? Talk . . . ! Talk! . . . Talk!' Mother started crying again. That was when I knew Ranu had become a stranger to me.

When she woke in the evening after sleeping soundly all day I almost threw myself on her, ran my fingers through her hair, cracked her knuckles, talked to her about Durga Puja. Of course I had to suppress the Ajay episode. But Ranu was only annoyed at my attentions. She hugged the pillow and shut her eyes. Where had she spent a whole night without me? My heart was bursting with curiosity and anguish. When did she become so grown-up, so mysterious? I sat still beside her while the night deepened. The pillow had burst and the escaping cotton was turning her hair white. I gently removed the white fluff and again begged her for an explanation. 'Where were you? Won't you tell me?' The wind rose. It howled under the eaves of the tin roof. A little later it began to rain. My blood pressure rose, making me feel suffocated. I was slowly drowning. The cool rain brought sleep to my eyes. 'My sweet Ranu,' I whispered. Did she have a secret as big as a book of fairy tales?

Late at night Ranu made a declaration at which I simply fell from the sky.

'I was at Majumdar's place.'

'Whe-e-e-re?' I couldn't believe my ears.

'You heard me.' She was totally unfazed. 'Look, don't tell Mother. Not that it matters. I don't care what others think.'

'No, of course, but you . . .' I began to tremble with nervousness. 'You used to be so terrified of him. Have you gone mad, Ranu? Spending the whole night beside that horrible monster! How could you?'

'Did he,' I asked again in Mother's idiom, 'do any bad things to you?'

'No,' Ranu answered calmly, 'he is far superior to Mother or Father.'

'What are you saying—he did nothing?' I almost screamed in bewilderment. 'Then what did you do all night?'

Leaving me all confused, Ranu fell silent again. I didn't have a wink of sleep. I could sense that Ranu was also awake. Yet, so strange was our embarrassment that neither of us could venture forward. At one point Ranu took hold of me like a grown-up, mature person, held me against the wall and said, 'Do you want to know what happened? Do you think I will be able to make you understand?'

'Still,' I ventured uncertainly. Ranu started talking.

'After school I was on my way to the grocer's, I was walking past his house. Suddenly I felt someone grab me from behind. I saw it was Majumdar. God, he is so strong! In one swift motion he carried me into his house and shutting the door forbade me to scream. Then he muttered some strange words and blew his breath on my face. I began to feel numb all over. Leaving me in that state he locked the room and went out. A while later he returned with a huge box. You have to see it to believe it. It was filled with food, biryani, sweets, fruit. He laid out everything before me and asked me to eat. I was still quaking with fear. Such a lot of food! I thought I would go mad. Anyway, I started eating, and he began talking. He has such extraordinary stories to tell. I felt a strange influence come over me. I kept looking at him.'

Ranu stopped. I stared at her in silence. She started talking again. 'Then he sat in meditation. Till midnight he made me sit there while he meditated. There was another round of eating and more stories. Do you want to hear those stories?' Since I didn't respond Ranu changed the subject. 'He is a very good man, do you know?'

'What if Father hears?' I asked stupidly.

'Father has entrusted him with all the responsibility for me, so that he can exorcise the evil djinn that has possessed me. It is because of the djinn that I am in low spirits and abnormally hungry all the time.' Ranu began to doze off.

I felt a venomous disgust for Father. Tears came to my eyes. 'Ranu, he is not a good man, and yet he has completely won you over. How could you bring yourself to like him?' My pleas fell on deaf ears. Ranu began muttering her own story.

'He told me so many things, the story of his struggles. Not that I could make sense of everything. He said one day there will be a big earthquake that will destroy everything. When he was building his house a pir warned him in a dream not to complete it, or else all three floors would collapse and crush him to death. That is why he sleeps under the bed. He is so sad because he doesn't have a son. He knows what I see in my dreams.'

'Crazy! A lunatic!' I screamed. 'You are not to go there again.'

'Apa, he told me he will protect me from the earthquake. He has that power. He loves me so much. In order to help me he has killed cats, rabbits and puppies by injecting them with poison. He cried inconsolably when he was meditating. I felt so miserable because I used to be repulsed by him. The man is terribly lonely. We misunderstood him.'

So Ranu had been bought over by Majumdar. I tossed and turned all night. From that point I began to hate my parents and brother and sister. From the next day Ranu was a totally different person. She began to avoid me. Always clad in new clothes, happy in her infatuation, Ranu became lively and cheerful. All her varied new clothes of course made me burn with envy. Side by side there was genuine anguish. Meanwhile, my parents' dependence on Majumdar increased fourfold. He had driven away the djinn that had possessed Ranu. Now she was a lively, sociable person. All the gifts of food and clothes she got from him were seen as evidence of his sincere affection for her. I wanted to ask Father, 'Where is your religion now?' I was all alone. I drew on paper, I painted. I was unhappy. My days of weary aimlessness began. Now I realize that till then

I had been a child. Poverty had prevented me from experiencing the natural sensations of growing up. As a child I had felt like a woman devastated by the struggle for survival. But at one point a certain physical change in my body literally altered my whole life. I had never before been so desolate and vulnerable.

I knew every girl went through this change. Without any irritation or pain, it occurred suddenly. But I had no inkling of its true nature.

I had fever for several days without let. In the middle of it I felt a strange warmth in certain unmentionable parts of the body. I was exhausted from activities outside the home and to that was added the physiological turmoil. I would curl up in bed and cry all night. There was no one in my life who, if they came and placed a hand on my head, could restore my confidence. From my fragmented memories of that time just after the Ajay episode, when my childhood was drawing to a close, I recall that distant male relatives had started revealing different facets of their behaviour. If they were visiting, because I was still so young, Mother would send me to sleep with one of them. In the middle of the night his breathing would become progressively heavy and if I fled hissed threats would follow me, 'You're dead if you tell anyone.'

I would sit panting on the floor of the next room. I wouldn't tell anyone. One night I dreamt I was being chased by some men. The road stretched to faraway places. My feet refused to move, I keeled over, stood up again. The men left. As I lay in the middle of the road, I suddenly saw Ajay . . . Amazing! At the very sight of him such waves ran through my body . . . His touch was so sensitive! Waking up from a romantic dream early in the morning I found blood in my shorts. I was astonished and felt silly. I was feverish all over. Gripped by a strange fear, I examined myself carefully for cuts! No, this torrent had erupted from deep down. My limbs trembled, I thought I was guilty of a terrible crime. I felt helpless, confused, though there was no pain or irritation. After a long time I felt close to Mother.

While teaching me to cut up old pieces of cloth to soak the flow, mother told me many things. My days of freedom were over. My behaviour would have to change, etc., etc. I felt desolate, tearful. Mother whispered, 'Be careful. If anyone does anything to you now you will become pregnant.'

Does anything—but what exactly? I was confused again. Mother had spoken so casually. Did she think someone had in the past done something? And Ajay? If he kissed me again, or if that kiss had been given now—would I become pregnant?

A weird, bewildering period began in my life. I didn't have a female friend other than Ranu. Who would I talk to about all these things? And Ranu had suddenly become distant. My boring days passed in insufferable uncertainty.

∼

'Hey, Ranju,' I called out of my bus window when I saw him walking along the pavement near Nilkhet. He kept walking nonchalantly, so I called out again.

He turned his head abruptly, but couldn't spot me in the crowd. I stretched an arm out of the window. 'Here!'

His face lit up when he saw me. He gestured at me urgently to get off the bus. I drew his attention to the people crowding the bus. 'Can't get off. Tell me what's new with you.'

'Come, get off, there's news.' His insistence put me in a quandary. I couldn't deny that after my break-up with Rezaul, Satyajit, Ranju and Salauddin had been extraordinarily supportive. Without their heartfelt sympathy, who knows where I would have drifted off.

114

But would I really have drifted off? I had faced crises in the past as well. Then no one had stood by me but I hadn't drifted away. Anyway, there was no denying that I was deeply indebted to these few friends who had helped me financially and emotionally in my crisis.

~

The whole of last night and all day today I was immersed in the past, which I normally avoided. But I couldn't help it, I had a bee in my bonnet. So many events had crowded together that, like it or not, my thoughts kept nudging them. Suddenly, while rifling through a file the thought struck me—where in the life of our family did Irfan Chacha fit in? But by the time I found the document I was looking for, I had forgotten all about it. Then I went to Sultana and asked for another loan. The next day was payday.

Sultana herself wasn't in very comfortable circumstances. She too was in a pickle over family problems and lack of funds. But she laid it on, I thought. I had to hear her out of course, or pretend to be listening and nod mechanically, while maggots grew in my brain—where were my two uncles at that time? Where are they now? One of them had landed a good job in Chittagong. Had either of them repaid an iota of their debt to their elder brother?

A chill descended on my heart. The joints of my hands and feet felt loose. Red and blue ledgers whirled around before my eyes. The clatter of typewriters gradually increased. It sounded as if the wind was knocking together the bones of a skeleton. I wanted to escape the noise, but a pointed finger emerged from the invisible skeleton and pierced deep into my chest. I pressed wet clay to my wounded face. Numerous crows were cawing in unison. Those murderous creatures in

The Birds were chasing me with horrible cries. I fled in terror and as I ran I slipped and fell . . . the crows pecked at my leg. I pressed my hands to my head. I pressed hard against the wooden table to steady myself.

'Are you feeling sick?' Sultana was bending over me. She began dabbing at the perspiration on her upper lip with a handkerchief. Then she brought her handbag and put her hand inside to look for something. 'Here's another two hundred—after all, you are getting paid tomorrow.'

And Rezaul? How firmly entrenched in my life had he become? In which phase had he entered my life and how much had he thrilled me? Before that? Did I love someone else? What sort of dreams had I woven around Rezaul? Did I really have any dreams? So many characters and so varied! I quickly lost track when I tried to think about them. I began to droop with fatigue. His face emerged as a form out of a totally abstract painting. How much had I got to know of that artist—his lanky body, eyes, mouth, his spiritual range . . . ?

'Thanks so much, Sultana.' I dragged myself back to the present as I put the money in my purse. 'There are so many bills to settle after one gets one's salary that we miss out on the pleasure of the payday. How the money will leave your hands is fixed beforehand.'

'You can pay me back two hundred this month,' Sultana said in sympathy. 'We are all in the same boat; sometimes I feel really miserable. The other two hundred you can pay back when possible, don't worry about it.'

And now I had managed to squeeze through the passengers and emerge, half-baked, on the pavement. 'Now you have to pay my rickshaw fare home,' I told Ranju sharply. 'I don't want to wrestle my way into a bus again.'

'How much do you need?' Ranju asked a little gruffly.

'Why, just because you have suffered a setback, have you taken to robbery or what?'

'Hell, no, no . . .' he burst into laughter. 'That is a much later episode. It is not necessary to go so far now.'

A lazy afternoon. Buses, trucks, cars rushing by. Red traffic lights turned on, green turned off, amber next, the traffic cop's sharp whistle . . . Ah, then the stadium in my brain comes alive with a weird football match. I remembered a nasty family squabble over Irfan Chacha. I had just joined the cultural organization. One day when I came home after a programme it was evening. A battle was raging, with Mother—my soft-spoken mother—screaming at the top of her voice. If there was a thermometer for measuring astonishment it would have registered 105° Fahrenheit. My feet came to a standstill on the sand spread before the front door and everything I heard is still clear in memory. Father was shouting, 'You have to see whose daughter it is. The mother herself is of a dubious character . . .'

'What are you trying to say?'

I had noticed earlier that on this particular question Mother was always aggressive in her own defence. Father sensed this and took advantage of it.

'If my character is so disreputable, why did you marry me? You had become quite desperate to marry me then.'

'I was mad, that's why.' Father ground his teeth together. 'You are no beauty. I took pity on you—pity. Otherwise who would accept someone else's discarded goods?'

'Is this what you call pity?' Mother set up a wail. 'Since we got married I have been toiling like a slave, but have you ever spoken two kind words to me?'

Mother didn't know how to counter one argument with another. When Father's unseemly behaviour would reach its climax she would simply accept defeat rather like Shanu. The

117

defeat was also acknowledged in a commonplace manner. She only said in the end that Allah saw everything and was the ultimate judge.

To me the whole thing was intolerable. I have often seen Mother shed tears. Had I received any affection from Father? Since he was my father how can I think there was no affection? But did I ever feel it? I examined every episode, every page in the book of my life. Alas, wasn't there a single tender moment that I had shared with Father?

'What's the matter? Why have you clammed up?' Ranju gave me nudge. 'Come, let's walk.'

We walked down the straight pavement. Dust swirled in the dry afternoon breeze, settled in a film from head to toe. Two half-naked ragamuffins dashed across the road. A monster of a car whizzed past their ear. I was about to sink into my private thoughts again when Ranju picked up a newspaper from a vendor. Rapidly scanning the headlines, he turned to me. 'Nina, it seems the Third World War is about to break out.' I surfaced from my private world. 'Do you think things will go that far?' Ranju sat down on the kerb. 'You have to admit, Saddam is a hero.' As he buried his face in the paper I said in some surprise, 'Do you support what Saddam has done?'

'Then, will I side with this Bush bugger?'

'No, no, I am not saying that.'

'Then what are you saying?'

'The world isn't so utterly lawless that Saddam can act on his whim and occupy another country. Now let him pay the price. Does he have the means to resist the Americans?'

My words fell on deaf ears. Ranju ignored me and started reading out the headlines and important news reports. 'Flocks of aircraft in Iraq's skies: U.S. Forces Ready to Invade' . . . 'Biggest American Deployment since Vietnam'. Though I was annoyed, some of the passersby were curious about what he was reading.

They formed a circle around Ranju. They enthusiastically urged Ranju to read more loudly. When he had read a few lines one among the audience ventured an obscenity and that too in verse.

Some say Saddam's one hell of a dude,
All I know is we're getting screwed.

Some laughed uproariously. Others rebuked the versifier for using an obscenity. 'And why shouldn't I?' retorted the rhymester. 'Saddam occupies Kuwait, and at once prices in our country begin to skyrocket!' Yet another person joined in. 'Shopping centres should close down at eight in the evening. Oil, electricity, everything is in short supply. Trade has dwindled . . .' Shouting everyone down came another voice. 'Whatever you say, our government has benefited from the war. Saddam's action has taken the wind out of the sail of the anti-government movement.'

While all this was going on and it seemed a big crowd was forming around us, I pulled Ranju to his feet. He threw the paper to the crowd, walked holding my hand and soon left the Gulf region far behind. 'Nina, I am in a very pleasant mood. I think I can overcome the setback I have suffered.'

'How?' I asked as I bit my nails.

'Thanks to Satyajit, I have got a partner.'

'Do you know your partner?'

'I have told you, Satyajit introduced us.'

Light-complexioned and curly haired, Ranju was turning grey in the late afternoon air. Amber sunlight wove a nest around him. We had reached the end of the stretch of pavement. Before us, the open road. Innumerable adverts, varied stores. Before us lay a crossroads. On the other side, a row of shops selling cosmetics and clothes, then a bakery. A sharp odour reached our nostrils: the fish market wasn't far. The crowd was dense. Suddenly a totally bizarre thought occurred to me: What if someone were to impale me on a bamboo stake at the crossroads? Damn!

'Listen,' I said, putting on worldly-wise airs, 'a business partnership is a risky business. Money is an evil thing. I don't have to explain it to you, even close friends who enter into a business partnership may end up with murder on their hands. Since you say your partner is a new acquaintance, I am rather apprehensive.'

'Not that I haven't thought about these risks,' replied Ranju, 'but my recent debacle has hardened me. If any bastard tries to trip me up I will kick him.'

'That again means you will not avoid trouble.' My voice showed irritation.

'Nina, will you come along to my place?' Ranju asked. 'I don't want to talk about such calculations. We've met by happy chance and see what we are doing instead of carrying on a pleasant conversation. Come, let's go.'

'Suddenly?'

'Yes, just like that.' Then he started on another task. 'Won't you marry again? Will you spend your life like this?'

'Haven't you spent your life like this?' A mysterious smile played on my lips. 'Will you marry me?'

Though it startled him, he quickly pulled himself together and started laughing. 'Your first marriage will make things difficult. Father will straightaway show me the door. As it is, I am ...'

'The two of us will enjoy life in the open air.' Now it was my turn to break into laughter. 'With only the sky above and the ground beneath.'

'If only you were a little prettier, I would have got you hitched with Salauddin. But he's the sort of nincompoop who won't mind the lack of grey matter in a woman as long as she's fair. The skin is all to him, the idiot! To think that he aspires to be a writer!'

'Why do you want to send me his way? Don't you like the idea of an open-air life?'

'Don't joke about serious matters.' Ranju gradually became serious. 'I have also been very flippant. Please don't take it to heart, Nina.'

Suddenly realizing we had come quite close to Arefin's hostel, I was sharply jolted back to reality. I asked Ranju on the spur of the moment, 'Can you lend me some money?'

'How much?'

'I know about your present condition,' I mumbled, misgivings beginning to take shape within me, 'whatever you can manage. Hell! I asked you without thinking. Now I'm feeling bad about it.'

'Don't be so formal,' Ranju said, putting me at ease, 'will a thousand do?'

'No, no, not that much. In your present difficulties . . .'

'I am starting afresh,' he said. 'No risk, no gain. When I have sacrificed one lakh taka, what's a thousand? Tomorrow I'll come to your office with the money.'

Saying goodbye to Ranju I went straight to Arefin's hostel, walked down the long veranda and knocked on his door. One of his roommates was sleeping. He opened the door and in a sleepy voice informed me that Arefin had left for home.'

Back on the street I began another debate with myself. Though he didn't have any money he went home without telling me! Surely I hadn't behaved that harshly with him? Rage and hurt made me choke. His pride and self-respect had become so robust! Whereas mine had been frittered away till I had come down to zero! I really had nothing in common with the members of my family. They in turn had used me according to their need. After sucking me dry they would dance on my skeleton and play a tambourine. How far would I demean myself for the sake of such selfish love? But the very next moment my nerves became alert. Was Father's health in a serious state? Why hadn't he died yet?

~

Lulla hulla lullaby . . . At night I made the bed and settled myself in it. Pillow beneath my head . . . running my fingers through my hair . . . sleep, Nina, sleep . . . how does the lullaby go? It had been taught to us during the year I was in the Girls' Guide . . . girls on parade in white uniforms with starched green dupattas, singing in chorus while miming—*Row, row, row your boat/ Gently down the stream.* How does the tune go? A loud humming, like ceaseless downpour. The image dissolves, the music fades. Enter Mahim. He had a show of his work— apprentice work—at 'Battala', the shade of the huge banyan tree in front of the Arts Building. There were a few scattered visitors. I stared in astonishment at one of the paintings. A demure girl in the rain, her eyes averted downward. Not a remarkable subject by any means. But the painting possessed an exquisite air of chastity . . . the raindrops on the girl's cheeks, it seemed, would drip if one touched them. I thought my index finger would involuntarily reach out for those raindrops. The novice artist couldn't remain aloof any longer; he came up to me. 'Do you like it?'

I was thinking of dismissing it with a show of childish disdain—'Not at all'—when my eyes fell on his face. Hair awry. A humble demeanour . . . that was the beginning. We walked together along so many roads . . . flew together in so many skies . . . drifted together in so many seas . . . Where was that boy now, in which distant land? An extraordinary love entered my life. I lost all track of time. I used to raise his little finger to my lips, and intone like a poem in a dream, 'Mahim, come and traverse me. I can't bear this starry light in this whirlpool; this is silent poison.' And then? Then I roamed the city's outskirts with him, in a rickshaw, many many times; stopped; went into a reverie; started off again. Was that merely the pursuit of pleasure in restless youth, I asked myself. I would die at his touch, crumble into powder at the soft rustle of his breath. What was that? He wrote in my notebook: 'No soap on earth can wash away the stain of a few drops of blood I've spilt on your hand. Even if you amputate your hand its salty tang will never leave you.' Was it all fake?

I remember that we were in the library when he first asked if he could kiss me. I agreed, then went through with it in a trance, only to spring back as soon as our lips had touched. I recalled Ajay, the half-taka. Ugh! How insulting! Now, here was Mahim, intoxicating Mahim. I hid my hands beneath my kameez and retreated. 'I won't even let you touch my finger . . . these things are wrong.' He said, 'My needle-sharp gaze has pierced right through that finger and traversed your entire body on a profane pilgrimage. Even if you put that finger in a thimble you won't be able to cover up the mark I've made.' He used to say these things to me in a deep, anguished voice. It made me cry . . . nobody had ever given me so much importance. 'Mahim, if you abandon me, my tear-filled nights, the railway track, the whole of nature—these will not forgive you.' I used to be haunted by the fear that I would lose him because even when he was sitting beside me I would get the feeling that he wasn't really there. He held my hand, spoke to me in a serious voice, but I got the impression that my image in his vision wasn't sharp and clear. It was sheer agony for me. I was like Durga's ten-armed image before him. Through me he worshipped a deity who stood beyond mundane life. But it was only much later that I discovered this.

'I love the clouds...the drifting clouds up there...I love those wonderful clouds.' And then: 'But there's my father's room. He lies paralysed...' I watched Mahim sit down on a chair with a broken arm. How can I escape the unhappy subject? There we sat in the dim light of a hurricane lantern, silent, unable to speak.

Ranu used to say, 'What a wimp! If he took my hand I would die of disgust. Are you in a relationship with him? What taste!' Her comments drove me to tears. It seemed as if Ranu had no conception of beauty.

Sleep, Nina, sleep. A gecko climbs the wall. The light is on. One, two, three geckos...Innumerable insects around the light bulb, one, two...O my, who is that coming towards me across the floor, on all fours? Does it have horns on its head as it forges through coiling mists and swirling smoke? I raise my head. Slowly, everything clears. A child squats on all fours in the vacant space of my brain. It grows in size and stands tall, occupying the whole room. A child, just one child. I pick it up and cradle it in my arms. It clamps its toothless gums on a nipple. I squirm in pain and push its mouth away from my breast. Then that deathless scream explodes. The breasts, swollen and heavy with milk, throb in agony. As if they were huge boils...I apply the point of a safety pin to prick the tip of the nipples. The mute breasts won't open their mouths, although they are brimming with milky words. Such agony! Why don't you have teeth, my child, to bite them off? The breasts vomit blood on to the safety pin. The doctor comes running: What are you doing? Ranu, when you marry there will be *pitan*...There's the flour mill, just a short way from here. The child's screams are unbearable! I toss and turn in bed, fling the child into space. Does it now sport white horns on its head? Strange! One's child is so exquisitely lovely, so affectionate! I can't ever escape its circle of attraction.

The baby crawls under the edge of my sari. With long nails it scratches my belly. It exudes the sweet smell of fresh milk. I can sense its breathing is inhibited. I drop it. Again the unearthly cry. I clap my hands to my ears. I run down the hospital corridor. Stop this crying, this deathly crying! And now? At midnight I prick my ears—where is that cry? Where is that wailing? All my senses grow restless, crazy, thirsty. O kite, can you give me my baby's cry?

No.

Rabbit, O rabbit, can you . . . ?

No.

O *mrigel* fish, can you . . . ?

No.

I turn off the light. Pressing my hands to my ears I dive into bed. Now then, why did my younger chacha hang himself? Such an iron-willed man! Damn, let me dance. What a gorgeous dress! I am Cinderella on her evening out. Alas, where are my shoes? Shit!

Nina, look, that's the Stadium, that's the Museum, over there is the Children's Park. There on the left is the Old Radio Station. This is New Market . . . Nina, there at last is Rampura TV Station. Sleep, Nina, sleep, it's late night.

The days went by in this fashion: tedious, unexciting, engaged every moment in a pathetic struggle to eke out a living. One afternoon Rezaul turned up at my office. The hullaballoo at work, the protest and whatnot had run out of steam. How everyone had burst into a flame! Then, like lamps running out of oil, they suddenly died down. That day I was at my desk as usual. Barua Babu had left his desk to sit in front of me and go on and on about his niggling domestic problems.

This ludicrous man was like a harmonium whose keys always produced the same boring notes: do re mi fa. He gave me the most boring moments I have known. I lack all interest in sports, still go on about Roger Miller's goal-scoring record, Maradona's childhood in a slum, at least for half an hour; or talk about films, not a single one of which I would see in a whole year—taking Bombay's Shabana Azmi alongside our very own Shabana, proclaiming our Bobita to be superior to Smita Patil; let such pseudo arguments take up another hour or so, even then I will listen, and attentively too, and from time to time even argue with the help of my limp logic. But if you talk about being struck with a broom by your wife, about your father's cataract surgery, Nina will at once turn into a statue. She will stare at you open-mouthed, deaf to all you say. No comments, no sympathy.

But didn't I too sing the same boring mosquito-songs? I could easily bring such allegations against myself. When borrowing money from Ranju, didn't I tell him about Arefin, my own miserable life, the condition of my family? Ranju was decent enough to bring the money to my office. He even expressed warm sympathy when he heard my story.

I am without equal when it comes to discovering reasons to justify myself. Of course I am not always making up hard-luck stories, and surely when it is embarrassing and even shameful to keep mum while accepting help from a generously extending hand. So what I said was for the sake of politeness, not to be taken seriously. Whereas the people I am talking about will spend hours analysing these embarrassing matters from various angles, till they are left completely naked. What help can I offer in such circumstances? Why do they demean themselves by talking like that? I have no idea. Perhaps it takes the weight off the chest—at least that's the only reason I can think of. Smash the stone squatting oppressively on your chest into little chips and scatter them all around! But when did I become so selfishly hard-hearted to think such thoughts?

When Barua Babu finishes the tale of his woes and leaves, I am literally dozing off in my chair. Just a few more minutes before the working hours come to an end. Just then I see Rezaul walking through the door. He comes in and in his characteristically restless way looks about the room. Looking for me, I presume. It was a year and a half since our divorce. This was the second time he had come to see me. His limpid eyes had sunk into their sockets. His cheeks had become creased. He had lost weight and his hair was awry; he looked miserable. I put the cap on my pen and stared foolishly. A cold-blooded serpent siphoned water from my breast. My breath stuck at my throat, making me feel cold.

Rezaul came over and stood before my desk. There was an air of desperation about him. A few moments of silence. I asked him to pull up a chair. The whirring ceiling fan disturbed my brain. Just the width of the desk separated us. Without a word he sat down and fixed me with a cold stare. It was the height of theatricality! It was really awkward for me. I pulled open the drawer, put the files in and locked it. I tapped the key ring on the desk as I waited for him to say something. An intolerable inhibition rendered both of us mute. I was about to break the ice with a 'How are you' when he said, 'Why didn't you come to Salauddin's?' I had forgotten about that altogether. Satyajit's revelations, my sense of humiliation ... everything came back to make my senses alert again. I replied coldly, 'The invitation was yours; whether to accept it or not was up to me.'

'You are still the same,' said Rezaul, smiling wanly, then went on naïvely: 'I thought you'd come, even waited a long time. It was a terrible day for me.'

'If you believe in someone that person gains longevity, but it is something I can't bring myself to do,' I said laughing, 'especially when it comes to believing in myself.'

'Can you spare me some time?' So he had now taken the direct approach. But what a polite tone! It made me feel good. How I would long for this when we were married.

'Very well,' I said.

We went to a small restaurant. But neither of us could start the conversation. Doodling with a finger on the tabletop I tried to think how long after that intense involvement with Mahim had Rezaul entered my life. How many years, months, days, hours? If I had wanted I could calculate the precise answer. After that break-up every day had scoured the dry soil of my consciousness inch by inch like a ploughshare. How could I deny that after the anguish of being rejected by Mahim, Rezaul had aroused me? It had been a profound experience. Amidst my heart-wrenching loneliness, the cups of insipid tea, empty afternoons, dark nights, rains, sleepless nights, Rezaul's cheerful presence pointed out a new path. The two of us then walked down the road I had earlier taken with Mahim and, as with Mahim in the past, went together on evening rickshaw rides. Only, because of the added years, the earlier excitement wasn't there—the childish weeping, the volatile emotions. I had definitely matured. But the strange excitement within was still the same. That's when I first realized that it is through continuous repetition that we become creative every day. I realized we aren't born to remain stuck at one point. No matter how painful it is to pull up one's roots, the natural tendency of mankind is to strike out in new directions. It was for the sake of survival that I latched on to Rezaul. I knew he only had a petty job and earned little. But I liked the way he had organized his life, renting a room in our small town, living a disciplined life all by himself. Besides, Father was in a bad way. For several months my youngest uncle, who had started working, sent us enough to support ourselves. Then Father had a stroke and became bedridden. Uncle left his job and came home . . . then came his death. These misfortunes had completely devastated our family. Meanwhile, Arefin had just managed to scrape through in his Higher Secondary Certificate examination and Baro Chacha threw him out saying he wouldn't support such a donkey any longer. The upshot of all this was that Rezaul seemed to possess a magical appeal amidst the harsh realities of existence. The bond between Majumdar and Ranu had grown loose. He had fetched his wife and daughters from the village to live with him. The effervescent Ranu had petered out like a wick that had run out of oil. These unfortunate turns of events had the effect of erasing Mahim's shadow from my inner world. I remember his desperate declaration of love: 'Let's get married, Nina. A simple verse from the sky and congregated stars will be our wedding mantra. One day the curse on us will lift and our disguise will fall away.'

I would burst into tears. 'What curse are you talking about? What have we done wrong?'

Actually he lacked inner stability, so to him my company would be more a source of pain than joy. 'Your lovely hands that I am touching,' he said sadly one afternoon, 'is their loveliness what I wanted to touch? Do I know the intensity of my desire for you in the depths of my heart? I am disturbed by the apprehension that I am deceiving you. I do not really know my true feelings about you.'

This is how he used to speak when his visits to our house had become rather frequent. It caused me anguish, though I had no idea what lay at the bottom of such a declaration. He had sketched me many times. But in those drawings I could never locate my own face. Instead, there was a face, a figure, a posture that seemed uncannily familiar. I tried to dip my hand into that tangle of colours, but they were like iridescent water that broke into ripples at the slightest touch, irretrievably scattering the image. Much later, after much research, when I realized everything, I discovered that Mahim had dredged Ranu out of my depths and constructed that image. My world collapsed into ruins. I gazed at Ranu's exquisite, pale features. My inner world crumpled into a mess. With a desperate effort I straightened myself, stood up. From that point began the phase where I clutched at Rezaul like a drowning person at a straw. I was certain that even though we didn't share a grand passion, he was the man to whom I mattered as an individual. Then—did the dream fade? I don't know. Or was it all a complicated blunder, one that I cannot fathom?

*Singara*s and steaming hot tea on a ramshackle discoloured tabletop. Me on one side of the table, Rezaul sitting beside me and sipping tea—could we begin all over again? Such a terrifying proposal was sprung so suddenly on me that I was simply rattled. I got a grip on myself and drawing the cup closer to me sipped at it slowly. With the other hand I squeezed the belly of the singara, forcing out a couple of potato pieces. 'Will that be a good idea?' I replied. Then limitless silence reigned. There were fewer people in the restaurant now, scattered pairs and groups, sipping tea, engaging in desultory conversation. Rezaul looked about, then spoke up: 'Listen, I am in a very bad way. It's not money matters I'm chiefly worried about, it's psychological. Life is so blank, so lonely, that on some days I feel I'm suffocating. I'll be quite happy with something less than "super".

'You are rambling like a fool.' I became rather irritated. 'Your only thought is your own well-being. But my opinion about your proposal, my decision on it, is pertinent—isn't it?'

'Are you happy now?'

'Yes,' I said firmly.

'Nina, you are being wilful. For a woman in your situation to be happy is unnatural.'

'You were married for quite some time. If my character was normal and chaste, then surely the question of divorce wouldn't have cropped up?'

'Will you still cling to your old, abnormal wilfulness?' Rezaul again sipped his tea.

'But giving in to wilfulness is also humiliating for you. It only aggravates the misfortune, doesn't it?'

Rezaul was carrying a newspaper. In order to distance myself from these annoying subjects I took it from him and spread it out. The headlines swam round and round. 'BUDGET CRISIS IN U.S.A.', 'SOVIET UNION APPREHENSIVE OF MAJOR CONFLICT', 'WE SHALL FIGHT FOR A THOUSAND YEARS—SADDAM', 'GUNFIGHT ON CAMPUS—1 KILLED, 8 WOUNDED', 'IRAQ PLANTS EXPLOSIVES IN KUWAITI OILFIELDS', etc., etc. I folded the paper and put it aside. Everyone in the restaurant knew the news. More people had come in, and at each table there was tremendous excitement. I imagined my dead body floating above a vast battlefield. Let a war start, I said to myself, let everything turn topsy-turvy. But impoverished people like myself were very opportunistic. We'd quickly traverse narrow lanes and alleys and within moments get back to our own lives.

'Look,' I said bluntly, 'I won't say I am very happy—that would be absurd. But I am wonderfully independent. I am much more healthy—at least psychologically—than I was when married. There is a strange joy in freedom. I hope you are experiencing that joy too.'

'Come on,' Rezaul dismissed me. 'Are you afraid I will not have a job? I haven't lost my job, you know. There was a bit

131

of a problem, but that's behind me now. The bottom line is, Nina, it has become impossible for me to live alone. Believe me, there are days when I want to die.'

'How glibly you can talk about these things.' I found myself getting angry as I spoke. 'Do you think a divorce is a joke? I am astonished you think I am so cheap. That I will naturally be affected by your joy and your anguish—haven't you been able to get rid of this medieval notion? The divorce took place because of a profound incompatibility, which had caused much suffering. Your feelings for me may keep swinging between attraction and repulsion; it is a matter of complete indifference to me. Don't destroy whatever little respect I have for you by expressing such bogus sentiments.'

'Bogus sentiments?' Rezaul became worked up. 'Are you calling these bogus sentiments? You have even learned to lie, I see. Where there is hatred, which leads to a divorce, can there also be a little respect? Cut out the clever chatter and just admit that in the name of freedom you are enjoying being promiscuous. You can do whatever takes your fancy, so marriage seems to be a prison house. You had always been like that. That's why married life was a burden to you. In marriage even the wildest man accepts certain restrictions.'

'You are exceeding all limits. You'd better say clearly what's on your mind.'

'Satyajit, Salauddin . . . so many well-wishers have gathered round you. No wonder you are enjoying your freedom.'

'Listen,' I said in a callous tone that came without any premeditation. 'I've slept with Salauddin several times. My relationship with him is purely physical, so the question of marrying him does not arise. You know that I have some problems. It is not unusual for me to indulge in various perversions. Now tell me, do you want to set up house with

132

me once again? Then I am willing. Though not at the price of denying the others.'

Rezaul quietly removed the teacup from my hand and gave me a mysterious smile. Then he gently pressed my hand. 'When you get angry you say such wild things. Very well, in spite of what you've told me, I stand by my word. When are you coming then?'

At this point I began to feel a certain pang. Long cohabitation had given him an insight into my nature. Even after all these days he had accurately interpreted my words. I bit my lip to conceal my reaction and smiled wanly. 'You think I have made up a story, so you are taking it lightly. Showing your broad-mindedness, eh?'

'Not at all,' Rezaul replied. 'I believed what you said.'

This threw me into a dilemma. After a moment's thought I presented the subject from another perspective. 'Why will this society allow me to go back to you? According to religious laws I have to marry someone else before I can return to you. Can you accept that?'

'First say yes to my proposal,' said Rezaul. 'The other things can be dealt with after that. The times are changing. If necessary we'll marry again. Now tell me another thing without being evasive: has Satyajit told you anything?'

'About what?' I asked, absent-mindedly poking at a piece of potato from a singara with my finger. Not finding the right words, Rezaul stammered, 'You know, your sexual . . .'

'What could Satyajit tell me about it?' I feigned surprise while suppressing the fires of rage in my breast. 'What are you trying to say? I don't know what you mean!'

'I asked because of your sudden revelation.'

'It seems you have told him something. Or else why should his name crop up?'

'For heaven's sake, stop playing detective.' He placed a cigarette between his lips. The match hissed as he lit up. 'I told him nothing. He is a close friend of both of us. We talk about everything under the sun, that's why . . .'

'What a lame excuse!'

Seeing that I was getting angry again, Rezaul asked gently, 'Tell me honestly, Nina, what you said about Salauddin is a joke, isn't it?'

This should have set off another upheaval within me. Actually, it was impossible for Rezaul to come out of his narrow groove. But he had correctly seen through my statement and that had aggravated my misery. Now his question afforded me an escape route out of an uncongenial enclosed space.

'No, I wasn't joking,' I replied. 'I have slept with him. Is that surprising, considering that I lead a lonely life? Besides, I am not pledged to anyone.'

Rezaul's cigarette burnt itself out. The waiter removed the plates and cups. The restaurant filled up with patrons and the air became stifling. Amidst the tinkle of cups and the incoherent hullaballoo dusk descended on Dhaka. When we stepped out of the restaurant, the city lights had come on.

As we parted Rezaul said, 'I don't believe what you said.' I replied laughingly, 'But you do, and your belief is concealed in your denial. You should say instead that you find it painful to believe it.'

Rezaul quietly switched the topic. 'Can I see you after this?'

'The less we see of each other, the better for both of us, don't you agree?'

'Now you are imposing your opinion on me. Anyway, I'm off.' His slight frame disappeared into the crowd. I stood still for a while.

When I got home, a tremendous row was in progress. Shanu was a champion engaged in verbal combat with the

134

landlord. Her husband brought up the rear. Her sweaty face, the sari edge trailing on the ground, her rapid breathing—these were clear indications that the matter was serious. I was standing in the doorway when the battle reached its climax. As a third party I just stood there in utter bewilderment.

'We will *not* leave, and we'll see what you can do about it. Do you think we don't understand what you are doing? Kicking up a fuss so that you can increase the rent again? Didn't you raise the rent three months back? You think you can do just as you please—one thing today, another the day after?'

'Shut up, woman,' the landlord shouted back. 'This is my property and if I wish I will ask you to leave. And I don't have to find an excuse to raise the rent for a cheapskate like you.' Shanu's husband now came forward. 'Remember your manners'—and then it seemed that my presence led him to go back to another subject. 'A young woman works to support herself. It is natural that she may come home late. Have you seen her come home in the company of all sorts of men, as you say? Why should an elderly man like you lend an ear to gossip? You don't even live here.'

'Enough, you don't have to speak so politely with him,' Shanu fumed. 'He says I have turned the house into a brothel. Why, have you in your old age got the urge to become a client? Don't I know you? It's only the other day you were absolutely cooing with affectionate concern! A young woman, you said . . . poor thing, without a husband, with no shelter . . . how you waxed lyrical . . . I'll tell everyone about your real intentions.'

Shanu kept up her spirited rant. She could go to any lengths. And me? I was the centre of this obscene squabble. I stood paralysed till Shanu dragged me in. 'Come, Nina, we'll see how the bugger drives us out.' Then more screamed abuse, absurd arguments and counter-arguments, the landlord's sudden departure at one point. Then deepening night, Shanu's unabated grumbling, my unbearable anguish. I felt disgusted with my life.

When I went to bed full of all sorts of feelings of loathing, repulsion and disgust, my thoughts took flight. What did Satyajit think about me? Was he first and foremost Rezaul's friend? And me—just his friend's wife? But how could I dismiss the person who at a ganja session at Salauddin's one afternoon smoked and waxed lyrical about the stuff, turning it into something sublime, and pledged that we were soulmates? How melancholy and tearful he sounded when he spoke of communal conflict! 'Isn't this my land, Nina? For so many years our blood and sweat has mingled with the soil, and yet, when some fellows on the other side of the border start demolishing a mosque we have to face such horrid taunts and persecution on this side. The landlord came yesterday to denounce me: You are sending all your money across the border, he told me, and then concluded: Why are you sitting here—just get lost. But who do I have on the other side? Can religion alone give you a home? Is Saudi Arabia your country, Nina? That day the people who chased me down the alley with stones were filled with such hate! See, I have a cut on the skull, and see here, it's swollen.' He presented his head for my inspection. He was unsteady on his feet. 'Will I survive if I leave this land? Nina, you'll never understand what profound anguish that would mean. Since yesterday I've holed up in Salauddin's stuffy little room. Nina, look, my blunt, soggy, mutilated heart is in flames, I am being burnt to a cinder—hold me, Nina. A person without a homeland is the most wretched beggar in the whole world.' I had hugged him tight. 'Satyajit, calm yourself, please, no civilized being is doing those horrible things.' Holding my face in both hands he had said in profoundly hesitant tones, 'You don't fit the picture of the yellow bird that bites its lips and flutters its wings in the cage but cannot fly. You've done a good thing, Nina—at least you've flown away.'

'What if I fall flat on my face on the tin roof?'

'You'll fly off again.'

'Then why are you crying?' I poked fun at him. 'You have allowed incidents instigated by a few fundamentalist politicians to drive you to despair.'

'This is a different kind of anguish. Will the soil on which I was born exile me, just for my religion?'

'The soil hasn't disowned you,' I said calmly. 'If you give in to weakness you'll only help those barbarians win a victory.'

'That's enough of your prattle. Now let me cry a little.'

And he had burst into loud sobs. Salauddin and I consoled him with great effort. Was Satyajit—a person with such emotional depths—just Rezaul's friend? Was all that mere pretence? I thrashed about helplessly. How could someone who had spoken so solemnly about flight be transformed by Rezaul's lament mingled with the sniffle of common cold into an ambassador of reconciliation? He must have given Rezaul my office address. Where would I find sanctuary?

∼

It was the morning of a public holiday. I thought I'd visit Irfan Chacha and fetch the easel he had promised me. Just then a flustered Satyajit arrived. 'Are you going somewhere?' he asked.

I was surprised to see him. Shanu's set-to with the landlord, and now his sudden advent so early in the morning— embarrassedly I pulled up a chair and asked him to sit.

'Salauddin had an accident yesterday,' he said. 'He has been admitted to the Postgraduate Hospital.'

'Where? How?'

The news was a bolt from the blue. I felt strangely numb.

'He was on his way back from the press with a few formes of proofs. He was about to cross the road near the Tikatuli crossroads when a son of a bitch of a minibus hit . . . lucky to have come out alive.'

'How is he now?'

'Not too good. Lots of cuts and bruises. He's in constant agony.'

I was more or less ready to go out. We went together. I wiped off the lipstick as surreptitiously as I could and tried to sit in as natural a posture as I could manage on the rickshaw. Neither of us spoke. This was the first time we had met after that disturbing encounter and I just couldn't feel at ease with him. On top of that there was the eerie silence imposed by the accident. I gazed at the passing scene to hide my embarrassment—the Abahani sports field and, later, the Science Laboratory, MSKO Shoes. The road on the left led to the Hatirpool Bazar, on the right stood Mujib Hall. We were still silent. Then Sylvana, the restaurant, on the left. When we stopped at the Shahbagh crossroads Satyajit again opened his mouth. 'Lost a lot of blood. I was in the Bakery. Suddenly a small boy came with the news. His parents live so far away, they haven't heard anything yet.'

'Can't we send a message?'

'All the way to Dinajpur! Let's see, I'll try. The bugger has ruined himself chasing his literary dream. There's nothing else in his head. For some days now he had forgotten everything in the world except his house and the press. Whatever he has saved working all this time is going on this book. This accident will mean added expenses.'

'How strange—he was printing his own book! Couldn't he find a publisher?'

We had to walk around a bit. The brightness of sun-reflecting glass all around: Dhaka's famous crows being thrown off-balance by the dazzling shafts of light. After getting past the gatekeeper with the help of a convoluted explanation we found ourselves behind a crowd of people waiting for the lift. We took the stairs instead, climbing slowly, step by step.

'What were you saying?' Satyajit said. 'With his own money? Well, he's a new writer, where will he get a publisher? He has no contacts at all.'

In hospital once again. We walk down the long corridor. My feet become weary, numb. The inescapable odour of Savlon enters my brain, makes me foggy. The death rattle of thousands seems to resound all around me. Invisible glass walls return my stare. The ceaseless sounds of lamentation derange my soul and drain my blood. In those arid spaces radiant human infants go round and round on all fours, walk, run, stumble and fall amidst loud cries. The continuous wail of the yellow-skinned infant is scattered over a meaningless blank stillness. How quickly lethal jaundice can be. Yellow—the only colour that casts a poisonous shadow on the world. My feet wobble, I feel faint as the smell of Savlon penetrates me. Yes, it was the smell of the hospital that clung to the child's body. The entire hospital was awash with the smell when the child died.

I dragged myself into the huge whitewashed ward. Beneath the vast white ceiling Salauddin lay motionless. His face contorted in an effort to suppress the pain. His legs, forehead, in fact almost his entire body was swathed in bandage. I placed a hand on his hair. He gave me such a pathetic gaze that I felt a little discomfited. He parted his lips slightly and smiled. 'Still smiling!' I said in mock anger.

'Why shouldn't I?' he said in a faint voice that was barely above a whisper. 'Today, for the first time, I have realized that I'm not alone in this world.'

'That's the pleasure of thinking that one is alone,' I said. 'When there's nothing to ask of the world, a little that suddenly comes one's way seems to be a great deal.' My white cotton sari grew moist with the smell of the hospital.

'No, no, no,' he said, waving a hand, 'you don't understand at all . . .'

'Don't try to talk today,' I advised him, running my fingers through his hair. 'I'll come again tomorrow. We'll debate the issue later.'

Some time passed in silence. When I prepared to leave Satyajit got up to see me out. 'You stay with him,' I told him. 'I can find my way out. Besides, something has to be done to send news to his family.'

'Nina, are you cross with me for some reason?'

'No.'

I was going down the stairs when someone called from behind. I turned to look. An ape-like man. Scraggly hair hung over his forehead. A tiny pair of eyes beneath the high bridge of his nose. An unsightly stubble. A discoloured shirt on a skinny, gawky frame. Trousers too discoloured. He looked terribly familiar. Yet I felt nervous on the lonely stairs. My dead child's smell still pervaded my whole being, and I was too confused to figure out who it was.

'How are you?'

'Fine,' I replied as I continued on my way down. I was certain I had never been acquainted with such a grotesque character. It was silly to dilly-dally on the stairs because he seemed familiar.

'You didn't recognize me?' He came down the stairs till he was level with me. 'You are so nervous and scared. You were scared that day too. And yet I see that you are generally on your own.'

140

'What do you mean?' I stopped. When did I get scared? He was talking with such authority and yet I couldn't remember him. Where had I seen him? I groped in the recesses of my memory. Damn—my groping hand touched my dead child's abdomen.

'Did you find the house that day?' He came down another step. I brightened up on hearing the question. 'Oh yes, that day . . . I say, mister, you had become tired and abandoned me. Then I went round and round . . .'

'Anyway, did you find the house?'

'Yes, that I did.'

'Actually, I had an important appointment. Someone owed me money. If I didn't go to meet him then I wouldn't get the money back. He was leaving the country for good.'

'No, you did a lot,' I said gratefully. 'But why are you in the hospital?'

'Last week my younger brother was stabbed by a friend. He was called out of the house late at night and then . . .'

'What are you saying?' I was shocked. 'Why are you calling the assailant a friend? He was a foe through and through.'

'Yes, of course. We were mentally prepared for such an event. My brother used to move in very bad circles.'

'Let's go and see him,' I said out of a vague sense of duty. As we went up the stairs the man wanted to know what had brought me to the hospital. I gave him a brief account of Salauddin's accident as we entered the spacious hospital ward. Such a young boy! The picture of innocence. He slept, a bandaged arm raised and attached by traction to a stand, chest bandaged too. An old man in the next bed lay under a ceiling fan and also used a hand fan to cool his head. His eyes were sleepy. I didn't quite know how to break the ice among strangers. A nurse in white headgear came and sat down on a stool. I kept standing awkwardly. The grotesque man rescued me.

'You were going home, I suppose.'

'Yes, how is your brother's treatment progressing?'

'Hospital treatment!' he said ironically. 'So-so.'

'How is he now?'

'Not too bad, but he complains when he wakes up. Let's go.' At the landing he asked, 'What's the number of Salauddin's ward? Since he's your friend I'll call on him.' I gave him the number of the ward and Salauddin's bed and stepped on the stairs. 'Will you come again?'

'Yes, of course. Salauddin is a very close friend. If I visit him I'll come and see your brother as well.'

'Oh, I forgot to ask, where do you live?'

'Rayer Bazar,' I said and started down the stairs.

'My name is Omar,' he called out from behind.

'Oh, I see.'

It was past noon now. I walked out swiftly and hailed a rickshaw. How dreadful it was in there. Groans of people in agony. The smell of poisonous Savlon. Limbs hoisted in the air with pulleys. Excreta, sputum, bandages, ineradicable memories, heart-wrenching cries of an infant, in every corner of the hospital I got the smell of the child's death. I was talking to people, but I was utterly disoriented. I felt numb all over. A bitter blue juice was being squeezed out of my heart. The whirling fans were unsettling the whiteness of the ceiling.

Out in the street I took deep breaths. Eventually the rusty air of our ancient earth washed away all the muck. Past traffic lights, people in a hurry, rows of stores . . . after a thousand twists and turns my rickshaw stopped in front of that old mansion.

An extraordinary coincidence: I have come to this house on two different days, and on both days I have met that man. First in the street, today in the hospital. What a hideous appearance. Of course, he was very polite.

That day I had been discomfited by the thought of meeting Irfan Chacha; today I was uneasy on account of his wife. So it was with the same degree of nervousness that I pressed the doorbell. The door opened after a while and the owner of the house himself stood there. He greeted me warmly: 'You— what a pleasant surprise.'

'I have come for the easel,' I said.

'But aren't you going to step inside?'

'If you wish I can come in for a while.' Our conversation started with such light banter. It was in the same room where I had sat the other day, with its Mughal ambience, slightly musty odour. I sank into the sofa, but couldn't find anything to say. Irfan Chacha, in a dressing gown, was quite cheerful, sprightly. Freshly shaved cheeks, warm smile. But what was conspicuous above everything was the wonder in his eyes, which I had obviously inspired. I stood up. 'Let me go in and pay my respects to Chachi.'

'You don't have to be so polite,' he said. 'It is not necessary in this household. You'll meet her by and by.'

I sat down again, but I was bothered by misgivings. 'It isn't a question of mere politeness,' I said. 'She was very affectionate towards me that day.'

'Very well, then, you can go in and see her later. Now tell me, how have you been keeping?'

'Temperate—neither hot nor cold,' I said, laughing.

'Well said. You are in the best possible state. It is the opposite with me; in summer I feel terribly hot, in winter terribly cold. I have never had temperate weather in my life.'

Interminable silence again. He was semi-recumbent on the sofa, lost in thought. I fingered my handbag, shuffled my slippers on the floor, surveyed the room again.

'Have you finished Van Gogh's biography?'

'No.'

'Why, don't you find it interesting?'

'The book is wonderful. But it plunges me into anguish.'

'Is art possible without anguish?'

'I don't know. But for some reason anguish seems monotonous these days. More than the anguish itself it is the monotony that I find intolerable.'

He had flicked his lighter. Whoosh! A cigarette dangled from his lips. Then smoke. The very next moment my nostrils picked up the smell of Savlon. It rose dancing to my olfactories. The hospital with its white ceiling, the stuffy room, merged into a single entity. I felt sick. Gasping, I stood up. 'Why do all the rooms in your house at times exude such a strong odour of Savlon?'

'That's the favourite scent of my missus,' he said. 'She has the floor of every room wiped with Savlon diluted in water. What's interesting is that it's not in order to disinfect the floor, but simply because she likes the smell of the disinfectant.'

'She actually likes the smell!' I gasped. Human beings are really strange. I couldn't stand the smell, which to me suggested bleeding and death.

'You are feeling uneasy!' He was concerned.

'No, no, it's quite all right.' I quickly controlled myself.

'You know,' he said, 'she has another peculiarity—regarding geckos as pets. To have every room fill up with geckos is her dream.'

I couldn't help laughing. How strange human interests can be. Then, like one in a trance I reeled this off: 'Do you know, the smell of Savlon is associated in my memory with the death of my child. When I smell Savlon I again hear the child's cry, I see the child's dead body.'

He flicks ash into the ashtray, puffs again. His face is obscured by a screen of smoke. After a while he gets up slowly. There

144

is a hint of despondency in his footsteps. How surprising that he hasn't reacted at all to my revelation. My soul became embittered. I found myself filled with self-loathing. Alone in that huge room, I wondered why I had exposed myself in this manner. Nothing like this had ever happened before. Why did that fact stuck suffocatingly in my throat force its painful way out? I felt helpless. Should I just leave? How would such impetuousness look? I sat alone, restless. In a few moments my host re-enters, beaming. He is carrying an easel. He sets it up in a corner and blows away the coating of dust. Then with a childlike twinkle in his eyes he asks, 'Do you like it?'

It was really quite exquisite. The base was shaped like a duck's webbed feet. The varnish was a deep nut-brown. The oppressive bitterness within dispersed instantly.

'Wonderful!' I exclaimed loudly. 'The case of the model's pose being more beautiful than the finished painting—some such tragic possibility is very real. Won't what I paint on it pale before its beauty?'

'Why do you suffer from such diffidence?' he asked. 'Try to have some faith at least in yourself. I haven't taken an interest in your painting out of my motive. Your work lacks restraint— that is because you lack academic training. Your painting does not follow any grammar. But your spontaneous brushwork, your choice of palette, are wonderful. Or do you think I am going over the top?'

'Why, are you beginning to regret what you have said? You are a stickler for grammar even in conversation! You have created such a barrier of decorum around yourself! You know, such calculation behind the spontaneous expression of feeling is anathema to me.'

'Very well, I surrender.' He raised his hands. 'I am telling you frankly that you have artistic talent.'

Truckloads of food arrived. The afternoon spread all around. I was famished. An art connoisseur's praise amidst all this was a bit disorienting.

'How well do you know Greek myths?' he asked as he picked up a slice of an apple. 'Are you interested in it?'

'I know little—what I've heard from friends.'

'It will help you a lot in your painting. Rodin's sculpture was influenced by Greek myths, and he wasn't the only one. You might think they are weird old tales, fun to listen to, though some might dismiss them as pure rot, but in either case, not without the power to cast a shadow on an artist's work.'

'Actually, at different phases of art history there has been so much experimentation, so many quality works have been produced, that one gets the shakes when trying to paint. What I am doing—or others are, for that matter—isn't anything new. Isn't it rather the repetition of what is old hat?'

'You aren't eating anything.'

At once I return to reality and pick up a plate of rice pudding. What a fragrance! Enough to make you ravenous. Yummy!

'Take that well-known story,' he resumed, 'the one about Orpheus. The intoxicating music of his flute stills the forests and enchants birds in flight, so that their wings are benumbed. I am retelling it in a simplified form for your benefit.' He picked up another apple slice. The entire room was now dark as a cave. He continued: 'The sudden death of Orpheus's beloved, the exquisitely lovely Eurydice, drove him mad. He began a tireless journey. No matter what, he had to find a way to bring Eurydice back to life. Or else it was meaningless for him to stay alive. He headed towards the Underworld, or Hades. His musical lamentation charmed Charon the boatman who ferried him across Lethe, and past Cerberus, the three-headed dog guarding the gate to Hades. Pluto, god of the Underworld, was overwhelmed by the lament of Orpheus's flute. "You may leave," he said to Orpheus. "Your wife will follow you, but beware, don't turn back before you reach the kingdom of light. If you do, disaster will strike." Nina, you can capture the next segment of the story in a painting with great success. This is the tragic part of the tale. Orpheus is walking ahead, flute in hand. There is joy in the flute, not even a hint of melancholy. Orpheus crosses many fields, many shady forests. After a long time doubt strikes. Is his wife really following him? Doubt makes him turn around before he has reached the kingdom of light. Alas! At once he sees his beloved wife fade away. You can capture the entire tableau in an abstract form: the youth with his flute, the indistinct form of the young woman behind him. Love has been a literary theme for thousands of years, but how you present it today can make a difference. The range of your imagination, your individual style, the choice of a palette that is in consonance with the subject and its ambience—these are the factors that endow your creation with the dignity of art. In this regard, to the extent you are your authentic self, to the same extent your art is bound to be distinctive. By the way, I hope I'm not pontificating too much before an artist.'

'You are excessively polite,' I said, laughing. 'The way you are promoting me, the Arts Institute students will laugh. Anyway, your words are wonderful to hear, though I have moved far from these aspects of life.'

'Scatter all the anguish and sorrow in your heart over white paper, and you'll see that anguish is not monotonous—it is wonderfully variegated. The disgrace of money problems will be washed away in the current of other worries. Then your anguish will seek greater achievements. The incidental discomforts of life will then seem laughable—'

'How well do you know me?' I asked. 'Why do you assume the centre of my agony is financial trouble?'

'You have misunderstood me,' he protested. 'Financial problems are only a fraction of your troubles.' Then saddening me, overwhelming me, he said, 'If someone has lost a child, even if I know nothing about her, I have to acknowledge the depth of her suffering.'

~

He took me to another room—a veritable magic chamber where my inner world came alive in wonder. What an extraordinary collection! Shelves with hundreds of books, exquisite paintings on the walls. He opened a locker and showed me many drawings and paintings on paper collected from all over the world. A film of dust had accumulated on the drawings. Some had been attacked by worms. An intoxicating odour pervaded the room. It seemed as if the doors had remained shut for a century, everything looked so antique. Porcelain ducks, bronze figurines. I was in a daze. A huge marble pillar occupied an entire table. 'What a large collection! Why don't you take care of it?' I muttered in amazement.

'I am tired of looking after it,' he replied. 'During the thirty years of my working life I sought out these things. But beautiful objects need connoisseurs who appreciate them. In this case, you might say I have been the only one to do so.'

There was a layer of dust on the wing of a bronze falcon. I blew it away. I suppressed a desire to ask about Chachi's feelings in this matter.

'If you wish, you can have this collection.' The offer was so sudden that I became flustered. 'To me they no longer mean as much as they used to,' he continued. 'Your interest is still fresh, it has an intensity that mine lacks, so in your eyes these things will retain their splendour for a long while yet.'

With what ease he was offering a painstakingly gathered collection to a woman he had met just twice! Then why had he preserved it for so long? Besides, there was such a thing as attachment—maya—wasn't there?

'You are a very impulsive man,' I said. 'But you'll have regrets later on.'

'All my decisions are taken on the spur of the moment, and I regard them as final. I don't feel any regret later on.'

'I don't attach much importance to impulsive decisions,' I said lightly. 'It's best if a wish to give someone a gift is slowly nurtured in the soul. At least that's how I feel. Who wouldn't be delighted to accept the gift of such a beautiful collection? But I cannot take it. The recipient must possess certain minimum qualifications—I don't have them at all.'

'I understand. You possess charming modesty.'

Gently replacing the porcelain duck he picked up a large packet and offered it to me. 'Brushes and paints,' he said. 'You don't need any groundwork to accept these, do you?'

I returned home with a profound impression made on my soul by a very special person, and there followed over time many more encounters so that I got to know him well, to discover varied facets of his personality, to talk and argue with him about art, sculpture, literature and life. One outcome of this was that Salauddin, Satyajit, Ranju and their ilk paled in significance in my eyes. They became relatively remote figures in my life. On Chachi's account I had once felt embarrassed in their house. Now that I became a regular visitor I did not know how she looked upon me. Because of what I had seen of her, I couldn't relax inwardly even after I had spent hours arguing with Chacha over something or the other: a niggling sense of discomfort would never leave me. At one point I discovered that a boundless gulf separated her from her husband. She was like a modern version of my mother. Clinging to their palatial home was her life's joy. Her sensibility cared nothing for art or literature. She suffered profound anxieties over her husband; he remained remote from her, beyond her reach for all time. I always found her sombre and silent, but that was her nature and not a reflection of her attitude towards me or, indeed, of any hidden sorrow. As I got to know all this, I became bolder. I started taking advantage of her indifference. On some days I wouldn't come across her at all, and I'd enjoy a long chat with Chacha. Then I would come home and collapse face down in bed.

One day Chacha asked a wily question. 'Your mother was terrific at embroidery, which is also an art form, you know. Does she still do it?'

'Mother's eyes are very bad,' I said. 'Everything looks hazy to her. At one time of course we used to see her embroider various things and sell them to neighbours. But if you think embroidery is an art form, so is cooking.'

Chacha became subdued and sat in silence, like one who had had a rude awakening. I rather liked to see his face in that state. Nowadays I enjoyed putting a damper on someone's hopes and illusions. Equally enjoyable was the activity of examining the pale face so as to tease out the subtle truths hidden behind it.

Around this time I went to the hospital again. Salauddin had almost recovered. I had largely overcome the strange disquiet that hospitals used to induce in me. Salauddin's wounds had nearly healed. I pulled up a stool and asked how he felt. He was more concerned about not being able to correct the proofs for his book. 'Literature has no value in this country,' he said. 'After hard work and spending money out of your own pocket, the book comes out at last—but will not sell. The author resorts to hard sell, and manages to palm off a few copies, that's all. For the poor, literature is a luxury, pure and simple.'

I have always had the habit of arguing, and launched into a protest at his weakness. 'The literary arena has always and everywhere been like this. You must have lifelong dedication. If you can create something of merit it will receive due recognition after your death. If you give in to despair, you might as well abandon the medium and take to one of the many easier ways of earning recognition and popularity.'

'But does that mean we have to put up with what is unfair just because it has been the norm for centuries?' Though he could not get up from bed, Salauddin became quite excited. 'Wouldn't we protest against such unfairness?'

'Sure, start a movement,' I said. 'You can do it on your own.'

'It seems you find such a painful struggle quite acceptable?'

'No matter what advantages and facilities you have, for the creation of great art you need to struggle. Of course, if you have those advantages, if art receives due recognition, the brute hardships of life are diminished, and your struggle becomes an individual, psychological one. The mental energy that is wasted on practicalities can be focused entirely on creativity. All told, I am not denying your right to be angry.'

'There, you've come round to my point of view,' Salauddin said and proceeded to doze off.

Then I went over to the ward where Omar's wounded brother lay. Silently, I walked over to his bed. A profusely bleeding patient was virtually dragged in and set down on the floor on a plastic sheet. He had left a trail of blood on the floor. Around him his relatives gave themselves up to lamentation. Flies buzzed merrily around the puddles of blood. I turned back to the youth lying in bed before me. A white sheet was pulled up to his chin. He directed a plaintive gaze at the ceiling. I could see fear in his eyes. His mother sat fanning him with a hand-fan. After a while Omar came with some medicines and on seeing me became so effusive that I found it embarrassing and incongruous in that setting.

'How extraordinary! I couldn't imagine you would come again.'

'Why? Didn't I tell you that I would?'

'People always say such things without meaning what they say,' he said, laughing. 'Really, one has to praise your affability.'

'Listen, I have come to see your brother, not you.' His effusiveness was so annoying that I wanted to put him down.

'Have I said that you've come to visit me?'

Now I burst into laughter.

However, considering the slightness of our acquaintance the conversation seemed out of place. Then there was the man's shabby appearance to consider, and his tendency to impose himself on you. No, he was quite an annoying character. His most brazen proposal came when I was leaving.

'Can I see you home?'

'What are you saying?'

'Didn't you hear me?'

'I did,' I said coldly. 'You needn't take the trouble.'

'Will you come again?' he wanted to know. 'Oh, I forgot to tell you. I went to see your friend and had a long chat.'

'That was very good of you.'

I stepped on the stairs.

'Was he your classmate?'

'Why do you want to know all of a sudden?'

'Because girls in our country hesitate to call a boy a friend unless he's a classmate.'

'No, he wasn't a classmate. Besides, I overcame such hesitations long ago.'

'Are you annoyed?'

'No.'

I could feel he was still standing behind me. But as I went down the stairs my annoyance began to ebb. The reason, which I unearthed through introspection, was this: no matter how irritating his personality, he had been paying me a great deal of attention. This realization was softening my attitude towards him.

Later, however, I was to learn how unbearably excessive attention can be. Before that my lonely nights were showered with the chill of winter. I curled up, stood up again, my blood became thin—diluted with saline water—no light, no dreams, only an invisible curlew before my eyes . . . When I was passing my days in this state, Arefin's roommate came to see me. He said that after Arefin had come back from seeing his family, there was a police raid and arms were found under his bed. Word reached him just as he was entering the hostel. At once he went into hiding. According to his roommate he wasn't into the sort of desperate political activity that would require the use of firearms. The weapons must have been planted by someone in a party opposed to his. He had a number of personal enemies who could have done it. The hostel had been sealed off by the police, so Arefin was heading home again. Father's health condition was very bad, and I should go to see him as soon as I got the news.

My spirits sank on hearing all this. I had got my salary, and some of it was still in hand. Besides, the money borrowed from Ranju was still intact: I had set it aside for Arefin, in fact. It would come in handy if I went home. Getting leave would be difficult though. There was suppressed resentment among the employees; the boss, on the other hand, was not in a mood to tolerate the slightest deviation from the norm. Then there was the profound unease over the arms. What a perilous situation Arefin lived in! But did someone really plant the arms—or was it being said to spare my feelings?

'Do you also belong to a political party?' I asked Arefin's roommate.

'Yes, the same party as Arefin.'

'This is something I do not understand at all. Why have you got mixed up in such dangerous political activities—is it in the hope of getting into power?'

'Come on, why should I get into power? My party will. But how can individuals like me remain quiet when there is such injustice?'

'What sort of injustice?'

'Harassment of students by the police, spiralling prices, driving the country into bankruptcy by borrowing billions— do you want to hear more?'

'But what is the chief aim of your politics? I don't really understand you. You have abandoned normal life, but in pursuit of what? Do you really want the country's welfare? Or are you merely doing what will serve your party's interests?'

'I don't have much academic knowledge of politics. We usually follow the ideals of our leader at the university. But it is clear to me that we are passing through very bad times. We are victims of a bad situation. You can't imagine what kinds of things are happening all around.'

'But, as far as I can make out, none of you wants power to work for the good of the country. A selfish greed drives you in your attempts to unseat the government—and the same selfish greed induces the government to cling to power.'

His reply had a caustic edge. 'Let us remove the glass splinters strewn on our path. If we ourselves scatter glass splinters, future generations will get rid of them, no doubt. An abomination is an abomination, no matter where it is found. You can see the terrible fallout of tyranny just by looking at Iraq, where thousands upon thousands are suffering.'

'Is the United States any less as a tyrant? Saddam merely occupied Kuwait, but is there any protest against the Americans, who are making the whole world dance to their tune?'

'Do you support Saddam?'

'I don't support any form of tyranny. The occupation of the Falkland Islands and of Kuwait both are equally reprehensible in my eyes. I am a great opportunist. I don't do politics, nor do I understand the intricacies of politics. I am caught up in the vortex of my daily struggle for survival, that's why I've asked you to tell me about these things in detail.'

'Don't you care about the hartals and demos in the country, the world's concern over Saddam?' he charged.

'Why shouldn't I care? But when I hear of arms being stashed away in hostels, of students sent to study on the hard-earned money of their parents turning into hooligans, then as an ordinary citizen I am filled with anxiety. And with scorn. For the city people are driven by passing fads. If they hadn't got so worked up over Saddam, your movement against the government wouldn't have fizzled out like this. Personally, I am not much affected by hartals; I can't go to work, so I have to face the tedium of being homebound—that's all . . .'

'Apa, we have our backs to the wall. When the knife runs you through you will wake up, but then it will be too late.'

I laughed. 'That's precisely what I fear—who knows when the knife point will prick the chest. Hence my worry over Arefin. You may be getting annoyed at my selfish thoughts, but the truth is, your party politics, with its selfish lust for power, doesn't attract me at all. But, if a student is shot dead, I am disturbed because I think about the bereaved family. His party will step over his blood to go to power. They will shamelessly enjoy what has been won in exchange for his blood. They wouldn't even remember the martyr. You haven't been able to reassure me that there is a healthy, alternative sort of politics. Do you have the education necessary to challenge my indifference?'

'I will come another day,' the boy said, getting up. 'I am rather upset by what you have said.'

'I am sorry if I have shattered your illusions. But please try to take care of Arefin.'

This long conversation did nothing to remove the dark misgivings that haunted me. They hung like a curtain around me. But for the first time I felt that Arefin appeared before me wearing a mask of innocence. I had no reason to feel complacent about him. He had provoked such enmity that he was ringed with adversaries. He had put himself at great risk. Everything had become topsy-turvy. Unsure, indecisive, I sat racked by conflicting emotions.

The next day I sent a leave application through Arefin's roommate and set off for home. I had been restless since the previous day: it felt as if the deepest roots of my being had been rudely yanked. From deep down emerged the question: am I a deracinated, homeless creature? Why hadn't I felt an inner urge to visit my parents for such a long time? If it was out of escapism, one should not indulge it. For wherever I went the atoms of escapism would accompany me, dissolved in my blood. The shadow that I wanted to shake out of my existence embraced me with doubled force. Then why not decide to combat it face-to-face by entering that shadow?

The wind through the train window continually dealt me stinging slaps. After walking long distances, after an interminable length of time, I stepped into the familiar old alley. I stepped on to the old, familiar doorway. I had no idea that standing there would trigger off the collapse of my whole existence, would set my frame atremble as I stepped in to encounter Father's bed. He lay like a corpse in the bed in the outer room. From the next room came Ranu's voice. There was no one with Father. A cat sat on the floor, yawning like a baby. The daylight had exhausted itself. I stared blankly at Father's bed. Mother came in from the next room, bearing a freshly lit hurricane lantern. Silently she placed the lantern on the table and looked in the direction of the door.

'Who is it?'

'Me.'

I could make out that Mother's vision was blurry. I stepped up. My hair bristled. Ceaseless waves from deep within broke at the back of my throat. I stood still, my bag still slung from my shoulder.

Coming closer, Mother became taut as a bowstring. An old, green sari clung to her body. Her face had acquired more wrinkles. Her hair was tangled. I got a whiff of a musty stink coming from her clothes. I felt faint seeing that Mother had wasted away to such a degree.

I lovingly grasped her bony, shrivelled hands. Balanced on those withered branches I advanced into the room and slowly went up to Father's bed. I could see Ranu standing at the connecting door between the two rooms. Behind her stood Montu—grown into a strapping adult since I last saw him. A strange shadow pervaded the room, and stuffy heat. Father lay under a sheet. I stared with lost eyes at his emaciated form.

I took one of his hands and called softly, 'Baba!' Once, twice.

He opened his eyes and stared. It was a blank gaze.

'How are you?' I asked—a heartfelt query. He opened his mouth to speak, but only a gurgling noise emanated from his throat. I squeezed his hand tighter. I felt terribly guilty. From behind me came the sound of the poor, endlessly harassed, hurt woman racked with sobs. How extraordinary was the light of the hurricane lantern—if it reached the ceiling, it didn't fall on the floor. The earth showed through broken patches of floor, which was a dirty grey. A few spiders swung from their webs. After a while Montu came forward on hesitant feet and asked, 'How are you, Apa?' I placed a hand on his head. 'Fine.' Ranu comforted Mother. 'Why are you crying? It is pointless.'

All your life you have only understood the calculation of debit and credit, I thought, and glared at Ranu. Her glamorous looks were gone, her face a little pale, the glow snuffed out. The decline, of course, had started even before I got married— when on the return of his wife and daughters Majumdar's shadow moved away from her. Arefin told me she had become rather weird. She had acquired a host of friends who visited her for the relaxed long chats of an *adda*. She never went out.

Cockroaches bustled about the floor. A dog sniffed its way in and began a battle royal with a kitten. 'Hey . . .' Mother's skinny arm waved in remonstrance. But no one else seemed to be bothered.

'Since when is Father like this—why didn't you let me know?' I asked Ranu, while I took out some apples I'd bought for him and handed them to Montu. Ranu answered me in a sing-song voice, 'His condition suddenly went from bad to worse one week back, so we took him to hospital. Since then he's been unable to speak. The doctor said there was no hope of recovery, so we brought him home. What would have happened if we had let you know?'

Ranu's outstretched neck was a taunt. My gorge rose instantly.

'What have you achieved by staying here? Your bad manners have become intolerable; you had better learn to speak politely.'

Montu restrained Ranu with a nudge: 'Don't say anything.'

But she continued in caustic tones. 'I have said the right thing. She comes as a guest here. She has to be invited to come and visit.'

Racked with rage and sorrow, I spoke through clenched teeth, 'Ah, yes, I have all the leisure in the world to keep track of what's happening in different places. I don't have your special qualification, so I can't stay at home and make a living by selling my physical attractions.'

Mother literally leapt up at this point. 'You have come after so many days, after such a long journey, you should wash and have some rice; instead, you are uttering all sorts of rubbish. Have you gone mad?'

'Splendid! Lend all your support to Ranu, as you have done all these years.' I swallowed back the tears. Montu led Ranu into the next room, and Mother placed an affectionate hand on my back. 'All your life you have had this misapprehension and vented your spleen against me. What has been the outcome— nothing but misfortune for you. Try to understand, I am a mother; to me all my children are equal.'

Thus a disconcerting episode came to an end.

At night as we lay in bed Ranu and I became extraordinarily easy with each other. After all these days we waxed nostalgic under that old roof, quite overcome with emotion. I felt profound affection for Ranu, something I hadn't felt while I was in Dhaka; it tugged at my heartstrings. My tears brimmed over. Ranu, however, couldn't become easy straightaway. She lay face down, sobbing. Coming home after such a long interval, the first thing I did was to go for her; it pained me. I could empathize with Ranu's inner agony, but this only increased my anguish fourfold. After the recent embarrassing event it wasn't easy asking her to calm down.

Arefin came home very late; his presence made the situation more difficult. He of course exuded pure joy on seeing me. Then he wanted to know the reason behind Ranu's sobs. Montu gave a detailed account of the incident and sat with downcast eyes. Arefin replied bluntly, 'If it is so hard to swallow the truth, then why sell oneself in the first place? If Ranu wishes to continue along the path she has chosen it is advisable to lop off one's ears.'

Arefin's words only intensified Ranu's crying. Like a helpless child she took to a corner of the room and wept ceaselessly, while I was torn by self-mortification. Why couldn't I put up with Ranu? Was it because of Majumdar? I couldn't find any convincing reason. Or was it Mahim who was behind it all? I remembered how one day he confessed in sombre tones, 'Nina, I will not be able to explain why I've become infatuated with Ranu. Her beauty encapsulates a strange desolation. It is so rare that one may spend a lifetime without encountering anything like it.' I sat in silence, knocking two pens together. 'I didn't want to tell you this,' he went on, 'but what am I to do? You are such a wonderful, frank, simple-hearted girl. It mortified me to cheat on you.'

As his words flowed like a stream Ranu's image in my consciousness was torn to shreds. His anguished passion drove the innocent Ranu out of my life and into such a deep abyss that very soon I found that even if I reached out I couldn't touch her. So, was that the main reason? I really couldn't tell.

Everyone turned in, Father and Mother in one bed, Montu and Arefin on the floor. I went to the other room and silently placed my irresolute hand on Ranu's back. At once she burst into uncontrollable sobs. Strange shadows created by the hurricane lantern played about the room. I was at a loss for words. I lay down beside her, my tremulous hand still on her back. A number of geckos ran on the wall in the smoky lantern light. The bed smelt of rancid oil.

'Can't you wash the pillowslips?' I asked in an attempt to lighten up the situation. Ranu didn't reply.

'Everything is in such bad shape that I got a shock on coming here. Our parents are terribly unfortunate—we haven't been able to do anything for them.'

As my words disrupted the silence in that stuffy place, Ranu gradually quietened down. Overcoming my inhibitions I said in a different tone, 'I know I shouldn't have said those things then, but . . .'

'That's okay; you don't have to be any more remorseful.' Ranu turned towards me.

'How are you?' I asked her.

She smiled wanly. 'Forget about me. Tell me about yourself. How are *you*?'

'What is it about me that you want to know?'

'Come on, all the news is with you. I was dying to hear you talk about yourself. Instead, as soon as you got in, you . . .' She was like a child as she wiped her eyes and slowly relaxed.

'I don't know what comes over me at times. Forget and forgive—promise me.'

'I have forgotten it,' Ranu said, giggling like a child. 'Now tell me about yourself.'

I felt a thousand nails dig into my throat. What would I say to her? The sharp-pointed spear that kept pricking me, my experience of marital life, that nerve-benumbing episode which I had put behind me, the reasons why I did so—was it possible to explain these things rationally? Could I tell her that there was never any physical abuse, that my husband never came home drunk, was not in love with another woman? Then how would I analyse his character, and to what extent would I be able to present myself in a clear light?

On our wedding night I was in a strange languor as I offered myself to him. Technically, I was still a maiden. What agony mingled with the ecstasy: I was agitated by the conflicting reactions. He had turned fierce and, breaking through my defences, ran me through, indifferent to my cries, and then at one point stood up, sweaty and exhausted. I lay inert on the floor. The sheet was soaked in fresh blood.

The sight seemed to rouse him again. How can I describe the hideousness of that scene? In a moment he seemed to be possessed by supernatural strength, and when he lifted me high in his arms I thought he had Majumdar's hands. Holding me aloft, he circled the room and muttered like a demented man, 'Oh, Nina, Nina, Nina, I am so happy!'

I was stunned. Had the sight of blood driven him out of his mind? The next moment his excited words were falling like hammer blows on my cold skull: 'You are a virgin! Amazing! I can't believe my eyes!' Then dropping me on the floor he went down on all fours, leapt like a monkey and exultantly rubbed the blood on his hands. 'I am the first man in your life. Ha! Ha! Ha! You are hundred per cent a virgin!'

'What do you mean?'—my empty, bloated body splashes into the water, all around there is moss, tiny worms, blinding sunlight, directionless waves without water, I keep sinking— 'What are you saying? What did you think?'

'You had so many friends. You were even in love with someone, but, I mean . . .' The joy of finding something precious made him incoherent.

Could I make Ranu understand that from the very first night my marital life had been drenched in limitless loathing? Like Sita as she faced the humiliation of the test by fire, I too wanted the earth to split asunder and swallow me. But the earth isn't my mother—so why should she offer me sanctuary?

There were many more distressing days and nights, culminating in my child's death. 'Ranu, my baby died. I felt my heart would burst in agony. But none of you came to visit me.' Ranu couldn't reply at once. I felt a new current emerging from the depths of my being. My limbs became numb but there was fresh anger brewing within. I was choking, as if there was water stuck in my throat.

Ranu began to speak very softly. 'You know about Father's condition. Mother cried a lot because she couldn't go to see you, leaving Father here. As for me . . .' She paused, then started again. 'I thought my presence would only heighten your agony. That's why, even though I felt so awful . . . I cannot explain it to you. I had to content myself by asking Arefin for your news.'

The wick of the lantern had been turned down too low, and the light suddenly went out, plunging everything into darkness. Ranu picked up a palm-leaf fan, which made a creaking noise as she stirred the air with it. Her old familiar scent reached my nostrils.

I changed the subject. 'Everything looks colourful from outside,' I said. 'Ranu, now tell me frankly about your life, of course if you want to. What's the whole truth about Majumdar? And then, who are these friends who come to flirt with you right under Father's nose? Who are you trying to punish?'

Ranu's fan stopped moving. I was stifling in the heat. In the next room Montu was muttering in his sleep. Presently, raindrops began beating a tattoo on the tin roof. A fine spray came through the ventilator. I stretched out my face towards it. Ah, peace! Rainwater streamed over the wooden windowpanes. My eyes had got used to the dark and I gazed at the water falling in a faint, straight line.

'What can I tell you?' Ranu began. 'My affair will not make any sense to anyone in the world. To them the whole thing will seem horrendous, and that is quite understandable. But, Apa, the man who has held me in his maw ever since I attained the age of awakening may be hideous to look at, but he has given me such love and affection, shown me so many extraordinary happenings, that to me he has become like the Creator himself. I can think of nothing except him.'

'You are the victim of an ugly situation,' I said calmly. 'You are now old enough to realize that. He has cunningly brought about your ruin, and yet you adore such a lecherous charlatan. How can you?'

'How do I explain it to you?' Ranu had been holding my hand. Suddenly I felt her body become taut. 'If I tell you about a few incidents, you too will be astonished. You will feel you are out of your depth. I couldn't tell anyone about them, lest they think I had gone mad. Like you, everyone else says he has cunningly contrived my ruin. The neighbourhood has been together in condemning me. We have become isolated as a result. Don't think it doesn't pain me. But how can I blame that man?'

I didn't say anything. If I expressed any indignation it would affect her frankness. Anyway, here was a mystery that I wanted to fathom. The night deepened. The two of us became more relaxed and easy with each other.

'You know, Apa,' Ranu began in a self-absorbed, listless tone, as if there was no one with her and she was talking to herself. 'Majumdar's greatest torment, his chief grievance, was that I reacted fearfully to his ugly appearance. He himself did not know why he felt such a strange attraction for me. Driven crazy by his emotional turmoil, one day he abducted me from the street and took me into his den. Then the whole night . . . you know all that. But spending that night in his company diminished the fear and contempt he used to arouse in me.

'Six months went by like this. The most extraordinary thing is that he didn't even once express any interest in my body. I had just finished primary school, so I wasn't all that young. I could understand that he was apathetic towards sex.

The realization made me feel boundless respect towards him. His hideous face at one point began to seem kind and beautiful to me. I no longer felt an aversion towards him. I would stay with him till late at night. As the evening deepened he would sit with eyes shut before a bowl of burning incense. As the smoke spiralled up and spread, he told me the pitiful story of his life, how as an impoverished young man of hideous aspect he felt tremendous hatred for mankind. But it was my loathing for him that he regarded as the ultimate sign of his failure in life. If I had continued feeling like that for a few more months he would have taken his own life.'

'Did you believe him?' I couldn't keep the scorn out of my voice.

'There are all sorts of analyses one can come up with now, but at that time I was really in a state of enchantment. I don't know why I am telling you all these intimate things. You have come after such a long time, such a long gap separates us. Tell me, do you hate me?'

'There is anguish'—I could feel a tightening of the chest as I spoke—'but not hate.'

'Any grudge over Mahim? Believe me, I found him very likeable at the beginning. But after being so intimate with you, whenever he visited us and met me—believe me, I found it quite loathsome. You know, even after you got married, whenever he saw me he . . . but let's not go into that.'

'He came even after my marriage?' A pained voice emanated from my vocal chords. I felt pale as an ailing person; an irrepressible tremor began under the skin. How clearly Ranu had learnt to express herself; experience had brought her maturity.

'Yes, he used to come even after your marriage,' Ranu said. 'How he cried one day, with my hand in his. The more I said that Mother might come any moment and that he should leave, the more he clung to my hand and swore that if I didn't show any mercy he would give up painting, he would go into exile. You must feel terrible listening to this. How immature he was.'

Immature? So this is the kind of personality he had! We had walked so many miles together. I was immature and restless then. Recalling the things I said would make me laugh now. And the quiet artist beside me? There was a wonderful languor in the way he smoked cigarettes. He would light one after another as he went on about exotic paintings and their colour schemes. When we stood face to face he seemed to become a huge tree, while I became all the more diminutive by comparison. And then he became immature in Ranu's eyes. His passion had led him into such dire straits, had lowered him to such a level! My heart was on fire.

'Talk about Majumdar,' I said fretfully. 'Let's drop the present subject.'

Ranu's body seemed to somersault behind the veil of darkness. With a supple movement she lay straight, turning her back towards me. Then she said certain things that plunged me into profound astonishment. We used to share a bed in those days. Sometimes Ranu used to come back glowing, sometimes sunk in absent-minded unease. From the very beginning she had tried to hide these things from me. As a result an unbridgeable alienation grew between us. She used to be so reticent and withdrawn, keeping her terrors to herself! Yet today, after all these years, at the slightest nudge she completely unburdened herself. All her thoughts, memories, torments and humiliation—everything was revealed.

'After six months it was I who began to change in a strange way. It's amazing to think how young I was then and how such desires could grow in one at that age! I was lying down. Majumdar, as usual, was running his fingers through my hair.

One day his hand strayed down my back and stayed there for a while. Then he got up and brought a bizarre book of fairy tales from which he began to read out to me. What tales they were—about the women in a dreamworld sporting in the water with men. Everyone in that land is nude. When one of them covered his private parts with a leaf everyone exclaimed, "Obscene! Obscene!" And he read more stuff in a similar vein. Listening to these induced an extraordinary languor. I beckoned to him to come to me.

'But he said it wasn't time yet. He was under certain restrictions. I felt so humiliated. But my respect for him increased a thousand-fold. One week after that we had sex for the first time. The first day it was very painful. He flung me aside, exclaiming, "Damn! You are too young." Then one day he said, "Of course you have an exquisitely different taste." After that we had so many days and nights together. I cannot explain to you what an extraordinary technique he had. He used to lift me ever so gently—it was unimaginable that one so fierce could be so tender. He'd say he had entered through heaven's gate, and now he could die without any pang. Getting me had freed him of the fear of death. Let there be earthquakes, let a deluge carry everything away. You know, Apa, even now I run to him like a beggar—though his wife and daughters live with him. I crave his touch. But a curious change has come over him. At my sight he clenches his teeth and screams as if he were driving away a stray dog. He says his guru has pronounced that I am the bearer of Saturn's malign influence. My touch will ruin him. The people in his family insult me mercilessly, still I keep going, because I know I am fated to do so.'

The rain had stopped. The moonlight came in through a chink and suffused the room. My heart, my nerves, felt numb. What I had heard was no tale, it was the autobiography of my sibling who had fallen victim to a subtle intrigue.

'Shall we go and sit outside?' she asked. Then, 'Apa, do you feel disgusted?'

'No.'

'You know Apa, once he took me to his village where his wife and daughters were living. You can't believe what an influence he wielded there. Everyone thought he was a supernatural being sent by the Creator. The most surprising thing was that everyone in his family treated me with respect. He had told his wife that I would be the mother of his son, so there should be no dearth of hospitality shown towards me. I was just a slip of a girl, but Majumdar's word was like holy scripture to everyone there. They told me Majumdar had dreamt that within a few years I would bear him a son.

'I was having a good time there. One day, as I was flying through the air on a swing hung from a tree, I felt I had become wet. I went quietly to the cowshed to check and found blood on myself. I was unaware that this happened regularly to girls after a certain age. I examined myself over and over again: no, I hadn't cut myself anywhere. For some reason I felt I was to blame for it. I had to conceal it. If I wiped off the blood that would be the end of it.

'I kept wiping it off, but to no avail. Suddenly I noticed Majumdar standing at the entrance. My soul froze. But he was overjoyed at what he saw. He went and whispered the news to his wife. She came, along with the other women in the family and the maids, and, anointing me all over with turmeric paste, asked me to sit down on a low stool set in the middle of the courtyard. They placed a *bodna* filled with water in front of me and asked me to see my beautiful face reflected in it and repeat to myself in an undertone, "May God give me a son just as good-looking."

'I said it as I nearly fell over, my body overcome with bashfulness. You cannot imagine what a sweet memory it is.

Alas! Where is that son? What happened to that dream? Now my monthlies seem to be nothing more than a curse sent by the Creator . . .' She paused for breath.

'What followed is even worse. I know you will not believe it, still I will tell you, because I cannot fathom its mystery. I don't know with what drug he put me in a trance and then made me see these scenes. I went to his house one day and found a boy wailing loudly. He was a handsome boy, light-complexioned, tall for his age. Such scenes were common at his place; they all had to do with moneylending. By now I had become used to them. But the boy was saying that his mother had just been admitted into hospital. She had lost a leg in a traffic accident. He had got her admitted and then rushed to Majumdar. He needed some money. Majumdar's voice was cold and hard: "First repay the earlier debt."

'The boy beat his head against that rock for a long time. Then at one point he gave up and left. I almost threw myself at Majumdar's feet. "Why are you so cruel?"

'He only laughed silently in reply. "You have seen such scenes before," he then said, "but you never reacted."

'"That's true."

'"Why are you reacting today? Because the boy is handsome, isn't it?"

'I kept quiet.

'"Your conception of beauty hasn't changed yet. Is this what you understand by beauty?"

'I became enraged. "The boy's mother . . . ?"

'"Ah, you have a lot of compassion, I see."

'Anyway, after this incident he found new games to play with me. I was like clay, a mere doll that he could reshape at will. He lectured me every day in an attempt to brainwash me. He tried to teach me that compassion is most harmful to life. It turned life into a torment. Those who harboured compassion

169

in their heart could not resist its demands. So things like pity, compassion, sympathy had to be exorcised from life. Then he tried to teach me that since time immemorial a particular conception of beauty had dominated the world; if I could now regard the ugly as the beautiful and vice versa, life would become better. This is because the accepted ideal of beauty is beyond the reach of man in this life. Then he began a series of strange tests. For instance, he took hold of a pretty parrot, burnt its wings and confined it in a cage. The bird cried piteously; I looked at it with amazement and my eyes filled with tears.

'"These cries express a desire to live," he said. "Isn't it wonderful?"

'He would tear off the legs of a dragonfly and then make love to me. He said that I must pass these harsh tests. But the most amazing achievement was his expertise in dream interpretation. All kinds of people would come and tell him their dreams. He would explain their meaning and charge a fee in return. One day I dreamt I was gathering gold nuggets by the handful. He became very disturbed on hearing about it and prophesied that I would shortly fall into grave danger. Believe me, Apa, that's just what happened: I fell into a well and broke my leg. For many days I couldn't walk straight. Then onward the man seemed to me like the Creator himself. I couldn't deny him. Gradually I got used to his way of life. The sight of blood even began to excite me. Hair was burnt off a chained cat, which kept jumping up and down in agony. Amidst my distress at the sight, I experienced excitement. The boredom of life dissipated. He landed a heavy slap on the cheek of a teenage boy. The boy howled. To me the incident was amusing.' Ranu paused. I had been listening eagerly, with bated breath, making no comment. Ranu let out a long sigh and began again.

'Since then many days have gone by. I have grown up in his shadow. Defying parental authority, I would go to see him. He became an intimate part of my daily life.

'Do you know, Apa, an extraordinary thing happened around that time—an earthquake. I was sleeping on the floor. When the whole house started shaking, he dragged me under the bed. He was trembling violently. I was choking with fear, but he tenderly covered me with his body so that if it collapsed the roof wouldn't fall on me. When the quake stopped after a while, he pulled me out and made me sit up on the floor. What a cruel face he made! Quickly, he brought an earthen pot filled with charcoal, scattered *dhoop* incense and lit it up. "Beware, don't move," he commanded, looking me in the eye with his bloodshot eyes.

'Then dementedly moving his hands in a circle through the rising incense fumes he muttered, "Come, come, come, you malign spirit. Come, you, who have been trying to scare me, come—" If you had seen his room at that time you would've been shocked. Straw and bits of wood lay scattered on the floor, a layer of moss covered the walls, wild creepers raised their heads in the broken brickwork. He would keep the curtains drawn at all times. A wild creeper even grew right through the wall and emerged triumphantly in the open air. The entire house had the appearance of a heap of ruins. As we sat there, suddenly a skull fell in our midst. His face turned pale with fear. "Here . . . here is that head. Where has it come from after all these years?" He held it in his hand and muttered frenziedly, "Son of a bitch, you would take money and neither pay it back nor give me your land—so how could you expect to live?"

'My blood had frozen. I was quaking with fear. What was I seeing? A lame, bleeding cat came ambling, then suddenly, a dog, its body too soaked in blood. They walked around

Majumdar and his bowl of fuming incense. The wingless parrot and the mynah screeched at the top of their voices. And then the skull and an odd sound: the sound of dripping blood. Red-eyed, Majumdar too kept up his continuous screaming . . . Then, as if seeing something in the dark, he stuck out his long tongue and shouted, "What do you want—to murder me? Ha! Ha! Ha! I will die in an earthquake. I am not scared of you. Come, I will kill you all over again. Here, I am sending out smoke to get you."'

Carried away by her own story, Ranu seemed to become unaware of my presence and entered the world she was describing. She sat up straight and like one in a trance stared into space and went on: 'Dense smoke came out of Majumdar's mouth. Then I seemed to see clearly, like a white shadow, a man standing in the darkened doorway. O my, what were these things I was seeing? Majumdar's face disappeared beneath the current of smoke. Shouting "Ya Allah, save me," I fell unconscious.

'The next morning I found myself lying in the street. Majumdar had thrown me out and shut the door on me. A crowd had gathered around me. Then . . .'

'Impossible!' I screamed out. 'It is all magic, or else he had drugged you with something that made you hallucinate. It was a trick to get rid of you.'

'The next day,' Ranu went on in a daze, 'I saw that an earthquake had brought down the unfinished upper storey of Majumdar's house—a pile of rubble covered the ground-floor roof.'

'Okay, I grant that it happened,' I said heatedly, 'but it was mere coincidence. An earthquake can happen any time. The whole thing was magic and hocus-pocus. I suppose he got rid of you just after that.'

'Yes.'

'You still go to him! Really, you are grown up now. How can you ruin your life for a man like him? Can't you see through his trickery?'

'What will I do?' Ranu broke down and wept. 'How I have demeaned myself in my attempts to forget everything. I flirt with all sorts of boys, smoke cigarettes. They look for opportunities to feel me up. But they are such wimps, their appearance is so childlike, their hands are so feminine! How can they take the place of those large, bloodshot eyes, the hairy arms, the strong yet tender paws? They are children, they make me puke, they nauseate me. How can I overcome the habit of so many years? He would lay out various dishes, feed me with his own hand, tell me wonderful stories—without them I pass sleepless nights now. Where will I find these now? Still, I chat with the boys, then withdraw into myself. Desire increases till my heart is desolate. Over and over again I rush like a madwoman to his house. He has become a big merchant, pretends to be very busy. He shoos me away with abuse: "Get lost! You are jinxed, you are trash!"'

'Ranu how can you tell me these things?' I held her cold hand and shivered. 'Can your life go on like this?'

'Surely one day he will realize his mistake . . .' On a note of such terrifying optimism Ranu fell silent, became passive.

And I? I stood up with a steel hook piercing my breast, opened the door and stepped out. It was a magical moonlit night, crickets chirping without a pause. Nature lay bathed in a glow of white light. I stood on the veranda. The air was so clean! Everything was wrapped in abstract shapes of light and shade. I abandoned myself to the open spaces. Fly away, let a fierce wind lift your wings and envelop the world before you with the wonderful colours and sunlight of outer space.

But was it ever possible to leave all behind and fly away, even for a moment? There was Mahim, who used to advise me to exorcise my inner restlessness and acquire a beauty of being—why couldn't I accept him? He had a role in shaping every iota of my personality, but when he shifted his attention to Ranu, why did even his existence become a matter of indifference to me? Didn't my attitude only prove that I wasn't a superior person? Even if I once occupied the centre of someone's heart, it was quite possible for someone else to supplant me. I had regarded this psychological truth as a perversion merely because it went against my personal interest and hurt my feelings. Surely someone who did not know the ABC of the way relationships waxed and waned was very petty as a person.

What a wonderful moon-blanched night. The moist earth seemed to be sweating in the moonlight. Majumdar stared unblinkingly through that unearthly light. I was gasping in sudden agony. I heard footsteps and turned my head. Ranu had come out and was standing there. The moonlight clearly showed her exquisite, melancholic, distressed face. I was used to seeing her always in colourful attire. Tonight she was in a faded grey shalwar kameez. The dupatta hung loosely round her shoulders. Most conspicuously dull were her eyes. Her complexion too had grown dark. Everything was incongruous.

We sat down side by side on the veranda.

'Apa, do you remember,' Ranu said with renewed excitement, 'when we went to look at the posters at the cinema? We tried to sneak in and were roundly rebuked by the security people?'

I brightened up. 'Yes, yes, and how the two of us ran!'

'I had stopped in front of a sweetmeat shop, and you were tugging at me . . .' Ranu laughed into her dupatta. 'Then I picked up a chewed sugar cane from the street and you gave me a hard slap.'

'What an appetite you had,' I said, laughing. But suddenly I felt a tug at my heartstrings. Both of us fell silent. The spectre of silence in the dark again took possession of us.

~

I woke up very early and saw Ranu squatting on the floor, a silent statue. Hair awry, eyes bloodshot from lack of sleep. I had gone to sleep with the complexities of this world stuffed into my brain. Now, on waking up, this was the first scene that met my eye. I remembered the painful, bizarre, dreadful chapters that had led us through the evening till we fell asleep late at night. Awake again, my nerves felt numb, as if they were ailing. I looked about. The door was open. Waves of white light came dancing in. Inside the whiteness of that light was Ranu's sketch. The sight of the sketch aroused another torment. Amazing! I hadn't yet started working on the painting! I remembered that I had left the easel at home, leaning against the wall. 'Didn't you sleep?' I asked, yawning.

'It is often like this,' Ranu said. 'I feel so restless that I feel like holding my breath till I'm dead. Well, not really, but I resolve not to go deep into anything. I won't let this boring, horrid old world leave a mark anywhere on my existence. I balance myself and stand up on the floor. Even if I die, the world will carry on with its spine straight and supple. The fluttering of my heart, the intolerable misery—only I would experience such punishment. I would tremble and thrash about and at one point become inert. What's the point in gathering these bits of agony and pain till life becomes unbearable? What would I gain by transforming myself into an intolerable, anguished creature? Would that stop this frightful yet pleasurable world from throbbing within me?' Ranu got up and walked away silently.

I collapsed in weariness in the wooden chair. Arefin came in carrying a packed handbag. 'I am off to Dhaka; when are you coming?'

'Tomorrow. Why are you leaving today? Your hostel is closed. After two or three days there will be hartal. Why risk going there now?'

'I will stay with a friend. I have a special reason.'

I remembered the police raid of the hostel and the discovery of weapons under his bed. Again I felt my body weakening. Nah! I wouldn't live very long.

'How are things at work?' Arefin lifted the edge of the mosquito net and sat down.

'What would you like to know?'

'I heard there was serious trouble. You haven't lost your job, have you?'

'No, both sides have run out of steam. The management had decided to start firing people. That provoked a huge outcry. Now everything has subsided naturally.'

'This is also like our politics,' Arefin said laughingly. 'When it's on it's intense, but for most of the year it's dormant. It's like a seasonal festival.'

'So you realize that, and yet you feel you can bring about change through politics?'

'Actually, the movement suffers due to lack of unity and coordination. Those in power and those in the Opposition are all characterless, mercenary scoundrels; no one loves the country. They don't know anything above self-interest. I also feel let down.'

Arefin changed the tone of his voice as he continued: 'The police have arrested one of our party leaders, the man who inducted us into politics, whose ideals we blindly followed. What is extraordinary is that our party chairman gave him away to the police.'

'Why?'

'He had become frustrated with the leadership and was planning to launch a new party. He has a large following, so the party would have been split down the middle. Believe me, I have no respect for any party or any leader in this country. They are all the same.'

'You understand everything, and yet . . .' I said in surprise.

'You are asking about me?' He laughed. 'All of us understand everything, know everything. Has a single murder on campus been solved? One has to patronize things to stay in power. Everyone of course effortlessly mouths patriotic slogans. They cry themselves hoarse on the subject of the nation. I don't want to live in such a vile world any more. Everyone wants the throne so that they can fill their pockets. Before their calculations I am small fry. Look at Saddam. The fierce American tiger is at his doorstep. Doesn't he know the limits of his own power? Yet, has that diminished his arrogance? Try and make him understand this. Because of his wilfulness hundreds of thousands will die. That is politics—it doesn't follow common reason like you and me.'

'Do you think America has entered the fray driven by altruistic motives of aiding Kuwait? Aren't they also motivated by wilfulness and greed like Saddam?'

'Yes, of course. That's what I meant—politics is like that. Think of the hartals which are having a devastating effect on our weak economy—do you think the Opposition is organizing them in order to rid the land they love of an autocratic government? If they get into power will not they too turn autocratic? But these considerations will not induce the people to condemn the wrongs being perpetrated right under their noses. People believe a better time will come and are willing to lay down their lives to make that happen. And look at what the government is doing—always fomenting strife between other parties, exploiting the religious sentiment of the people to create a chaotic situation in which they can further their own selfish interests. If the present restlessness persists, people will turn their eyes to alternative forces. The government of course wants the opposition parties to squabble among themselves so that they can continue in power and reap the nefarious benefits of power. This tendency to cling to power—do you think it comes out of love for the country?'

Saying this Arefin burst into frank laughter. 'There! I have lectured you just like one of our leaders. You see, everyone is on the make. Except for self-interest they have no other motivating force.'

'If that's the case, how can you carry on in such life-endangering politics?' I asked anxiously. 'No matter what you say about me—that I am stupid, concerned only about saving my own skin, in short, a typical lower-middle-class person; but why should I knowingly risk my life for attaining an unprincipled objective?'

'It is a dream,' Arefin protested. 'Even though there are no principles, you know what my dream is? To forge ahead and usher in a better time. Those of us who are still innocent and uncorrupted have been sustained by political ideals . . .'

The conversation flagged. After a while I asked anxiously, 'I hope a world war will not start, Arefin.'

'World war?' Arefin was surprised. 'If I could die in such a big war I would count myself lucky. We will die under the pressure of rising prices, in the battle to land a job . . .' Our conversation drifted thus, rambling, disjointed. But when I couldn't contain myself any longer I blurted out, 'I hear some weapons were discovered under your bed. What's the matter, Arefin, why do you lead such a dangerous life?'

'Believe me, those were not mine. It is the work of a rival party. I will deal with them.'

'Leave all this and come back,' I appealed to him. 'When such a situation exists at home these things are hardly befitting. You should also accept some responsibility. I cannot manage by myself.'

'Politics has entered my bloodstream,' Arefin said in serious tones as he slung his bag on his shoulder. 'It is a strange addiction, being looked up to by junior students at the university, the protest meetings, battling the unjust lathi charge of the police. I cannot leave these. At times I feel that with a single punch I'll be able to crush all evil forces on my own. I am angry at myself. There's no love among us, no unity. We squabble among ourselves and allow the autocrat to get stronger. It's disgusting to see that those without an iota of love for the country call a hartal for trivial reasons in order to prove that the government is ineffectual. In spite of this I am unable to find a way out of politics.'

'I don't understand you people,' I said. 'You say you find life in politics, and passion. I have neither any knowledge of, nor respect for, politics. And I have not a little loathing. I don't know how these feelings can coexist, I only feel their tug, and that's why I'm filled with apprehension and fear.'

'That's common among Bengali women,' he retorted, 'so why should you be an exception? But enough of these useless topics. I have got a private tutor's job. I have to teach a group of four students. That's why I'm rushing to town. If you can't earn enough to feed your belly it's all up with you.'

'You don't have any money on you—why aren't you asking me for any?'

'Where will you give it from? Just stay here and you'll see how quickly money disappears. The group I'm going to teach are a decent lot. When they heard about my experience with pickpockets they paid me an advance. I'll manage the rest.'

'I'll probably go back tomorrow,' I said. 'I'm a little anxious about things at the office.'

When Arefin left I went to see Father. He was still asleep. His breathing was laboured. Mother sat on the floor, slicing vegetables. She sat in the familiar posture, only the shoulders were a bit more rounded, so she seemed to bend too far forward over the blade of the *boti*. I gazed at her, but in my brain Majumdar's head tossed about relentlessly. What a cruel, devious, artistic murderer! He was slowly murdering Ranu. And Mother was silently slicing vegetables. She was absorbed in her work. But a giant termite had got in and was eating into everything. The woman was plastering the wall, varnishing wood. But did she try to see even once what she was applying these on? What was underneath? Didn't she know? If she took a look her life expectancy would diminish; the longer one ignored it, the better for everyone. Whether out of weakness or the will to survive, they themselves had facilitated the termite's entry.

I pulled up a low stool and sat beside Mother. 'Ma, do you have any of the embroidery you did?' I asked.

Mother was concentrating on the vegetables, still she was startled into asking, 'Why do you suddenly need to know about them?'

'When I was young I didn't pay them much attention. I would like to take another look, see what they were like.'

Mother's hands stopped working. Unsteadily, she set aside the boti and stood up with the bowl of sliced vegetables in a strangely listless posture. 'Do I have any of those? They were all sold a long time ago.'

Mother went to the kitchen, rather subdued; I went and stood by Father's bed. A tube had been fitted under the lungi to convey the urine to a plastic bucket. He stared as if his eyes would pop out of their sockets. I could sense the gentle rise and fall of his breathing. 'Are you in great pain?' I asked in a whisper. In reply he twisted his mouth and groaned. Saliva ceaselessly dribbled down into his beard. My heart was desolate. I looked away and sat still. The plaster had flaked off the walls, cobwebs covered the bamboo ceiling: our stuffy, old, sweat-drenched, familiar home.

Montu came in whistling. 'The physiotherapy that was given—didn't it produce any results?' I wanted to know.

'That was a long time back. It was stopped after five days. It cost a full sixty taka per day.'

'The hospital just discharged a patient in this state?'

'They didn't discharge him. We had him released when we heard the final prognosis. If something were to happen, it was best it happened in one's own home. There is no good or bad death.'

How simple everything was to them. How effortlessly they accepted the bitter truth. They planned accordingly, laid out pathways. Taking life in this manner worked wonders for their longevity, no doubt.

'The two rickshaws you invested in—do they bring in anything?'

'Yes, but one has to put up with a lot of bother. Every couple of days they ruin some nut, bolt, chain and whatnot. Shouting continuously at the rickshaw-wallahs has turned me into one of them.'

'Where did you get the money?'

'What money? To buy the rickshaws? I managed to find it.'

'Managed? How?'

'Mother sold some ornaments and gave me two thousand; I begged a thousand from Uncle, the rest I managed.'

'The rest is nearly the entire amount,' I pointed out, driven by a compelling disquiet into scrutinizing every detail. 'Where did that come from?'

'I didn't ask you for money, did I?' Montu rejoined heatedly. 'Why are you playing the detective?'

'If you had asked me I wouldn't be asking these questions.'

'By raising donations,' Montu answered arrogantly. 'Four or five of us got down to it in the name of a society we claimed to have formed. We did it for seven months straight, collected a lot and split it among ourselves.'

'Did you carry a pistol?'

'That wasn't necessary. If I hadn't bought the rickshaws, with the market what it is, Father's pension wouldn't have supported a beggar. You were lucky you escaped. Even if the whole family sold its blood, it couldn't have fed itself.'

The conversation stalled. In such cases, the more one sidetracked the issues, the better. I thought it wasn't nice of me to grill Montu like that. But sometimes a stubborn obsessiveness took hold of me. Didn't I know its origin? What was pushing the broken-down car forward? Was there any sense in trying to confront these things? But I had realized one thing. I didn't feel like stirring from home. So many memory-laden streets, the ambience in which I had lived since birth. I used to be passionately attached to them when I was away, and they seemed far away, beyond one's grasp. Yet, coming here, I felt that if I could stay away from here, keep myself concealed, I would have peace. The road of memory had better be in the distance. If one went close to it the result was only heartache.

It became clear at noon one day as I stood in the street before our house. Anam Chacha from next door came with his lungi hitched up to fetch water from the public tube well. On seeing me he opened his eyes wide in an odd way and said, 'Who is it?' In a hesitant voice I replied, 'It is me, Nina. How are you, Chacha?'

'How are you? You have come after such a long time. Have you forgotten us?'

'No, it's just that I don't get any time for myself. My job takes up all my time.'

'Over here I am worried sick about our Muslim brother Saddam. It seems a world war will break out. Anyway, hasn't your husband come? Have you come alone?'

'Yes, alone,' I said, feeling hot all over. Such pretence! As if he knew nothing. Presently, the pointed questions would prick the roots of my being. I was about to turn around when he said, 'Try to control Ranu; otherwise this neighbourhood will become unlivable.'

'What has she done to you?'

'Nothing to me personally, but personal harm isn't the only consideration. Wouldn't you consider the atmosphere in the neighbourhood? But what's the point of telling you? I hear you have had a divorce. We have daughters too, that's why we are worried. What a father and what offspring! Who knows what sin your father is paying for—but let's change the subject. Tell me about the support for Iraq among people in Dhaka.'

I couldn't take any more. My familiar world had died. Probably we were its assassins, or victims—I don't know which. I felt physical distress at the mention of these venomous matters which were causing me enough pain daily. Now, the open interrogation, the revelation of my past in all its nakedness, was impossible to bear. I didn't feel like carrying on the conversation.

I went in and found Father lying still on a wooden plank. His eyes were bloodshot and weird noises emanated from his throat. His entire body was rigid as steel. In his agony he was trying to shake his head. He turned terrified eyes upward, as if he had seen something sinister. His face was turning blue.

I rushed to Mother. At first she tried to brush off the matter, saying it happened often. But my inner eye could see that he was engaged in a battle with a supernatural power. I literally dragged Mother to come and have a look. She too became nervous on seeing him. She sat down beside him and raised his head to ease his breathing. It was clear that for him breathing had now become an agonizing effort. I sat down on the other side. We wanted to lift him up—Ya, Allah! There were bedsores down the entire back. Pus had glued the oilcloth to his back. There was a vile smell. I was at my wit's end. 'Lift him along with the oilcloth,' Mother said. We did that. Father wasn't heavy; he had been reduced to skin and bones by continuous illness. Yet, when Mother and I tried to lift that body, we literally broke out in a sweat. We took him by his extremities and somehow hauled him on to the bed. My hands were smeared with pus from his back and from the oilcloth. Just then a roar of agony startled us. Father's eyes turned upward as he made frantic efforts to breathe. With his left hand he tried to point out something he had seen in the doorway.

At this Mother started shouting for Montu.

Montu was nowhere to be seen. Ranu came in. But her behaviour was the strangest I was to witness. 'Ranu, open the window,' Mother shouted, 'Your father is gasping for breath.' Ranu didn't move a finger and impassively stared at the movement of Father's head.

'Ranu, didn't you hear what Mother said?'

I saw Ranu's face gradually harden; then a mild tremor set in. But she didn't move an inch. Leaving Mother to look after Father, I rushed to open the window, then flung open the door. 'If he dies, she stands to gain, so why should she do anything?' Mother complained. Opening the window brightened the room a bit and brought in a hint of a breeze. Saliva dribbled down Father's beard and on to his chest, and the groaning did not diminish. 'Send for the doctor, Ranu,' I said anxiously. 'See where Montu has gone.'

But Ranu stood like a tree, her keen eyes fixed on Father. At first I thought she had become so nervous that her brain wasn't functioning properly. But when Father raised an arm and, twisting his face, let out a long groan, I saw clearly that Ranu was thrilled. Her eyes stared unblinkingly. A tiny bright light played about them. Someone seemed to suck out all the fluid from my heart through a straw. I was dumbfounded. In that state, I gritted my teeth and ran out into the street. Luckily I found Montu there, chatting with an odd group of boys. I called out to him and, briefly describing Father's condition, asked him to fetch a doctor at once.

Father's condition remained unchanged. Mother raised his head and placed it on double pillows and ceaselessly exercised his inert right arm. I fanned him vigorously near his nose with a hand-fan. Taking my lips close to his ear I whispered, 'Baba . . . Baba.'

But his eyes were empty. The paralysed side of his lower lip hung pendulously, the other side was trembling uncontrollably. If Mother cleaned up the sores at one spot with moist cotton wool, the flesh would come off in another part of the back. At the same time, blood and pus rolled down the sides. Father's eyelids drooped. Noon gave way to afternoon and the whole room began to look a filthy brown. The floor was wet and muddy. On the wall a procession of red ants carried the trophy of a dead gecko's head. Ranu sat in the same posture. When Father's distorted voice rose suddenly, she thrust her head forward to look, but her face was expressionless. I shifted my attention from Father to Ranu. Whenever Father's agony rose, her expression became strange. It was like the look on her face when she used to see the things on display at a fair or the arrangements for a grand wedding or an elephant swaying along.

Nah! I couldn't waste time on Ranu. The doctor had arrived. As word of Father's worsening state spread, some of the neighbours dropped by. Seeing them after such a long time I felt ill at ease and withdrew into the background. But their anxious, busy movements, expressions of concern, their conversation removed the stuffiness in the air.

The moment after the doctor stepped in, Father began shivering like someone chilled to the bone, went into spasms and then lost consciousness. A shock wave shot through my bloodstream. On the doctor's instruction Montu rushed off to get saline and some medicines. The thin wad of banknotes I had brought became noticeably depleted in making the necessary purchases.

It was evening when the arrangements were completed. A bag of saline water was hung from the bedpost. The bed itself was awash in faeces and urine. All along, Mother had looked after the patient's toilet. The doctor left after giving some additional words of advice and collecting a fat fee, thereby bringing my financial situation down to a precarious level. Anyway, it was pointless to dwell on such things now. I could clearly sense one thing—Father had probably set off on the great journey. Montu of course did not take the matter seriously. Over the past year or so he had seen Father go through many such ups and downs. Mother's reaction was impossible to gauge from her face, but even she seemed to be stricken with hopelessness.

As the evening deepened, the crowd of visitors thinned out. Only a few, mostly relatives, remained. A distant aunt began chatting with the wife of Anam Chacha from next door. Father's emaciated body lay flat on the wooden bed. The rise and fall of his chest could be seen clearly. The smell was revolting. Mother pulled out the soiled oilcloth with practised hands and asked Ranu to help by lifting Father's legs. Ranu surprised me again by getting up promptly and raising both legs so that Mother could take out the oilcloth. Mother carried the soiled object out to the tube well, while Ranu used a wet rag to wipe off the bits of faeces that clung to Father's legs. The stench was overpowering. Yet Ranu's face showed no reaction at all. Montu came in with a hurricane lantern which he lighted and placed on the table. A sliver of light fell obliquely on Father's body.

A few more neighbours came in. The aunt inserted a paan into her mouth and declared before the gathered neighbours that her brother-in-law had been a real angel. When he had started working he used to visit their house bearing oranges, chickens and other gifts. He never said anything that would hurt anyone and was always wrapped up in pious thoughts. If any *habiya* sins had accrued to him it could only be on account of his children's wicked deeds. On saying this, she looked squarely at me. In order to emphasize her words, she waved an index finger in a novel way. 'Yes, I am addressing you,' she said to me, 'but what can I say to you? Arefin has had a passable upbringing because he used to live with your elder uncle. We are related, but I cannot visit even once a year—you know what shame is the reason behind this.'

There was nothing that could be done except face the unsavoury situation. Ranu still sat serious-faced on a low stool. Not the slightest change of mood showed on her face as a result of Chachi's words. I sat near Father's head and fanned him continuously. The entire room was intolerably airless. I felt suffocated. Taking the cue from Chachi, some of the neighbours added their comments. They too had some moral responsibilities. Taking advantage of our silence, they raised their voice—'It is impossible to tell if the family has a mother. You live far from here, so you don't see what goes on. Unspeakably obscene things. Because of Ranu, we are always anxious about our own daughters. When only a child, an unweaned child so to speak, she started hanky-pankying with that old Majumdar character. If she wasn't a filthy beast, would that fellow have been able to carry on so scandalously? And Montu? He has become a regular thug. The family is ruined.' Chachi's hoarse voice now joined in resoundingly. 'You haven't seen anything yet! There is much more to see. It all started with his uncle. He is my relative; it is shameful to go on about him. His elder brother brings him up, gives him an education, and what does he do? Gets a job, goes off to Comilla. Fine. Then what?' Profound stillness descended on this 'Then what?' No one uttered a word. I too became eager to listen to this story. After a long time, that terrible episode again roused my curiosity. An involuntary tremor rippled through my body as I recalled the scene.

'Then he leaves the job and comes back,' Chachi continued. 'For some days he mopes about like a ghost, then one night puts the noose around his neck. Later we hear that he had an illicit relationship with a married woman—these things do not remain hidden for long. How sinful! How utterly sinful! The bastards should be drummed out of the neighbourhood. Or else *qiyamat* will soon be upon us.' Chachi stopped here. Our neighbours carried on. But I had no ear for their sugar-coated venom; I had transcended all that to plunge into a bottomless sea. The story I had heard was new to me. I did not know any unambiguous definition of an illicit relationship. If the relationship I had heard about had actually existed, it involved two souls, or else the question of suicide wouldn't have arisen. And if souls were involved, no matter how much sensuality was also present, by what logic could I condemn it as illicit? I wondered about that uncle of mine, who used to be so withdrawn. He would leave in the morning, return in the evening and go to sleep after dinner. Outside of that we had no interaction, and he would never deviate from the routine. How could he just leave his job, such a hard-to-get job it was too. He came back from Comilla and sat in morose silence for some days. One evening he called me and asked, 'Do you still paint, or have you given it up?'

The fact that Uncle knew about my hobby was enough to make me feel faint with surprise. I became doubly dumbfounded that evening as he handed me fifty taka and said, 'Here, buy art materials with this.'

The next morning I woke up early. I was stepping towards the bathroom. Ya Allah! Right here, in the outer room, where Father was now lying, an old, rusty ceiling fan used to hang. Uncle's inert body was hanging from it by a *gamchha*. His tongue protruded from a distorted mouth. I vaguely remember letting out an earth-shattering wail and feeling unnerved by my own voice, trembling. The floor tilted and rose towards the ceiling, and Uncle's body, together with the ceiling fan, collapsed on the floor. A loud crack and the wall with flaked-off plaster advanced in a terrible whirlwind . . . Then I remember nothing. Now Chachi had revealed a complex reason behind the death. After seeing that sight I wasn't normal for many days. For days and nights on end I tried to fathom the reason, without getting anywhere. Father sold off the fan. After that, even he subsided into a terrible quietness. Whatever concern he used to have about the mundane requirements of the household was now wiped out and replaced by thoughts of the Creator and the afterlife.

Learning the hidden reason behind the event made me feel feverish. How everyone was raving! They were sitting in our house and rattling the bones of the skeletons in our cupboards. We did not owe them anything—not even five paisa. Still, I kept quiet, did not utter a word of protest. In this ramshackle room, haunted by an unnatural death, where Father's devastated body lay pale and bloodless, my blood felt cold. How these people were taking easy advantage of our distressed, polite silence. Ranu, Montu, Mother—everyone was being examined by turns, analysed from various angles. Though she heard everything, Ranu was still expressionless. Why couldn't she turn everyone out? But then, the words had to bite before the question of protesting arose. Ranu loved the perverse, she loved agony, she was utterly ruined.

Eventually the neighbours left. Mother sat limply with her back resting against the wall. Montu stood by the saline drip. The lantern's rays pierced through the belly of the stagnant darkness. Mother's faint sobs broke the silence from time to time.

A heap of dust from the termite-ridden leg of a chair lay on the floor. Ranu sat in it, relaxing. Mother's distressed voice sounded like death—'Will he live?' Then a shadow darkened the doorway. I turned away my face quickly. The heat of my body turned into cold sores. It was as if a giant had descended from air. I directed a hard, spiteful look that way—it was Majumdar.

Slowly and steadily he walked over to Father's bed. On seeing him, Ranu became taut as a bowstring. Her joy was so outlandish, its expression so obscene, that my breathing halted out of sheer disgust. Ranu got up hurriedly and placed the chair near Father's head. A long spell of silence. Then Majumdar pronounced in a deep voice, 'Time has run out.'

These wise words thrilled Ranu, who declared beamingly, 'It is possible only for you to know that. You have that power.' In Father's present state, Majumdar's statement could have been made even by a child, but there was no way to make Ranu see that. After this frightful fairy-tale monster came in, my flesh and bones seemed to become crushed together, and hordes of leeches leapt on my injured body. Cobwebs trembled in a slight breeze. Majumdar sat with a stern expression on his face. The night thickened. I sat leaning against the wall and stared unblinkingly. Montu hung a new saline bag. Father's body lay motionless. Two geckos had been swirling their tails for a long time: first one, then the other, both showing infinite patience. I directed my gaze towards them. They take so long even after arousal. They were still as death. At times, the rise and fall of the tail carries an obscene suggestion. After a long time one of the geckos becomes violent and, rushing to bite the other, runs away. It goes very far, where the darkness is deeper. I stared hard. The other followed and re-enacted the scene. The dance of the tails went on. I got fed up. Majumdar's hideous face was near Father's. Only Ranu was restless. She paced all over the room. My eyes went to the ceiling again. Even after being in intimate contact with the male, the female gecko ran off again. Father was in a limbo, suspended between life and death. Not the hurricane lantern any longer. Now the light of five fairy-tale lamps shone all around. Like an unbridled horse, my imagination ran in contrary directions. The line of sindoor on my forehead . . . a magic veena on my shoulder . . . maiden, who are you? . . . The maiden Kalavati am I, with tresses like monsoon clouds, why don't you send your son to my home?

I descend from the magic circle of the five lamps. A desert storm is brewing around me. Why is there a monkey in front of me? Where is the handsome prince? Whose face is Mahim painting with such concentration? The youth who touches the traceries on my feet is covered all over with needles? Taking off his lungi, Rezaul leaps into bed. I crunch Ajit's head with my jaws, I chew the yolk of an egg. But what is this? Out of the yolk comes a human child. By mistake I have eaten it up. Who is peeping through a chink? What a huge king cobra! I look around—end of fantasy. The geckos are making love on the wall. Mother's pale face is without tears. Majumdar stands up like a witch in the dark. Running out of oil, the lantern flame flickers, goes out. At midnight Father dies.

~

Two more months went by. The familiar poverty and life's other sordid realities continued to rack me. At times I would become disconcerted and feel I was out of my depth. I had virtually lived alone, my family existing only in my dying memory. But since I got back from my parents', responsibility for them had re-entered my sense of duty. I asked myself, how m ch more can I bear? Yet, it wasn't possible to evade it. B sides the struggle for survival, I had access to a tiny world of y own. But everything in this personal world began to disin egrate gradually. My thoughts were now centred on a single en money. These past two months, as soon as I got my salary, I sent home a thousand taka. Then, after paying the rent, I was left with virtually nothing. I borrowed a little from Shanu, and even from Barua Babu. My wedding ring, which I h d hung on to for a long time, was sold yesterday, thus removi g the last remaining sign of my failed marriage. After settl ng a part of my debts, with the rest of the money I bought five kilos of rice, a kilo of dal, a soap, a kilo of potatoes and a kilo of sugar. There! No more left. I told Shanu that for a few months I wanted to cook for myself, as I couldn't afford to eat with them. 'Please don't mind,' I begged.

Shanu was surprised. 'I don't understand how that will help you. Wouldn't you have to spend more money if you cooked for yourself?'

'You will not understand these calculations. Please, let me be on my own for a few months. Don't mind, angel.'

Actually, during the previous month, I hadn't really paid them for my food. The amount I gave at the start of the month was enough for only a week to ten days. After that, I paid a few measly amounts. I felt greatly embarrassed and ashamed about it. As it is, Shanu lived amidst a million problems. Lately, Kamal Bhai too had become a bit of a gadabout. Sometimes he wouldn't come home at night. He said he was looking for new business opportunities—he had a grocery in mind. Of course Shanu couldn't for the life of her figure out what that had to do with spending the night away from home; still, she made a point of insisting that her husband's character was spotless—reiterating this was a way of calming her fears. 'If there are no children there is nothing to draw men to their homes,' she said. 'So I cannot blame him. He could have taken a second wife by now, which he has not.' People resort to extraordinary devices to preserve their sense of security. If one panel of the window closes, a person hastens to open the other panel: it was nothing but a means of preserving peace of mind through self-deluding tricks. This was an easy way to hide from oneself and from others. Amidst all this, I was becoming a burden for them. It was because of the intimacy and affection that had grown over a long time that we still shared a household. But how much longer? I couldn't go on like this either.

Dhaka was excited over one topic, it was seized with one fear—was a Third World War imminent? The sharply incised headlines were chilling: 'SITUATION SIMILAR TO FIRST WORLD WAR, GET READY TO FIGHT—BUSH'; 'FINGER ON THE TRIGGER: BOTH SIDES READY FOR WAR'; etc., etc.

Besides, the series of hartals organized recently by the Opposition had diminished in intensity but had not entirely stopped. What a danger we ran into when Arefin and I returned from home. We had decided to risk it even though we knew a hartal was on. I had to extend my stay by a few days on account of Father's death, amidst mounting anxiety regarding my job. Arefin reassured me that if we arrived in town we would at least find a rickshaw at the station. It was a day-long hartal. When we got off at the station we felt like a pair of fools. The city was deserted. The rickshaw-wallahs were all sleeping in a row. What to do—we picked up our luggage and started walking. It was fun—deserted city streets have a charm of their own. But I began to tire. Arefin took the big bag from me and hurried me along. Suddenly we saw that a huge procession was headed our way. Blocking its path at some distance was a police cordon. I could sense a rising excitement in Arefin. I gripped his hand. The slogans became louder and louder. Seeing the procession up close made me feel faint, it was so big. I stood open-mouthed on the pavement. Presently someone stepped out and dragged Arefin, bag and all—'Son-of-a-bitch Arefin, you are having a lark!'—into its seething mass. That's when the trouble started. A deafening explosion, and instantly the air became unbearably pungent. I desperately looked for Arefin, but the gas shells kept on coming, though they could not stop the procession. Smoke, screams, streaming eyes. I ran dementedly this way and that. Just then the sound of a gunshot seemed to resound inside my heart. I ran madly and caught sight of two bleeding youths being spirited away in a police van. A little way off a red Toyota—on which the demonstrators had decided to vent their rage—was up in flames. My eyes and nose burned with acrid smoke. How I moved my feet and with gas-blinded eyes managed to find my way home still surprises me—it was a dreamlike experience. Two hours later Arefin turned up, clutching the bag to his chest, bedraggled in appearance, and was overwhelmed with relief on seeing me—'Good show, girl . . . so you are still in one piece!'

In the last two months I visited Irfan Chacha twice. That was the only place where I discovered a reason to live, at least partially. I found escape from the horrible penny-pinching and suffocating existence, if only for a while. I recall with what eagerness I rushed to Chacha's house after I returned from home, when my mind was fraught with thoughts of Father's death, Ranu's anguish, Montu's wayward ways, Mother's affectless stare, the futile struggle to make ends meet. The silence of that house and Irfan Chacha's habitual calm felt oppressive, and almost as soon I had reached there I felt an urge to leave. 'Wait a while,' Chacha said.

I sat down, but I was restless.

'Have you started painting?' he asked.

'No,' I replied in a combative tone, 'my life is too messy to let me do that.'

'If you are to paint you will do it, whatever the circumstances.' His cold eyes impaled me. 'Why are you so restless? Relax.'

'You are fortunate because you have the power to remain calm; you can make people condemned to a life in the gutter dream of paints and brushes,' I blurted irritably. 'But painting isn't for me, so please don't mention the subject again.'

He kept turning the pages of a magazine languidly. I got up and breezed out of the house. He didn't utter a word.

That night I mounted a sheet of paper on the easel. I dipped the brush in the loaded palette and stood for a long time. At one point my body began to give way to weariness. More time passed; I began to feel drowsy. The rooftop looked desolate. I packed up everything and collapsed on my bed.

On two other days I smartened up with care and visited Irfan Chacha. We debated a thousand topics, elaborately discussed human proclivities, the population explosion, social anomie, and also his own life—how he developed through struggles and conflicts, and so on. But nothing was said by either of us about my painting. My attitude was that if I could paint, I would. His attitude was the opposite: circumstances did not matter. If I had no worries relating to basic necessities like food and shelter I could have considered painting for my own pleasure. But my life did not allow me that luxury.

'Nina,' he said once, 'if you ever go to Santiniketan, you must see Ramkinkar's sculptures. What an extraordinary control over form! All standing figures, without any softness, utterly black, as if the bones had been burnt and only anthropoid ash was left standing. You cannot imagine, Nina . . .' His patience made me chuckle.

Salauddin had been released from hospital, I heard. I felt duty-bound to visit him, but there was no inner urge. Arefin was taking up a job in a high school on the city's outskirts. The interview was over, and he was supposed to join on the first of the following month. There was a lot of scope for offering private tuition, but he wasn't thinking of that at present as he had to complete his university studies. He was confident he would manage to pass the exams.

I had been out of touch with Satyajit and Ranju for a long time. After coming home from work I would simply lie in bed and stare at the roof. There would begin the perennial duel in my inner world—why wasn't there the faintest dream of a beautiful transformation in my life? Wouldn't it be better if I simply went under? Let me be buried beneath an earthquake-demolished seven-storeyed building: one leg beneath rubble—can't pull it out; broken walls around my head; not a sliver of sky to be seen; not even an iota of pale sunlight. Deprived of food, light and air, my struggle will subside and I will be overcome with drowsiness, then die amidst agonized cries. That would be a lot better than my present suspended state, in which I could glimpse a bit of the sky through a chink or two, and feel a desire to fly, but couldn't even stretch a hand upward.

Why not seal the chinks so that the question of seeing anything through them does not arise? No desires would be kindled and I will, in time, forget how the sky looks.

With what hopes I had begun my married life. Then I came out of it of my own volition. With a little compromise, by remoulding myself to fit the requirements of society, I could easily have passed this lifetime. Most women in this country lead far more unsavoury lives. Unless their husbands kick them out, they don't think of any change. What did I have beneath my feet by way of support?—neither an affluent family nor much education, nothing at all worth mentioning. I hadn't finished my honours degree, yet I walked out of my marriage with long strides; I was the one who asked for the divorce. Where did I get the courage to do so? In return, had I found the person I couldn't touch while I was married? Wasn't life repeating itself, wasn't I fighting the same battle?

Or was it the same? I tried another tack: hadn't I left behind those excruciating agonies, the complex mental torment of living side by side? As life drew on, a man who, in a profound sense, was indifferent to joy or sorrow would excitedly plunge into the game of proving his manhood, like a day labourer who after work had nothing but to swoon on a piece of flesh. Whether I was happy or wretched was irrelevant, as if I were merely a lump of clay—that's how he treated me, chucking me about. I'd grit my teeth and put up with it. Still, he wouldn't find satisfaction; he'd toss and turn all night. What an intolerable sight! The thought of it makes my blood run cold even now. As soon as he got back at the end of the day, the polite, healthy young man in shirt and trousers would show such a repulsive aspect, as if he were entering a lavatory. Here, there was no need for decency. First he would change into a lungi, which he wore folded to knee-length. The ceiling fan wasn't enough, so he fanned his paunch in a curious style with a palmyra-leaf fan. But what was really atrocious is that as soon as I shut our door at night, he tore off his scanty covering and advanced on me like a wrestler. I would hold my breath! What a horrible, ugly, naked beast . . . Sometimes we would quarrel about this, abuse each other, or else I would allow the beast to ravage my tender body. That's how I adjusted to life. Marriage taught me that the physical relationship between man and woman meant gulping venom to maintain a formal, social bond. Gradually I was learning to accept everything in this spirit. Even then I would sometimes explode: 'Aren't you ashamed of yourself? You strike such obscene postures! Don't you regard me as a human being?'

'Ashamed in front of one's wife? . . . Ha! Ha! Ha!' He would explode in laughter. 'You're turning into a mental case.'

Many days went by like this. What a perverse creature, how weird was his nature! Perfectly composed and practical by day, the same person underwent swift change at night. Sometimes he grabbed a tuft of hair by the root, sometimes he shoved me off the bed, but he would still not find satisfaction. What restlessness! I couldn't fathom the reason behind this. At times a real rumpus would break out, with me screaming: 'You are a beast, you dog, you'll be the death of me one day!' He would remain undaunted, his desires imperious as ever. He would mutter: 'You are sick, or else why should a woman be indifferent to a man's touch? Looks like you'll drive me to the whorehouse. You are the one who is sick, you should see a doctor.'

That 'should' was the end of this line of conversation for the money that was inseparable from medical care was the object of his intense possessiveness. Indeed, it was this aspect of his personality that was the chief reason why married life became anathema to me. He was impossibly stingy, and he was deeply attached to money. Yet, he was lazy when it came to earning money. I am not sick enough to say that a man who lacks the drive to make more money should desist from sex with his wife. But isn't a man supposed to set aside a certain minimum out of his income for household expenses? After coming home from work the first thing my husband did was sit down with his back to me. He would take out his money and proceed to count it. If the figures did not balance because of a difference of just one taka, he would spend the whole evening going over his calculations again and again. On the other hand, every morning he would put just twenty taka in my hand and disappear. I had to run the household that day on those twenty taka. Was it possible? After spending a bit on this and a bit on that, by nightfall I would feel rather off my rocker. When I showed him the daily accounts he would sit up straight and demand to know why I couldn't manage in the amount given. I would account for every single paisa. We had enough rice in stock, but I had to buy a quarter kilo of potatoes for Taka 1.50; a quarter litre of oil for Taka 8; a quarter kilo of dal, Taka 7; sugar, Taka 3.50. After that, the only tea leaves we had were what was there at the bottom of the teapot, and as for onions, garlic, fish and vegetables, we had none. I had borrowed onions from next door. For lunch I had mashed potatoes and dal; dinner would be the same.

Rezaul looked worried. 'Be a little economical, Nina,' he said. 'If we can't somehow survive on the money I earn, after a while I'll be forced to run away.' I would remain calm: there was no point in reading an ulterior meaning into his words and getting angry. But after spending the whole day in that stuffy room, I would feel suffocated by evening. Not a single day came when he would say, 'Let's go out tonight.' Whenever I suggested such a thing he would begin an elaborate dissertation on rising rickshaw fares and whatnot. How often, and how sweetly, he explained to me on more than one occasion: 'Nina, in Dhaka city, believe you me, rickshaw fares determine everything. From here to Crescent Lake is a neat eight-taka ride, then there's the return trip. While you are there, you can't let your mouth sit idle—you must have snacks and drinks. As for buses, one would have to be utterly mad to go by bus on an outing with one's wife.'

Satyajit ragged him a lot about his attitude. He shrugged it off. Someone like me, who has romped around the city streets, was then leading a life of compromise as a housewife. Every moment your attention is directed towards your husband's capability to generate income; it makes you loathe yourself. One day Satyajit made a suggestion—why didn't I get a job? Rezaul's attitude towards the matter was straightforward. He was all for women's rights, but before looking for a job I must finish my honours degree. Better work on that first.

I have to admit he did not show any conservatism on the question of my freedom. In most marriages this is the chief problem. In many cases, I have noticed, a girl after she gets married is hesitant about introducing a classmate as a friend. Rezaul's friends used to call me by my name and use the familiar form of address, *tui*. The contradictions in his character amazed me. Satyajit and his other friends came many times when I was alone at home. Rezaul came and saw us engrossed in an adda, and would join in himself. But did my freedom extend over such a small area only? Suppose I went out to visit some place and walked a large part of the way back, Rezaul would return home from work and find me missing. When I got back he wouldn't kick up a fuss over it, but he would want to know where I had got the money to go out. That's why I didn't get around much. As for the hassle of getting an honours degree, it didn't depend on my wishes and disinclinations. So many bothersome things were involved—the admission procedure, the monthly fee, filling up examination forms. Rezaul was utterly callous about such matters.

So, he did allow me freedom, but he also had a device to prevent its expansion into new areas. The upshot was the same:

Here, girl, see a patch of the beautiful sky through the blinds; now fly if you can!

The same man, when he came home from work, did not offer me a single kiss or a sensual touch—he would get down to his daily accounting. Else, he would lie flat under the broken fan or fiddle with an old bulb. And when he came to bed at night, his terrible show of strength, as if he was a victorious general back from a war of conquest. After that he would inquire like a moron, 'Didn't you like it?'

'No, no, no, how many times do I have to say it?'

'You are an insensitive, rhino-skinned woman. It is nothing but bad luck that I have married someone frigid as ice. You cannot appreciate my vigorous foreplay. Any other woman in your place would have responded a hundred per cent.'

'Then why don't you carry out your sexual experiments with other women?'

'I have no experience in that line, or else you think I would have suffered such rebuffs and still salivated for you in this manner?'

His confession was reassuring, and I responded accordingly. 'Try to be a little tender. Believe me, I find sex unbearable. If you wish to make it so, it can become beautiful quite naturally.'

'Someone who understands beauty will find it in this,' Rezaul retorted. 'I like it this way. You say it is bestial, but in these things the more bestial one is, the more pleasure one gets. To my regret you don't appreciate this.'

After this I didn't have the energy to argue. I tried to maintain my equilibrium by reminding myself of things such as these: Rezaul was attached to his home; after work he did not dally anywhere else; I was the only woman in his life; he did not drink; he was frequently driven to despair because of his inability to provide me with creature comforts.

Life was going on in this fashion, at a slow tempo. Then one day I discovered another facet of his perverse nature. I found a magazine on the table. Opening it at random I saw pictures of young boys: nude, delicate and graceful as maidens. When I asked Rezaul about it he replied breezily, 'I brought it to show you. What do you think of them, do you feel any attraction?'

'What are you saying?' I exploded. 'They are children!'

'You know nothing about their beauty,' he said with a mysterious smile. 'It seems you are enthralled by so-called manliness.'

I began to tremble, everything grew dark, but I managed to ask calmly, 'What are you trying to say? Say it clearly.'

He subtly changed the subject. 'Nothing, really. They are such attractive youths, but you are calling them children! I was just noting what elderly airs you can put on.'

This introduced a new source of anxiety. I began analysing him closely. Why was he unsatisfied even though he would turn me over and do what he wanted? Satyajit had lent me the biography of Rodin in which there were reproductions of nude sculptures. Turning over the pages, Rezaul enthused, 'Have you seen these male nudes? Don't they have wonderful figures?'

A forest fire was raging through my head. But without discovering a definite link I couldn't launch an effective attack. That's when I realized that though he looked ingenuous he was actually very cunning. Though he had revealed certain things in a state of excitement, I hadn't yet scratched the surface of his wayward nature.

My days passed amidst tremendous restlessness. Once, at night, we were lying side by side in bed. The whole room was dark. I placed a hand casually on his thigh. I said to myself that everything I suspected was an illusion. My psychological instability was behind it. I asked in a voice different from the normal one, 'You know, I know nothing about your school or college days. Tell me about school today.'

Rezaul was amazed. 'You are curious about that after all these days! You are a strange girl.'

'There's nothing extraordinary about it,' I said. 'This episode is crucial in shaping one's life. Yet we don't know anything about each other's schooldays.'

We had a long chat that night. He told me the whole story of his upbringing in a pious, superstition-ridden family. That was the first time I learnt that after class five he had to live in the hostel. His roommate was a bad sort, had many perversions. Be that as it may, Rezaul matriculated while living in the hostel.

'What sort of perversions did your friend have?'

'We did not like the boy, that much I remember. After matriculating began my days in a "mess". They lasted till I got my BA.'

'There was no girl in your life till then?'

'I used to detest girls,' he said firmly. 'You know I have no sister. I lost my mother when I was very young. Then the hostel, the mess . . . everywhere there were only boys around me. I don't know why, but from boyhood onward I disliked the weakness and softness of girls.'

'Strange, then why did you like me?'

'Don't try to play the detective. You were a bit of a desperado, you had less than the usual tenderness—these attracted me. If someone calls you "Bhabi", I feel annoyed. You are Nina, a strong woman; that's how I saw you at the beginning. Of course, later, the reality—anyway, I can't say anything more.'

Rezaul fell asleep. I spent a sleepless night. Why had a fear taken possession of me? When he went to work I shut the door and windows and sat alone, like a ghost. In my distracted state I began looking for more evidence of his perversions. I scrutinized the lanes and bylanes of his life. I pondered the lack of continuity between aspects of his previous and present behaviour, and felt an intolerable pricking in my heart. It was clear that he wasn't happy with me. He was desperately seeking pleasure in my body, but to no avail. The realization was so shocking that my hair stood on end. For him, marrying me was an experiment, pure and simple. I was a guinea pig. Venomous loathing filled my being. When he reached out to touch me at night I stood up at lightning speed, extricated myself and sat down on the floor.

'What's the matter with you?' he asked roughly and tried to drag me into bed again. But I sat tight. He got down on all fours and advanced towards me like a beast of prey. I sat with gritted teeth. He lay down beside me and astonished me by declaring, 'I have given it up.'

'What are you talking about?'

'What you have suspected. That's why I left the mess. Actually, it had become a strange addiction. It is only much later that I realized it's a harmful addiction.'

'When did it start?' I asked in a tremulous voice. 'I mean, when did you first do it?'

'In my schooldays.'

'What if I say you haven't been able to give it up?'

'Then there's nothing I can do about it,' he said, twisting his lips as if to show that that absolved him of the responsibility. 'I felt you had come to know about it. Still, I thought I should tell you. How you take it is your business.'

I wept disconsolately till I was overcome with drowsiness in the small hours. Now I knew for sure that it made little difference to Rezaul whether I lived with him or not. He had no remorse or regret, no feeling of shame. Calmly uttering those terrible words made him light-headed with the delight of being honest. If he had tried to suppress the truth, or tried to explain it away, I would have known that he was scared of me, that he gave me some importance. This realization was enough to justify my walking out on him. But he knew it was not an easy matter, and even if I did do it he wouldn't be bothered. Of course, all this was the outcome of my anxious speculations. My nerves began to fail me; I felt numb. Then suddenly he yanked at me to turn me towards him. 'If I hadn't told you? What would you have done? I hate such overacting.' As he spoke, the same old game started. He pulled on my sari, then gradually mellowed and began to implore: 'Believe me, my family is all-important to me now. I don't want to lose you for anything. I cannot explain to you . . .'

We were in the midst of profound darkness. He became desperate. I pushed him away violently. His mellowed-down personality plunged me deeper into the foam of intense loathing. My head hurt. I heaved out endless tearful sobs. The strength to protest also began to ebb out of me and I gradually became limp. That night my husband raped me and fell asleep, exhausted.

As these unbearable memories resurfaced, the veins in my temples throbbed madly.

Shanu had bolted her door and gone to sleep a while ago. Once again her husband had not come home. I got up unsteadily from the floor. What had happened next? The child came into my womb and drank water in large gulps. The easel with its blank sheet stood in the middle of the room. I sent it clattering with a shove. I sat down on the bed in order to compose my thoughts. It often occurred to me that marrying Rezaul had been a blunder. Money was a major problem of course. If someone dropped in I would often pretend to be sick so we could avoid offering refreshments. Plans had been drawn up many times to buy certain badly needed household goods—only to be scrapped in a moment. Anxious about sudden emergencies, Rezaul sometimes skipped a meal in order to keep a secret fund at the desired level. As I dwelt on these matters I crumpled in rage and anguish, but only to turn on myself the next moment: getting involved in these things had turned me into a lifeless bore. He used to sleep with his lungi hitched up in grotesque fashion. But didn't I also turn my bare back towards him and ask him to scratch the prickly heat? Wasn't he too a victim of disappointment? His touch had become unbearable because I no longer felt any attraction for him. But in that situation wouldn't he have thought that I was just a lump of flesh? Wouldn't he have thought that the daring and dynamic personality he had fallen for was a sham and the reality, terribly disillusioning?

Of course I could argue that the change that had come over me was the result of his crude behaviour.

What if he countered it by claiming I had failed to appreciate his needs, so to him I was the one who was crude? I did not want to think further. I sat clutching my head tightly. Intolerable pain in the temples. These headaches were frequent and came on mostly at night, and made me feel like going berserk. I got up and stepped out on to the roof to pace up and down. Shanu opened her door and came out. 'What was that noise?' she asked. The next moment she saw the easel lying on the floor. She gently pulled up the chair and sat down facing me. Her eyes were red—clearly she had been crying all this while. I said nothing. She too sat quietly. I had been going round and round all by myself; now another person had joined me. I began to unwind, my limbs relaxed, I felt drowsy. I looked through tired eyes at Shanu.

Shanu placed an affectionate hand on my back. 'You'll sleep in my room tonight,' she said.

~

I took a rickshaw after work. It went smoothly along a straight road till a red traffic light forced it to halt and it got

206

caught in a jam. That's when I remembered that my salary was in my bag. Going straight home with the money would have been the sensible thing to do. But for some days I had been contemplating a visit to Salauddin. Today I took a decision and headed towards his place. But now I was gripped by fear. The way mugging had increased, my money might change hands at any moment. However, I loved motion in every form. I didn't have the tendency to give up a plan out of fear. So I just put my trust in fate. Eventually the rickshaw came to a stop in front of Salauddin's dingy quarters. I paid the fare and knocked on his tin gate. Whenever I came to his place there would always be a roaring adda in progress, so the gate would not be locked. Today, the place was quite still.

Salauddin greeted me with radiant eyes.

The plaster was still on his arm, a scraggly look on his face and a dark and deep scar above a brow. His room looked as if it hadn't been inhabited in a long while. A banana peel lay rotting on the floor, spreading its stench all around. The chaotic papers on the table were coated with dust.

The thin tendrils of a money plant climbed the tiny window. Countless cigarette butts were strewn all over the floor. The crumpled bed sheet was sticky with oil.

I pulled up a chair and sat down silently. Salauddin sat on the bed, leaning against the wall.

'Strange, don't you have any visitors?'

'Yes, once in a while,' Salauddin replied. 'Mother came and stayed for a few days.'

Profound silence. I didn't know what to say. Salauddin made a request. 'Can you change this bandage for me?'

I noticed now that the upper part of his leg was bandaged. I got up with alacrity, took out cotton and bandages from a packet on the table and tenderly lifted his leg.

Salauddin sat quietly till I had unwound the whole bandage.

Now he broke the silence to declare a strange indifference to the world. 'Chatting isn't as pleasurable as it used to be,' he said. 'After a while I feel exhausted. Even my friends are fed up; they hardly come. No one came in the last three days. I just lay quietly in a darkened room. If I find a boy in the street I send him for bread and bananas from the neighbourhood shop. I have been living on that.' As he spoke his head sank into the pillow.

'What did you have for lunch?'

'Nothing,' he said with his eyes closed. The expression on his face seemed to show that the world had collapsed around him. Like a silkworm he had sought his last retreat amidst dark cobwebs.

I rushed out and walked till I found an eatery. I ordered rice and curry, packed it in a polythene bag, but when I got back to Salauddin's room I found his water jug empty. There was no water in the kitchen tap. I gave half a taka to a boy playing in the street and asked him to fetch water. Salauddin just sat with a dazed look on his face. When I brought a plate from the kitchen and, arranging the food on it, offered it to him, he burst into tears like a starving beggar. I held his hand and asked him to compose himself.

By the time he finished eating and I washed and put the plate away and sat down, the afternoon had fled. Inside me was the niggling anxiety over my salary. This visit was a very risky affair. As I got up to leave, Salauddin blurted out in emotional tones, 'Why don't you move in here, for good?' So I had to sit down again.

The room was in deep shadow. As I pressed the light-switch, the dust-encrusted bulb gave out a greyish light. Looking at his anxious face I laughed to make light of the matter. 'Why are you letting your weakness get the better of you? You will regret it later.'

'I have said this after careful thought,' Salauddin replied. 'You need not worry about future regret.'

'No, you haven't thought about it at all,' I said amidst growing distress. 'It is only the impulse of a passing moment.'

'Maybe you are right,' he said, subsiding again into listlessness. 'You know, in the past I used to socialize a lot with you, but I didn't really hold you in esteem. The business of the divorce in fact aroused disgust. I used to think your unrealistic desires and your inability to live and let live had brought it about.'

'How come your view has changed so quickly?'

'I don't know, maybe it's just a question of feelings. Feelings don't arise or change through a rational process.' Salauddin paused. 'To me there was something obscene in your relationship with Satyajit. I don't know why I am telling you all this today.'

I sat stunned for a while, then got up. I controlled my inner turmoil somehow and said calmly, 'Why are you telling me all this? If we don't know something it cannot hurt us. It is only when we take off our clothes that we become naked. You may be deriving pleasure from being truthful, but truth that is uglier than falsehood had better be kept to oneself. Far from feeling happy, I feel insulted by what you have said.'

'Nina, I am sorry . . .' Salauddin limped behind me up to the gate. By then all the excitement within me had dissipated. An intolerable tumult had begun in my heart.

'When you have recovered, you may bring your proposal to me. I will then decide about moving in here.'

The suppressed rage in my words was lost on Salauddin. He gazed at me passionately. I was about to step out through the gate when he took my hand. I turned my head and noticed a strange expression on his sweaty face. His lips were quivering. His breathing was heavy. Dusk had descended on the outside world.

My hand was in his grip for a while. Softly but with sarcasm in my voice I asked: 'Feel like a kiss?'

Startled, Salauddin let go of my hand and composed himself.

'Then go ahead,' I said, pouting and thrusting my face forward.

An electric shock convulsed Salauddin. 'Nina, really!'

And I was back in the real world.

On the way home I was hardly conscious that I was carrying my salary in my purse. Pain, loathing, rage, shame—all mingled in my consciousness. Why couldn't I accept his honesty with ease? In order to calm down I said to myself: if he hadn't said those things to me he wouldn't have suffered any loss. Maybe he had blurted them out because he had a nagging sense of guilt. If that was the case, why did I insult him?

After a while I realized that the cause of my distress lay elsewhere. He had concealed his feelings and mixed with me in a spirit of cordial intimacy. On many occasions he had hailed my decision to live on my own by declaring, 'You are extraordinarily radical! Every woman married to a stupid, useless, inconsiderate and abusive husband should walk out instead of desperately hanging in there.' Besides, he was full of sympathy over my divorce. He had said so many comforting things. 'I respect Satyajit,' he said, 'because he wasn't influenced by your husband into showing disrespect towards your friendship.' No one had thrust on him the burden of hiding such hatred beneath an actor's mask. Could I trust anyone in this world!

As soon as my rickshaw turned into my lane I noticed a rough-looking youth hanging around a lamp post. His clothes were shabby, his eyes somewhat red. Large pimples covered his cheeks.

Instantly, my head was cleared of all chaotic thoughts. A cold current coursed through my body. I gripped my handbag tightly. The youth was staring at me with wide-open eyes.

When my rickshaw crossed the lamp post my body felt like cold steel. I had to hold my breath and cover some more distance. My spine tingled. I held my head rigid, not turning around.

As it stopped at the gate of our house I realized my entire body was drenched with sweat. With profound relief I felt that Salauddin, his words, the hideous turmoil in my brain— all these had melted like camphor into thin air.

Clutching my handbag to my breast I let out a carefree laugh. I paid the rickshaw-wallah, and on entering my room was overwhelmed with a sense of well-being—*Om Shantih*—as I saw that Shanu and Kamal Bhai were there, playing Ludo. I merged into the waves of their excited laughter. I felt so light, weightless. Ha! Ha! Right now I was on top of the world.

~

After many days, as night fell I became addicted to the marriage of paint, brush and canvas. Gradually my brushstrokes brought to life a scene preserved in my mind. The stuffiness of the room, the unsightly spots on the walls, everything around me simply receded from view. My brushstrokes created a darkened room in which a naked lamp burned fitfully. It was as if I were standing at the door of the room. Profound darkness spread over the canvas. At a touch of my brush a long tongue of flame glittered in the middle. Inside it lay a comatose young girl. The light from the lamp fell on her face, and the play of light and shade revealed her pale, terror-stricken face. Nearly a whole night passed in an attempt to paint this subject.

When I set the unfinished work aside and got ready to turn in I realized my entire body was throbbing with aches and pains. My throat was parched. I drank a lot of water and lay down flat. I felt feverish, restless, because of an unbearable suppressed excitement. After the long gap my hand was extremely stiff, amateurish. I didn't know what was going on within me, but the fact that once again I had a desire to paint—this dream kept me in a trance for a long time.

The next day at work I was driven by the same urge. Even amidst the pressure of arduous work I felt the magnetic attraction of my room—and the delicately poised canvas standing in the centre. I was in the process of wrapping up for the day when I noticed a man's shadow across my desk. I looked up and at once my brows creased in surprise and irritation—Omar.

'I have been standing here for some time,' he said, pulling up a chair, 'but strangely enough you did not notice.'

On the basis of our slender acquaintance he had unearthed my work address and landed here without warning; I thought he was way out of line. I sat down, deliberately unsmiling, not saying a word. Not that this had any effect on him. 'You must be surprised at my presence here, because you hadn't given me your address,' he said breezily. I opened the newspaper and held it up to read. 'MEDICAL STUDENTS STRIKE: PATIENTS DYING.'

'I am not surprised at all,' I said coolly.

'Annoyed?'

'No.'

'I cannot make a mystery of things,' Omar said frankly. 'Your friend in hospital—what's his name?—anyway, I got your work address from him. Strange that you didn't go to see him again.'

'Did you regularly ask him about it?' I said, while my eyes perambulated the newspaper. 'DEAD RAT IN WATER SUPPLY.'

'It seems you are offended. Of course that hardly matters to me. My attitude is simple: if I value something, I show it, even if it may seem I am going overboard or making myself ridiculous.'

'It seems you are very indulgent towards your own feelings.' I couldn't keep my annoyance in check any longer. The newspaper had pictures of a procession: agitating university students had taken to the streets.

'Maybe,' he said. 'As I've admitted, my behaviour has a bad side, which may provoke irritation in many. But that does not upset me.'

Some of my colleagues were glancing in the direction of my desk. My visitor was dressed in a bizarre fashion. His beard scraggly as usual. That no comb had run through his hair in days was obvious to everyone. He appeared to have lost some of his vitality. A person was entitled to call on an acquaintance, and if that person was immune to insult there was no point in trying to put him down. The bell rang, announcing the end of the working day. Everyone got ready to leave. Some were yawning. I lowered the newspaper. 'ACCIDENTS IN THE CITY KILL NINE IN ONE DAY.' As I folded the paper and put it away I asked: 'Have you taken your brother home?' At once he became lively—'Damn, while we were bandying words around, I forgot the reason why I came here. Lately, my brother's behaviour has astounded everyone. I will not go into details, but you will no doubt be surprised to learn that he is desperate to see you.'

A bloody lie! The fellow was shamelessly trying to give our acquaintance a family connection. When this thought entered my head I could no longer suppress my annoyance. I said sharply, 'Your brother did not even see me properly, he does not know me at all, so please tell me what is your true intention? Why use a ruse like a brother's wish to see me?'

'Believe me, I am not lying.' His face looked pathetic. 'I have already told you; everything about him has become rather strange. He did see you. Whatever the reason, your face is lodged in his memory. He has repeatedly asked to see you. Day by day he is also becoming more and more abnormal. Often in the middle of the night he walks out of the room on crutches. Mother keeps a close watch on him, but to no avail. He sneaks out of bed, unbolts the door and makes off. If he gets caught he says incomprehensible things. "I am a dead man," he says, "so I go to meet other dead people."' Omar's expression became sombre as he finished speaking.

I sat still, like one benumbed.

Omar began talking again. 'The most extraordinary thing is his claim that once as he sat till the end of night inside a graveyard, he met our grandmother. She stroked his head and chatted with him about lots of things—like Father's early first marriage and the death by drowning of his child bride; then Father's marriage with Mother. When Mother heard all this she almost went out of her mind. She was the only living person in the family who knew about these things. My brother said that Grandmother had a dark birthmark on her forehead; Mother confirmed this. Grandmother died before we were born, so we couldn't have known about it. Stranger still, my brother keeps his eyes closed and mutters, "Where is that dead body? Tell me whose dead body is it?" I asked him many times, but I could never get a reply out of him. Did I tell you— often I too sit by the graveyard?' Omar's face darkened. 'Of course that's another story. Anyway, my brother's case has baffled all of us.'

'Now look here,' I said, 'I do not believe in any irrational theories. He must have heard somehow about your grandmother and your father's first marriage, and in his illness he is repeating it. He has come back from the jaws of death, so it is natural for him to think about dead bodies, isn't it?'

'But his midnight walks?'

'I am no psychologist, but I think the matter is related to the attempt on his life. Fear can produce strange abnormalities. At least that's what my common intelligence tells me. You should take him to a psychiatrist.'

'Will you visit him?'

'Tomorrow is a holiday. You can come the day after—I will go with you.'

'Why not today?' he asked a little hesitantly.

My brain was teeming with images of the canvas mounted on the easel. It drew me like a magnet. There was an intoxicating smell of paint in my nostrils. It seemed ages since the last time I had felt such excitement. Ah, that dream-inspired painting!

'There is some problem today,' I said. 'Please come the day after tomorrow.'

When I reached home, my ardour dissipated wholesale. First, I noticed the woman from the basti standing silently with her son in her arms on the lichened stairs. I hadn't seen such rapid physical degeneration in anyone. The bones were barely contained by the frame of her skin. And her belly had swelled like the bladder of a *potka* fish. On seeing me she became nervous and quickly made for the basti. Kallu perched on her hips and cast a doleful glance at me. My heart gave an agonized lurch. 'Hey listen,' I called out . . . But the woman pressed the edge of her sari to her face and disappeared into the basti. I placed a heavy foot on the stairs.

When I stepped in I got another shock. Shanu was muttering curses like a madwoman. On seeing me she literally hurled herself at me. 'I want this month's rent!'

I was startled. Sari in a state of disorder. Sweaty face. Aggression oozing in her attitude. 'Even after getting your salary you aren't paying the rent,' she said. 'I haven't opened an orphanage here. You are saving your money while I spend out of my pocket to look after you.'

'Really! How can you . . . !' I exclaimed in protest. 'In which month have I not paid you? Can you mention a single month for which you paid the entire rent? As for this month, Arefin has just got a job and said he needed something to tide him over till he started getting paid. That's why . . .' Tears rose to my eyes before I could finish. I put down my handbag, pulled open the drawer and, flinging the money at Shanu, declared, 'I'll get out of here tomorrow.'

'Why did you throw the money?' she screeched. 'Am I asking for charity? Besides, are you trying to scare me? Of course, a woman like you will not be short of places to stay at—don't I know about your character?'

That was it. I hurled her on the bed with a push. 'You stupid bitch, don't I know why you are taking it out on me? Who is the father of the child in that woman's womb? Do you think you can cover up the scandal like this? I'll tell the police about it.'

My blood was on fire. Rage and loathing drove me out of my mind and I wound my sari's edge around my waist to do battle. 'I'll strangle you to death,' I shouted. 'You cannot control your own husband and I am to blame for it! Even if I hadn't employed that woman you think your husband would have remained chaste? Doesn't he know where to find women like her?'

Instantly, all the pent-up fire turned into water. Shanu started wailing loudly. 'How can you insult me like that? Then you know everything, don't you? You all are my enemies—keeping things from me. Doesn't the bitch have a husband? Just because she once had it off with my husband . . .' Shanu began to hiccup like a child. 'She came to squeeze some money out of me. Don't I know her type? Shameless opportunist. She says her husband has kicked her out. What do you expect, a bitch like her . . .' Shanu couldn't finish her sentence. She

216

collapsed on to the floor, sitting with legs outstretched and began to howl.

The theatricality of the whole incident was astounding. Even a moment back I had no idea I would make such a telling guess about the paternity of the child in the woman's womb. I felt dizzy: what a situation to face after a day at work. My muscles went slack. Still, I yanked Shanu to her feet.

'Why are you howling like that? If people get to know what has happened they will make your life miserable. You seem to be a victim of an inner weakness. Why should that woman's word count for anything? You know very well that she has a husband. But you are in such a state that if the local people see you now they will force Kamal Bhai to take that woman in his arms. You must be firm.'

Such commonsensical advice was enough to make Shanu calm down. She dragged me into her room. 'These people are terrible. Do you think they will blackmail us?'

'They will, if they see you are weak,' I said. 'First, get your act together.' I had to make an effort to control my irritation.

'No, no, they will not try blackmail,' Shanu said, suddenly blowing her nose noisily into the *anchal* of her sari. 'You did not see, but I gave it to her like a real shrew.'

After all this, when I stood before the canvas at night there were knots in my brain. I couldn't get started. This way I would get nowhere. I began to feel a benumbing sense of bitterness. I had handed over the rent to Shanu in a fit of anger. And she had taken it. I hadn't yet sent money home. Then there was Arefin. I had thought that if I could avoid paying the rent this month and took care of the other emergencies, then next month I would somehow manage to clear the rent for both months. By then Arefin would be able to help. For a couple of days I had kept such thoughts at bay. Today they again converged on me like crabs with snapping claws. My patience was on the point of collapse. I tried to get a grip on myself. I mounted the half-finished painting on the easel. Gradually, the stubborn knots loosened up. At one point, a feeling of tenderness brought a pervasive sense of calm to my breast. I dipped the brush in black paint. Now there was a lamp to one side of the darkened canvas. On the other side was a monstrous face, like that of a black giant out of the *Arabian Nights*. His eyes stared blankly. There were more dismembered heads of cats and dogs—floating amidst light and shade. Somewhere a clock struck three. I came back to my senses. Impossible nervous pressure almost paralysed me. A weird city of preternatural creatures had sprung up on the canvas. There were chaotic scratch marks. An arm manifested itself amidst thick paint, only to be obscured by more paint. Sometimes a profile . . . the way we often see people, bit by bit, all these images composed through my amateurish handling of the brush brought a tale alive to my mind's eye. In the darkness of the night the canvas seemed to depict the varied life of a cruel, terribly fierce beauty. It wasn't just a picture. It seemed as if my brushstrokes were drawing blood from the depicted scene . . . blood spurted amidst death throes . . . glissandos on the *santoor* played thrillingly amidst screams of agony . . . At one point I come out of the trance. And my last glance at the canvas makes me feel hollow within. You haven't got it—this thought is so intense that I feel drained of vitality. My lips are dry. My feet have gone to sleep. My hand is stiff, aching. I stagger to bed and collapse. I will rip it apart. I will not finish it. I will start again—with a fresh conception.

That night I was visited by strange dreams. My burial had taken place and everyone had gone home. A cold silence pervaded the grave. The darkness was like a black buffalo. Suddenly I noticed a railway track in front of me. I could not figure out how one end of the track had merged with the grave. I ran like a crazed person over the wooden sleepers. A fog-like white darkness lay all around.

I saw a train drawing near, whistling furiously. It stopped abruptly. Every coach was filled with decapitated heads. Dead bodies lay piled up in the engine. It was horrifying—I turned pale. The next moment a yellow-complexioned child stepped out of the train. He was my baby. I let out a deafening cry. The child was small, but his teeth were disproportionately big. He walked confidently. I clasped him to my breast like a madwoman. But he effortlessly disengaged himself and in a strange, languorous manner walked ahead a considerable distance. He casually gestured to me to follow. I followed the footsteps of that tiny, naked form. The road was endless—I was soon panting. My body was on the verge of collapse, yet the baby kept on moving. Suddenly I heard a voice like an echo: 'Do you believe in God?'

'Yes, I do,' I said in a tremulous voice as I looked around.

A youth. His skin was so fair, it seemed that if I pricked it with a pin, milk and blood would ooze out. He was dressed in something like a cassock. He picked up my child and thundered, 'You are lying.' The youth's face struck me as being very familiar. Where have I seen him? I groped in the fog for an answer. He stood still. The child in his arms was laughing. I recalled with surprise that I had seen him in hospital. He had been stabbed. He was someone's brother—damn, I couldn't remember whose. I stood shivering. Whose brother?

Suddenly, I woke up. I looked around frantically. What was this, tears in my eyes? The pillowslip too was soaked in the brine of tears. But I didn't cry in my dream! Or else, if I did cry I couldn't remember. Currents of agony flowed through my breast. An extraordinary solitude all around. The dawn was breaking in through the chinks in the door. But why did I cry so copiously? And why did the nothingness in my breast kick up such a whirlwind? I sat thinking. My existence froze at the discovery that I stood face-to-face with my son for the first time in many days. I had suppressed all these memories for days. Gradually, even the wound caused by my anguish was acquiring a scab. That face surfaced in dreams to prick me and make the weak spot bleed afresh. I did not want to dwell on that episode of my life. I sat up nervously. The ghost town on the canvas lay before me. But it had come to nothing—there was nothing in it but the trickery of impasto painting. I wanted to get up and get rid of it, but my benumbed body crumpled once more on the bed. I had never seen the child give a smile—only ceaseless cries were let out. Today, I was astonished to see what large teeth the child had. And such a sweet, tender smile. I gazed after it.

It brought back to life the painful memories associated with its birth. The entire period of its growth from an embryo passed in extreme restlessness. The day a urine test revealed the existence of the embryo marked the peak of Rezaul's joyous excitement. But by then I had lost all respect for him—not to mention affection. All my dreams centred on the growing foetus. The first three or four months I was on the point of dying. I threw up all the time. The bathroom floor was always awash with vomit. Everything stank—fish, vegetables, bhaji, sweets. The harrowing, sleepless night passed in agonized tossing and turning. The most painful was having Rezaul sleep beside me. His whole body had a fishy odour. It made my stomach turn, I felt I would suffocate. In order to avoid him I decided to sleep on the floor. But he would come down too, begging me to let him stay there and make love. This compromise weighed on me heavily. But I knew that continuous rejection would threaten our marital ties, so even in that delicate physical and psychological condition I had no choice but to give in.

I had another serious problem. I developed an appetite for foods that we could ill afford. Roast chicken, *pangas* fish, ghee, *halim*. Usually Rezaul used to say they weren't available or he did not have enough money, but every week or two he would bring them for me, as if they were a rare gift. Lack of a regular and nutritious diet made me increasingly weak and emaciated. I was perpetually irascible. Rezaul, however, showed no distress or remorse for his inability to buy these necessities. In fact, I often had the feeling that he was quite contented with his lot. I never saw him trying to improve his situation. He answered these questions with either defeatist resignation or listlessness. With the passing days, perhaps because of the restrictive circumstances, I may have become somewhat abnormal. I began to think obsessively that my baby would be born with congenital defects. I thought it impossible for a healthy child to be born amidst this life of deprivation.

A corrosive fear fastened on my breast. It seemed my unborn child and I were continually slipping into a dark abyss. I would reach out to touch Rezaul for support. But, instead of showing sympathy, he callously brushed off my anxieties by scolding me. 'You are a very weak person,' he would say. 'Try to increase your endurance. The way you behave, it is hard to tell that you grew up in a family that had to struggle with poverty.'

Amidst such anxieties I realized that the foetus had nearly reached full growth. At one point I began to rebuff Rezaul's nocturnal advances very forcefully. The foetus would crawl from the left to the right of the womb. Rezaul would place his hand on the mound of the stomach and be thrilled. It would arouse him. But I would firmly refuse his advances. This happened once, twice . . . gradually he became aggressive. Our nights began to witness ugly scenes. I felt so much pressure, as if I were suffocating.

The conflict reached its climax one day when he came home accompanied by a handsome youth. He said they used to be roommates in the mess when they were boys. The youth had come to Dhaka for a week and would stay with us. 'You cannot imagine, Nina, what a shy fellow he is,' Rezaul said. The mention of the mess chilled me from inside. The conversation of that other night came alive in all its tangled complexity. Rezaul had narrated the story of his long period of deviance. He had begun with his initiation at the hands of another boy in the mess. Behind the mess lay a wide sandbank, then a river. 'Moonlight on the sand possesses a supernatural beauty,' his friend told Rezaul, who was persuaded to go along. That night the moon was really like a limpid eye. The extensive *char* was deserted but for foxes barking in the pumpkin fields. As the wind whistled around them his friend took Rezaul on the sand. Rezaul said in a subdued tone that there were other boys who were also interested in this game. 'You know, I wasn't active at first,' Rezaul confided in me. 'I was used as a passive partner. One day I went with my friends to a sweepers' colony. There was nightlong singing and dancing, as we guzzled on bottle after bottle of country liquor. Some of the sweeper girls would make themselves available—for money, of course. I was dead drunk. I had my first fuck with one of them, but as I ejaculated I realized that she hadn't really given me much pleasure. I felt that a male partner would be more satisfying. Gradually I too became an active homosexual.'

Why did Rezaul have to tell me all this? So that I would respect his honesty? Or that because he told me all I wouldn't feel he was deliberately insulting me? I stopped him with great vehemence. 'I do not want to hear any more, do you understand?'

And so, now, at the mention of the word 'mess' I lost my head. Besides, I did not trust Rezaul at all. I withdrew into the kitchen and gave vent to my suppressed rage.

'Bear with me for a few days,' Rezaul begged. 'I used to be very fond of him. If you take the bed, the two of us can sleep on the floor.'

'You could have carried on outside,' I hissed. 'Why bring him home?'

'What are you trying to say?' Rezaul asked with a stony face.

'Don't you understand?' I was just as bitter. 'In your delight at sleeping together on the floor you may forget that it is obscene to have a woman sleep in the same room with two men. That too in this weather. When I cannot keep my sari on while sleeping because of the heat. But I cannot ignore *that.*'

He stood fiery-eyed for a while. Then he suddenly dragged me into the room. The boy was reading a magazine. Rezaul threw him on the bed and began kissing him with wild abandon. Rezaul's hands groped his body all over. I stood in a state of shock, with an expressionless stare. Rezaul began to pant from the exertion. The boy was dying of embarrassment; he glanced at me and quickly left the room. Barely conscious, I sat down on the floor. My throat felt dry. My body trembled uncontrollably. Hatred, fear and the tears of self-pity prevented me from looking at Rezaul.

Five days after this incident I was admitted into hospital. I had been experiencing slight pain since the morning. After midday the pain increased a little. I had had similar pains once or twice before, and had dragged myself to the Outdoor Patients' department of the hospital, where the doctor reassured me it was a 'false pain'. But now the pain really was of a different sort. Night came on soft feet. The pain steadily grew. Rezaul's anxious face hovered over mine. I shut my eyes: the pain was unbearable. It went on increasing relentlessly. With the deepening of the night the spear-point grew sharper. It kept pricking me. The nurse came round every few minutes to take a look. I was drenched in sweat. My body was being twisted and shredded. At one point my pain-racked body was placed on a trolley. Before this the doctor had come to check and saw that the passage along which the baby would travel had not opened. But the sac had burst. The anxious doctor urged me to push: 'Push hard, with all your might!' But did I have the necessary strength? At the slightest exertion the spear-point became sharper. Meanwhile, the baby seemed to become still. Strange, had it died? 'Let it die,' I screamed. 'Doctor, cut me open! Rezaul, you son of a bitch, what have you put inside me?'

Where were they taking me? Was it the open mouth of a furnace? Even amidst the torrents of sweat I was burning.

Then the baby's staggering cry. Because it was expelled in a flood of amniotic fluid caused by the premature bursting of the sac, it had had terrible breathing difficulty. After he was born a fresh problem arose: the placenta would not come out. I understood little of these complications—or the way the doctor handled them. My entire body was by then in a state of collapse. When the baby was cleaned up and set down beside me, Rezaul came running. The sight of the newborn face gave me a sense of meaning in life, despite all that had happened. Then came the child's illness, and death. For this I blamed Rezaul most of all. Anguish and despair tormented me ceaselessly. The baby's cries shook every part of my being. I clutched at Rezaul's shirtsleeves: 'Get some money, medicines, saline.'

'Where from?' he replied, at which with weak, trembling hands I gripped his collar. There was no effort on his part. Couldn't a man who was out all day find money for the treatment of a newborn baby?

He roamed all day. In the evening he came to the hospital to find me in a crazed state. 'Can't you beg?' I screamed at him one day. 'Or else you stay with the baby. I'll go and sell my body to get the money.'

'Have you gone mad?' he shouted back. 'I am bringing what I can.'

What he brought wasn't even enough for a bag of saline. I cried hysterically, 'Save him, please!' The outcome was that Rezaul stayed away for longer. He sank into despair and took refuge in Satyajit's adda.

One day the turbulence ended for good.

The thought again makes me feel hollow inside. The child is laughing. There he is, squatting on the table, sleeping on the floor, sitting in the chair and swinging his legs; sometimes, he floats in space. How extraordinary is that smile of his. I keep gazing with thirsty eyes. Inside me goes on a continual analysis. Why am I blaming Rezaul for the death? Can I hold him responsible for his poverty? Is a father's concern for his child any less that the mother's? But then there are varieties of concern. Some hug their children to the breast, some abandon theirs in the street because they lack the means to bring them up. Both actions spring from affection. In the latter case, the mother cannot bear the thought of watching the baby's gradual decline and entrusts its fate to the void.

There was a knock on the door. After Kamal Bhai left in the morning, Shanu sank into deep sleep. They had squabbled till the small hours.

I was immersed in painting. I had learnt to ignore their fights. I straightened my sari, but my hair was still awry when I opened the door. As soon as I did so I was overcome by embarrassment. With a broad smile on his face Irfan Chacha stood on the doorstep. 'Can I come in?' he asked.

'What is this?' I exclaimed in astonishment. 'So early? You are a strange man indeed. But do come in.' Warmly welcoming the guest, I went into the bathroom with a clean sari. I spruced up and came out to find him standing before my painting. What an embarrassing situation! The painting hadn't yet been filled out. There was work still to be done, and here he was examining it while it was showing all the signs of amateurishness. I felt I was shrinking. I broke into a sweat. I thought he would be pleasantly surprised that I had started painting again. Instead, here he was, saying in a very serious tone, 'This is where the delight of your painting lies. It does not care for craftsmanship. You can add thought to amateurishness and create beauty. Perhaps I too am an amateur connoisseur.'

I did not quite know whether to be pleased or disappointed. He sat down in the chair and began rolling up his sleeves. I sat on the bed. 'Grotesqueries all over the canvas,' he said. 'A young maiden with the face of a corpse gazing at the flame of a lamp. The darkness of death is devouring her. The severed heads of cats and dogs, a monstrous face, somewhat hazy, a pair of hands raised upward. Presumably he wants to lift the girl. No, it is terribly complicated.'

'No, no, he does not want to lift the girl,' I countered, 'though the painting will not suffer if anyone thinks so. The entire idea is centred on a real incident. The girl is my younger sister, Ranu. She was an adolescent then. Actually, for lack of competence I could not express anything of that idea.'

'Giant, severed heads'—he looked surprised—'Ranu in their midst: is it based on her dreams?'

'No,' I said impatiently, feeling a little disoriented at recalling the whole episode. 'Actually, she is a strange victim. That monstrous man is called Abdul Ali Majumdar.'

Irfan Chacha fell silent. Strange! Not expressing curiosity seemed to be a mark of politeness with people like him. Neither of us spoke for some time. Then he said, 'I am glad you have started again. I ask only one thing—don't lose faith in yourself.'

After a pause he continued. 'At one time I travelled a lot, especially in neighbouring countries. I first realized that a born artist can create something original when I visited the

Sun Temple in Konark. Horses, chariots, elephants, dancers in diverse postures . . . such extraordinary works of art! Sculptures hewn out of stone; men and women in coitus. Such lifelike representations of warm passion—even looking at them lifelong would not satisfy the thirst of the eyes and the mind. Yet the artists who created these had no formal training. They did not even have mentors to advise them. Who knows how they could create such exquisite sculptures in deference to their royal and feudal masters? Or take the case of the sculptures in the Old City in Kathmandu, the Krishna Temple there, or the 1600 terracotta figurines of *gopis*—who made them? Nina, there is nothing comparable to spontaneous creativity. Knowledge can only enhance it. But knowledge without creativity? It can only be pedantry. The beauty that lies in every corner of the Taj—did Shahjahan create it? No, behind it lies the talent of artisans. Don't you see the paintings behind rickshaws? Who paints them?'

I listened spellbound. Here was a lovely individual whom nothing could touch, neither the Gulf War nor hartals nor terrorism. That's why I loved to immerse myself in his words. There was a calendar on the wall with the photograph of a pretty girl. He laughed. 'There is something heartless about calendars,' he commented. 'A beautiful picture is hanging in front of you, but you can see it only for a month or two. When the time is up, turn over the page and move on to another pretty picture . . .'

At once I engaged him in a debate. 'Since the primary function of a calendar is to show the date and not a picture, I see nothing heartless in this. Time flies—you have to accept this truth.'

He laughed. 'You think I don't? I have been turning the pages till I have become an old man. Now let me come to the main point of my visit: are you busy today?'

I shook my head.

'Then let's go out. Let life have a little variety today, what do you say?'

'Where?' I felt suppressed joy and the spark of surprise within me.

'Don't ask where, the main thing is to go out. We can decide later where we'll go.'

My guest seemed to be quite a bohemian! He was another manifestation of my wilted dream. Many a time I would feel an urge shaking me awake—Venture out, Nina, go . . . But nothing would come of it. Every footstep had to be carefully calculated.

I was thrilled. I gazed at those eyes, so calm; that man with a placid exterior and a restless soul. But his gaze shifted to the canvas. As if he was carrying on an autopsy of the whole picture. Suddenly that young man occupied my vision—dressed like a Catholic priest, Omar's brother. After the dream I actually felt an urge to see him. Again, melancholy began to gather inside me. Not laughter but a child's wail came drifting. It was endless. I stood still. A little later I gave myself a shake. I turned inward. I gave in to the very different thrill of stepping out into the unknown.

≈

And so we went. Once out of the filthy, congested lanes of Rayer Bazar, the rickshaw was flying through the open space. 'You know,' he said, 'I used to have a car. I thought then that I would never be able to do without one. But I had to sell it when there was a financial crunch. After the crisis passed I never got round to buying another car. So I am like the king in a folk tale who has a palace but no throne'—he burst out laughing as he spoke—'and the pleasure of such imaginings is that one cannot place oneself lower than a king.'

I smiled to hear him ramble but said nothing.

A strong breeze was blowing. Trucks, buses, cars sped this way and that. Irfan Chacha's broad forehead was uncovered as his hair flew in the breeze.

We sat in silence, observing the passing scene. But in this open space I was a different person. I felt like throwing up all the accumulated bitterness within. The sun was in the belly of a cloudbank.

'Nina, have you read the *Arabian Nights*?'

'Bits of it. Strangely enough, when I was painting Majumdar I was reminded of an African giant.'

'Your general interests will provide you with plenty of subjects to paint. In most of those tales you will find beautiful women betraying good-looking husbands and indulging in orgiastic sex with black men. When the husbands get wind of what is going on, they don't ask any questions and with their swords slice through the lovers while they are at it. In those days, physical pleasure and murder both played a conspicuous role in life. There are many more strange tales. They are full of wonderful raw material for painting. Of course I am saying this because myths and legends fascinate me.'

'I need to study art thoroughly,' I said. 'I have virtually no education in this field.'

'Well, who is this Abdul Ali Majumdar?' he asked. 'Of course, if it is too embarrassing for you, you need not say anything.'

'Your lack of interest in him earlier irked me,' I said. 'It seemed like a put-on. It is against my temperament to be so calculatingly civil.'

'Why do you think a certain aspect of my personality is a put-on?' he protested. 'This is how I have grown up. I believe if someone wishes to say something they will do so willingly, spontaneously. Listen, why aren't you more frank? If you want to say something you need not wait for others to show interest.'

'Come on, shall I babble if there is no one willing to listen?'

'You should simply have your say. Why allow the audience to destroy your spontaneity? Besides, you surely have some idea about whom you can tell certain delicate things to. You will not go around telling them to all and sundry, of course.' After such a long preamble began the story proper. The rickshaw was travelling past Dhaka College. Soon after came the traffic congestion around Gawsia Market.

'There used to be a man called Majumdar. He was a moneylender. Since her very birth, a young girl called Ranu used to be terrified of his hideous appearance . . .' I narrated the story in this style, as if it was far from me personally. As for the age and the time when the events took place, I removed myself from the pain associated with them and calmly said to myself that in such open spaces there could be no pain, no suffering—I should forget all about yesterday's world.

I don't remember when the rickshaw crossed Eden College and entered the warren of streets in Old Dhaka. The streets were extremely narrow. As we moved between the crumbling old houses I experienced a peculiar pleasure. Though the atmosphere was claustrophobic, the age of the buildings lent it a romantic thrill. I had never visited these places. I was struck with wonder as I pondered how the people here could grow up without access to even a slice of the sky.

Irfan Chacha's reaction to the tale I had been narrating was frank astonishment. 'Barbaric!' he exclaimed. 'Murder is far better. Majumdar is also a cunning murderer with a novel method.' Irfan Chacha looked grave. Clearly, the incident had a profound effect on him.

'I am reminded of a form of murder that used to take place in Dostoevsky's age. A band of assassins have encircled a mother and her child. They devise a novel way to murder the child. First they cosset the child, make it laugh. The child laughs.

At that moment they hold a pistol to the child's face. The child laughingly reaches for the pistol. Just then it is shot dead. This is bestial cruelty. But in those days it was interpreted differently. Beasts cannot kill with such artistry. Only humans are capable of such terrible cruelty.'

He became pensive. I too felt depressed. There was no point broaching the matter today. For today I was out in the open air without any prearranged plan. Life's harshness had become intolerable, that's why.

'Perhaps you are feeling bad because these things have come up on a day of leisure—it is quite natural. But, Nina, I have learnt from experience that it is not possible for one to escape from oneself and be happy—even for a moment. If you want to be happy, you should from time to time take your sorrow out of your heart, hold it in your hands and examine it, then put it back, but make a space for joy beside it. That will make the joy more intense. But if you try to uproot your sorrow you will only be able to feign joy—you will never experience genuine joy.'

'What if I say you are guilty of it yourself—you are pretending to be happy while trying to escape from yourself?'

After hurling this sudden accusation at him I turned my gaze towards the narrow lanes we were passing, in an attempt to conceal my self-consciousness. Our rickshaw was slowly weaving its way through the press of people. Ahead of us lay a huge, ruined mansion. The brickwork was hanging loose in places. Innumerable banyan saplings had grown through the walls. One had the impression of a heap of bricks touching the sky. No stairways were in sight. I turned my head and noted with surprise a curtained window right at the top. Did human beings live there? Yes, actually. I was reminded of the saying that everything was possible for human beings. My companion had lit up a cigarette with his lighter. 'No doubt you were

231

hinting at my relationship with my wife and my family,' he said while exhaling smoke.

I had nothing to say in response. He exhaled more smoke as he continued. 'There are certain things one can never explain to anybody. I am not used to talking about personal matters. I have many friends and well-wishers, but they could never find out even a fraction about my personal affairs. Of course I am not claiming my habit is commendable or acceptable.'

'I am sorry,' I said. 'My curiosity was probably unseemly.'

'You need not be so polite,' he said. 'There is no lack of modesty in you.'

The rickshaw came to a stop at Sawari Ghat, beside a muddy road. Before us stretched the Buriganga. The river was so close by, yet I had never come here. The sun had forced its way through the clouds, but it was without ferocity, rather mellow. After the rickshaw-wallah was paid off we walked down the muddy road and stood near the ghat. Numerous boats bobbed in the water and people jostled all about us—so many that the river seemed to have lost its mystery.

The waves went surging past. The smaller boats were tossed about. A fresh breeze blew apace. I found the scene charming. But the mood of enchantment was shattered by Irfan Chacha: 'It will be too dangerous to go for a boat ride in this current,' he said. 'Let's go elsewhere.'

I had a ready rejoinder. 'There is a vast expanse of water before us. We may not be able to swim in it, but going back with the disappointment of not even having a boat ride would be utterly absurd. This is the first time you have given your age away. At this age one does not take any risks.'

He reacted spiritedly. 'Did you start thinking I was a boy? Do you think any mature person would approve of the youthful habit of foolishly plunging into activity without weighing the risks?'

'Youth does not care for approval,' I declared—feeling a certain thrill at his show of anger. 'Of course it doesn't apply in the case of all youths,' I added. 'Some young people are very calculating in every aspect of life. Even if they give up all arithmetic in the heat of love, everything is accurately calculated in the event of a marriage.'

'Are you speaking from the perspective of your own life?' he asked.

'No,' I said firmly. 'Why are you pretending not to understand?'

As a dinghy came forward he gestured at me to get on board. I did so with a spring. He followed. The boat negotiated its way by the other craft and made for the open water. The water was cool to the touch . . . and the breeze . . . and how lovely the roll of the boat!

'Who initiated the divorce proceedings?' he asked in a low voice. I felt annoyed because he was avoiding the main issue. Anyway, why should I show any interest if he wanted to avoid the subject?

This was the first time he had asked about my married life. It was an embarrassing subject for me, I realized, especially when I was asked to reveal anything about its private aspects. But under the open sky, amidst the restless waves I felt like uncovering everything, letting it all hang out, the sin and the shame, the bitterness, and if I could not explain everything rationally, perhaps I could convey it through the language of feeling?

My companion had a bag with him; he took out a packet of chips and offered it to me.

'Do you keep such things in your bag? That's very interesting.' I opened the packet and conveyed one of the chips to my waiting teeth. 'It was I who initiated the divorce,' I said unabashedly.

'Why?'

'I cannot explain those things to you.'

'Was it a love match?'

'Yes.'

'How long were you together?'

'Why are you interrogating me like this? Anyway, it was for about two years.'

'You got to know someone within such a short time? If I say that you began conjugal life without knowing what it was and also destroyed it without knowing it properly? To you marriage was a joke...'

'What do you know about it?' I countered heatedly. 'Who has given you the right to comment like that without knowing anything about the case?'

He gave a mellow laugh.

'You are very young, Nina. That's why you are quick to take offence. Just think for a moment and you will see what folly it is to comment on an event from a distance. Something may be sullied within or it may be decent and attractive, but it must be first observed directly from within. In the account of courtship and marriage that you have given, your perspective is very narrow, cheap. I did not expect such an analysis from you.'

A motor launch went by chugging deafeningly. The waves in its wake struck our boat so fiercely that it rolled alarmingly, throwing us both off balance.

It was obvious that if we ceased bickering, our relationship would become more frank and open. Besides, the battle of wits was tiring me out. I relaxed, lowered my guard. Such a stance would be better for us both. After all, everyone needed a place where they could weep without inhibition.

'Listen,' he suddenly started talking again, 'our conjugal life was never a very happy one. That is the first, simple truth.

And, without going into the complexities, another simple statement that can be made is that what I did with your mother is commonly called being deceitful. But there is no connection as such between that and my marital unhappiness.'

I was munching the chips, watching the restless water. He lit up again, expertly shielding the flame from the wind. 'But I have already told you I have no regrets. My relationship with your mother was profound, and it was entirely the passion or infatuation—whichever you prefer to call it—characteristic of a certain age. At one point I came out of it and analysed it. Your mother's dream was limited to a house with a veranda and a garden. She did not know, nor was she curious about, the vastness of the world and its variegated beauty. Her thoughts never flew beyond the narrow circle she had drawn around herself. The purchase of luxury items, collecting rare objects, the thirst for travel . . . such things seemed to her a waste of money. Bitterness or indifference, either is enough to destroy love. At one point I began to tire of the relationship, you understand? I realized that I wanted my wife to be a friend. If I married her out of deference to society it would only be a show of pity. At least I could not be disrespectful towards her love. I went through a tremendous inner struggle over this. I struggled with my conscience, with my feelings, till a time came when I couldn't face up to it any more. You might say I fled. I had become strangely attached to her, so that when I came to Dhaka I became anxious and restless. It was quite some time later that I first met my future wife at an art exhibition. In those days women were hardly to be seen at such places. The way she carried herself, her taste in artistic matters—these attracted me powerfully.'

Irfan Chacha paused, flicked the half-smoked cigarette into the river's current. He looked sad. But he started talking again.

'One day we got married. But then I observed a certain abnormality in her. If I asked her to go with me to a get-together with my friends or some public function or even to the park, she felt I wanted to display her everywhere because of her good looks. As a result, she began to avoid me. She started sleeping separately. She stopped going out with me or appearing before my friends if they called. I spent hour after hour explaining that her ideas were delusional and should not be indulged. But she clung tenaciously to them.

'I began to think that she perhaps did not find me attractive, or else there was something I did not know. I began to search desperately for some hidden reason. She was an only child and after our marriage came into a lot of property. I found that she was full of self-conceit on that account as well. It found expression in the innuendos she hurled like lances straight at me. For instance, she would say I hadn't married her for her own sake—I wouldn't have if she wasn't an heiress, if she were poor. There were many unseemly quarrels over this. I cannot tell you, Nina, how desolate I felt at the time. Much later she told me that I could take lovers—she wouldn't mind as long as I did not want to marry them. All she asked for in return was that I let her live with me as the lady of the house; otherwise she would lose face before her family.

'Once I angrily demanded to know why she had got married at all. "Because it was what was considered socially desirable," she answered, before breaking down into uncontrollable sobs. She then told me without suppressing her sobs that as a young girl she had fallen in love with a youth. She used to think of him as her husband. When her parents were out she would call him over and they would make love. They were so passionate about each other that their families agreed to the match and fixed a date for the wedding. But before it could take place the young man quietly left for Australia and soon after married someone else. She could not imagine another man occupying his vacated place. Actually, Nina, every person's life is as dramatic as a hero's or heroine's, only some get known about, others remain concealed.'

It seemed that the doors to Irfan Chacha's soul had been flung open today. As if, in a few moments, he wished to unburden himself of a rock that had been weighing down on him.

'Meanwhile, we had a child,' he continued. 'He was growing up in a state of utter helplessness in the stifling atmosphere of his home. So when he was seven I sent him to his uncle in America. Since then life has been a grind. Of course I have also gained something from all this . . .'

A hint of excitement crept into his voice. 'People who are cheated in one area dedicate themselves to something else and find compensation there. The same happened with me. I became passionate about collecting works of art and antiques, and during holidays I became a compulsive traveller. But to be frank with you, Nina, even in that unhappy situation I did not feel any regret or remorse over my relationship with your mother. It is not that one was a better alternative to the other. For me, neither was really compatible. If I had married your mother, within a few days I would have become thoroughly bored, and her life would have become sheer agony. It is just as well that I did not plunge her into unhappiness. Now I can at least treasure that memory of her untrammelled love and the extraordinary simplicity of her nature.'

I was experiencing a strange anguish, my heart felt a pricking sensation. I stared at the river current. Suddenly, he seemed to come out of a trance and changed the subject by pointing a finger. 'Nina, look, that's the Nawab's Palace.'

I came out of my reverie and saw the pink walls of the aristocratic mansion built right on the river. The anklets of nautch girls rang in my ears, and the tinkle of bottles. The nawab was coming down—I could hear his footsteps. From my cheery dreamworld I exclaimed, 'Wonderful!' Irfan Chacha laughed. 'You are saying it's wonderful. But these feudal lords did not treat common people as human beings. Zamindars would wager over the gender of a foetus and have the pregnant woman's belly slashed open to determine the winner. There are so many stories of varied cruelty. Yet today we find their world wonderful.'

I came out of my rosy reverie. 'Let's forget these things.'

'I have finished my life story in twenty minutes,' he began again, hesitantly. 'That's why I don't want to talk about it. Everything is touched upon superficially. The whole thing turns into a little story. No matter how sensitive the listeners, it is impossible to make them realize the subtleties of daily life or the intensity of feelings.'

I went back to the main question. 'But did you know that the day I first went to your house I noticed an extraordinary change come over Chachi's expression the moment I mentioned Mother by way of introducing myself? It is possible that your reading of your wife isn't accurate. Had she been indifferent towards you she wouldn't have shown any sign of jealousy.'

'That might have been your misperception,' he replied. 'Surely, you had assumed that when you would mention your mother my wife would become a little flustered.'

'How can you assume she hasn't changed at all in thirty years?' I protested. 'Perhaps she has learnt to accept many things over time. Why did you settle into a rigid attitude? Why didn't you try to find out if she was changing? Why wasn't there any effort on your part to improve things?'

'Listen, the fact that she told me everything about her past didn't mean that our relationship came to a dead stop. We sat down at the same table for our meals. In all these years of marriage I have spent many nights in her room, but that was to satisfy a purely physical need. In real terms she had no life but for her hatred and contempt.'

'How can you think these are the only emotions to have dominated her all this time? Have you tried to find out if there has been any change in her? It is possible that making the confession induced extreme self-consciousness, and you mistook that for contempt.'

When I finished I looked up at the sky, which arched over the river's waves. It was now afternoon. The large motor launches that sailed between Dhaka and Barisal lay quietly in anchor. At a signal from Irfan Chacha our boat made for the ghat. I could see the pink palace of the nawabs upside down in the water.

'Nina,' he began again, 'human feelings and beliefs cannot really be explained in terms of reason. I am caught in the midst of my life, seeing things from my perspective. Maybe you are right and I haven't tried to find out if my wife has changed. But how can I believe that my senses are so untrustworthy that if there was any change in her, I would not have felt it when I touched her?'

The riverbank was muddy, crowded with rows of boats. There was the stench of rotten fish. It began to drizzle. We stepped from boat to boat and then on to muddy, garbage-strewn land. Two bamboo poles one foot above the ground had to be carefully negotiated to reach dry land. A motley crowd milled about, exuding the odour of sweat. When we had crossed over to where the rickshaws stood, he said, 'I think we should be feeling hungry by now. Let's go to a local restaurant— what do you say?'

This was a basic necessity, before which a tiger was no different from a mouse.

'Let's go,' I said, climbing on the rickshaw we had hailed. Again we traversed narrow, winding lanes. Because of the drizzle we had to put up the hood and cover ourselves from chest to feet with an oil cloth. Had the rickshaw shrunk in the rain? Sitting huddled together was quite discomfiting. We sat in silence as we passed through Laxmi Bazar, Patla Khan Lane . . . eventually, after a thousand twists and turns the rickshaw stopped in front of Star Restaurant. It was a large eatery. We walked down its entire length to a private cabin. He ordered plain rice and fish and asked what I would like. Without a thought I said, 'Chicken pulau.' At once I remembered how long it was since I had last eaten the dish. It was depressing. We never cooked anything like it at home. Back from work, I would get down to chopping the veggies, boiling rice, frying an egg—that would make a full meal.

Silence for a while. Then he fished a gilded photo frame from his bag and handed it to me. It had a somewhat blurred black-and-white portrait. 'It has been with me for many years,' he said. 'It's the fruit of the passion of those years when my affair with your mother was turning everything upside down. That's when I took the picture and had it framed in gilt. I came upon it the other day while looking through my things. If you don't mind you may give it to her.'

The excited chatter of the people in the next cabin reached my ears, along with the tinkle of teacups and saucers.

'Why are you embarrassed to express your emotions at this stage of life?' I asked archly. He looked shocked, hurt. I turned the photo frame over and over in my hand to examine the picture. A sense of desolation spread over me. Such an exquisite pose: holding a pigtail and smiling. Mother. She used to look so sweet. I had no recollection of that face. Had she started degenerating right after marriage?

'As far as I know you are not conventional in your attitudes.

You have a frank and open relationship with your mother. I hope I haven't made a mistake.'

'There is one mistake you have made,' I said laughingly. 'You would realize it if you saw my ageing mother. I am sure she would throw away the photograph and sell the frame.'

His face darkened. He sat in silence for a while. The food arrived in this interregnum. I could clearly see the rice beneath his inert fingers turning cold. The whole thing produced an unsavoury reaction within me. I was turning bitter, but I didn't know if it was because of anger towards my mother—or envy.

'Nina,' he said calmly as he finished his meal and wiped his hands on a handkerchief, 'you may have an arsenal of weapons, but you should not use them all.'

'Since you understand everything perfectly,' I said somewhat brusquely, 'why do you talk of youthful passion? Why don't you admit that you still love my mother?'

'I don't understand why you are getting worked up.'

His words brought me back to my senses. I relaxed again, let out a little laugh. 'Am I getting worked up? I only wanted to bring you face-to-face with a truth. I am sorry if I have ended up being rude.'

'Nina, the day is nearly done. Now it's not pleasant to stir up anything. That's all I have to say.' He became serious.

I was confused. But it was time to take a rickshaw again. For a long while we sat in discomfiting silence. This was followed in my mind by a growing sense of shame. Suddenly he commented that I was looking very tired. 'Listen to this little story,' he went on. 'Two ancient rishis were having an argument. One asked who was the loveliest woman on earth. The other replied that a woman who wasn't tired from a journey could never be beautiful.'

The story revived me. 'Really, you have a way with words.'

'There! You are smiling again,' he said, laughing.

At once I felt like a child in his presence. A strange, distressing, painful, joyful, memorable day thus drew to a close.

~

Then began the days of my worst financial hardship. After a long stretch of fugitive existence Arefin returned to his hostel. The high school where he had got a job was beyond the airport, in distant Azampur. It was a daily struggle to get there, first by a three-wheeler van, then by bus, and finally on foot. When he came to me for help I could only give him 500 taka; he was quite disappointed. Besides, my conscience was also pricking me for being unable to send anything home to Mother. After paying the rent, helping out Arefin and repaying the 200 taka loan from Sultana, I was nearly broke. At work I sat in a state of depression. There were murmurs of rebellion again; nobody paid attention to their duties. The old problem was resurfacing. The boss was in a towering rage. My sympathies were with the rebels: perhaps a stand-off would result in a pay rise. But what if the rebels lost? After all, there was no unity among them. What if the entire staff were sacked? There would be so many more queuing up to take their places! They would be grateful to have any job, even if after their travel and daily expenses they had only 300 taka left to see them through the month. In just one hour they could find fresh staff. The very thought was enough to make you feel ill. I buried my face in my papers, oblivious to the surrounding disquiet.

Alone at my desk I became a citizen of the world. To my colleagues Bush, Saddam and the Kuwait occupation were now old hat. But the incongruous headlines I read daily sent a chill through my spine: 'US BOMBS DESTROY MOSQUES, NURSERIES, HOSPITALS'; 'BUSH–GORBACHEV TALKS FAIL'; 'RIVERS OF BLOOD WILL FLOW THROUGH SAUDI

SANDS—DECLARES IRAQ'. Even though I had no direct connection with this conflict—happening in a corner of the vast world—the fact that it disturbed me proved that I was not outside its influence.

Amidst all this Rezaul turned up again at the office. After much beating about the bush he again begged me to reconsider my decision. 'I have realized,' he said, 'that there is no point in a life of penny-pinching. I have to do something in addition to the regular job, some moonlighting, and have a budget for one's entertainment.'

'Are you trying to tempt me?' I asked in irritation. 'Are you going crazy?'

'You have never been able to see things in an uncomplicated way,' he declared. 'Why not relent and see for once if we can rectify our errors?'

'We did not make any errors,' I retorted. 'I didn't walk out of our marriage because of any error. Why are you after me like this? Is it because it is too much bother to cook for yourself? I have a job now, it is not possible for me to do any cooking.'

'Listen,' Rezaul said harshly, 'there are many maids available for doing the cooking if you pay them a little.'

'Ah, but you have a problem with spending money. I don't want to waste words on such petty matters. I have simply resolved that you may remain in touch with me if you wish, but I am never going back into the cage I have vacated—is that clear?'

Rezaul now resorted to angry mutterings—my attitude had precipitated his decline, I had now got a taste of the wider world and revealed my true nature, I had been merely play-acting as a housewife, and so on. And when I pulled him up sharply, telling him that he should at least be aware he was in a workplace, he stood up and shamelessly informed me that he would come and see me at home for a comprehensive and

243

frank palaver. If one thought of marriage as a cage, the question of imprisonment automatically arose: I ought to extricate myself from this mode of thinking. He might have married again; instead, he was trying to come back to me, so I should appreciate ... Having had his say in this vein he prepared to leave. He looked back once, then he was finally on his way out. As I glanced at his retreating shadow, the image of Rezaul in the nude surfaced in my inner vision. Those disgusting thoughts returned: how people in bed behave exactly like animals. I have seen the street dogs at it: humans behave just like them. As I desperately burrowed into the files, an illuminating thought occurred: we could also say that animals behave just like humans. What a strange bind; we were in quite a pickle. The household I had walked out on appeared before me to be subjected to a detailed analysis, which only left me utterly exhausted. Back home in the evening, I simply collapsed in bed. My lunch had been chapatti and bhaji. But the thought of cooking dinner made my limbs go on strike. Still, I somehow dragged myself to the kitchen. Put on the rice and dropped in a few peeled potatoes. Then some salt, a drop of oil ... Frequently I had to borrow these from Shanu. She advised marriage: Could a woman live alone?

'Oh yes, eligible young men are queued up in the street outside,' I would reply banteringly to deflect her words. For some days now, Kamal Bhai's income had gone up noticeably. Shanu too was lately quite wrapped up in herself. The bickering and screaming had diminished. Kamal Bhai bought her a new sari or two from time to time, kept her busy cooking special dishes, and increased the frequency of his overnight stays away from home. I was pottering about my room when Shanu came in quietly and stood before me. 'Listen,' she said, 'Kamal has an elderly uncle, long a widower, quite rich too— why not latch on to him? What does a man's age matter? Besides, your life isn't an immaculate sheet either. Think about it.' I seethed with rage. I felt like grabbing her by the roots of her hair and hurling her down. But I suppressed my anger and got on with my chores.

There had been no contact with Irfan Chacha since the outing. I had desisted from calling on him out of a strange sense of anguish. His personality, his exquisite taste, his age, his sense of well-being—all these induced the anguish. But I couldn't fathom its source. I had brought the photo frame, but I couldn't be enthusiastic about giving it to Mother at this colourless, declining hour of her life. The whole thing would be cruel and ridiculous at the same time. In the meantime a new problem had shown up: I would often feel a pain in the left side of the stomach. I just gritted my teeth and put up with it. Probably an ulcer. I didn't dare see a doctor and kept on working as usual. In the office, I sat quietly amidst the protesting voices of the others. There they were at their desks, stretching their necks towards me. The faces attached to the necks would collapse in a moment in an expression of despair. Surely their voices, ever engaged in describing their financial distress, would burst on me in a moment. Or else they would resort to such crude humour in an effort to hide the boredom and suffering in their lives that the atmosphere in that closed space would become polluted with obscenity. My time passed in apprehension.

Still they came. Barua Babu, Sultana, Kibria Shaheb. They sat across my desk and talked about the situation in the office. They even asked me teasingly, 'We don't see the boss summon you these days—has anything happened?'

This was hardly something I had noticed. The gentleman in question seldom called anyone to his office unless it was for an express purpose. 'No, nothing has happened,' I said in reply to their query and fell silent. Then they switched to such topics to which I could respond only like a statue. 'That's right, he fell right into a manhole, my cousin, he was returning home late, and right in front of his house, where the street lamp had been missing for days and it was pitch dark, he fell right in . . .'

'Really?' I felt excitement rising in me as I listened. 'Did he die?'

'You give too much importance to death,' my interlocutor said in a disappointment tone. 'His bones are all broken—does he have anything left? He is crippled for life. A row of his front teeth have been knocked off. Death would have been better—he was the only one in the family who was bringing in some money.' Then the subject was taken up by everyone in the room. The nuisance of petty thieves, the bulbs supplied for street lamps. I ignored the reverberating voices and buried my nose into my files. Just then Barua Babu came up and said in a guarded undertone, 'Kibria Shaheb has a roving eye, so keep the anchal always wound around your body. As soon as he comes to know someone doesn't have a husband he begins to salivate.'

Impossible! I held my breath in rage and disgust.

At one point the summons did come from the boss. He looked relaxed, with his hair neatly parted, clean-shaved, wearing a spotless white shirt. Sitting down across his desk, I was at a loss for words. 'I have often noticed a clutch of people near your desk, and there is a hum of conspiratorial voices. Are you also ganging up with them?'

My heart leapt into my mouth. But when there's no truth in an accusation one naturally feels emboldened. 'No sir,' I replied, my head held high, 'when they come, I try to avoid exchanging words other than what is necessary. Still they come. I cannot force them to keep their mouths shut.'

'I don't want to know what they say,' he said calmly. 'If they talk like that again, just avoid them. I will not tolerate gossip in the workplace.'

As soon as I came out of his office everyone crowded round. 'What is going on?'; 'Why did he ask to see you alone?'; 'Any solution to our problem?'

I sat down at my desk and got busy with the paperwork. But their curiosity was irrepressible. Some bent over my desk to ask, 'Come on, why aren't you saying anything?'

'Please do not crowd around my desk,' I replied. 'Our boss does not like it.'

This stunned the whole room. Everyone crept away to their own desks. Then began the susurrus of varied malicious remarks. 'Is a job everything in life?' . . . 'If you don't have any dignity, what can a job give you?' . . . 'Don't we know the boss's character?' . . . 'Here we are, dying of dysentery and cholera, and the firm's owner gives him an air-conditioned car! Drive to work in cool comfort! And don't we know what all he does in his air-conditioned office?' . . . 'He is the owner's henchman. And when women enter the picture . . . what can one say? . . . A woman with a husband has one provider, but if she leaves him she has ten providers.' When the office hours finally drew to a close I dashed out without looking right or left.

I jostled my way into a bus at the Motijheel bus stop. Then came the obscene thrusts of elbows, a tug on the hair—I hung on with my face upturned. This was part of my daily routine, but even after all these days I hadn't got used to it. The gorge rose every time. Vehicles honking all around, the ceaseless human chorus . . . a long way to go. The fountain at the Shahbagh crossroads gave out a hissing sound. As soon as a few passengers got off I hurled myself to occupy a vacated portion of the seat in front. The road stretched on. As we passed Nilkhet I thought of Arefin, whether he had bought the mattress and pillow he

247

needed with his earnings as a private tutor. Travelling so far to work, and earning only 500 taka—how was he managing? Then we were at the Science Laboratory turning. People hurried to get off, others rushed in. It was a drowsy evening. The motion of the bus was putting me to sleep. On and on and then, in this fuzzy state of mind, I had reached Shankar.

Shops crowding all around. Turn right then the mosque. It brought back memories of that dream. A padre asking me, 'Do you believe in God?' And then in my befuddled consciousness rose the recollection that the last time he saw me Omar had promised to come again after a day. A week had passed by. Strange fellow. To hell with him! Then another stretch of road. In a field on the left some boys were flying kites. One boy's pair of shorts, held in place by a loose elastic band, was continuously slipping down. He held it up with the left hand, while the right hand managed the bamboo spool of his kite. I stood and watched for a while. Everything was lightening up. Winter was approaching on soft feet; I could feel the subtle change in the folds of my skin.

The next day, just as I was getting ready to leave after work, Omar barged in. His clothes were shabbier than usual. A dark, oily smudge was conspicuous in a corner of his shirt. He began talking in a very serious tone: 'What a load of work I have had to deal with these past few days. Haven't had time to breathe, you understand? Still, every day I thought about what you might be thinking. It was so many days ago that I had promised to come.'

I said something deliberately insulting: 'Don't worry, I had forgotten about your promise.' His face fell. He pulled up a chair and sat down quietly.

'And how is your younger brother?' I asked.

'No change in his condition,' he said, and immediately was off again on a jabbering spree. 'You think I have had the

248

time to look after him? What with all the time spent on the garments factory, the press, the household . . .'

'Are you working in a garments factory?'

'No, after passing my BA, I have been loafing about for some years now. A week back I ran into a childhood buddy. He is filthy rich. Owns a garments factory. He suggested that I take up a contract to supply his company with the printed stationery they need—things like letterheads, visiting cards, timecards. I would be able to make some money he said. I got down to work the very next day. I took on the job because a printer in Old Dhaka was an old friend.'

'Any sign of profits?'

'It's too early for that. But I made some money when buying the paper. If it hadn't been my friend's company I would have had to lay out the money for the paper from my own pocket. But for friendship's sake he made the concession.'

After work I set off in Omar's company. The sound of crisp banknotes began to play in my brain. Of course it was an utterly ridiculous matter, but I was in the grip of an irrepressible curiosity. So as soon as we were seated on the rickshaw I asked Omar how much he had made on the paper. 'The first time round I didn't get a big order. The bigger the order, the bigger the profit. For instance, if I buy twelve reams of paper and if I can make twenty-five taka on each, it comes to 300 taka. It all depends on how sharp you are. And also on how much your party trusts you. Am I making sense?'

But other thoughts suddenly began playing in my head. This seems to be my innate tendency. When I lie dying I might remember to ask myself if I had bought the groceries. Or, if I won the ten-lakh-taka lottery I might pause to see if I remembered who had bought my first painting. In the same disconnected way I posed Omar a question: 'What are your thoughts about the Gulf War?'

Without batting an eyelid Omar replied disinterestedly, 'If Saddam doesn't vacate Kuwait, another world war is inevitable. And if he does get out no one will ever be able to drive out the Americans. But what the hell! There is a war in remote Iraq and we are getting worked up. What business have we to think about ships? We are minnows, let's think about our little pond.'

'Everyone is born only once, so what's the point of this bloodshed? If another world war does break out, how ridiculous and paltry our calculations over groceries will seem.'

Omar burst out laughing. 'I would consider myself lucky if I died in a world war,' he said. 'It's like the death of an ant in a great deluge. But just think, long before such a grand death, there is a rickety motor-rickshaw headed your way and you may die beneath its wheels. So focus on today. What will you have for lunch? Think about that.'

Omar certainly had a point there. I pondered the matter for a while, then switched very naturally, effortlessly, from the Gulf War to the printing press: 'How long does it take to fulfil a contract?'

Our rickshaw ran bumpily down an old alley. 'You seem to find this sort of work very interesting,' Omar said in reply.

'Listen,' I said frankly, 'my salary is not enough to live on. It occurs to me, and this is a thought prompted by your words, that I could try to do a second job.'

Omar almost leapt with enthusiasm. 'Then join forces with me. The two of us will be able to do things much faster.'

It struck me at this moment that he was very naïve. His own business had no firm foundation, and here he was exulting at the thought of someone to share his income with. It made me laugh. 'I'll go around with you for a couple of days. I need to get acquainted with the world outside the parameters of my office. If I find the situation encouraging I will think about the direction to take.'

'You are more practical than I,' said Omar, suddenly becoming serious.

'More than you, perhaps,' I rejoined, 'but not in comparison with anyone really practical. I am just as practical as one is forced to be under the pressures of life, but no more than that.'

Both of us sat in silence on the rickshaw. He took to biting his nails, and then suddenly said, 'Oh yes, I haven't asked anything about your life. Do you live with your parents?'

The rickshaw entered an alley. There hadn't been any rain, yet it was awash with filthy water from an overflowing drain. The stench was overpowering. One's very life was at risk in this badly damaged thoroughfare. Stale leftovers lay in small heaps. The rickshaw knocked against the walls as it made its way. An uncovered manhole gaped at us. I remembered the colleague who had described the crippled man. If someone fell in at the dead of night, who would know? Would he not rot and mingle with the filthy drain water? This unfortunate accident brought to mind the image of my dead uncle, hanging from the ceiling fan. My blood ran cold. I tried to get a grip on myself.

'I have sublet a room from a family living here. Mother lives in our family home. Father is dead.'

Silence again. At one point I decided to dampen Omar's curiosity by adding, 'In case you want more details, I had got married four or five years back. Two years back it ended in a divorce. Since then I have been working. You might say the responsibility for a whole family rests on my shoulders.'

'I know,' Omar replied casually. 'Your friend in the hospital told me everything.'

'So you've started making inquiries about me! Then why the pretence of not knowing who I live with?'

The rickshaw came to a stop in front of a house made of tin sheets whose paint had peeled off. Before I could put my hand in my bag Omar whipped out his wallet and paid off the rickshaw-wallah. This single action suddenly raised him in my esteem. It was enough for me that a man in dire straits did not wait with his eyes on my purse.

As the rickshaw drove off he turned an unfamiliar glance towards me. In a voice that did not go with his personality he said, 'If a person has many well-wishers it isn't necessary to make inquiries about her. One gets to know just like that. When I went to see your friend in the hospital, there was another person present, whose name I do not remember, but I think he is the owner of a bakery. He seemed to be very keen on literature. Anyway, that's not important. The two of them talked a lot about you, your personality, your divorce, and there was quite an argument. They forgot that a third party was present. I will not analyse the substance of their arguments, but I could gauge they were great well-wishers of yours.'

'Are you trying to be sarcastic?' I retorted. I was really incensed. 'You are guilty of spreading gossip.'

'You think so because you have an inner weakness. I am not condemning them. I haven't said anything to approve of or condemn what they said. Why do you think the substance of their debate was critical of you? I have also asked about you elsewhere. I have got to know you, at least to an extent. I did not want to say all this, but since you accused me I had to defend myself.'

A small anti-government demonstration was making its way through the alley. The dramatic hartals and violent showdowns of a few days back were no more. Gradually the movement was losing momentum. This demonstration was more for the sake of routine than anything else. Utterly pointless.

Omar knocked on the ramshackle tin door. I had to admit he could argue quite cleverly. It had been wrong of me to suppose that he was thick-headed. But his words now caused a strange disturbance within me, making me feel listless, exhausted. I thought of the intimate world around me, the people who showed such affection and sympathy when strolling beside me, but as soon as my back was turned, changed their tune and passed ugly comments on me. It was distressing.

The door opened to reveal a girl standing in the doorway. What a devastated face! A long, scrawny neck, a wrinkled face precariously balanced far above the shoulders, a pair of sunken eyes. A kameez hung loosely. It seemed as if worms were sucking out everything from her body, drop by drop. Fixing me with bewildered eyes, she stepped aside.

On a wickerwork mat spread on the mattress lay the youth I had seen in hospital. The floor was uneven and it was hard to tell if it was made of cement or packed earth. On it squatted the old woman I had met. She was slicing up a pineapple and was dressed in a sari that wasn't even good enough to be used to make a *kantha* quilt. A naked six- or seven-year-old child sat beside her, chewing on pineapple peel. A couple of rusty trunks, a mildewed clothes horse, and a discoloured chair and table were the only items of furniture in the room. The old woman paused to cast an impassive glance at me. I sat down on the bed beside the young man. The stench of sweat was nauseating. It was the same youth I had seen in the dream, carrying my infant child. I felt drawn to him in spite of everything; he elicited from me a strange affection. This young man seemed very close to me. Dreams, I suppose, can inspire such novel feelings. He looked at me dispiritedly then looked away. His expression was one of utter indifference towards the whole world. Now the skinny girl draped in a dupatta fashioned out of a piece of an old sari came forward.

'My sister,' Omar introduced her. The old woman stood up, a world of roughness on her face. She went up to the young man, very close to him. He spoke now, in a broken, uneven voice . . . she pricked her ears to listen. But the voice was very indistinct. At that moment it seemed that he belonged to the land of the dead. How his eyes popped out! This is what I had also seen in my dream. He cast fearful glances to the right and left. He pointed at the door—'There!'

We all looked in that direction. It was getting dark outside. The young man's eyes were opened wide—'There, they are coming!' We looked again. Everything was deathly still. The entire room was in a shadow. The sister came up anxiously. She held out a cup of tea that looked like the wine of a jaundice patient. Something came over me, and I rushed out of there.

Omar followed me. Out on the street I said to him coldly, 'You lied to me.' He didn't say anything. My nerves relaxed. I felt slightly relieved. 'Everything was not a lie—only what I said about my brother wanting to see you.'

'I don't understand why you wanted to take me to your house, and why such a pretence was necessary.'

'I wanted to see how contemptuous you felt towards me when you saw me in the surroundings of my home.'

'Strange! Why did you suddenly become keen on discovering yourself through my eyes? I realize that you are interested in me, but trying to gauge me through such ludicrous tests is downright humiliating.'

Omar walked on with heavy footsteps. I hailed a rickshaw and started bargaining over the fare. The potholes in the street brimmed over with thick mud. I raised the hem of the sari and stood on two bricks lying in the street.

'Will you let me accompany you to your place?' Omar asked.

'You are evading the issue.'

'You know, my sense of pride is terribly undeveloped. Don't you understand that I dragged you along to find out how you would look upon me after having seen me in such a situation? You are feeling awful, aren't you?'

'My situation isn't any better,' I said. 'Having been in such a situation since birth, I am quite fed up with it. It does not mean I hate your poverty. This whole charade was quite pointless.'

When I got on the rickshaw Omar said, 'You haven't told me if I can come along with you.'

'If you get to know my address I will have a problem on my hands. Your character being what it is, you'll come and disturb me every other day.'

Leaping on to the rickshaw and sitting down beside me, he burst into loud laughter. 'Well, you've really come to know me.'

The next day after work I went out with Omar. Once again we entered the narrow lanes of Old Dhaka. I recalled the boat ride. For long I had had no contact with Irfan Chacha. My sudden enthusiasm for painting had also diminished. I needed to get to know the world outside the confines of the office. The office was in such a state that no one knew what the next day would bring. Today the lift wasn't working. We had to drag our feet up the stairs. On entering the office I saw that no one was in their place. A few of the employees had been sacked. Everyone was in a state of high excitement. I advanced on unsteady feet. Through the glass wall of his office the boss's face looked cold and stern. When I entered his cabin, despite the air-conditioned chill, I broke into a sweat. Beneath the glass top of the desk lay many photographs and calling cards. I directed my gaze towards them. He said, 'The office is pleased with you because of your sincerity. You will soon see the result. Just carry on in a disciplined manner. I am taking steps to deal with the present situation effectively.'

Inwardly, I felt quite overwhelmed. It only increased my nervousness. I mumbled my thanks and was about to get up when he said, 'I may need your assistance in a matter—be mentally prepared. Mehjabeen has not been coming to work for three days now. Tomorrow, as you know, we are expecting some important visitors from New York. Dealing with them is not your job, but if Mehjabeen does not come to work tomorrow . . .'

I turned pale. The boss's voice lost its enthusiasm. My throat felt dry. Mehjabeen was the much-talked-about disreputable character among the women employees. She did not even have a desk in the office. She was responsible for all outside PR jobs. How she dressed! And her language—obscenities were always on her lips! One encounter with her still gives me the creeps whenever I remember it. We were the only people in the lift, going down. Suddenly she flicked a cigarette lighter and, swaying drunkenly while fixing me with an irate stare, she nearly set my pigtail alight. As I screamed in panic she blew out the flame and burst into hysterical laughter. And now I would have to fill her shoes! I had harboured the notion that the boss respected me as a person. Something crumbled inside me. He noticed my distraught countenance and said, 'Now look here, there is nothing shameful about receiving a visitor at the airport. For the office to arrange it is a mere courtesy.'

I knew that I had been given an order, and it had to be obeyed. But I had no knowledge of the true nature of such duties. To an outsider such duties might well appear to be demeaning. The employee entrusted with them would be the butt of snide remarks. Out of desperation I said, 'I am not sure why I am needed for the job.' At once I realized that for an employee it was a naïve thing to say. I corrected myself: 'But, very well, sir. I will be ready to go the airport.'

Since then I had been full of misgivings. Omar was going on about his work: how clever he had been at handling the job, how he could maximize profit, how he had taken five or six days to get the hang of the thing, and so on. It was annoying.

My thoughts were about my own job, how it had transformed me into a helpless creature without any strength of character. I knew my limits. Not to mention just an airport visit, if the boss had asked me to accompany him to the seaside for a week's holiday, would I be able to fling a letter of resignation at his face as easily as I imagine? Actually, faced with such a situation, wouldn't I withdraw into myself? Wouldn't thoughts of my family, my life of struggle, my critical existence occupy the centre of my consciousness and lead to such rationalizations—it is only a question of relaxing for a few days by the sea, so what if I go? It is not by a stinking gutter, after all. What extraordinary thoughts. Omar's words did not register at all on my consciousness. I had no inkling how I would cope with the next day's assignment. Suppose I went along and the office authorities were charmed by my smart handling of the situation? Then such experiences would become more and more frequent. I would become known as Mehjabeen's substitute. But what if I proved to be inept? Who knew how important the next day's guests were? What if I floundered and drowned in salt water?

The rickshaw stopped in front of a printing press housed in a small room. Buildings towered above it on both sides. The surroundings were intolerable, what with crowded rickshaws and pushcarts and the stench of refuse and filthy gutters.

Inside, we were in a different world altogether. The tiny room was filled up with machines and workers smeared in ink. The factory owner did not look any different from his employees. He sat in a chair pushed against the wall. A table was before him. Omar was clearly on good terms with the owner, who greeted him warmly. As if to impress me by a show of intimacy he slapped the owner on the back and said, 'I have brought along a guest today.' In reply the man openly expressed his amazement. 'A female guest with you—you have really taken me by surprise.'

Omar was evidently proud of himself. The glance he cast towards me seemed to say, 'Just because I have been following you around does not mean I am like that by nature.'

Inwardly, I have to admit, I was feeling a little pleased that this man whose life was utterly devoid of women should be so keen on pursuing me.

Standing in the press Omar proceeded to lecture me on his new business venture. 'It is in this press that I place orders for printing ledgers, calling cards, timecards, letterheads, etc. Of course, I would have got nowhere if it weren't for Kashem Bhai,' he said, gesturing towards the owner of the establishment. The latter, far from being flattered, kept making his calculations.

Turning to me Omar continued, 'First of all you must familiarize yourself with the press itself. That one over there is a treadle machine,' he said, pointing with a finger. 'There is another machine for offset printing, an automatic machine, and that is a paper-cutting machine.'

I felt a stabbing pain in the left side of my stomach. There was no avoiding a visit to the doctor, it seemed. Who knows if the ulcer had become acute. I felt frantic. 'I will get to know these later,' I said. 'First tell me if I can get jobs for the press.'

'For that you must be on good terms with those running a garments factory, or the owner of an NGO,' Omar sagely commented. 'An artist friend is also a big help. Say, you get a printing job for an NGO. First you need to prepare a design, which is then made into a block or a plate for offset printing. For a block, of course, you need a different machine. Now, where do you get the design? If you have an artist friend he might do it for you for free.'

'Listen,' I said unenthusiastically, 'where do I have the time for all this?'

Omar became subdued. 'Lack of self-confidence will not do,' he said in a serious voice. 'When you start getting contracts you can leave your job. You cannot shine in business unless you take risks.'

The entire space of the press was scattered with torn rags filthy with machine oil and ink. The smell of kerosene was nauseating. The place was suffocating.

Taking leave of the press owner, we stepped out. 'I have no inkling where I may find jobs,' I said, 'and already I am meeting press owners.'

Omar walked silently alongside, then suddenly said, 'You could be a private tutor if you wanted. I myself have two or three students whom I tutor. In fact, for several years now, that has been my chief source of income. Or else, on my father's pathetic salary . . .'

'I have already thought about that,' I said, 'but if I do that after working in the office till five, it will be very late by the time I get home. I am terrified of the city after dark.'

'You have to control that fear,' Omar advised. 'You cannot be independent and give in to fear. In that case I would suggest that you hang on to somebody's shoulders.'

'If I found strong shoulders I would do just that,' I said, laughing. 'That's what I have wanted all my life. But the shoulders I have found have all been slippery, without strong bones inside.'

'Give up the idea of hanging on to someone's shoulders and everything will come out right,' Omar pontificated. 'It is this mindset that's holding back our womenfolk.'

'O my! That puts an end to the argument.'

Evening came swiftly today. A chilly wind started to blow. Once on the main street, I began to breathe deeply.

The next day when I came to work I was relieved of a haunting anxiety. Mehjabeen had reported for duty. What a debate had raged in my soul the previous night! I dreamt that I was flinging a letter of resignation at the boss. I woke up in the middle of the night with a pounding heart. Wasn't I making a mountain of a molehill? It was only a question of receiving a few guests at the airport. The office hadn't asked me to do anything more. If the question of reputation and honour was so sensitive, why work at all? Why would others busy themselves to smoothen the path for me? Even after these thoughts my misgivings did not disappear. It was such agony: surely, I thought, this was the beginning of my slow descent into darkness.

I came to work in the morning with my face all rouged up. And then . . . enter Mehjabeen. Ah, what a relief! For the first time I took her by the hand and made her sit down before me. 'Well,' she said with a wink, 'I hear the boss dangled a bait before you?'

'Is that what he told you?' I asked, feeling cold all over.

'He did not quite put it like that,' Mehjabeen said, as she dabbed around her lips with a handkerchief. 'He said, "If you do not turn up I will have to send Miss Nina Tarafdar." I hear you were feeling very nervous.'

'Why are you calling it a bait?' I asked, fixing her with a wintry look.

'This is how it starts,' she replied. 'Anyway, I am here now.' She scrambled to her feet, spreading a superb perfume all round. It was intoxicating.

'Miss Nina Tarafdar, you will not have to move from the place you are occupying now—isn't that wonderful? Your sari is quite extraordinary, you look lovely in it. Why are you so simple? A touch of make-up makes you look very attractive—hasn't anyone told you that?'

Clicking her high heels Mehjabeen went out of the office.

Then began a new reaction within me. Why should I be glad that Mehjabeen had reported for duty? My appointment letter made no mention of the kind of work the boss had asked me to do. The problem had only found a temporary solution because Mehjabeen had come to work. Otherwise I would have had to do the job myself. I had already suffered all the humiliation I could be made to feel. There was no room for complacency—or was I exaggerating everything?

In the afternoon I took a bus and then a rickshaw to get to Irfan Chacha's. The drawing room was open and he was reclining on a sofa, his eyes closed. A santoor was playing on a cassette. Vapour spiralled up from a cup of tea that had just been left before him. The whole scene was so charming that I quietly walked in and sat cross-legged on the floor beside his feet. The tremulous vapour from the tea and the soft notes of the santoor moved in tandem. Irfan Chacha's calm, saintly expression induced in me an overwhelming feeling that but for this man I had no one in this world to provide me with sheltering shade. Only before him could I lay down my soul, body, bones and flesh. I took his hand in mine and, pressing it to my breast, burst into sobs. As soon as he opened his eyes I controlled myself and got up. I walked straight down the long veranda. In passing, I had glimpsed in his eyes an intolerable indifference. I entered Chachi's room and found her lying down for an untimely rest. Her wavy hair was spread out on the pillow and a maid gently massaged her scalp. On seeing me she sat up, her eyes wide open in surprise.

I pulled up a chair and sat down quietly. There was a glow on Chachi's face, a strange blend of many colours. There was something special about her. Pride was befitting in her. Even the folds of her loosened hair revealed artistry. It was perplexing that Irfan Chacha had failed to touch the depths of her being. What inner strength she must have!

'What's the matter?' she asked. 'Have you had a tiff with your Chacha?' Her voice was easy and natural. All the self-consciousness I had felt about coming to this house was erased in an instant. A little bashfully I said, 'No, today I have come to see you.'

'Do you want to make peace between the two of us in our old age?' Then she added laughingly, 'I have known you to be an intelligent person. Isn't it advisable not to rake up the muck?'

'I haven't come on a peace mission,' I said. 'I've only come for a chat.'

'That is something I am not good at,' she said. 'Indeed, to be absolutely frank, making small talk is positively irritating to me. Your Chacha can do it very well. He must have bored you that day.'

'Which day are you talking about?' Now it was my turn to be astonished. 'The day you went on a boat ride,' she replied. 'He told me that he touched upon every aspect of our lives. How he can go on! How can you bear it?'

I left Chachi abruptly. How strange is human character! Actually, I know nothing about the world. When it comes to matters of experience, I am still in the foetal stage.

Back in the living room, I sat down calmly. Putting down the magazine he was reading, Chacha asked if I had done any new paintings.

Flames were devouring me inside. Everything was taken so lightly by this man. What a complex marital relationship he had described that day. I had saved the memory of that day with the utmost care. But he had come back to give that explanation to his wife. What Irfan Chacha had said did not seem to reflect the real state of their relationship.

'Have you had any fresh thoughts about the Greek myths?' he asked. 'Have you done any new paintings?'

'Let me tell you something,' I said in a mounting rage.

'I admit you are a man of wide experiences. Nor do I deny that as an artist I am a novice. You may understand everything, but an artist, however modest his talent, will resent any attempt to impose a subject on his work. No spontaneous, beautiful picture can be created in this way. Why do you imagine that I will warm to the subjects that interest you?'

He turned pale and listless. A ripple seemed to be playing under the folds of his skin. A vast silence spread all around. In its midst I was all atremble. A stabbing pain beneath my ribs on the left. I pressed my hand on the spot. 'I am sorry,' he said. 'Actually, people learn a little from each other every day, and in this way they become indebted to each other.' I drew a foolscap sheet out of my handbag. It was a female nude drawn with a signature pen, the outcome of doodling in the office. Till a moment ago I had no intention of showing it to him. I spread it out on the table and examined it coolly.

He bent over and silently gazed at the drawing. Then he asked in a mellow voice, 'Has your anger diminished? Can I say something?'

'I am not angry at all,' I said calmly. 'If you take my behaviour so lightly I'll feel more insulted than anything else.'

'Then why aren't you being open about yourself?' he asked. 'Since you came in you've been engaging in a childish game of making yourself impenetrable.'

'That is your game,' I riposted. 'You enjoy cultivating obscurity. But deep inside you are very ordinary. If you had honestly expressed this ordinariness it would have acquired a certain beauty.'

'What are you trying to say?'

'First tell me, am I a child? Or a guinea pig? After gallivanting around all day you come home and report to your wife that you have played a game and it has been an experience of mingled joy and sadness. Are our conversations and our intelligence so crude?'

I looked up at him with tear-filled eyes. The nude fluttered in the breeze from the electric fan. It was getting dark outside. A mild chill was slowly setting in. Irfan Chacha's face reflected a terrible blankness. I had never seen him looking so depressed. He spoke in a broken, hollow voice, 'I am terribly lonely, Nina. When I am with her I have nothing to do besides go over the day's activities. It has no meaning. It has become a habit. Believe me, I do not say anything to belittle anyone.'

I sat quietly for long in a distraught state. I leant forward and, wiping my eyes, asked him to say something about my sketch. Our conversation now flowed along another groove. We talked a lot about the casually drawn portrait. He referred to Venus, who was born on an island off Asia Minor. A vibrant yet serene goddess. Nude, exquisitely lovely, the essence of purity. Such artistic beauty within such vitality and nudity that one felt like touching her. We entered a trance and felt that if only it were possible to touch her, dig into her, it would be the ultimate fulfilment. But there was no way to reach into that beauty. He even showed me a reproduction of that image of Venus. I looked at it intently but decided that I didn't like such smooth perfection in a thing of beauty. I told him that I found the rough surface of Indian sculpture more attractive.

This led to a vociferous debate. Many things were said about art, like war was the chief weapon of art. Nothing on earth could silence an artist. 'The pictorial depiction of living creatures was once banned in Arab society,' he said. 'Have you noticed that the Arabic calligraphy in mosques and posters of that period seem to portray different creatures in an indistinct, suggestive manner? One can make out, say, a bird's wing, a camel's face, a deer's tail.'

At one point the conversation veered off in another direction. Once again we were arguing over my marriage, its break-up and that old rigmarole—while 99 per cent of women in difficult marriages were coming to a compromise with their husbands, why couldn't I, how intolerant I must be, how insulted I must have felt, how radical my stance was, whether I could have waited a bit—my considered opinion on these, whether I had left before my back was really against the wall, etc., etc.

'How do you know you would be in a soup again?' he asked. 'The reverse could happen: you might find things improving. Human beings change. Or else why is he desperate to come back to you?'

'Reason can only be used to make up pretty arguments,' I said. 'The human capability for feeling and apprehending is extraordinary. Do I have to cut my finger to understand the pain of bleeding? Today, because I am beyond my ex-husband's reach, his desire for me is intense. It is in the nature of some to long for what they have thrown away.'

There was an exchange of arguments and counter-arguments over these points. I remember thumping the table in my excitement, even leaping up as I shouted. He was calm and unyielding.

At one point I sat down and lapsed into silence. After a while he went in and came back with an envelope. In a commanding tone he said, 'There is some money here. I have chosen the amount with due consideration of your ability to clear a debt. It is a loan. If you take it amiss I'll be very hurt.'

I froze. 'I did not ask for money, so why are you giving it?' I asked.

'You know, Nina, if you want to keep our relationship formal, I can only feel hurt. But people can never conceal their main problem; it will surface from the depths of the unconscious. Didn't you angrily shout at me about financial distress: If you owed money to others, if you had to shoulder the burden of a family, if you had to live like a fugitive because of a 2000-taka loan ... With these words you drove me into a corner, but you don't remember because you were in a rage. For the time being you can settle your 2000-taka debt; you can settle your debt to me later.'

That brought me to my senses. Could such a fiery argument slip my memory just like that? My financial problems were really acute now. Sometimes at night I would simply munch a biscuit and gulp water and hit the sack. His words brought me face-to-face with my miserable life with all its demeaning penny-pinching. Because of this I was avoiding Ranju and I had stopped visiting Satyajit. It was only the twentieth of the month and I was out of pocket. I had even exhausted the money I had borrowed. Shanu was leaving the next day on a visit to her parents, and she had said it would be nice if I could pay her the outstanding rent. But my crisis was so acute and the anxiety it induced so intense that I felt utterly helpless. I had decided to go home and tell Shanu I did not have any money. She could do what she liked. But the thought sent a chill through my body. I had borrowed a tidy sum from a colleague as well. While vociferously arguing with Irfan Chacha I was also telling myself that I would soon start giving private tuition. Now Irfan Chacha's offer set off within me a strange interplay of shame, embarrassment, delight. There was even a sense of humiliation. I said quietly, 'Wouldn't you let me come out with a spontaneous account of my condition? Do you think I said all that with the intention of getting something out of you?'

His face darkened. Silently, he took the envelope and placed it under a magazine. I was overwhelmed by a sense of extreme uncertainty. Who knew where I would be dragged by my indigence? I felt a twist in my chest. Amber light was scattered around the room. Irfan Chacha was sombre, silent. I tore through the expanse of light and stood up. In a helpless, agonized voice he said, 'I did not want to give the money as largesse.'

Hot sunlight flickered in my breast. Ignoring the baffling complexities, I raised the magazine and picking up the envelope put it in my handbag.

I walked towards the door, a smile hanging from my lips. He too advanced towards the door. 'I am keeping your nude sketch,' he said. 'I had no idea a woman's hand could render a nude so sensitively. Keep painting, Nina. You don't have to win fame. Paint for yourself. I shall say no more.'

'You love me, and so my defects escape your eye.'

I was about to step out into the evening when he asked me to stop. Presently, I entered yet another mysterious realm conjured up by his whimsy. He took me to the old chamber decorated with various objets, as if it were a museum. I was entering the room after many days and I was overwhelmed. I inhaled the old, musty smell, glanced at the curious collection. He opened an almirah and took out a foot-long coloured candle. It was shaped like a snake, with the wick coming out of the mouth. He placed it in a candle stand and lit it.

'I want to read out something quite extraordinary,' he said. 'That's why I'm detaining you. Everything needs the right ambience.'

He began rifling through a pile of books. I was all aflutter inside. The paper rustled as he turned off the electric light and sat down beside me; the trembling within me grew worse. Images of Ranu, Majumdar and the candlelight amidst the darkness—everything kept whirling round and round. The horrid images inscribed in my breast just wouldn't disappear.

But shortly after, I was enveloped in a strange beauty. Opening a Bible, as if he were a padre, Irfan Chacha began reading in a deep, steady voice, 'I will read you a few passages from the

Songs of Solomon. I suddenly felt like reading them out to you. Are you feeling uneasy?'

Overwhelmed, I shook my head. He began—

"'I sleep, but my heart waketh: *it is* the voice of my beloved that knocketh, *saying*, Open to me, my sister, my love, my dove, my undefiled: for my head is filled with dew, *and* my locks with the drops of the night.

"'I have put off my coat; how shall I put it on? I have washed my feet; how shall I defile them?

"'My beloved put in his hand by the hole *of the door*...'"

The candle flame burned steadily. Irfan Chacha's voice was charged with passion; it created a strange music in that play of light and shade. In the furrows of the currents of my blood played a wonderful scent. I gazed at his God-like face. What a lovely scent! It seemed as if he were sitting alone in a city square in ancient Greece, reading to himself.

"'I rose to open to my beloved; and my hands dropped *with* myrrh, and my fingers *with* sweet smelling myrrh, upon the handles of the lock.

"'I opened to my beloved; but my beloved had withdrawn himself, *and* was gone: my soul failed when he spake: I sought him, but I could not find him; I called him, but he gave me no answer.

"'The watchmen that went about the city found me, they smote me, they wounded me...'"

He stopped reading. Silence gathered around us. He shut the volume and looked at me. I was in a daze. I couldn't understand how an old room, a large candle flame and a middle-aged man's calm voice could weave such magic—it spirited away my sordid, miserly life and my troubled past till they were remote from me. I gazed calmly at their nasty images. If only I could immerse myself for a lifetime in surroundings like these! If only it were possible.

'And then?' I asked.

Breaking the trance-like state he turned the pages and said, 'See what Solomon wrote in another passage—

'"We have a little sister, and she hath no breasts: what shall we do for our sister in the day when she shall be spoken for?

'"If she *be* a wall, we will build upon her a palace of silver: and if she *be* a door, we will inclose her with boards of cedar."'

He shut the book.

'Then?' I mumbled.

'That's it,' he said and, quickly controlling himself, seemed to prepare to say something. Flustered, I stood up. 'Please do not say you have been childish,' I said. 'That will destroy the entire dream.' This made him smile in such a way that in my relationship with him I was transformed once again into a child.

He wanted to turn on the lights but I objected. Oddly enough, I remembered a childhood story that used to move me to tears. 'Have you read that fairy tale about a mermaid's unhappy love for a human prince?' I asked him. 'When the prince fell into the sea and was nearly drowned, she nursed him back to health. She then went to a sorceress and even though it was a painful process had her tail cut off so that she could get a pair of human legs. But when she went to the palace she found the prince's wedding in progress. He did not even recognize the mermaid. The sorceress had warned that if she tried to return to the sea after acquiring a human form, she would be reduced to foam. The sea stretched away to the horizon. The prince was sailing with his bride to their honeymoon. The mermaid stood on the edge of the deck and wept copious tears. Finally, she leapt into a huge wave and at once turning into foam, merged into the sea.'

Irfan Chacha sat impassively in his chair. His face was radiant. I went round the whole room. I stood in front of the almirah chock-full of small statuettes. I said, 'Imagine that this is a ship and I am the mermaid. I am bleeding where the tail was amputated and my new human legs were fixed. Let's imagine this is the railing of the ship.' I dragged the huge chair with carvings to the middle of the room. With eyes closed I intoned, '"What a vast expanse of water before me, and such swift currents—O waves, take me back." I sink, turn into foam . . .' I slipped from the chair and sat down on the floor with head lowered. From that position I cast my bewildered eyes towards Irfan Chacha. His glance was as innocent as the sage Rishyasringa's. His look was the look of surprise on Rishyasringa's face when the latter came face-to-face with Tarangini deep in the forest. Then it was all dark. Fog shrouded the path ahead. And a terrible silence suffused the world around. I buried my face in my knees.

Irfan Chacha lifted me to my feet. The lights were on. My face was drenched with tears. What was the matter with me today? Why wasn't Irfan Chacha crushing me to his chest? After a long time I would have cast myself adrift today. I was being burnt to a cinder. Why wasn't he taking me? He only said, 'Let me escort you home.' As usual, his voice was controlled, steady.

As I stepped out of the room a shadow seemed to disappear swiftly. I glanced in its direction and caught a glimpse of hair hanging loose over the shoulders. Irfan Chacha's wife. She seemed to be heading for her room. The inside of my breast gave a lurch. I looked bewildered at Irfan Chacha. He was silently locking up the room. So the lady of the house was eavesdropping! Nothing was said about this after we stepped out into the street. I couldn't make head or tail of it, no matter how hard I tried. Really, his wife was a strange character!

The rickshaw travelled through the dimly lit streets shrouded in light fog. I became immersed once again in the complexities of the day's happenings. He said, 'I used to be like this too. I used to lose myself in some episode or tale. Coming out of Star Cinema I felt I was William Holden or Uttam Kumar. As I walked down the street I used to cast proud glances to the right and left. Never for a moment did I imagine I was separate from the character that the star had played. One day this led to a row with my wife. We were returning from the cinema. It was a film starring Greta Garbo. Imitating a scene from the film I buried my face in her back and whispered, "Oh, Garbo, Garbo . . ." You can guess what happened.'

Strange how age devitalized the mind. Around us lay the silent night. At this moment it struck me that my companion was talking about his days to someone belonging to the succeeding generation. He had aged.

'Didn't you ever remember my mother when you were with Chachi and become all confused?' The question emerged from the grey depths of an anguish harboured in my soul. But as soon as it was uttered I realized that such questions made no sense. The street was sunk in the coppery glow of sodium lights. For a long while neither of us spoke. Then, for the first time, he took my hand in his and, gently pressing it, said, 'Such a thoughtless question ill befits you. You are too mature for this.'

In our alley the surface was uneven and the air always noisome. As we neared my place he said, 'I will take this rickshaw back. I will not come in tonight.'

I got off the rickshaw slowly. A chilly night breeze swirled round. I said with a laugh, 'I have been very childish, perhaps.' As the rickshaw turned around he laughed loudly and replied, 'See, it seems childish to you now—I am not saying anything.'

∿

There was a rude shock waiting for me. A sombre-faced Shanu opened the door. There was Rezaul smoking a bidi. Satyajit was sitting cross-legged on my bed. I felt drained of energy. When I put down my bag and with a perfunctory greeting went in, Shanu said loudly, 'Kick them out. Now, even talking to your ex-husband is sin.'

The introductions were over, then. I went to my room and sat down, surly and erect. No doubt I would soon have to swallow a homily on the lateness of the hour at which I came home. No, Rezaul's expression was mellow. Like someone very close he said, 'You are looking quite tired. Besides, we have been here a long time. I'll be off. I'll come another day.'

'Why are you so formal with Nina?' Satyajit chided him. 'People are strange. You lived together in the same room for so long, and now you are behaving as if you were newly introduced.'

Rezaul got up and started putting on his sandals.

'Been busy all day, trying to make ends meet. I'm fagged out.'

'You go on, I'll have a word with Nina.' At this, Rezaul walked towards the front door.

'Did you plan the whole thing?' I asked angrily. 'Once I come in you take leave and Satyajit stays back. Why the charade?'

Rezaul stopped in his tracks. 'You don't have the ability to see things as they are.'

Satyajit got up. 'I'm also leaving. You have insulted me, Nina.'

'How can you have friends if you are so sensitive?' I burst into laughter. 'You too sit down, Rezaul. I too have to slave to make ends meet, you know.'

Even then Rezaul's voice dripped affection: 'Not today, I am really not feeling well. I'll come another day.' His behaviour did not seem unnatural, though all negotiations regarding our relationship made me very uneasy.

272

As soon as he left, a profound loneliness settled in the room. Rows of breakers before me . . . O Sea, accept me, O Wave, transform me into foam . . . Then completely overwhelming me, after many days, the newborn child cried, making me clasp it to my breast. My young uncle's dead body rotated as it hung from the ceiling fan. I felt helpless.

'Nina, you have been avoiding me after that day's conversation by the lake. May I know why?'

Satyajit's question brought me up from the depths to the surface. I cast a sleepy look at him but said nothing.

'Regarding what was said, you neither agreed nor protested,' continued Satyajit. 'What is my fault here?'

'Have I blamed you? Actually, I am terribly busy. Talking about these things is distasteful to me.'

'Have you thought about Rezaul?' He moved subtly towards the main question.

'Thought about what regarding Rezaul?' I feigned ignorance.

'He wants to get back with you.'

My turn now. I sat back in the chair. Raising my arms I began taking off the rubber bands in my hair as I spoke. 'Am I not supposed to be having some sexual problems? Does he think I have overcome them and turned into a new Nina?'

'Maybe those are no longer important to him. People change, you know.'

'Didn't he say I had certain perversions that living alone had exacerbated?' I continued uttering my words slowly and deliberately: 'I will give him an analysis of that transformation, detail by detail, and if he still wants me back I will accept him.'

'You get riled up very easily,' Satyajit complained. 'Isn't it true you couldn't tolerate him in bed?'

'A man shuts the door behind him, strips in front of me with the light still on, and advances like an ape. Can I respond when

273

he lies down with me? Everything must have a modicum of artistry in it.'

I was again exuding vile miasma. Tears tried to force their way out. It seemed as if the splinter I had removed was again entering my body, piercing my flesh, spleen, liver. Satyajit sat down on my bed, leaning against the wall. I felt uneasy because Shanu was at home. Like any conservative woman, I too felt a twinge deep within as I openly criticized my ex-husband before a close friend. I felt very ordinary. Must one speak about someone with an admixture of hatred and disgust just because they have been divorced? But I was deep into the subject; it wasn't possible to go back on what I had said because I would be contradicting myself.

'The problem lies in you,' said Satyajit. 'If you survey a thousand couples you will find that they consider it normal to strip before each other. After all, their relationship isn't that of young lovers.'

'When there are a thousand women like that why should he want me again? I seek beauty in everything, naked animality is repugnant to me.'

'You used to be suspicious without any reason. If his younger male friends visited him you did not behave cordially with them. Losing a child is sad, but it is not uncommon. After the death of your child you began to ignore him completely. This way you made his life miserable. He too is human—shouldn't you have been sympathetic towards him at a critical moment?'

'Didn't he tell you why I did not behave cordially with his young male friends? Is that also one of my perversions?'

'I know about that as well. He gave that up long ago. You cannot keep harping on the past and make the present intolerable.'

'He did not tell me about that aspect of his past before we

274

got married, so one could say he cheated me. He told me only when I expressed my suspicions. I am willing to admit that 95 per cent of our women pardon past misdemeanours of their husbands. But what if that past destroys my happiness in the present? What makes me obliged to accept that as well? I know it is not uncommon for people to lose newborn babies—for a third person like yourself it is easy to remind me of that. But I gave birth to the baby, and everyone is not equally resilient in the face of bereavement. There I was, distraught, almost half-mad, and within five days of the child's death he became hungry for my body. If I protested angrily he would implore me. This happened almost daily. Sometimes he would try to pounce on me like a beast. Gradually I began to lose all respect for him. In that crisis he gave me no psychological support. Wasn't he the child's father? Shall I deny him the right to mourn? I have told you everyone is not equally resilient. I do not belong to the 95 per cent.'

The tirade exhausted me. In the dim light my trembling body became listless. The flame of the tall candle flared into life before my eyes. What a calm figure, reciting steadily—'my soul failed when he spake' . . . Then the sculpture of Venus rose in my consciousness—such perfect beauty could not be touched. Beauty glowed like a still silver star. I felt like tearing into shreds the animal instincts of mankind. When I came back I found I had brought back nothing save this desire. Beauty remained as it was, steady and radiant.

How much of life would I have known if I hadn't met this man? Then there was another chamber: delicate, lovely Ranu in the grip of a huge monster. The entranced Ranu lay with eyes shut. What a strange and terrible smell! Where was it coming from? *Agarbatti!* Father's dead body lay in bed. Smoke swirled around it. Everything was unclear, hazy.

'He has altered a lot,' Satyajit said, getting off the bed to squat on the floor. 'As we were coming here he told me that in his relationship with you he did not give due importance to decency and beauty. He acknowledges it was a grave error. Nina, are you unwell?'

'Just feeling a little dizzy. It's very late.'

Satyajit walked towards the door. 'I will not try to pressurize you,' he said. 'You could still give the matter some thought. He is terribly lonely.'

An unbearable pain spread itself through my breast. If I lay on my side, from time to time I could breathe properly. One night when I had a severe headache, Rezaul had massaged my forehead for a long time. Memories of that scene put all the dirt in the shade. I was emotionally overwhelmed. That night a tender, loving Rezaul had so passionately taken me into his arms that remembering it in the context of the present squabble brought tears to my eyes. I had only raked the muck of his life. Wasn't I to blame as well for being intolerant? Suddenly I remembered something else. I opened my bag hurriedly and gave some money to Satyajit.

'Give this to Ranju. It is a long time since I borrowed it.'

'He was saying the other day that you had done the right thing. He isn't in very good shape. Ran around for days trying to form a business partnership. Now he is a punctured balloon once again.'

'Tell him to come and see me.' Again I felt tired. I felt like sleeping. When Satyajit left I got down to calculating how much I owed Shanu. She and Kamal Bhai were leaving for her parents' home in the morning. When I had settled the account Shanu turned to me and said, 'You should be cautious about letting these young men visit you. People around us have started gossiping. The landlord came again today to give us a piece of his mind. "Don't I know what the character of a divorcee is like? A woman who has had a taste of male flesh . . ."'

'Please, please, Shanu,' I begged her to stop as I was racked with sobs.

The next few days I was all alone in the house.

∽

The following afternoon Omar turned up at my office in a state of high excitement. 'An excellent private tutor's position has been found for you,' he announced. Then he pulled up a chair, placed it under the ceiling fan and flopped down in it. He undid some of his shirt buttons. His appearance was even more ragged. It was painful to watch. Without waiting for my response he went on: 'So, you will join tomorrow?'

'Why have you grown a Hanuman-style beard?' I couldn't help blurting out. 'Young man, if you aren't more careful . . . Doesn't anyone tell you anything?'

'Sure, why won't they?' He burst into laughter. 'Ha! Ha! You have told me just now. But so what! You know, charcoal is black by nature, nothing can change that.' Then he changed the subject and said casually, 'You will not believe what I saw on the way here. A minibus ran over a young girl, right in front of my eyes. Such a lot of blood!'

'Did she die?'

'Heh! Heh! Such a huge minibus and such a tiny slip of a girl—how can she survive?'

His callous attitude made me suddenly lose my temper. 'What's so funny about someone's death? You are a weirdo.'

'Shall I cry, then?' Omar's attitude did not change. 'Death is no big deal. Today or tomorrow, we all have to enter that furnace. Worrying about it means dying before one's death.'

It was impossible to carry on a conversation about such matters with this guy. Better talk about practical matters.

'Can I have the details of the tutoring job?' I asked. 'Why have you kept quiet about it after simply mentioning it?'

'Kept quiet?—I haven't.'

'Do you realize you talk too much?'

'Is it much too much, enough to grate on the ear?'

'If you don't realize that, at your age no one will be able to make you realize it. How is your business doing?' I asked, swiftly changing the topic.

'So far I have only seen profit. If I had ready cash to invest I would have done much better. My self-confidence has gone up.'

'Yes, money enables one to achieve a lot,' I said. 'See how far you can go without it.'

'Now, let's get back to the tutoring job,' Omar said briskly. 'The only daughter of a wealthy man, a little wayward. The pay is good. A thousand to start with. If you can handle her it will go up. The girl has no interest in studies.'

'How did you get to know them?'

'What's surprising about that? Is there anyone I don't know? From a sweeper to ... Anyway, when it comes to doing something for myself I am lousy. Perhaps it will not be a bad idea if I start a private tutors' agency.'

'And what's that?'

'Take this instance. I've got you a pupil. It helps you out financially. So you give me something. In the same way, anyone else I can fix up with a pupil gives me something, and this way...'

Shit! No point wasting time prattling with him. I held a newspaper open in front of my face. Murder, rape, mugging, extortion rackets! Arms discovered in university hostels. Barua's voice rose above everything: 'Just see what's going on. There are riots in India and the government in this

278

country tries to divert attention from the anti-government movement by hiring goondas to vandalize some temples. What a dirty game!' In order to avoid getting into the intricacies of the matter, I turned back to Omar. 'Will you start your tutors' agency with me?'

'Will you give me something?' he asked solemnly. 'Very well,' he continued, 'in your case, maybe, you could treat me to a Chinese meal. It has been ages since I last had one.'

'And who treated you to that one?'

'Now you are babbling too much,' he said solemnly. 'Tell me if you are going to start today.'

'Today?' I expostulated in surprise. 'You just said tomorrow.'

'Procrastination is the bane of Bengalis,' he pontificated.

That decided it: we set off at once.

Light from chandeliers, rooms with imported furniture. To reach there we had crossed a vast lawn trimmed like a carpet and met a shaggy foreign dog. I stared fascinated at the marble fireplace. In a corner stood a lifelike statue—a full-breasted female nude. The other day I had seen a serpent-shaped candle—its head silently melting when it was lit. Today there was a still more curiously shaped vase: a glass python with mouth opened wide to accommodate numerous narcissi. And what a lovely scent in the air. Freshness! I sat in a state of enchantment in that exquisite living room. Omar was definitely the odd one out in that ambience. He had sunk into a sofa, picking his nose. At one point he said in an irritating voice, 'Bugger has made quite a pile. He has grown fat on bribes.'

'How do you know he has taken bribes?' I hissed at him.

'He was a bureaucrat. Can one build a paradisiacal palace like this on a civil servant's salary?' Omar bared his teeth in laughter. 'Alongside his job he used to do illicit business. You have no idea about what goes on in our society.'

'Look here, I did not come here to listen to these accusations,'

I said coldly and sat in silence. I became very upset by this loony's attempt to shatter my enjoyment of this cool, otherworldly chamber. At this moment this glittering world was the truth. What was the use of listening to the dark episodes in history?

After a while an exquisitely lovely girl came and stood before me. A beautiful tune was playing somewhere. In this gorgeous setting the girl's appearance was a lyrical event. She had a smooth, peaches-and-cream complexion, wonderful silky hair and a lilting gait. I ogled at her with a near-masculine hunger.

Without casting a glance at me the girl busied herself with a huge doll. She leapt into a sofa across the room. I sat uneasily. 'She is probably your pupil,' Omar whispered to me, 'since the gentleman has only one daughter.'

The girl's carelessly worn clothes reflected superior taste. I gazed at her attire, while my heart turned into a desert. Everything in the house had an otherworldly aura. Looking at my attire, I felt like a beggar. A profound sense of inferiority hemmed me in from all sides. I had no idea of the rich melody of English songs. The marble fireplace vibrated to the song being played. The lovely girl seemed to float in the cool, air-conditioned air. She swayed to the music. There was a haughty indifference in her demeanour. After all, the world was beneath her slippers.

What if this music, this song, were playing in my room? What form would it take? With what unease would it play in my stuffy room, with plaster flaking off its walls, a rickety chair, an uncomfortable bed?

Just then an impressive-looking, serious-faced gentleman in a dressing gown entered. At once Omar sprang from his chair and like a humble servant salaamed him with a low bow. I felt even more inferior now.

Gesturing to him to sit down, the gentleman sank into a sofa. Omar bared his teeth in a humble smile. 'Sir, your clerk Kader Ali is a friend of mine. You might have seen me in his company.'

'Yes?' The gentleman wanted him to get on with whatever he had to say.

'I believe you were looking for a private tutor for your daughter,' Omar explained. 'Kader Ali told me.'

'Yes,' said the gentleman calmly. 'Is she the teacher?'

'Yes, sir,' I answered meekly. 'Of course I do not have any experience. This is the first time . . .' I noticed that the girl had slipped out of the room.

The gentleman stood up. 'So far no one has been able to manage her. I am a little frustrated. You can start from tomorrow. See if you can do anything.'

In order to give myself a sense of importance I said, 'But tomorrow is Friday; I will start the day after.'

'That's fine.' The gentleman took a step, then stopped. 'You'll have snacks before you leave.' He left the room with an air of supreme insouciance.

I relaxed but couldn't fathom the whole thing. He hadn't felt the need to conduct even a perfunctory interview. Strange are the ways of the wealthy. 'See!' Omar exulted, 'It's done.'

Back home, I felt my unease quadruple. That palatial home with its trim green lawn and glamorous interiors assailed my thoughts. If only I had been born in that palace! A mere accident of birth had placed me where I was. And I would have only this one life. Not even knocking my head against the wall till it bled would afford me access to the life of that palace. Things that to me were remote as the sky were at their fingertips. I was tormented continually by my stuffy, musty room with its tiny, shut window, its hard bed and above all by the vast, silent night. For the first time the longing for an expensive sari, a pair of smart sandals brought tears to my eyes. The silence of a tomb engulfed the whole house. From a distance came disjointed snatches of old Hindi and Urdu songs. I kept the light on, tossed and turned in bed. My anguish drove me to desperation. What was the point of this life of loneliness and deprivation; this chaste body? My thoughts aroused sensual hankerings. I recalled the landlord's words—a woman who has had a taste of male flesh . . . Naked flesh, ah! No, I hadn't had a proper taste of it. But the desire to have a proper taste of it was there. Why deprive yourself, Nina? Start a relationship with someone tomorrow. Cast yourself adrift . . . To hell with so-called . . . O God! I dug my nails into the hard mattress. The scent of that air freshener was in my nostrils. That music played in my ears—I entered a strange, trance-like state. O Allah, I don't want anything after death: Let there be endless void. All I want is to step into that palace with the haughty indifference of that doll-like girl, pet the shaggy-haired dog on the trimmed lawn, touch that air-conditioned car with blue-tinted glass that was parked outside, drive out in it with the engine roaring. And then?

I don't know. Why are you stabbing me beneath my heart? What have I done to you? I got down on the floor, sat with head lowered, tore to shreds the picture set down beside the easel. At least this was within my power!

I woke late. A lazy weekend morning. Hugging a pillow, I lolled in bed for a while. I was dying for a cup of tea, but felt too lazy to get up and put the kettle on. As for breakfast, I would ask a boy from the basti to get me some dal–puris. At this moment I felt it wasn't so bad after all to not have the responsibility of bringing up a child. The whole day was free, without complications. But one had to be financially solvent to enjoy that freedom. If one had to count every coin one spent, everything was spoilt.

I was about to get up when there was a knock on the door. It was Arefin; it was many days since I had last seen him. He had grown a beard and looked very grown-up. I was delighted at his appearance at such a lonely moment. 'You have become so busy with school-teaching that . . .' My snide remark made Arefin act even more busy. 'Won't stay long,' he said. 'But you could give me a cup of tea.' My spirits dampened somewhat, I went to the bathroom to splash water on my face, then put the kettle on. When I got back to my room I noticed the shredded painting. Why did I get so upset over some silly desire? It made me laugh now. Arefin looked restless. 'What's wrong with you?' I demanded.

'I am thinking of leaving the hostel.'

'Why?'

'Too much of a bother travelling to my school. I have also lined up a few private tutoring assignments.'

'Will you drop out of university?'

'That's what I am thinking; don't like it any more,' he said without hesitation.

'Anything else that's bothering you?' I wanted to know. 'You can be frank with me.'

'Actually, I am in a crisis. I have been involved in a political party for so long; I've given it my labour—both physical and mental. Now I find that our leaders are allying themselves with the corrupt forces against which we've been fighting all along. But even after seeing everything, even after losing my faith and confidence in the leaders I cannot make myself break away. My disciples, those who joined the party because of my influence, will not leave me. Meanwhile, the leaders are threatening me. Don't rock the boat, they say.'

After some minutes of silence I said, 'There are only one or two leaders. Why should a couple of people make you lose faith in the party? Can you identify a few individuals with the party?'

'Is that what you think?' Arefin was surprised. 'Should I go back into the fold? Do you know, the university has become a haven for robbers and thugs? Every day there is violence or even a murder.'

'Why do I have to tell you to go back to the party? I know there can be no party without individual members. But if you believe in an ideal, I see no reason to give it up because of one or two individuals.'

'Our adversaries have become very aggressive and control our hostel. It is risky to stay there.'

'In that case you can leave the hostel. You have only one life, so be cautious.'

There was the hissing sound of the kettle boiling over. I ran to the kitchen, made the tea and brought it to the room. Handing a cup to Arefin I said, 'Kamal Bhai and Shanu have gone to the village. It's terrible being on one's own.'

'When did they leave?'

'Yesterday.'

'You are alone at night as well?'

'What else—have I married again?'

Arefin gulped down the hot tea and stood up. 'Don't misunderstand me, at least,' he said. 'There are so many problems all around. It's today more than ever that I have found it reassuring to talk to you. I'll go to the hostel now to get my stuff. I'll come and stay here at night.'

'Will you?' I was delighted. 'You are a real saviour. We'll chat to our heart's content.'

When he left I had the entire lonely day ahead of me. I had been feeling feverish since dawn. I was unable to breathe because of a stuffy nose. Instead of having breakfast I had a long shower, hoping it would make me feel light. It had the opposite effect. I became sluggish even before it was midday. Still, an imperious desire drove me against my wishes. I cleaned the easel and stood it up. A long sheet of paper came out from under the mattress. The colours on the palette had dried, so I cleaned it up. Putting everything in order, I squeezed paint out of one of the tubes gifted by Irfan Chacha. After rearranging everything I began drawing and painting without any preconception. A weary moon, a maiden just a little above the ground. A sunken body within a paper envelope. The bright index finger seemed to be trying to touch the pale moon. The subject took shape slowly and I was driven to complete the painting somehow, applying layer after layer of paint, and the whole day went by, leaving my limbs aching. And yet, the painting I had conceived did not find its true form. Instead, my brush had dismembered the maiden's body, separating her raised arm from her shoulder. My thoughts were not finding any visual form here. I kept on stubbornly applying paint. My eyesight was stagnant as a puddle. Sweat beaded my forehead. I was trembling from my soles to my throat. I felt like throwing up. It made me double up and squat on the floor.

The door and window were shut. I turned off the light and opened the rickety window. A sliver of pale light brightened up a corner of the canvas. I found it hard to breathe. I don't know why, but suddenly a dark shadow seemed to impose itself on me. I was devoured once again by that white house—like a gigantic swan—that carpet-soft lawn, that swaying girl. Again I was filled with disgust for my own surroundings. Why had I pushed Arefin towards a life of danger—something I never wanted for myself? Was it in the faint hope that he might play a role in bringing about some social change?

Change, my foot! Did I really think before I spoke? I was only matching argument against argument. Would change ever come in this land of opportunists? My head was splitting. My fingers became stiff. My tongue scraped dry lips. At one point I collapsed, almost senseless, in bed. It began to drizzle—

a cold, wintry drizzle. I shut the window and lay sunk in a reddish haze. I was famished. As I lay I could empathize with Salauddin's pathetic condition. The drizzle turned into ceaseless rain. Gathering my strength, I staggered to the kitchen. I dropped a potato into a pot of boiling rice and came back to bed. I felt so helpless I wanted to cry. The day seemed to drag on and on.

Dusk fell eventually. After eating I sat quietly surveying the results of the futile exercise with paint and brush. Just then there was a knock on the door. Rain was still pattering down. I was chilled to the bone. I opened the door with a shaky hand.

Rezaul burst in, drenched from head to foot. Without a word he quickly surveyed the whole house and then stood beside me in an agitated state. 'So they have left?' he muttered.

'You knew that—that's why you came.'

He fixed me with a stare, making me nervous. His eyes looked strange, unfamiliar. 'Why are you trembling?' he asked.

'Fever,' I said.

He placed a hand on my forehead and gave a start. He helped me to the bed and made me lie down. It was getting dark. He took a kantha quilt from under the pillow and draped it over me. His actions were so caring that I was moved. He went to the bathroom to fetch a mug and a bucket of water, then poured the water over my head. It was a long time since I had last surrendered myself like this to someone's ministrations. When he undressed me and sponged my body I could not remember the document that had separated us. After a while I began to feel comfortable. It was followed by racking sobs. Did I know this man? My long period of deprivation and anguish gave way to an outburst of sensuality. I burst out of my shell to bare myself in all my primitive passion beneath the all-encompassing sky. Was it the first real sensual contact in my experience? Where was this emotion concealed all this time? Was it the first time this man had stood under the sky?

As my body thrilled, its warmth could not disentangle the complexities enveloping us. It did not know when its boundless thirst led it to surrender itself. I could clearly see my lifeless body floating in the sea. In front stretched the moon-blanched water and the waves reaching the horizon, while the silent night kept deepening all around . . .

After the rainy spell that night, the cold weather set in rapidly, and a murky shadow fell on my life, making me a victim of absurd ups and downs. An unearthly force seemed to have sucked away all my anger, pain, aversions. Gradually I seemed to be turning into an inert entity. Indifferently completing my tasks in the unwholesome atmosphere in the office I descended into vast, faceless crowds. The street lights came on. Crossing the pretty lawn, on which the master and lady sat in cane chairs, languidly sipping tea, I walked up the steps and into the aristocratic living room. I had so far been unable to act naturally with the girl. She had on her fingertips detailed information about a world very different from mine—the latest videos, romances, gossip over fashionable parties, the personal lives of supermodels, things like that.

My ignorance about these matters had from the outset marked me in her eyes as an ignoramus. Consequently, I had adopted a mask of high seriousness in her presence. Far from winning her over, I couldn't even touch her little finger. Still, I carried on my efforts. Hemmed in by financial problems, I had no alternative. She continuously jabbered in English, like an American. In using English I was like a deflated balloon. In self-defence I progressively emphasized the study of Bengali.

I warned her that she did not exist outside the framework of this country and its language. To make my point I referred to those who had become martyrs for the sake of this language. But these lectures were of no interest to my pupil. Eventually, both of us were fed up.

A massive poster showing a nude couple kissing hung on the wall of the girl's room. From where I sat my eyes fell directly on them. One day I blurted out, 'Doesn't your father ever come here?'

She kept on shaking her leg and lazily turning the pages of her book. She replied with a characteristic shrug.

'Why did both of them have to be nude in order to kiss?'

'You should ask those who produced the poster. Besides, at one stage people have to become nude as they kiss.'

'But why have you kept this in your room?'

'Because I like it.'

'Don't you like to study?'

'No.'

'Then why go to school?'

'It's the fashion, so one has to go.' There was a chewing gum in her mouth. While her jaws worked mechanically she suddenly leapt into bed. Soft satin sheets. Subdued lighting spread over her. She sank into it and shouted, 'I don't like you, you peasant woman. You are not eligible for entry into this house.'

'Cynthia!' It was almost an anguished cry.

'If you scold me I will give you a tight slap.' As I busied myself trying to exercise self-control, she burst into merry laughter.

I have to adopt a different strategy, I thought at once and was amazed at my own patience.

When I got home my brain was resounding with clamorous bells. Rezaul had come sometime before this incident. Arefin was supposed to stay the night, so as soon as I was out of the trance I got rid of Rezaul. I lay inert all night, almost dead from shame and self-disgust. Arefin did not turn up.

Rezaul came again the following day. Without a word about the previous night's happenings, a man like him went to the kitchen to make tea for me. At midday he went out to fetch rice and other things. He even complimented me on my half-finished painting. Finally, when he asked me to decide on his proposal I said I needed a few more days to think about it.

Since then I have been thinking about it. Should I start all over again? The man had undergone a sex-change, but how much of it was genuine? People could always change . . . I took the cue from Irfan Chacha's pronouncement. Involving me in a profound bind, Rezaul left.

The next day he was back again. Had he got the old smell of flesh? I tried to talk naturally with him. But his expression was always distraught, hair dishevelled, eyes bloodshot. Since my defences had crumbled he could take liberties. Taking advantage of my naturalness he leapt on me in bed. Though I felt angry and insulted at first, I couldn't hold myself back after a while. I had married a man who had no finesse in lovemaking; where had he acquired it suddenly? His behaviour was gentle, he was tender. Besides, for days and nights on end I had been a starved woman. I surrendered to his every touch, without a care for caution or conscience. Before leaving, Rezaul fell silent; then in a sad voice he talked about his early years, his failures and his inability to fit in anywhere.

I listened with bowed head, without making comment. He left. Before that he asked, 'Why do you always let your hair hang loose. Can't you do it up neatly?' His words prompted me to analyse him anew. He was still the traditional husband. Had he been a lover he would have liked loose, flowing hair. But what had been his attitude towards my hairstyle in the past? Had I done the right thing in offering myself to him? I was in a quandary. Had I given myself to him? Did I know where and to whom my hungry body had responded, without any reason? I was on the point of forgetting even my own, fundamental anguish through role-playing—with oneself, with others, with my soul, with my adversaries. I did not know myself any longer.

Lazily to work the next day, boring bus journey, then back in my lonely den, as if I were a primitive human, sitting like a spectre. A knock on the door. Rezaul again, carrying a b x of ice cream. 'You used to like it,' he said. My body responded eagerly to his presence; it made me angry at myself. He wante to know my decision—whether I still misunderstood him. How much of his change was convincing? No amount of thought revealed a satisfactory answer. The net result was that I opened myself to him again. Once more he took me in a sensitive manner. Then we had a long conversation. He ran his fingers through my hair. If we had been in a small town there would have been a roaring scandal. Thank God we were in Dhaka. There was no sense of community among the inhabitants. People did not pry into each other's intimate lives. Still, the censorious landlord made me nervous—what if he suddenly turned up? As the night deepened, Rezaul left after declaring he would come again.

What was my decision then? Gradually, I seemed to gain a third eye. I had the impression that his tender touch, his erotic finesse, all this was painfully put-on. He was always wary, lest his original wild nature found expression again. He presented himself before me with great caution—and cunning. Because of that, our lovemaking lacked spontaneity. In the throes of excitement the realization escaped me: he was the same man, no matter how smooth his manner. Then why did I respond so eagerly? Abandoning myself to him I had discovered one truth—he was forbidden, hence the attraction.

The couple in the next room came back from their holiday. The night was shrouded in mist. My tremulous body sank beneath the blanket while my brain was an arena for commotion. Who did I want to go to? Didn't that mean I was becoming tired of bearing my own burden? Why did I spread myself beneath him night after night? On those nights didn't I impose someone's shadow on someone else? Whose shadow, on whom? Did I even know that? Did I just want to spread myself— whoever the available man? Is that the real truth? Who knows? In the shadowy room I could only hear my sighs. I felt as if someone was pressing downward on my chest.

～

Irfan Chacha gradually turned into a sad and sombre personage. He shrank before the winter chill. Age began to take its toll. He had a bad cough. Surreptitiously, he wiped his nose on a handkerchief. He wrapped himself in a huge shawl and sat in silence. He waited eagerly for me to speak.

The urge to speak seemed to have steadily diminished in him. I came home, racked by misgivings, and stretched myself in bed. Meanwhile, my eyes had started giving me trouble. They were always tired. If I started reading, the print soon became hazy. My head ached dully. My chest pain had aggravated considerably. Should I see a doctor? The professionals charged such large fees! Then there would be urine, blood and a thousand other tests. One day I felt so helpless that I told Omar about my condition. 'Don't worry,' he replied, 'we'll take you to the hospital tomorrow.'

'I know I cannot afford the fees the doctors charge from private patients, but what's the point of going to a government hospital? Will it provide any treatment? It is a waste of time.'

'For beggars like us, whatever we get is good enough.'

It hurt my pride to place myself among beggars. But pride wouldn't fill my belly. I had to survive somehow.

The next morning I went to the office and took the day off to go strap-hanging on the bus with Omar. Getting off at the Azimpur crossroads, we walked through the crowds to save the rickshaw fare. Omar seemed to skim like a dragonfly as he walked. Once he stopped to ask in a show of politeness, 'Shall we take a rickshaw?' 'No,' I replied laughing, 'it's quite pleasant to walk.' Near the Shaheed Minar I remembered Arefin. He had said once that seeing the monument always quickened his blood. He thought of the language movement of 1952. He was regretful that he hadn't been a young man back then—he would have plunged into the movement. As for me, except for 21 February, the anniversary of the day of martyrdom, when a tidal surge of people washed around it, the monument standing by itself had no emotional impact.

Often I have analysed myself to determine whether I am self-centred. I am not terribly excited over political jiggery-pokery, revolution, anomie, the independence war or democracy. On the other hand, Arefin would burst into tears of rage and helplessness when he talked of the corruption endemic to the country. He was still largely innocent, uncorrupted. The wickedness in student politics had not infected him. Yet in me, his sister, there was no sign of political awareness. Had I got stuck in the rut of the struggle for survival, the struggle to obtain the basic necessities? I felt the prick of my conscience. My thoughts led me to ask Omar which political party he supported. 'Too busy trying to feed myself,' Omar said flatly. 'Never thought about which one I might like.'

'Still—even a little?'

'No, none of them. Every bugger is only interested in getting into power. As soon as they get it they are all the same—only interested in grabbing whatever they can . . . Anyway, that's too much of a lecture. We are desperately trying to make ends meet. At times we don't even know if we are alive or dead . . . Ah, here's the Outdoor Patients' department. Wait here, I'll go and see where they are issuing tickets to patients.'

I walked along with Omar. The whole place was crowded with patients, mostly people from the villages. An unbearable stench pervaded the place. There was filth everywhere. If a hospital was so dirty, would the patients survive? At a table next to a bench a clerk was bent over, scribbling away.

'Name?'

'Nina Tarafdar.'

'Age?'

'Thirty.'

'Ailment?'

I became confused, 'Eye strain. No, no, gastritis.'

Omar sagely remarked, 'One doctor will not treat all your ailments.'

He reached forward and volunteered the necessary information: 'Gastritis.' And turning to me: 'The eye doctor hasn't come in today.'

Someone who had been groaning stopped momentarily to give me a stare. When we got to the right place there was another queue. Omar inveigled me on to a bench already harbouring a number of impoverished patients.

'You sit here. I'll keep your place in the queue.'

Sputum, urine, paan juice, the smell of Dettol, the damp odour from somebody's sari, sweat, ogling eyes, loud chorus of voices, patients leaning against walls, sound of breaking glass—all these were driving me to distraction. I noticed that Omar in his easy-going manner had moved to the head of the queue where he was sharing a bidi with the *darwan* and indulging in a merry chit-chat. That meant he had won over the man. He finished the bidi and scurried over to me with an urgent exhortation, '*Arre!* Come on,' and in a split second he had hustled me through the door despite a chorus of protests from the other patients in the queue.

I found myself in an odd situation. The doctor was brusquely dismissing a rustic youth. 'Ear diseases are not treated here. Go to the ENT department. Really!' At my sudden advent the doctor looked at my ticket and asked, 'What's the problem?'

He was bald. A face like that of the poet Jibanananda Das. His eyes widened—perhaps decently dressed patients rarely ever came here. I have always been particular about dressing well when going on a journey or paying a visit to the doctor. I pulled up a chair and began describing my symptoms. When and how the pain attacked me, its intensity, etc. The doctor listened with a serious face and then asked me about my personal particulars. Since the interview was being prolonged unnecessarily I became anxious thinking of all the people still waiting in the queue. At last the doctor informed me that the hospital was not the place where one could get proper treatment. All the pathological tests had to be done elsewhere, anyway. If I went to his private chamber in the evening he would be able to deal with my problems. Since he had the face of a great poet, one couldn't protest against what he said. I left in an irritable mood.

The upshot was that my ailment remained untreated. The pain in my stomach became a regular phenomenon and in time even began to subside. Life went on in its old rhythm. I would rush to Irfan Chacha's house and as usual chatter about my experiences: my childhood and adolescence, the man who stole a sudden embrace when he found me alone (he prevented me from even squealing, but when a cat leapt noisily he nervously let go and I ran). There were other memories from this time, like the folk song we sang in a circle around a girl who was being given away in an arranged marriage, in order to cheer her up.

Irfan Chacha just gazed at me, an enchanted listener. It made me a more enthusiastic prattler. I talked about the walk to the flour mill with Ranu, Ajay's kiss at the puja, my first period ... I didn't feel any embarrassment. Then came the affair with the artist: I grew depressed as I went on. 'Everywhere I have suffered defeat,' I said in melancholy tones. At one point I mentioned Omar. Hearing a detailed account of his personality, Irfan Chacha became interested. 'Bring him along one day,' he said.

'Really? As if I had nothing better to do!' I said, laughing. 'Then he'll cling to you and get on your nerves.'

But a time would come when these subjects became tiresome. Then Nina would pad about the rooms, in the grip of a strange fascination. There was no way she could bring herself to talk about Rezaul's sudden advent that night. Regarding this matter she was constrained by a hundred sensitivities. She couldn't feel at ease about it. Restlessly perambulating the rooms she again came face-to-face with the gentleman. 'I say, you look very distressed,' she said to him.

He found it very amusing. 'I see you are getting bolder,' he said, laughing. 'I can't be all that formal and respectful,' she replied archly, and took another turn round the room. Nina hummed a tune. She recited nonsensically: 'Insect walking in blood, on flesh, in arteries, the sun shines on darkness, or there's load-shedding in the sun ... What all am I saying? ...' Nina sat on the floor ... There was a bed in the middle and they were playing in a circle around it. The girl was laughing heartily, and at one point she suddenly caught him. Rezaul hadn't ever physically assaulted Nina, but now over this incident he was banging her head on the wall. He held her by a tuft of hair. Could it be called physical assault—or manhandling of the hair—or head-bashing? Or what? . . . The child had forgotten its tears and was looking at Nina. Its gums were being pierced by milk teeth. It was growing bigger in her arms. Nina gradually withdrew into herself.

I dragged her out through the smoke and stood her straight, facing me. There were only Nina and me, taking up the whole room. I gazed steadily at her. At one point, disentangling the knots, Irfan Chacha stood up straight. 'Are you all right?' he inquired. I opened my eyes wide. A silent observer was gazing at me. I walked slowly to the sofa and sat down. His breath was making a slight sound because of his cold. A long time passed. He did not say anything more. I stood up again, leafed through magazines, paced up and down. For a while I talked about my crackpot of a pupil, Cynthia. I said I might give up the tutor's job.

'Will you admit defeat?' In his characteristic way he was giving me encouragement. 'You accepted the responsibility knowing full well what it meant.' His words gave me renewed inspiration. That's why coming here was such a calming experience.

Once he brought up the subject of death. He said he had a recurring dream in which he was frogmarched through a vast field by Death. Or he saw a black shadow shoving him from behind amidst a violent whirlwind, and then his body floated lifeless in a torrent. Or else someone would confine him in a dark chamber and with a long pair of forceps attack his eyes—he suffered gruesome wounds. Or else . . . it was fatiguing to listen to all this. The sunlight cast murky shadows on the veranda. Once, with his eyes closed, he said in a slow, weary voice, 'At one time I committed the folly of attempting fiction. I remember one of the stories.'

I pulled up a cane stool and sat facing him. 'Let's hear it.'

'There was a sannyasi,' he began. His hair was awry, his head bent low. 'I don't remember everything, but I'll try. The sannyasi was walking alone in the dark. He had a long way to go. After some time he came upon a lonely cottage. Peering in he saw an exquisitely beautiful maiden singing with a *tanpura*. Her eyes were moist. This isn't my road, thought the sannyasi, withdrawing quickly. The maiden, hearing a noise, came out and caught a glimpse of the retreating sannyasi. In the gathering shades of evening his shadow was disappearing in the distance. Why, she exclaimed, it is he, the man I have been longing for. She ran after him, calling him to stop. Her voice battled against contrary winds and reached his ears. He stopped when he heard her, but soon resumed, for he was a liberated being. He had to carry on to reach his own world.

'A vast field. Both of them ran through it. Eventually both were overcome by weariness. They stood face-to-face and the woman said she would go with him. Where do you want to go, and why? the sannyasi asked her. This is the path I have to take, she replied, this is what I have been waiting for. The sannyasi tried hard to dissuade her, while the lonely night listened with a bowed head, but to no avail. Drenched in moonlight the two of them advanced side by side. In front of them lay the sea. Wait here, the sannyasi told her, I will visit the other shore and come back to you. The sea was roaring. The maiden said, what if you come back and find that I have merged into the foam of the sea? Casting on her a cool glance he said, then so be it.'

As he reached the end Irfan Chacha seemed to doze off on the sofa in a semi-reclining posture. Soon he slid into profound slumber. He had become increasingly prone to lassitude.

I was restless when I got back to my room. Why did he tell me the story? Who was the real-life figure behind the character of the sannyasi? What was he hinting at? I grew tense. The next day I went back to Irfan Chacha's.

'Who is this sannyasi?'

'You are a woman of the turn of the twentieth century,' he commented, 'and you want to know who is the sannyasi? It is a story, pure fiction.'

'Why did you narrate it to me?'

'Very well, I will not do it again.'

'Still, you must tell me . . .'

He shook his head solemnly. 'At times I am the sannyasi, at times it is you. We two cannot be confined by anything.'

Still, the tangled confusion did not unravel. I pursued other preoccupations. Things at home were dismal. Arefin sent small amounts of money, but lately it had become impossible for me to do anything. I was sweating in a futile effort to bring my debts down to zero. Montu had grown into a goonda. Arefin gave this depressing account when he came to explain why he couldn't come that night. He told me Ranu had become a decrepit woman. She was doing a typing and shorthand course somewhere. The rest of the day she would simply lie flat on her face in bed. Mother could only shed tears. One of these days a letter from Ranu led me to the verge of death. She did not write anything about herself; indeed, it could hardly be called a letter. It was as if she were mumbling—

Apa, let me tell you about something. Father is supposed to have become so enraged at Montu's birth that he tied up the three of us (brother and sisters) in the graveyard. She said it was all in a fit of rage brought on by our poverty. He did not want any more children. He also wouldn't dare to thwart God's design and hence prevented his wife from practising birth control.

Ranu

Could one call it a letter? Still, why was my breast so desolate? The ethereal air of the silent, haunted graveyard shut all the doors to anybody. I held my breath till I was in danger of collapsing. These were not matters I could talk about with everyone. Noticing my condition, Shanu advised me to go to my ancestral village. I don't know what came over me but I replied I did not want to see any more cremation grounds. These subjects, far removed from the sensory realm, wore me down, made me slothful. Sobs heaved up. What did they want—that I should commit suicide?

My relationship with Cynthia, too, had altered radically. We talked of everything under the sun—except textbooks. The rise of Aamir Khan, descriptions of Kimi Katkar's characteristic poses. I asked one day, 'How do you like Amitabh Bachchan?'

'A bit too old,' she said and went on to tell me about a crucial chapter in a recently read thriller.

One day she made me sit on her bed and showed me her huge make-up box. Hairspray, blush-on, eye shadow—while I buried myself in these treasures, she tried in vain to discipline my long hair with the help of her hair drier. Irritated, she said finally, 'Why don't you get your hair trimmed—this is awful.'

'Will I look good in short hair?'

'Of course. I don't understand how you can stay calm with so much trouble on your head!'

Amidst such exchanges I slipped in a trivial query. 'Who loves you more?'

'Haven't had time to figure that out,' she said, turning up her tongue. 'But my parents lead a charming life. Parties, drinks, dances . . . Run, run, run—life is so fast. But I haven't even turned seventeen. I don't have the right to enjoy anything.'

There were lots of papers in Cynthia's room, mostly weeklies. They were stashed in a corner, gathering dust. 'Do you read them?'

'Hell, no! They aren't fit for human consumption. Utterly boring and monotonous—who's dead, who's stolen what, where diarrhoea has broken out . . . Rubbish!'

Cynthia twirled round and round as she spoke. An old song was on her lips . . . *I love you more than I can say.* Suddenly she asked excitedly, 'Have you seen Madonna's latest show? Wow, so sexy!'

Without waiting for my response she hurried over to whisper in my ear: 'Do you know, at a party the other day Chinnah Uncle put his hand inside Mother's blouse. And Father was fixated on Mrs Ali. Mother has such heavy breasts—she used them to give Chinnah Chacha a powerful shove. How he laughed as he struggled to regain his balance! Isn't Mother wicked? I saw it all through a window.'

My head was all hot, my arteries throbbed. What could I tell this girl? Were they inhabitants of this country? In an attempt to get a grip on myself I spread the papers on the bed and read the disjointed headlines—'BAGHDAD: HUNDREDS DEAD IN SHELTERS'; 'TREMENDOUS BATTLE BEGINS'; 'INNUMERABLE CASUALTIES CLAIMED'; 'AMERICAN INTELLIGENCE BUSY TRACKING SADDAM'S SECRET LAIR'; 'ANTI-GOVERNMENT MOVEMENT GAINS GROUND'; 'SHAHNAZ FROM KHULNA FAILS TO SET EYES ON DHAKA'; 'HARTAL ON 19TH AND 20TH'; 'IRAQ REPULSES ATTACKS'; 'EXTORTIONISTS BLIND RECALCITRANT SHOPKEEPER'.

My drowsy eyes focused on Cynthia as I asked, 'Since you don't enjoy your studies, have you decided what you will do with your future?'

'Future?' It was as if I had opened a wonderful door for her. 'Like Father and Mother, it'll be London today, Paris tomorrow . . .' She laughed heartily. 'My mother is only high-school educated, but has that been an obstacle? Besides, whether it's today or tomorrow, I'll leave this country—what a horrid country it is. If you step out there is urine and shit at every turn—it's really hopeless. I'll settle abroad.'

Faced with her attitude, the naked child crying on the first page of a paper under the headline 'DROUGHT' was nothing but pure pornography. Cynthia laughed uproariously. 'Father thinks I'm an idiot and sends me these papers. His mentality is really weird. Forget those and get your makeover done.'

Acting on her words, she handed me her loose shalwar-kameez outfits. Once again I was on her level, albeit a little sceptical: 'Will these take me back to your age?' I asked as I tried them on.

'You should bleach regularly—at least once a month.'

'What's that?' I asked like a simpleton.

'You don't even know that! Where do you live, I wonder. You can find out the details if you go to a beauty parlour. It looks like flour, it's liquid, and very sharp. If you put it on your face you'll feel your skin is burning. You have to wear it for fifteen–twenty minutes. If you do it regularly you can stay young for a long time.'

'If you wear a mask like that won't you look like a ghost?'

'Come on!' She laughed out. 'There's a strange beauty in your face, but there's a dark shadow on it. You'll get good results from herbal facials as well. How strange—why don't you use any make-up other than a little kohl?'

'Why, I use lipstick—very lightly of course.'

When my 'punishment' was completed I stood before the mirror: someone I had never seen before. I looked at myself from head to foot. I had been metamorphosed into a strange European girl. I went nearer. Such profound unease; my existence had evolved too rapidly. Dress is a strange thing. I had broken out of one mode of being; now I was a different person. Was it grotesque? I stepped closer to the mirror. A dark hint of a shadow beneath the eyes. Hair done up. Gradually I began to see myself in a different light: This is Nina. She has two ears, two eyes, hair, nose, lips. Two arms and two legs, and a mouth as well. It's a human being.

'You've changed a lot, Teacher . . .' Her words brought me back to earth.

'Do you like me?' I asked her.

'Very much,' said Cynthia enthusiastically. 'You are very innocent. Sorry, I didn't know you earlier.' She slowly leant towards me. 'Teacher, I'm lonely.'

The days went by like this, with an all-embracing shadow in my breast. As far as possible I came to a compromise with myself over the long, lonely nights. And then I was faced with an inescapable fact about which I wasn't the least prepared. The suddenness of it was devastating. Amidst anxiety and spine-tingling sensations I became aware of the presence of a child in my womb.

I was bewildered by the abruptness of it all. There had never been any anxiety over the few sexual encounters in each month of conjugal life. There had been months together, especially before the birth of the child, when we had taken no precautions. I could never have dreamt that when I didn't have the slightest anxiety or apprehension I would be faced with a complication like this. My blood froze at the thought of having to deal with it. I tried to make calculations, work out the dates of the encounters and correlate them with my menstrual cycle to determine the degree of risk involved. Who knows, the uncontrollable retching, the days after the due date, the dizziness might all be false signals. One could not be certain without a proper test. But such thoughts would hardly steady the heart's pendulum.

I passed distraught, sleepless nights. I could clearly see the world before my eyes undergoing rapid change. Would my generally problem-free life of monotony and boredom suffer an eclipse? I stared impassively at the mellow light gathering outside.

My days passed like this. Nights of unending anguish, when I chastised my folly. The twentieth century was coming to an end, and here I was, no better than a peasant woman, letting myself go without any protection. What had possessed me? For some days now I couldn't sleep at all. I would doze a little and then be wide awake again. My heart would begin to flutter. Once I swallowed two sleeping pills. And in the drugged state that followed I was haunted by that scene: Father had taken the three of us to the silent graveyard and made us lie down there. All because of one unwanted birth. Why did I not remember it? We were born in close succession, I know, but how old was I then?

Even under the blanket it was terribly cold. I tossed it away and silently opened the door. The sound of crying came from the far end of the basti. It was a muffled groan that kept rising in volume. I stood on the veranda. The smoke-filled northern breeze touched my soul. Pale moonlight dribbled through a gap above. It seemed to be drenched in thick fog. The mellow light falling on this street-lamp-less area gave it a mysterious, melancholy look.

My heart fluttered. One cat chased by another almost trampled my feet as they rushed by. Then there was nothing. Only the irrepressible sobbing from the basti held me in its grip for a long time.

I gulped some water and went back to bed. The blanket was cold and at its touch my skin trembled. Suddenly I heard groans near my nose, as it were. I sat up hurriedly. They came from near the window; I got goosebumps. But the next moment came the sound of two cats wrestling. I lay down quietly, but the battle cries of the two cats kept me awake the rest of the night. Early in the morning the news came that Kallur Ma had died in childbirth during the night.

~

After work I went out with Omar. He had shaved—his face looked smooth and shiny. But his clothes were the same as before. One day I had ticked him off over his unsightly beard, and now he had got rid of it. I would have to tell him about his clothes and sandals separately. What a royal ass! He had grown even skinnier. He said his 'printing business' wasn't going very well. He had persuaded somebody to invest 5000 taka, and now he was unable to pay back even the capital. An incongruity in Omar's appearance suddenly struck me now. His face looks middle-aged, but from the waist down he is a young boy. His trousers too are queer. They flap about when he walks. On examination everything about him looks atrocious.

I thought I should tell Omar about the impending rapprochement with Rezaul. I started the conversation in a roundabout way.

'You haven't told me about your brother—how is he doing?'

'Oh, yes, of course—he has gone mad.'

'What? When?'

'It's been a month or so.'

'But we have met since then, and you haven't told me about it.'

'What if I had—would that have cured him?'

'Don't talk like an idiot. Where is he now?'

'He is at home—tied up.' Omar burst into hysterical laughter. 'If you only saw how he jigs about in that trussed-up state.'

'Please get off this rickshaw at once.'

'Listen, if I go with you I'll be able to save the rickshaw fare. I have to go there—the gentleman has assured me a job.'

'Have you taken him to a doctor?'

'We took him to the government hospital. They referred him to the Pabna Mental Hospital.'

'Why aren't you taking him there?'

'No point wasting time on this subject. He has gone mad and at one point he will get well too. There is no sense in others going mad worrying about his case.'

'But why aren't you taking him to Pabna?'

'For the simple reason that we cannot afford to put him in a paid ward. You have seen for yourself what kind of free treatment is available in hospitals.'

Omar became solemn. 'Not that I am not trying to improve my situation. I have been tirelessly lobbying Cynthia's father—something is bound to turn up. Now tell me about yourself.'

After what he had said I lost the urge to tell him anything about myself.

We were both silent as we entered the palatial house. Omar sank into a sofa in the living room. I went up the massive staircase and along the wide veranda, where I came face-to-face with Cynthia's distinguished-looking father. I paused nervously. He took off his glasses and after taking a look at me asked a question that took the wind out of my sails.

'You are still carrying on?'

What did he think? 'Yes, sir,' I answered, feeling rather hurt. I was about to walk past when he said, 'If necessary, don't hesitate to ask for an advance.' My sense of pride made me say, 'Thanks, it will not be necessary.'

I found Cynthia happily puffing on a cigarette and dressed in a diaphanous nightie, admiring herself in the mirror. In my annoyance I asked bluntly, 'Tell me straight whether you want to study under me.'

'No,' she said causally.

'Shall I give up this job, then?'

'That's up to you.' She started humming a tune and tapping with a foot to keep time. I went up to her and affectionately placed a hand on her head.

'Cynthia, try to understand, this is not the way to live.'

'Please get out,' she commanded coldly, without raising her voice.

Now it was my turn to work out a compromise. In due course, as the night descended, I came down the massive staircase. I was startled to find Omar still waiting in the living room. I went up to him and asked, 'You are still here? What's the matter?'

'I sent a message twice,' he replied. 'The shaheb sent word that he was too busy and asked me to leave.'

'And you didn't?'

'What else can I do? I need a job badly.'

As we went out, crossing the broad lawn, I asked tartly, 'Will you get a job if you demean yourself like this?'

'Then how will I get it?' he asked innocently. 'I will lobby the gentleman day after day. Why did he give me the assurance of a job when I met him in his office the other day?'

'Assurance of what job—of polishing shoes?'

'You seem to be getting angry,' Omar meekly pointed out. 'Isn't polishing shoes a job—why are you showing contempt for it?'

'Enough of your lectures. Then why did you bother to acquire an education?'

'Astonishing! If I don't get a job where I can use my education will I fold my arms and sit tight? Will you feed me?'

The road stretched away before us. Buses did not stop here, so every day I had to spend a little extra on rickshaws. For two months now I had earned a bonus from the office by doing some simple designs for advertisements. My only remaining debt was the money I owed Irfan Chacha. But that was enough to worry me at times. For a long time neither of us said anything as the rickshaw pedalled along the badly lit streets. Omar was sombre. Suddenly he blurted out, 'Do you know, I went mad once.'

'Do you consider yourself normal at present?'

'No, no, I am quite all right now.' And he launched into his story with gusto. 'My father was a petty clerk, and he used to evade responsibility by simply staying away from home as long as possible. He would come home late at night and straightaway go to sleep. Once the whole family was without food all day. When evening came I grew desperate. I was then sixteen or seventeen. I went out and made an inept attempt at picking a pocket. You can imagine what happened. I got a taste of mob violence. I had to stay in hospital for a few days. After that I went mad. Both my brother and I went mad as a reaction to physical violence. Ha! Ha! Ha! Isn't it amusing?'

I felt hollow inside. 'You are laughing! Is it something to laugh about?' I was almost imploring him to stop.

'What else is it? If you hear what I did after becoming mad you will laugh too.' Omar's laughter continued unabated. 'My mother says I once gobbled up my own shit. Ha! Ha! Ha!'

'Stop!' I almost screamed. With all this behind him, how could the man lead such an apparently untroubled life? Sobs heaved up from my breast. Amazingly, there was a profound similarity between Omar's family and mine. It was painful to think about it. The chilly wind penetrated my soul. I wrapped the shawl tightly around myself. The air was murky with mist and smoke.

'I don't know why I've told you all my secrets today,' Omar said. 'Towards the end of last month my sister had an abortion. She had got entangled with someone. Now she is in such poor health, it's painful to look at her. Are you annoyed to hear all this?'

After Omar took his leave I was overwhelmed with thoughts of so many similar tragedies. Kallur Ma had suffered the same fate, even though the circumstances were different. Two or three days before her death that bastard of a husband had kicked her in the belly, but even then ... For the first time I began to worry about Omar. He appeared to me now as being simple and straightforward, as well as mysterious. Then there was the matter of his sister's abortion, which he talked about with complete frankness. It tormented me, hurled me into an abyss, brought me face-to-face with a harsh truth. It made me worried and nervous, for the same seed had been fertilized within me. Was that the reason I had given in to Rezaul? Wasn't that the reason why I felt that the ground beneath my feet was giving way? But where had Rezaul vanished after that day?

One day Arefin turned up bearing a sari as a gift. I was overwhelmed. 'Bought with my own earnings,' he said shyly. I held the sari to my face to inhale its fresh smell and burst into tears. 'What's the matter? Why are you looking so sad?' Arefin looked disturbed. I came out of my daze and told him about Ranu's letter. Arefin laughed and said he didn't remember the incident either. But Ranu had exaggerated—Father did not rope us together. Arefin had heard about it from Uncle; it was something silly Father had done in a fit of rage. Strange that everyone knew about it but not I, though I was the eldest of the children. 'Why are you taking the incident so seriously,' Arefin asked, a little annoyed, 'after going through so many struggles in life? Strange!'

'You don't understand, Arefin. No matter how angry he was, how could our father take us to a deserted graveyard and keep three children there all night, in the company of corpses? I don't want to live any more. What dreams keep Mother alive still?'

'Calm yourself, Apa,' Arefin said soothingly. 'What's gone is gone. Besides, who said we were there all night?'

After Arefin left a shadow appeared on the veranda. I was about to enter my room but stopped short. I leant over to take a look. It was Kallu, sitting in the dark like a ghost. I felt a sudden tug on my heartstrings. I put a hand on his back and called him softly ... Kallu ... and pulled him to his feet. He had grown considerably since I last saw him. His features were obscured by the darkness, but his sobs could be heard clearly. His eyes were swollen from prolonged crying. I led him into my room. His anguished face looked terribly pale. As usual, the sight of him made Shanu livid. Puckering her forehead into a thousand creases, she disappeared into her room.

'Hungry?' I asked Kallu.

He wiped his nose with the back of his hand and nodded. His torn shorts hung loose, his body was bare, his expression piteous. I was overwhelmed with sympathy. I left him sitting on my bed and was going to the kitchen when the silence was shattered by a loud cry ... Kallu! O Kallu!! ... And the boy stood up with electric speed. 'Bajan?' he answered and ran towards the door. Quickly, I fished out a ten-taka note from my handbag and gave it to him: 'Buy something to eat.'

When the door was opened he seemed to disappear in an instant. I stood transfixed. Almost at once Shanu emerged. She had been preparing for this. 'Why did you let him into your room?' she demanded.

'The boy's mother has died,' I said. 'There is such a thing as sympathy.'

'If you want to make a fuss over such things do it elsewhere. I know you do it to insult me, but I will not tolerate it in my house.'

'I did not take him into your house,' I said. 'Please do not squabble with me, I am not staying here for free.'

I knew Shanu wasn't one to swallow such a retort. She kicked up a royal rumpus, accompanied by tears. She said I had the habit of striking at her weak points. Today I was bringing up the matter of sharing the house and the expenses. Not any longer; she said she'd talk to Kamal Bhai about it. I sat in silence. How selfish these people could be in order to conceal their own weaknesses. After dinner I was all alone in my room. In the next room Shanu and Kamal Bhai were talking in a low voice. Impossible! But what alternative was there? For a single woman to live alone in this sprawling metropolis was a trying experience—who knew this better than me? Still, at times we got into a tiff because it wasn't possible to maintain constant self-control.

My head had felt heavy all day. Suddenly, as the night deepened, I began feeling nauseous. I was doing a urine test out of fear. The confirmation of pregnancy would shake me to the roots of my being. Better to live with anxiety and uncertainty. But the nausea made my chest feel hollow. For this reason alone I would have to think about Rezaul. There was no alternative available. I was painfully helpless.

What a terrible danger I had slipped into! My days were going by smoothly. What was the point in getting entangled in such complications? But I should first know for sure how I felt about Rezaul . . . Ugh! I ran into the bathroom and threw up violently.

The next day the landlord came and straightaway announced his intention to raise the rent. I told him bluntly that he had no right to do so in the middle of the year. Then began a debate over rights and privileges. When he became enraged, I adopted a mild approach. Rather like a supplicant I told him about our economic hardship. He too mentioned the rising prices. Shanu came in suddenly and created a hitch in the discussion. She took a characteristically hard line: 'We will not pay a paisa more, let's see what you can do.' The landlord too adopted an aggressive stance. He went out to spit paan juice and came back to declare loudly that we would have to vacate the house by next month. Or else he would put the local goondas on to us. Then came that old infuriating subject— what had we turned the house into, with all sorts of people coming to visit. After all, there was such a thing as the prestige of a place. The strangest thing was that in the face of these snide accusations Shanu sang a different tune today. 'Please address such complaints to the relevant person. I will not tolerate any blanket accusations.'

'You have to understand,' I said calmly, 'I work in an office. People I get to know professionally may come to visit me. There are not many who do. You must have heard exaggerated rumours. There can be long arguments over the issue.'

In the end he announced that from the following month we would have to pay at least another 200 taka. That meant an additional 100 taka out of my pocket. Shanu went in grumbling: 'Won't he put up the rent? It is an added tax. Someone will play hostess and I'll have to pay the price. Don't I know why the suggestion of marriage is so unwelcome? A divorcee is like a cow let loose; once it gets a taste of the greenery outside, will it . . . ?'

Deliberately, I ignored such comments. Without retorting I sat with my head buried between my knees. Facing the appearance of a child in my life the landlord's pugnacious form began to explode in indecent abuse. I felt nervous, fearful. Then Majumdar's face appeared. Fragments of his head flew about. The entire room was spattered with his brain. He fixed me with a bloodshot stare and the next moment began advancing upon me with the head of a boar. These animals used to wallow in the mud in the sweepers' colony: what a foul odour! There was a sweeper's daughter called Chandana who used to ferment rice to produce an alcoholic drink. While passing by one could catch a glimpse of respectable young men entering Chandana's hovel. In childhood we would get to observe this whenever we went to spend the night in our younger uncle's house. The sound of qawwalis would keep me awake all night. Sometimes the heavy rattle of trains would make me sit up nervously. I would look out the window and notice men swaying drunkenly and mouthing obscenities as they came out of Chandana's place. She used to deck up with care. Seeing her made me want to be a young woman. She would have ribbons of many shades in her hair. Her laughter rang at all times. Only once did I see her cry. When her favourite pig was run over by a train she flew like an arrow and collapsed on the rails. She beat her chest in mourning. Perhaps her bereavement was no less than that of one who had lost a child. So much love was present in the breast of one who was so light-headed! I was amazed. What if she had seen Uncle's hanging corpse?

Time flowed on through many circles like these. Gradually, a violent current of water flowed through the depths of my chest. I buried my head in a pillow. The pillow steadily became wet. There were deep shadows all around. How intolerable the morning, noon and night! I went through the days like this and one day Rezaul turned up.

Was it the same Rezaul, though, the one I knew even a few weeks back? His Adam's apple was jutting out. His eyes were sunken, and his clothes were spattered with dark spots. His hair hadn't seen a comb. He sat down in the chair in a crumpled heap. He gazed at me distractedly; it brought my heart to a standstill. What a profoundly weary figure! The light threw my giant shadow on the wall. I hid my inner turmoil by gazing at my shadow. Should I give him the news? He too was eager to say something. Would he welcome any news regarding me? Yet that is how it was supposed to be. Whatever the reason, I had been waiting for him, and his pale visage made me depressed. But in this Rezaul I could clearly identify the Rezaul of my married years. It was as if he had taken off the new attire he had recently wrapped around his entire being. No, I could not imagine his intimate company even if the alternative was death. Oh, the stabbing pain beneath the ribs! Should I go to a doctor's private chamber after all?

'Do you have some money?'

'How much?'

'Say, 500,' he said, clearly embarrassed. As I opened my handbag he said in deliberate, mellow tones, 'For some time now I am without a job. I was one of the victims of retrenchment. I have been lobbying a company all these days, to no avail.'

In the pale yellow light my limp hand steadily searched the bag. The faint noise of dewdrops registered on my subconscious. Putting on a cardigan, I emerged through the smokescreen of narrow-mindedness.

'I am thinking of going to live in the country,' he said. 'I'll see if I can do anything in a mofussil town.'

For some reason I experienced a sense of decline. I was standing at the limits of tolerance. I thought I was a fallen angel. What had I learned so far? How far had I prepared myself? I surfaced from deep down. When I offered him the money he muttered a question, 'Have you reached a decision?'

I burst into laughter.

'What's the matter? Why are you laughing?'

'You keep the money—you need not be formal.'

'Am I being formal?'

'Ah, Rezaul,' I mildly chided him and sat down on the bed. Some time passed. At one point he got up to leave.

His steps were light. He smiled shyly. I went up to the door.

In order to hide his weaknesses he drew himself up straight. He stepped into the vast, dark world.

~

I kept floating like a kite whose string had snapped. Though in dire straits, after many days I strongly felt that I was free. Rezaul's net had long kept me thoroughly entangled. I did not enjoy autonomy in anything—distressing squabbles lasting all day, problems created by indecisiveness, and finally my wish to get back with him as a result of the steady growth of an embryo in my womb. Now it was my turn to face the void and take decisions absolutely on my own. Should I destroy the embryo?

While watching the mind-deadening dance videos in Cynthia's palace, taking in the office gossip or walking the lonely wintry streets, within me there was only the tidal rise and fall of a single question: What should I do now?

My lonely, heart-piercing, tremulous nights were infused with a single thought: Should I kill the embryo? When I said yes, I was harried by an opposed awareness: the sad fate of my first-born. Its cry resounded again all around me. I was tormented by this question: Did I want to be the assassin of my second child? I couldn't stand straight and steady.

Besides, even amidst the strange conflict experienced while waiting for Rezaul there grew within me the realization of the birth of a tremendous source of strength—a wellspring of warm affection. It was unasked for, sudden. It was only natural that the suddenness of this realization left me benumbed for some days. The natural means to obtain relief from the torment into which I had been suddenly plunged would be to promptly and suddenly uproot the embryo. But my mind was then working

314

out a means to restore my social standing, and in this Rezaul was a key factor. Consequently, the ground beneath my feet did not shift at once. But while waiting for Rezaul I overcame the shock of the sudden appearance of the embryo. Many moments went by, many hours, days, months. I could no longer call it an embryo. I gradually felt that it was acquiring a definite shape; the shock that had prompted the thought of destroying it had been absorbed.

Let's say a beggar woman steals an expensive piece of jewellery and is caught. It is discovered that she had been starving for three days. She did not even know the value of what she stole and only wanted to sell it for money to buy food. The lady whose jewellery had been stolen waited for a decision from her husband, who had gone to another district on business. After the beggar had been detained for seven days the husband returned and decided that her punishment should be a sound thrashing. Would the owner of the jewellery be able to deliver that thrashing with the rage that she had felt seven days back? Where did my independence and autonomy want to take me?

Besides, the being who had appeared in my blood, so to speak, had not sneaked in like a burglar. I had cleared the path for its advent. O Allah! How strangely the world swayed. The floor was awash with vomit. Shanu came running from the next room. Her startled eyes engulfed me from all sides. I took hold of her and stood up. I washed and came back to bed.

The following day, in the grey light of the evening, I made my way to Satyajit's bakery. Ranju and Salauddin were there, engaged in a tumultuous adda. On seeing me they shouted in unison: 'Some friend you are!' Their friend Shahtab, whom I was meeting after many days, was more formal: 'How is life with you?' They were extremely cordial. I joined them happily. Satyajit had extended the bakery. It was very spacious now. Obviously, his business was thriving. I pulled up a stool and sat down.

The whole world was being dealt with in the adda: Gorbachev's welcome rise; how the Nobel Prize was being rigged these days; Maradona's tearful exit; Madonna was really rocking—was Juhi Chawla any less? But Tagore's songs undoubtedly possessed an extra dimension. Chittagong University had been held hostage for twenty-four hours by the Islami Shibir cadres. The anti-government agitation had run out of steam; calling hartals for several consecutive days was only harming the economy.

The topic shifted to Iraq. Satyajit cried out that Bush had destroyed the entire stockpile of Iraq's chemical weapons. Clearly, he did not approve. 'Serves Saddam right,' Shahtab countered. 'Why do you have to occupy a neighbouring country? Saddam has no right to jeopardize the lives of millions of ordinary people. Now look at the outcome: over sixty miles along the Gulf, oil tanks are ablaze.'

'Our government has also sent troops,' said Satyajit. 'What's the news about them?'

'They are a handful,' replied Shahtab. 'Think of the Bangladeshis trapped in Kuwait. No food, no rest . . . A cousin of mine is stuck there. My aunt—his mother—has become half-crazed. She has set up camp at the airport and we can't persuade her to go home. There are innumerable people who have suffered a similar fate. Whatever you say, Saddam has done a terrible thing.'

But Satyajit would not accept this. 'You are lickspittles of the Americans,' he charged. 'How will you understand that it isn't wilfulness on Saddam's part, but a protest against American hegemony? He has guts, that man. He has even captured some outposts in Saudi territory.'

Satyajit kept shouting in Saddam's support. The result was a huge rumpus, shouts, screamed arguments. It was impossible for me to penetrate the massive wall of noise and articulate even a modest opinion. I sat in silence, wrapped up in my own thoughts. Our murderous father was dragging us to the graveyard and laying us out. The next moment there was another scene: we were eating rice to our heart's content and he was watching through tears of joy. That was replaced by an image of Father on his deathbed. Then there were the censorious harridans. I stood before them with a bulging belly.

'Bitch! Adulteress! Disgusting!' They showered me with gobs of spit. Then came Rezaul . . . Infatuated with Mahim, did I not deceive Rezaul? I had married him merely to solve a personal crisis. There was no love when we set up home. Every day I imposed the fantasy form of Mahim on Rezaul—was it any less than his homoerotic attachments?

And now?—Now both Mahim and Rezaul were dissolved in the vortex of a vast shadowy force. As for me, I was thinking of accepting responsibility for the one in my womb in order to set my life in order—was it sensible? Where would I find a place for myself? After he had proved everything false why had Mother's old lover now appeared before me as the embodiment of a noble truth? Why couldn't I walk alone? To what fresh depths would life's complications now lead me?

Rows of jars of biscuits, Pepsi, Mirinda, chocolates, coconut sweets, plastic flowers, cakes, pastries, dolls, hot patties—it was like a medley of songs in varied languages, Bengali, English, Hindi . . . and a chaos of varied scents. It was like being caught in a whirlpool. After a while Salauddin's easy-going nature seemed to be the most congenial. Changing the topic from war he said, 'I have started writing poems. Do you want to hear?'

Satyajit screamed at him. 'The presence of a woman always triggers the spontaneous overflow of poetry in the bugger. What a trick to get their attention!'

Cowed down, Salauddin complained: 'You have reduced Nina to a woman pure and simple. Yet at our addas all of you used to declare she was a friend, first and foremost.'

Now Ranju began to shout, 'Of course she is a woman! Are you claiming she's a man? Why don't you live with her and see who becomes pregnant?'

Unbearable! I scurried away. Was this the reach of their intellects? Far in the distance a brilliantly lit window cast shadows all around. The more I advanced, the deeper the shadows spread. I could hear the nerve-tingling music of moving water and sniff the suffocating odour of a decomposing body. Frantically, I tried to move away. Then a sudden gust of wind propelled me on to the road.

The pavement was well lighted. I took a deep breath—clean, wintry air. A crow flapped its wings on a Krishnachura tree. Mechanical monsters ran up and down the road. The wind penetrated my cardigan to wake up the pores with its ticklish touch.

Satyajit came up and stood beside me. A tobacco-brown complexion in the glow of sodium lights. We walked side by side. 'We didn't think you would be so sensitive. Ranju's joke . . .'

'Please, let's forget that,' I stopped him. We walked on in silence.

At his appearance my restlessness diminished considerably. I got a grip on myself. After a while I broached the big question hypothetically. 'Satyajit, I'll ask you to suggest a solution to a problem faced by someone—but on the condition that you don't ask prying questions.'

Satyajit did not say anything; kept on walking silently. I began without waiting for a reply. 'Suppose an unmarried girl suddenly becomes pregnant. But the man involved is far away. What should she do?'

'What do you mean, far away?' Satyajit demanded. 'Has he deceived her and made off?'

'Let's say, yes, roughly speaking.'

'How old is the foetus?'

'Say, two and a half months.'

'Then have an abortion,' Satyajit promptly replied. 'How can a twentieth-century woman like you ask questions like a royal ass?'

It was cold. We were walking on a lazy stretch of grey pavement. All around was a screen of amber fog. A sharp wind sprang up.

'Are you the girl?'

'You are prying.'

'I did not say yes to any conditions.'

'Can a divorcee be called unmarried?'

'Worrying about somebody else's mess? Whoever it is, the wise thing to do is to terminate the pregnancy. That's the only solution in my opinion.'

The conversation could not branch out after that. Satyajit left, carrying certain obvious suspicions with him. I could tell from his body language. The long winter night stretched before me. And the agony of lying awake. My heart quivered. The smell of rotting discards of fish. Sometimes I just lay like a stagnant pool. Sometimes a huge shadow confronted me and read poetry out of the Bible in the light of a tall candle. I listened with a bowed head. This is how my melancholy nights went by.

The following day I traversed a narrow alley and, somehow evading the terrible stench of the drain, reached Omar's house. The house looked even more decrepit today. The smell of urine pervaded the whole house. His mother's sari was worse than rags. On seeing me she became flustered and hurried inside. Fixing the knot of his lungi, a bare-bodied Omar came into the outer room. He just came, it seemed, without giving any thought to his appearance. I felt uneasy. But worse—hurtful, indeed—was Omar's behaviour. He laughed as if he had known about my impending arrival. 'So you have come at last.'

'Were you expecting me?'

'No, I had thought you would not come again.'

'Please put on a shirt and trousers,' I said. 'We'll go out.'

The legs of the cot on which I had to sit were so shaky that a well-built man sitting down would invariably suffer a bone-breaking fall. But where was his younger brother? His sister was peeping through a grey curtain. Omar went in without saying anything. I made use of the time to take a good look at the sister. Skinny, with the appearance of a wrinkled old woman. It seemed that neither a breeze nor a ray of sunlight had ever entered the room. The girl's eyes showed complete indifference. Now my eyes travelled upward to the false ceiling of bamboo, which was totally hidden by sooty cobwebs. An army of red ants was lustily transporting a dead cockroach.

The girl approached nervously. Her eyes were so frank and trusting that it was quite obvious she wouldn't be able to say no if a youth were to proposition her.

'Where is your younger brother?' I asked.

'An uncle of ours has taken him to Pabna,' she replied and self-consciously rearranged her short dupatta. But if she covered one side properly the other was bared.

So they had an uncle who would volunteer to take the boy to Pabna. But the air in this house was so foul that it was impossible to stay long. The moment Omar emerged, we left.

As soon as we were on the street I asked, 'Who did the abortion on your sister?'

'Mother.'

'Did you want it too?'

'You have to understand, the boy had done a bunk. We had no choice.'

It was a brilliant Friday morning. I walked the sun-toasted street with heavy feet and then, instead of finding a quiet place where we could sit and I could bring it up, I blurted out my sad secret right there, amidst the congested traffic. 'Listen,' I said, 'I am pregnant.'

Omar darted a keen glance at my eyes. 'A couple of months back my husband came . . . you understand, don't you . . . and from that . . . but what shall I do now? I can't decide.'

A shadow settled on Omar's face. The huge metropolis lay benumbed in crisp sunlight. Waves of strange sounds played around us. We ducked into a roadside tea-stall and sat on either side of a corner table. I put my bag down and looked him in the eye.

'Don't you want to go back to your husband?'

'That is my intention.'

The table between us was black with grime. A brisk adda was on at the other tables. The warm scent of tea mingled with the mild winter air—and the arrhythmic tinkle of teacups and saucers.

'What shall I say?' Omar began. 'But I have one suggestion— get married. This is really quite horrid. If you don't you will have to pay a heavy price.'

'Why aren't you suggesting I destroy the foetus?'

'That's a delicate question,' he replied. 'I don't understand these things very well. I cannot explain the nature of my respect for you. I feel an affection for your unborn child as well . . . No, I cannot think of the child's death. One should consider oneself fortunate to be the child's father.'

'But the primary question is, who would knowingly accept the responsibility? And if someone did do so, he wouldn't be the child's father, so the question of being lucky does not arise.'

Our dal–puri and tea arrived. The vapour spiralled up from the teacups. For the first time, Omar seemed to be very steady and stable.

'If someone does not knowingly come forward, someone else will do so unknowingly,' Omar said matter-of-factly. 'In that case you will no doubt raise the question of deceit. I do not understand these things very well. Perhaps because I grew up in the sordid environment of a basti, my brain is very dull when it comes to dealing with sin and virtue and deceit. If one can perform a great deed only by getting involved in what society regards as sin, so be it—I don't see anything wrong in it. Anyone can engender offspring—even cats and dogs do—but bringing them up is the true mark of a father, in my simple understanding of the matter. Besides, I still do not know what exactly is sin.'

Omar started laughing again. 'Let me tell you a tale. It is probably written by somebody famous; you may know the writer's name, but I'm not one to remember such things. The tale has no connection with the theme of the present discussion, though. I am narrating it simply because it left a profound impression on me. A girl said to her lover, "What proof is there that you love me deeply? If you can bring me a red rose within seven days, I will know for sure that your love is pure, unexampled." The lover went in search of a red rose, even though it was not the season for red roses in that land. The lover looked frantically, but in vain. On the seventh day he sat crying under a banyan tree. Just then a nightingale was pouring forth its song from a treetop. It was bursting with sympathy for the hapless lover, and it begged the rose plant to produce a red rose: "Can't you hear the desperate cry of a lover? You can produce at least one flower for him."

"'Very well," replied the rose bush, "I will produce a rose, but where will I find its red colour?"

"'I will provide the red colour," replied the nightingale and impaled its breast on the rose thorns. Blood oozed out and dribbled into the rose plant. Thanks to the nightingale's blood, a bright red rose blossomed at first light. In the morning the nightingale was dead.

'At the end of the week the crazed, despairing lover was beside himself with joy when he found a small red rose on the rose bush in front of his house and rushed with it to his beloved. Do you know what the girl said when she saw the flower?'

Omar cast an inquiring glance at me. There was a subtle commotion deep in my consciousness. I sipped my tea.

'The girl said to her lover, "You call *this* a *rose*?"'

Omar started laughing uproariously. 'No doubt you are thinking that the moral of the tale is: There is no true love in this world. That's what I also thought at first.'

Does one laugh after telling such a story? I felt like crying. If I went down on my knees with all I had before that calm man, saying, here's my pain and shame and joy, now take me, and if he flung me into the sewer as he had flung my mother, saying 'You call *this* a *Nina*?'

Omar lit a bidi and shouted, 'Why do I smoke a bidi? Because it gives me first-class satisfaction.'

'Why don't you stick to one brand? . . . Omar, is this what love is?'

The scent of tobacco. Vapour from tea and bidi smoke produced a fog around us. Omar laughed again. 'You have only seen the beloved's callousness, then? If this is the whole of love, why did the nightingale sacrifice its blood?'

I held Omar's hand. 'Why are you giving me this interpretation?'

Omar became subdued. 'I am a silly fool; what do I know about interpretations? Compared to the nightingale's sacrifice the complications in your life are trivial. Open your eyes, Nina, try to understand yourself. You have grown up in bright light, you have been able to develop yourself mentally. I have grown up amidst urine and excrement. What can I tell you? But I can repeat what I have already said: If you cannot survive alone, marry someone, or go back to your husband. You may not realize it now but you will soon—how vulnerable is your freedom.'

My anxiety had reached a peak by now. I somehow managed to mumble: 'Let life take me where it will, but I will not go back to him.'

Omar seemed vexed. 'Then marry someone—whosoever you wish.'

Omar sipped his tea. I stared at him through the haze of the vapour. Did he know what he had said, even if playfully?

I pressed my lips to the warm cup. My heart was strangely agitated. With his tousled hair Omar shook everything off in a moment and returned to his original position. 'What a load of serious patter. Please shake it out of your head. Let's gallivant around today. You have your tutoring of course, but give it a break. Do you have money on you?'

I sipped the dregs and put the cup down. My smoke-filled eyes looked into Omar's. 'But who will I marry just like that? Is there a man waiting at the street corner?'

Omar became mellow. He gave me a bewildered look and in an uncharacteristically sober voice said, 'Please do not ask me such a question. I do not want to exceed the limits of my audacity. That will be too much to ask of me.'

What should I do? Back in my room, my heart burned.

Didn't I know what would be the outcome of the crisis I had fallen into? Huge pincers would try to grip my throat from all sides and try to suffocate me. My existence would be ripped up and hung up in the void—how would I find a way out of this? Shall I murder the growing embryo? But when I place a hand on the stomach, a strange affection wells up, soft waves exert a profound fascination over me.

What did I actually want? Where did my entire being want to surrender itself? Didn't I know Omar's wishes? Didn't I know where he had grown, and how much—this man of the gutter? But my entire being wanted to stand in the shadow of the man who had grown to a lofty stature through all these days of my burgeoning dreams. I knew now that apart from him there was no other truth before me. But if I stood before him in this state, what would he say? My breathing was brought to a stop by anxiety and turmoil. The retching threatened to start again. My entire body trembled. All around was gentle sunlight. I hadn't felt like gallivanting with Omar. I couldn't steady myself anywhere these days. I held my mouth and sat bent forward in bed. Just then Shanu came in and sent me deeper into the abyss with her words. 'We will live here only the next month, and the month after that we will move out of here.'

I looked at her through blurred eyes. She was happy. 'We are moving to a bigger, better house. Your Kamal Bhai's business is showing an upturn. If you wish you can move in with us there. Of course, it will cost more.'

Ugh! I threw up on the floor. Shanu quickly gripped me. 'I have had my suspicions for some days. Tell me honestly, what's the matter?'

Something was heaving up. Bitter liquid again rushed out and splashed on to the floor. Everything turned dark. My chest was burning. I felt hollow inside. Shanu kept shaking me. 'Don't keep it suppressed. I am not a stranger, tell me what has happened.'

'Nothing,' I said, and collapsed on the bed.

I hadn't been to my pupil's for two consecutive days. I had barely managed to get through the office hours. After giving 500 taka to Rezaul I was out of pocket. One consolation was that the office was quiet. There was a chance I would get a raise next month. The boss had given his assurance. But I was not in the frame of mind to enjoy these developments. Flies seemed to buzz in the folds of the brain. The days were lazy.

One afternoon on a holiday I set out for my tutoring job. It was still bright and sunny. The sunlit road took me to the large gate. I found Cynthia dozing. I suspected she had acquired a drug addiction. Coming to this house gave me an added source of anguish. What I was doing was akin to chasing an unbridled horse.

I was about to cross the lawn back when I heard laughter and turned to look. Cynthia was awake and she was playing on the lawn with her white, shaggy dog.

I stood still. There were high boundary walls on all sides. It was a strange scene on the neatly groomed lawn. Could this girl have sunk to such depths? Bright sunlight fell on her face. A fair-faced girl floating in hearty laughter playing with a white dog—could there be a lovelier scene in the world?

I stood and watched, fascinated. Cynthia threw a ball which the dog returned with a stroke of its muzzle, and then Cynthia would dive and roll in the grass to retrieve the ball. Her trimmed hair spread over her perspiring face. Again she threw the ball, and the dog ran after it. Catching it finally the dog was coming back with it in its mouth. Without any reason Cynthia laughed uproariously and rolled in the grass.

Now Cynthia put the ball away in her pocket and shoved the dog to the ground. I approached slowly over the green

carpet of grass. The girl did not notice me at all. She leapt on
the dog, then hugging it ʰᵉ kᵒ laughing. Cynthia's ceaseless
laughter rang iⁿ ⁺ˡ   ʳast lawn.
    But ᵧ   ʸnthia's face turning red?
                                ᵃs running her fair fingers
                                ʳaces. Cynthia's eyes were
                                ᵢs. She was turning the
ˌ   ˡ sometimes hugging it
tᵢ

                                ldn't believe my eyes.
'Cy   an unnatural voice.
But   ɑnd disgust rapidly
brouₗ
    I rₐ   home.

At office t   itedly. 'I hear
you are geₗ
    'Oh no, tₗ   nd that too
is not confir.
    'Everyone iₗ   ₋ₐₙₐ said. 'They have stopped
up the chinks ₍   ₋ₜₕₒusand demands with a single finger.'
    I did not know about the general pay raise, but I was glad
to hear it. There wouldn't be any snide remarks about mine.
The misunderstanding over Mehjabeen and the boss had
also become inconsequential. It was quite possible they really
had a problem at that time. Right now, there was a massive
accommodation problem facing me. Last night I told Shanu
the truth. She was anxious, abusive. Finally, she cried because
she hadn't conceived. She begged me to have an abortion.
I had committed a sin, whose punishment in Islamic law
was horrendous. Then there was the question of social

condemnation to think of. She left nothing out. What was most painful was that her respect for me came down to zero. There was contempt in her eyes as she chattered away.

Mother sent me a brief letter. Every line was filled with lamentation because of my indifference towards my family. I must send some money as soon as I got my salary. But I had acquired a new problem. Perhaps because of the risks involved, Shanu withdrew the offer to share her new house. I bent over my files. My heart gave a start as a vast, green lawn emerged. That girl, tender as a flower, an innocent dog. What a horrible experience that was. Then, following my confession to Shanu, her frightful monologue—and after I went to bed came image after ugly image. But where was the ugliness located? In the girl? But was she of an age to be branded guilty? The scene had filled me with torment. I decided to give up the tutor's job. That would solve one problem. But with the passing days my life became more and more hazardous. What to do about that? How would I face my neighbours? Anxious thoughts were poisoning my blood. My clothes had a thousand tears. How many could I conceal with safety pins?

'Office hours have been extended by thirty minutes in the morning,' reported Sultana. 'Now we have to be in at eight, understand? It is a trick: give a little raise, and get it back another way. What can one say in response?'

Last night I took out the photo frame that Irfan Chacha had given for Mother. My shaking hands touched its very being. An innocent face, like that of a girl wrapped in gilt. I examined the face minutely. The woman in the picture was my rival, and looking at her brought up venom in my heart—this too I saw clearly. But there was no way I could connect that woman with the old woman of today. The night deepened. I realized what a profound influence had been exerted on my life by that man—his youth as well as his mature and middle years—who had induced stability in me. But had I really become stable? Didn't immersion in the secret waters of stability mean being swayed by deeper, stronger currents?

I had a headache since morning. Come lunchtime, I took the rest of the day off. For much of the way I stood impassively in the crowded bus. Then there was some distance to cover by rickshaw. Standing at Irfan Chacha's door I felt the same excitement as on the first visit. Such intense doubt and unease! Today there was a flame just beneath my fingers. It was the supreme test of my life. Needless to say, my pulse raced. I knocked on the door.

The gentleman had no job to attend to. His chief source of income was rent from his property. As a result he usually spent the whole day at home. In the past he would go out in the evening and come home late, after a long adda. Now that too had become a rarity. He greeted me with his usual cheerfulness. 'Arre, it is Nina Tarafdar. Do come in!'

I overcame my self-consciousness and relaxed. 'How do you spend the whole day—don't you get fed up?'

'People work all their lives in order to sit quietly in old age,' he said laughing. I said to myself: Everyone has a ready reason to justify their way of life.

'Have I come at an inconvenient time?'

'Didn't you go to work?'

'Took the afternoon off—I was feeling awful.'

'You have done the right thing. I am not feeling well either.'

Then a stretch of silence. I made myself comfortable on a sofa. It was early afternoon, yet he had his pullover on and a scarf around his throat. His face was splotchy and had darkened in places. 'Are you ill?' I asked.

'Yes, I feel feverish. Besides, my son has written saying he has a tumour in the stomach and is going to have an operation. It has made me anxious.'

I had almost forgotten that the gentleman had a son. Of course, he hadn't ever presented himself to me as a father. What a delicate matter. I felt a little subdued. Still, I tried to comfort him. 'This is an ordinary operation. In advanced countries it is a simple, routine procedure, and you know that very well.'

'But from far away everything seems to be more serious than it is,' he said. 'I have only fathered him. Since he did not live with us there were long periods when I forgot his existence. But as I am growing older certain fears have arisen, making me nervous. I don't know why, but I fear I will die alone in a dark chamber. Even if I shout myself hoarse no one will bring me a glass of water. Sometimes I take out the boy's photograph and look at it minutely. I feel a surge of affection. Where was it all these days?'

What could I say in response? I was being devastated inside. I sat in silence. Then I got up abruptly. 'I'll be off. Actually, I am really not feeing well.'

'Why?' For the first time he tried to dissuade me. 'You have taken time off to come here, and you will leave now? Nina, what a whimsical girl you are. You tend to indulge your restlessness.'

'Please, I will come another day,' I said, moving towards the door. 'Please don't take it otherwise. I am not okay.'

'I will not oppose your spontaneity,' he said, 'but I will not hesitate to tell you that your behaviour has hurt me.'

At these words, I turned about at the door and again sat down on the sofa, covering my face with my hands. Very affectionately, he covered my hand with his. 'You probably came to tell me something. Go ahead and lighten your burden. Why do you expect a situation to be exactly the way you imagine? Often, you have to adapt and get on with what you want to do.'

'Actually, I have slipped into a terrible crisis,' I almost whispered. 'I don't know how to put it,' I said, casting distracted, bewildered eyes at him. As on other days, he listened calmly. He sat in his own chair. Shifting to one side of the sofa, I gently wiped the dust off the plastic flowers in a vase.

'One evening I came down with a bad fever,' I began. 'There was no one else in the house. I did not know how to go on. There! I've lost the thread. Why are your eyes so calm?'

I braced myself again. 'What happened is that I was utterly desolate. As the evening deepened, Rezaul turned up out of the blue.'

There was a damp, musty odour. A sliver of light penetrated the window and glittered on the table. I placed my hand in the warm light.

'After a delicate incident that day I can feel something growing within me.' I looked at him with complete trust . . . 'What will I do now?'

As my words trailed off he turned into an unmoving wooden statue. He sat self-absorbed. There was no flicker of emotion in his expression, nor a reassuring impassivity. A tray filled with tea and snacks arrived. The maid left the things and quietly withdrew. Having made my confession, I felt light. The next episode was entirely my interlocutor's. Without touching anything else I picked the teacup and held it tightly in both hands. I raised it to my lips and sipped nervously.

'Listen, Nina,' he began after unobtrusively picking up his cup of tea. 'I will not raise any questions regarding the start of this business because I am not familiar with the situation or your position. But I have to admit I was not prepared for this, so I feel nervous talking about it, and I am amazed because I knew that in this one matter you could not stand Rezaul.'

'I will not be able to explain it either,' I said in a tremulous voice, 'but in that situation nothing else could have happened.'

I began to feel cold. With numb hands I replaced the cup on the tray.

He was half reclined on his sofa. Deep within, my soul resonated with the sound of water. My lips were parched. A continuous, mild tremor played over my entire being. I gazed at him in profound agitation. His decision would decide heaven or hell for me.

'Have you heard the story of that magician?'

'For heaven's sake, please don't tell me any more stories,' I objected.

'Relax,' he advised and became relaxed and easy. 'Listen, I believe that any kind of firmness helps one overcome many complications. If something originates in weakness, instead of allowing it to thrive in weakness one should firmly nurture the simple truth within oneself so that it grows naturally. Am I getting across anything?'

'No.'

'If I want to acquire comprehensive knowledge about how the body has grown or how this world functions, it will take thousands of years. When the life that throbs in us is snuffed out the world that we see also vanishes. Understan ing this process will take up millions of lifetimes. But you can destroy an embryo or a soul with the single stroke of a weapon, and this is entirely your own decision. Just as I cannot pounce on your enemy with the rage that you feel, I will not be able to embrace someone with the love that you feel for them. So the decision is yours.'

The chips were pulverized between my fingers. I picked them up one by one and crumbled them. I felt feverish. Often my interlocutor surreptitiously used a handkerchief to blow his nose. Still, I wanted him to be attentive towards me and made efforts to direct his attention.

I felt like sitting cross-legged at his feet and praying to

him to come down as well. Awareness of this desire brought a cluster of dark shadows into my heart. My heart raced, I could not speak.

'Have you read Sudhin Datta's poem, "Camel-Bird"? Some of its lines go like this: "You hear me well: and yet you try/ To hide within the desert's fold./ . . . This ruin is our heritance:/ A line of spendthrifts went before;/ They picked the pounds and left no pence:/ Now both of us must pay their score."'*

A storm brewed in my mind. I almost screamed: 'Why are you making me listen to this? I can't figure out which path I should take, where I will find myself. Besides, I have no idea who has incurred a debt or how I have to pay it back.'

'First, determine which path you will take. Then that path will take you to your final destination.'

'You are being frivolous . . .' Again I was nearly screaming. 'Can't you feel what a state I am in now? Are you resorting to pretence to evade responsibility?'

'Have I ever taken on responsibility?' he rejoined patiently. 'Nina, why belittle yourself? Is it possible to take responsibility for you? The question of taking such responsibility arises only in the case of one who leans on someone. You are sufficient unto yourself. I have never seen you lean on anybody, nor have I thought of you like that.'

'I am also human, I can be worn out or exhausted.' I seemed to implode; I laid down my weary head on the sofa.

'Nina, the world's most amazingly complex text is a human being. One does not know what is within one's powers. At this moment you must overcome weariness, more than anything else. Let me explain. In the situation in which you find yourself, you will be publicly pilloried by society, by the religious

*Translation of 'Utpakhi' by the poet.

establishment, by your neighbourhood. Will you submit to their persecution?'

'Then what will I do?'

'You will fight.' His voice was loud and clear. 'The foetus that has taken shape can be easily destroyed. Nurturing a child is the real challenge. The child will grow in your womb, you will give birth one day. And all the social battles that will erupt over the child have to be faced—and by yourself. That is the position in which I want to see you.'

'That is very difficult,' I said, subsiding into a dark abyss.

'The Nina I know,' he went on with resolution in his voice, 'will traverse this difficult path. Why should something that the civilized world accepts, and even celebrates joyously, arouse disgust over here? Why should we even countenance such reactions? I want that the struggle should start with you.'

Hazy shadows lay before my eyes. The way I was being inwardly fragmented, it was becoming difficult to keep myself in good trim before society.

'Have you stopped painting again?' It seemed he was trying to lighten up things by changing the subject.

'No,' I replied without raising my head.

'Nina, I am an ancient tree. Worms have devoured my roots.' His voice was solemn, melancholy. 'My branches break off at the mere flapping of birds' wings.'

Shadows had spread all around. With distracted eyes I glanced at the off-white distemper on the wall. The falcon on the wall sat still, plumb in front of me.

I got up from the sofa and went over to Irfan Chacha. What a wise, affectionate appearance. I took his hand, sat on the floor and drew his hand to my face. Sobs heaved up from deep within. My eyes were smarting. He silently ran his fingers through my hair. 'Nina,' he addressed me in a steady yet despairing tone, 'after spending a lifetime on a futile quest

334

I have found what I was looking for. If I had made the discovery at a certain age I would probably have imprisoned it in the hope of possessing it completely. But now I am happy just to watch it from a distance. That I have discovered it is happiness enough.'

'What if I turn into foam?' I rejoined, emerging from a dark crevice.

He gave a tender smile. 'To be able to say "So be it" the sannyasi had to be of mature years. Age lends one the courage to accept or to ignore. Do not lean on anyone, Nina. Now is the best time for you to know yourself, to discover yourself. Be completely alone. Keep the world with you, but never set it above yourself.'

'But is it possible to survive alone while the world is with you? Will not cruel loneliness propel me towards death?'

Irfan Chacha's tender hand was still on my head. His melancholy voice resonated in the entire room. 'Have you ever been anything but alone? A devotee makes an idol. After days of unrelenting toil, when the idol is installed in all its glory, brightening the space around it, the devotee exclaims ecstatically that he is its maker. "Here is the embodiment of divine beauty before which I shall pass my days." But who is then face-to-face with the idol? A decrepit shadow of the devotee. He has grown impoverished giving all he had to shape the divine form. He wants to contemplate the idol's divine loveliness. He reaches out his hand to touch her. But why should the exquisite goddess allow the doddery old man to touch her? He will touch only the clay or stone, pigment or painted coir with which he had shaped the goddess.'

My senses had become dulled. I stood up.

Irfan Chacha was still in full flow. 'If I could regain my youth and had your opportunity, I would get into the fray without any hesitation. Ninety-nine per cent of people become householders and give birth to potential householders. There is no creativity in this.'

I went up to the door. He came up with slow, steady steps and stood still in the dark doorway. Then, as usual, I descended the steps into the world of the evening. In the amber glow of sodium lights, through massed fog, I walked alone, as usual.

∾

I returned to my room and broke down in tears. After many days I cried ceaselessly till late at night, when exhaustion overwhelmed me. It seemed that the world had become empty. But the source of that emptiness could not be found, no matter how hard I tried. All I knew was that I was now alone. The massive tree that had stood like an umbrella shading me had been uprooted and removed. Utter loneliness stretched throughout the world. There was a knock on the door. Shanu had come out, perhaps because she had heard sounds from my room or had seen the light. I sat up in bed. She sat down close to me and asked what I had decided.

'Nothing,' I said and turned my face to the wall.

'Just as you are an expert at doing wicked things, your stubbornness is one hundred per cent. There is time yet; get rid of it.'

The folds on her forehead swelled with annoyance. I remained quiet.

'Your Kamal Bhai knows a pir,' she continued. 'Come along with us tomorrow. Go to him and humbly beg the forgiveness of Allah.'

'Will the baby in my tummy vanish into thin air, then?' I said sarcastically.

'Just listen to her words!' Shanu was getting worked up. 'There is such a thing as penance. Not in my wildest dreams could I imagine you to be so characterless. Your Kamal Bhai is downright apprehensive that he might become a scapegoat. He says you are a dangerous character.'

'Go to the pir and pray for him,' I said. 'After all, a woman has died because of him.'

Hardly had I finished before Shanu launched a counter-attack. While launching a broadside of typical abuse she virtually pounced on me. At one point Kamal Bhai came out in a lungi whose knot needed redoing. He dragged Shanu away and told me bluntly: 'You have got to move out soon. That's my final word.' Then their door slammed shut.

Shanu's ceaseless muttering reached my ears. I clutched a pillow and lay like a corpse. My head was spinning. There was smoke around the place. The battle was about to start then. Thousands of irate figures had lined up in front. Mother's terrified, pale face, Arefin's startled eyes, Montu, Ranu . . . Then the stage décor changed. Trembling with fear, I fell right in front of Father. Just before his death he was showing something through the open door.

There was such terror in his eyes that in that moment I realized what death was. No, I had to live! Who knows when my insomniac nights would make me raving mad? I turned off the light and clung to the bed, desperately closing my eyes. A gorgeous idol came to life down a path plunged in endless darkness. The retching started again. There was acute pain in the arteries at my temples. I sat up hurriedly. I felt so utterly destitute. There was no sky above me, no earth beneath. Where would I stand? Did I really want to stand in the shade of a tree? Has anyone been deceiving me? Do I myself know what message I had hoped to hear when I ran to the door?

Everything was okay with the world, everyone was okay. I was the odd one out. Again I felt a twinge of pain to the left of the stomach. I rolled on the bed. At one point I began to get exhausted and then I heard Mother crying. When Father lay paralysed, the closed end of a condom was cut open; one end of it was fitted on his penis, the other on a pipe, and that is how he could pass urine without getting out of bed. He was worse than a child then. Mother used to strip him and clean him up in front of everyone. But he had become so bloody-minded that he would upset everything with a sweep of his good leg. As a result the whole room stank horridly. He wasn't allowed a normal diet, so to compensate he would ask a boy to fetch things from the local shop, and the invariable result was a bad attack of diarrhoea. Unable to cope, Mother would cry softly all day, making our lives even more miserable. Another aspect of Father's irritability and peskiness startled us when we discovered one day that even in his decrepit state he desired sex with Mother. So strong was the urge that in reaction to Mother's irate unwillingness he had taken to upsetting the pipes and tubes and containers. He would then put his hand under the lungi and openly start to masturbate. Mother's deep sobs would shake the atmosphere . . . Tonight I heard exactly those sobs in my room. In this lonely night, wasn't it possible to magic away the baby beneath the skin with a mantra? No, let me instead talk to Mahim there—Mahim, who in his friend's palatial home first thrilled me with a kiss and then said, 'You are Nature. Your hair is grass. Your skin, flesh, bindi . . . these are earth, sunlight . . . I want to kiss . . . no, not lips, for these are the hallowed steps of a temple . . .'

These were suffocating thoughts. As a result of his irrepressible urge to extend his tactile explorations on the sofa, one of my earrings fell off. A search followed, on the sofa, in the whole room, but where was the earring?

I fell asleep and dreamt I had strangled the baby as soon as it was born. Waking up in the middle of the night, I felt my stomach in a panic. A thousand pigs from the sweepers' colony leapt over Chandana's wall of wails to rush towards the railway tracks. The horror of infanticide stunned me completely. 'After murdering your friend Atish in a dream why were you desolate for days on end even in your waking hours? My question is, why are you a murderer even in your dreams?'—Where had I read these words?

A mosquito had got in through a tear in the mosquito net. It sounded like a factory siren. The wailing from the basti gradually became a melancholy whine. Mahim made a woman of me, but there must have been something amiss, otherwise how could Ranu replace me so suddenly? He did not love me. Is it because I had no place in the depths of his being that his shadow within me became dead, spectral? The thought had already occurred to me—has that shadow died, has it vanished even now? An adolescent girl who had just been initiated into love used to drench the moonlight with her ceaseless, anguished cries. No matter how rude the reality that occupied her subsequently, could the early memories so easily be wiped away? Was Irfan Chacha, then, an evolved manifestation of Mahim? Were human beings such lifelong pessimists that they could only seek the shadow of one person in another? I had offered the whole of my being to Mahim. He could have had his way with me just as he pleased, but he would take my hand in his with such delicacy, as it if were a child's hand, liable to suffer injury at the slightest carelessness. I was not in the world of his love. Then where was I—in his affections? Driving me into the shade, was Ranu the one really full of love? O Allah, why was that man knocking on my door now? Why are his paintings flying around me, fading away, disappearing?

One day the two of us took a long rickshaw ride. He was extremely self-absorbed. We left the huge hospital buildings behind. I wanted to know what the matter was. He gazed at me in such a way that his eyes were filled with wonderful affection, as if I were a little girl and he was in a dilemma, trying to figure out how he could break the news so that I would be least hurt. He told me of his own inadequacy, he said he did not know of its source. Somebody had lifted me up into space and hurled me down. That's when I discovered that the girl that was me had left no shadow on his existence. That tremulous kiss, those endless rickshaw rides, the childish excitement over drawing and painting . . . the whole thing was my solitary dream. Superseding everything, Ranu had grown up. Then a long time passed by. Ceaseless tears were shed over Maitreyi Devi's *It Does Not Die: A Romance*. Having lost a Mircea from my own life I repeatedly muttered the name . . . Mircea, Mircea . . . How did Rezaul dredge me out of such a shameful, dream-laden anguish? 'Do you want to be Mircea?' I asked Mahim. He pirouetted in space: 'Yes, yes, I do.'

'Then take my child in your arms. Be the love-dad of this love-child.' I opened up my stomach to take the child out. So much blood! I looked about frantically. Mahim had decamped through the window. Laughing hysterically, I thrashed about in a deep ditch, helplessly. The mosquito netting seemed like earthen walls and earthen ceiling. I was in a grave. I raised the sides of the mosquito net. The odour of salted hilsa fish came in from somewhere. Good grief! I sat up, pressing a pillow against my nostrils. The chill intensified. My teeth were chattering. The falcon with glowing eyes sitting on the wall suddenly advanced on me. I stood up on the floor. Why was my heart burning like this? My mouth filled with bitter water. My head swayed. Staying so long in the dark made the shadows look lighter now. I pulled up a chair and sat down, put my head down on the table. 'Ma, Mother . . .' After many days I uttered the heart-wrenching cry. If only that scrawny old woman would place an affectionate hand on my head.

I stared at that hand with a beggar's longing. A thousand waves racked me inside. What had I gone to ask from Irfan Chacha? What was the true shape of his influence on my life? I could not fathom such questions.

Where did these strange, disgusting smells come from? My nose automatically shrank. I stood up. Timidly, I opened the front door. I inhaled the chilly breeze. I stood on the veranda. In the grey half-light I noticed that a creeper at the other end of the veranda was wet with dew. I pulled the shawl tightly around me. In front lay the silent, dark basti, rows of hovels, the mellow light of lanterns, heaps of garbage and Kallur Ma's dead body. My body tingled. Why didn't I go to see the woman's body? Why did my attempts to escape complications only entangle me in more complications?

And yet, at one time I had walked the muddy path through the basti, gingerly stepping on bricks laid out at intervals, and sat down on a sheet spread on a tacky floor. How dirty the place was! Polythene had been used to reinforce the bamboo ceiling of the hovel. Whenever I went there, the skinny woman would be flustered no end, and when I took her son in my arms she gazed at me as if I were a superhuman or a generous dispenser of relief goods.

Did that superhuman being become scared of her dead body?

Why did Uncle commit suicide by hanging himself from a ceiling fan? How strangely the body had hung. Damn!

I got up very late. I was shocked to see what time it was. I threw away the quilt and leapt from the bed. My head felt heavy. Going to work in winter was sheer agony. If only I could sleep all day. I was so weary. With one hand I brushed my teeth and splashed water with the other. There was some rice left over from the previous evening. I would fry an egg to go with it. When I went into the kitchen I found both cookers being used by Shanu. And yet, her daily habit was to finish her cooking before I got up. Breaking the egg into a bowl I said, 'Please take down the pot.'

'I'm cooking rice in it.'

'What's on the other cooker?'

'Bhaji.'

'Look here, don't try to start a fight. One of the cookers is for my use.'

'Buy your own cooker. I bought this one.'

'Then I'll also buy a double cooker. You'll have to move yours to make room.'

'Very well,' she said and calmly went on stirring the vegetable. I shoved her aside and replaced the pot of rice with my frying pan. Before I could pour in the oil she gave me a push, overturning the pan. That did it. The blood rushed to my head. I hurled her to the ground. Before her howls could bring Kamal Bhai to her aid I stomped out of there.

I walked for some time in state of stupefaction. Gradually I came back to my senses. Shanu was surely broadcasting the news of my sinful act to the whole neighbourhood. My feet slowed down at the thought. To hell with the office, I thought. Let me go back and make up. I stood still for a while. Then I had a flash of illumination. After Kallur Ma's death Shanu had become even more aware of her vulnerability. She wouldn't dare tittle-tattle about my personal life, because she knew her own weakness vis-à-vis Kallur Ma.

I got on a bus. I was burning from head to foot. Still, there was a sense of unease over Shanu: What if she had lost consciousness? Then my life as a fugitive would start right now.

I ate a bun and a sweet at the office and buried my face in my restlessness. I couldn't concentrate on anything. I had just taken my first sip of tea when Barua Babu came up laughing and asked, 'There is a Hanuman-like fellow who often comes to see you. Who is this creature?'

'I presume you are talking of Omar.' I cooked up a lie. 'At one time we used to live in the same neighbourhood. The two families are very close.'

'Some character,' Barua Babu added, pulling up a chair and sitting down. 'He seems to come out of a coal mine every day.'

'He is like that,' I said.

'What is the matter—the boss isn't paying you much attention?' . . . Barua Babu was off on another track . . . 'He used to call you all the time for some work or the other.'

'Maybe there is no work he can ask me to do.'

The person we had been talking about, the Hanuman, suddenly came in. I was red hot with rage from head to foot. Barua Babu got up with a snigger and left. Omar sat down. 'I have come to give you some news.'

'To hell with your news. Please get out.'

'Why. What have I done?'

'This is an office where decent people work. Your filthy rags may be all right in a basti but not here.'

He listened in silence. 'You could explain that in a soft voice,' he said calmly.

His reply further inflamed me. 'Are you a child? Am I your guardian? Explain in a soft voice? Just get out. Don't come to my office again.' My head was splitting. My eyes shot flames at Omar. A couple of colleagues turned their heads to observe the tamasha. Omar silently got up and left with a pathetic, hangdog look.

After sitting still for a while I began to feel remorse. I had done something really nasty. Now began fresh anguish. I became angry with myself on account of my disquietude and instability. Wasn't my behaviour dragging me down into worse loneliness, into a more terrible void?

After work I dragged myself down the stairs. Why couldn't I be stable and calm? Standing on the front steps of the office

I faced a vast crowd of people. And among them, to one side of the steps, I spotted Omar, cowering meekly. What a relief! I beamed at him. That was enough to bring him round. He hurried over. 'I got a real scare! Still, I did not go away. After all, how long could anger last?'

It was getting dark. We got on a rickshaw. It pedalled against the cold wind. 'What news did you bring?' I asked.

'Two things,' said Omar enthusiastically, 'My younger sister has got a job in a tailoring establishment and I have got a job in a garments factory. It is nearly final. I join next month. A supervisor's post. Strange similarity in the jobs of brother and sister. We will stitch up all the doors to evil in this world.'

I was delighted. 'Really great news. Is it the same garments factory that belongs to your wealthy friend, the one who gave you some printing jobs?'

'Yes, yes,' Omar nearly screamed. 'After I couldn't make any headway in business I fell at his feet. "Please do something," I begged. "Or else there is no alternative to death."'

I felt depressed. This fellow knew nothing of the trick of standing tall and proud. Or else, even if he did fall at his friend's feet, he wouldn't have mentioned it so frankly. The rickshaw was going through an alley. Omar said he would get off nearby. 'Will you be able to go alone the rest of the way?' I ignored his question and was sunk in my own thoughts. 'Please look for accommodation for me,' I said suddenly as he was leaving. 'As soon as possible—a cheap one-room flat.'

'But where you are staying . . .' Omar hesitated.

'The atmosphere there has become intolerable,' I said. 'They cannot accept anything about me in a natural way.'

A shadow passed over Omar's face. He stood stock-still, thinking. This still posture of his was very attractive. He

344

seemed to come back to the real world gradually. 'Will you live alone?' he asked.

I laughed. 'First let me move in alone.'

I found myself in front of Cynthia's huge mansion. I couldn't tell when I had changed my own decision. A complex turmoil had been set off within me by the scene I had witnessed. Of course I couldn't find any connection between that and my decision to give up the tutor's job. Besides, I had the additional burden of the loan from Irfan Chacha. Arefin was doing a very ordinary job, and yet I had relinquished the responsibility for the family to him. As a result, for the past few months I had been leading a relatively easy life. Anyway, how long could one live on potato, *potol* and *chorchori*? The mattress and sheets had been reduced to tatters. It had been days since I last bought anything. In this situation, how could I justify giving up the tutor's job?

While crossing the lawn I heard the sound of loud conversation and waves of exciting music coming from within. White orchids clambered up from the veranda. Through the open window I could clearly see a party in progress. There was a continuous tinkle of glasses and bottles. The world's handsomest and loveliest people had gathered there. Some were in conversation in pairs or groups, others were dancing. What a glittering scene! It was enchanting. The women had strange hairdos and varied attire. As far as one could see, it was a different world altogether. A grotesque-looking fellow was also dancing, swaying his massive hips, while he held a glass in one hand. Liveried servants scurried up and down the veranda. One of them stopped when he saw me. When I put a finger to the lips, counselling silence, he hurried away. Only one part of the party was visible from where I stood. Such laughter! Even if it was forced laughter, it would surely add to their longevity. Everyone was laughing. That unfamiliar rhythm bewitched me. What exquisite perfumes! Those elderly women who were concealing their age with the help of close-fitting attire and trying to drown everything in screams and loud chatter; the hideous-looking man who was unconcerned about his appearance as he danced—how many people were capable of doing such things?

Anyway, by now my attention had shifted to my own person. The sari I was wearing, the clerkish tiredness in my face—it would be a disaster if these were noticed by someone from the household. And if I were to reach the party in my present state—well, may the earth split beneath me and swallow me up. I was about to turn back when I heard the shrill laughter of Cynthia's mother. I could see her through the window. She was in a white chemise and pink dhoti, and had presumably permed her hair at a beauty parlour. With her buxom figure she was quite a sight. As she spoke to a gentleman her laughter too was broadcast all round.

I re-crossed the lawn and left. The night was foggy, the road deserted for some distance. The habit of getting back late had diminished my fear of the night somewhat. Still, a lonely spot always made me nervous. A mangy bitch was whining as it walked down the street. I wanted to walk fast till I came to the main street. Suddenly there was a voice behind me. My heart began to flutter. Two casually dressed boys with earrings and drugged voices asked, 'Are you Cynthia's tutor?'

'Yes,' I said nervously.

'Do you have 100 taka?' one of them wanted to know. 'After all, you are Cynthia's tutor, so we are not mugging you. We need the money badly.'

The road was deserted. One or two pedestrians passing by walked straight, without noticing anything. In spite of a chilling fear in my breast I asked, 'Why, to buy drugs?' One of the boys, who had a scar on a cheek and wild hair, laughed uproariously as he took the money and then said, 'Can you help us in connection with Cynthia?' I stole glances to the right and the left. The crowded main street was a short distance away.

'Help with what?' By now my blood had begun to evaporate!

'We want to teach her a lesson.' The other repeated the original request, 'Can you help us?'

'What kind of help?' My voice was shaky.

I could clearly see that the boys were swaying drunkenly. The void of the entire road was inside my heart. Then one of them threw a few words at me like a knife. 'This place is not safe. You come with us.'

My feet had become glued to the ground. In my anxiety and terror, sweat had congealed on my body. Meanwhile, another youth had joined the first two. Noticing my inertia, one of them flung away the mask of politeness and hissed through clenched teeth, 'What's up—doesn't sound reach your ears?'

I forced myself to walk along the concrete road. Suddenly I recalled an incident in our small mofussil town. A couple were returning at midnight from the late-night film show. At knifepoint the husband did not make any noise. A group of boys dragged his wife to a school playground. The incident caused a sensation in the town. Curiosity drove me as well to the hospital to see the woman. She lay with eyes shut, deliriously shouting, 'Move away, move away from top of me. Oh, I cannot breathe. Move away . . .'

I felt as if someone had driven a nail into my skull. While following the ruffians a sound like a groan escaped my lips. 'Please let me go.'

'Why are you scared?' The scar-faced boy asked in a rustic accent. 'We'll only explain something important.' A short way from the street they stopped at a half-built wall. Seeing the wall my heart seemed to come to a stop. With a piteous look I fell at the feet of one of the boys, 'Let me go!' Swaying as he pulled me to my feet, the boy elbowed me in the middle of my chest. At once the two others came up and putting their hands on my trembling body said, 'Why are you scared? Come, we will not harm you.'

They walked ahead. Behind them my nearly dead feet moved timidly. In the dense solitude of the place the faces of the three youths swung round. One of them went through a space in the wall.

I was trembling uncontrollably. The limitless fear accumulated through all these years was now a reality facing me. Suddenly the fellow with the earring looked at me and yelled, 'We are showing respect and it means nothing to you? We'll just shove it in. Come...' When his grotesque yell was about to drive my soul-bird away, a car drove down the lane with the headlights on. The two boys ran through the wall, and I ran desperately in the opposite direction.

The car sped away. The incident was exactly like something in a film. A zigzag light dragged me out of an abyss. I do not know how I covered the long distance. With my sweat-drenched, weightless body and tremulous heart I paused in the brightly lit main street and took deep breaths. Suddenly there was a sound behind me. In a panic I turned around. A man power-walked by. The darkness was deepening. Did I have a nightmare, from which I had now woken up? My whole body was swaying in an animal stupor. Everything was becoming shadowy. Eventually, staggering in a terribly confused state, I stood before my own door.

Where was I at the end of the day? My brain was still throbbing to the hideous rhythms of the music in Cynthia's house. After all that had transpired, what kind of peace was waiting for me? My eyes brimmed with tears. I couldn't knock at once.

Kamal Bhai answered the door. As usual, he did not speak to me. The thought was enough to disgust me thoroughly—

how could I live with these uneducated people all these days? As he withdrew I put down my bag and went straight to the bathroom. The day before I had braved the stench of the fish market to buy pomfrets. I had fried them last night. I couldn't heat them in the morning. It being winter, the fish hadn't gone off. There was just a hint of staleness in the smell. I fried it till it was crisp and mixed it with rice. Not a bad dinner.

When I was in bed after washing up, I heard Shanu in the kitchen. With the light on I held a two-day-old newspaper to my face. Large headlines declared that the occupying forces of Saddam Hussain were facing a debacle. In some time I had got over the shock of the attack by the boys. I folded the paper and turned off the light. I placed a hand on my stomach. It wasn't yet time for the foetus to be palpable. It lay there quietly. Still, I touched here and there to see if I could feel it. What a thrilling experience. I saw myself walking along a long country footpath. A sharp breeze whistled around me. Rice fields stretched away, one after another. At a brick kiln I saw a peepul tree reach straight upward. Beneath it sat someone like a pir, meditating. I drew near on nervous feet. His thunderous voice rent the air: 'Beg pardon from Allah!' I pierced the dark to take a stand, 'For what?'

'Bitch! . . . Heretic! . . . If you don't admit guilt you will end up in hell.'

I woke up feeling cold. I pulled up the blanket and lay motionless for a long while. At one point I tore through the amber shadow of narrow-mindedness and arose. I had reached an unenclosed hamlet. But why was I dreaming of the countryside? The connection between my childhood and the country was very slight. My grandparents died before I was born. Among my memories the only ones associated with the country were the long flame of a *kupi*, heavy rain outside and my step-grandmother's white anchal covering her head.

It was in another life that I had visited the country. The pir's cosmic voice rent my breast. I tossed and turned. But my suffering abated as a burst of breeze touched me, and in my dream I could rebel and ask why I should apologize.

After that, with every passing day my life became poisoned by crisis after crisis. The child was growing. A terrible fear gripped my entire being. I couldn't reach any stability. A few days ago I gave up the tutoring job. An impossible affection welled up for Cynthia. She was walking a razor's edge. Did she understand anything? But even though I stopped going to her, a hidden fear remained. What if I ran into those ruffians again? Would the police help me? Arefin had said to me that when there is a gunfight on campus, the police stand idle and watch the fun.

At Satyajit's adda one day the talk was on related matters. 'Every government gets into power through election-rigging. Would democracy ever come to our country? . . . Rubbish! All fake!' Satyajit slammed the table. Shahtab's argument was different. 'Shall we fold our arms and sit tight? Shall we condone the chaos day after day? Will we not protest?'

'Yes, go ahead and protest. You are your mother's virile son. When you get shot your parents will not even get your dead body.'

'But we are the living dead—what is the solution to that? Better to protest and die. Have you noticed, Satyajit, that with its burden of debts Bangladesh is worth nothing on the world market? Are we alive? Even dogs and foxes are more alive than us.'

'Whichever party comes to power, it will have the same character. The same rush to grab benefits. Show me one party with which you would like to replace this one. Is there anyone with character?'

Such arguments went on all the time. I was a silent listener. I felt one had to know politics well in order to accept or dismiss something. Since I knew nothing about it I was completely indifferent.

I stopped going to Irfan Chacha's. There was a spear always stuck in my chest. At work I continuously fought nausea, looking about fearfully lest someone noticed. I hid behind a newspaper. Thousands of Iraqis died at the hands of American soldiers and disappeared without a trace. Sultana was absorbed in her files. If only I could eat some raw mangoes?

Under the headline 'Bestial' there was a report on a youth who had raped a three-year-old. The office was calm today. Even Barua Babu was busy plying his pen. The retching became more violent. Surreptitiously, I felt my stomach. The ice cubes have started walking through the current of blood. The President standing in front of a mosque: a huge photograph. He is shown praying with other pious Muslims. A woman dies at the hands of muggers. No sign of an end to the bloodshed provoked by the demolition of the Babri Mosque.

'At last Saddam has agreed to an unconditional withdrawal from Kuwait. World heaves a sigh of relief.'

Amidst all this there were a thousand words screaming about the birth of my child: 'A woman has claimed that she is the father of a child.'

The retching was more violent than ever. I felt like ducking under the table.

'Youth lynched for stealing a light bulb.' Barua Babu walked over. 'Can you lend me a hundred?'

'I can manage fifty.'

'That'll do.'

For some days now the child has become desperate to eat sweets. I was again nauseated. I lowered my head. Barua Babu took the money and left with a 'thank you'. 'Bus plunges into a ditch near Aricha, killing fifty.' And statements by various parties. 'The movement to preserve democracy must be sustained at all costs.' Omar and Shahtab shared the same view: Are we alive? When I folded the paper there was another anxiety: What if Arefin is shot dead? This thought was rent by three wild-haired boys revolving like ghosts and flashing knives in the light. They dragged me towards a wall.

The next day as I sat down in my chair a sharp wind from the river pricked me. The pink palace of a nawab. Tears rose to my eyes. Why was I so sleepy? On a whim I went over to Sultana's desk and sat down opposite her. 'Why do you look so fatigued?' she asked. Instead of replying to her question I asked her, 'Do you know anything about M.R.?' At once I realized I had committed a blunder. 'Why?' she asked in surprise.

I checked myself. 'No, I mean, the people from whom I have sublet a room—the woman wants to have it done. She was asking me to find out how it's done.'

'How many months?' Sultana wanted to know.

'Two and a half or three.' I broke into a sweat as I spoke.

'Then it's not very developed. Especially if it's under three months old. But why does she want it out?'

'They have two children . . .' I felt I was suffocating. Did I ever talk to her about Shanu's inability to conceive? Sultana's expression was normal. 'It's done in clinics all the time. She can have it done in hospital also. It's a simple procedure. A thin tube is inserted and twisted and then a spray is used to clean up the womb.'

'Does the tube penetrate the child's body?' I mumbled.

Sultana looked at me with doubled astonishment. 'What's that? What are you calling a child? It has just become a foetus. Two and a half or three months—isn't that what you said?'

352

I came out to the street full of chaotic thoughts. After walking a considerable distance in a troubled state I asked myself what I really wanted. Why was I scattering the venom that was inside me? Suddenly on the right I noticed the sign on a clinic. On it was written: 'M.R. Done Here.' I asked the rickshaw to stop at once. In order to know the details I asked the rickshaw to wait and put a foot on the steps. My head was throbbing. Sultana's amused eyes were hanging in space. As I was about to go up a huge tube went in, piercing my child's body and then twisting and turning it mashed up my child, its faint heartbeats ceased with a horrible spasm.

I came back to myself. In a strange imaginary game I make Nina squat facing Irfan Chacha. His heavy yet gentle hands are wet with my tears. The rickshaw pedalled along. Somebody had stuffed all the office files into my head. Crushed beneath that pile, I was invisible. If only I could hide like that! Suddenly it seemed that a shadow was following me. Dusk had fallen as soon as I came out of the office. The lights had come on. A half-dead half-moon floated above the light. Someone was hurling me through the office window. Last night a throbbing headache had kept me awake till the small hours. As soon as I dozed off there were nightmares. Sometimes my dead child would assume another form in my womb. This gave me a thrilling sensation beneath the skin. Sometimes he walked unsteadily and then had a pratfall, but more often, because of his growing size I was detected by the world's eyes in a terrified posture. One night I clearly saw some kurta-clad men bury me up to the throat and then stone me to death. Since then I have had a continuous headache. These horrid dreams left me drained of energy.

As soon as I left the office one day, the pain seemed to move away. I went past the rickshaws, cars, people, to reach the bus stop. Again, the pressure on the head. You have the pampered body of a nawab, do you? I chided myself, but had to take a rickshaw eventually. Besides, I realized how risky it was to wrestle in and out of buses at this stage. And soon after I sensed that the ruffian with the earring might be tailing me. My blood ran cold. For much of the journey I sat trembling. After a while I could not see the boy any more. I was relieved that we had reached the wide road in front of the university. I could not take the usual route because digging was going on there. I inhaled deeply and looked up at the sky. The dying sun had painted it in magnificent colours. The spreading black leaves of the *koroi* trees had spotted the sky like flocks of deer. The rickshaw turned left, again draining me of blood. That boy was on a rickshaw behind mine, smoking a cigarette. I observed carefully—no, it was another boy. After a while it went off in a different direction. Though I stopped sweating, for a while after I got home I could not calm down.

Shadows of this sort continued to startle me. At night the nightmares got worse. One day I felt like knocking on Shanu's door. I felt like hugging her and humbly making peace. But her behaviour had crossed all limits of tolerance. If I touched anything of hers in the kitchen she started washing it at once. That drove me round the bend. In such a situation the hassle of shopping in the fish market, the privation involved in sending money home, the inability to buy a new bed sheet or a cotton sari sapped all the strength out of me. How much could one ignore?

Above everything, there was an all-encompassing anguish that cannot be expressed in words or in the form of familiar pain. I am not habituated to using the telephone. Phoning from a coin box is irritating, so I try to avoid it. I don't recall when Irfan Chacha had given me the number. I stood in a telephone booth in Motijheel. Excitement filled my eyes with tears. I dropped a coin and dialled the number. I heard a woman's voice at the other end. But after I asked for him there was a long silence. People in the queue outside the booth were getting restless. Just then came the indescribably robust voice—'Hello.'

'Hello, hello . . .' An anxious voice at the other end. I listened to his rich baritone in silence. I hung up, my hands shaking. I walked all the way back. When I got home I lay face down in bed. Shanu and I had stopped talking. The atmosphere at home was unbearable. The retching and dizziness had decreased. Instead, there was a feeling of heaviness in the middle. An iron hook had fastened itself on my liver. A monstrous preternatural creature pressed me from below. On top of all this there was a psychological complication—I could not attain any goal.

Amidst such fragmentariness, I came upon Omar one day. 'Will you take responsibility for my child?' I asked. The words startled him. He looked at me in bewilderment. We were sitting in a tea-stall. Vapour coiled up from the cups. 'You have a problem with the child's paternity, isn't that so? But do I have the ability to do anything?'

I felt weak and sleepy. It was smoky all around, and a complex mental torment weighed me down. The eyes gazing at me were round, vicious. What if the boys had dragged me behind the wall?

'Why are you asking for pity?' Omar asked. 'I know I am an utterly insignificant man. I would never have had the guts to want you. If it is society you are afraid of, then I am willing to accept paternal responsibility for the child. That would take care of the child. But what about you?'

'You all know how to play with words.' I was growing somewhat irritable. 'Words only put up walls on all four sides and I cannot find a way through.'

Omar's face was obscured by clouds of smoke. As the

waiter was removing my cup I ordered more tea. My throat was getting dry.

'I have little sense of pride or sensitivity to insults.' Omar's voice mellowed for the first time today. 'At least that's what I have always heard from others. I have sold myself in so many ways, in so many places—just for a little cash. Getting shoved and kicked around has made me thick-skinned. I do not complain about anything. But what you have said is really humiliating. You too are trying to use me. You see, it has brought tears to my eyes.'

Right in the middle of the tea-stall crowd I tightly pressed his hand where it lay on the table with both my hands. 'Believe me,' I said, 'that's not true. Don't misunderstand me. Everyone has deserted me one by one. Omar, there isn't a single man in whom I can find a companion who will enable me to live. Do I know if I love you at all? How can you presume that I will come to stand alongside you only with the inertia that you can see? I have to understand the situation bit by bit. The whole of life stretches before us.'

My tea arrived. I started sipping again. Omar was soon his usual self. 'I don't have the ability to make out the deeper significance of your words. All I can say for myself is that even if you try you will not be able to shake me off. You may call me spineless, shameless or whatever. Remember the nightingale's tale? I too can sacrifice my blood, if only because I have nothing else to give. But I cannot change myself.'

What could one say to that? What was there for me to do save turn into colder ice? But there was a worse chill awaiting me. I wiped the corner of my mouth with a handkerchief. Omar in his characteristically cheerful way said, 'Let me tell you about a tragic incident in my life. It is not something I can tell the world. Those who know me well have witnessed it at first hand, but you are the first person

I am telling it to. Then if you wish you can be even more contemptuous of me.'

Suddenly the radio in the tea-stall was turned on. A loud cinema commercial forced me to lean forward a little to be able to catch his words.

'I had a friend,' Omar began. 'I have of course told you that there are no friends in my life, that I cannot mix intimately with anyone any more. We were in class eight when we became bosom buddies. You know how poor we are—we were just as poor then. Though we were equally enthusiastic about playing truant and gallivanting about, my friend had a gift that gave me a terrible inferiority complex. He was a marvellous painter. Once he locked himself in for days to work on a painting. If anyone knocked he did not respond. When he came out for a bit he looked dishevelled and strangely self-absorbed. Every day I came back without having met him. Several months went by like this. I was lonely, companionless. Then one day my friend completed the painting. The two of us had a whip-round and raised enough money to have the picture framed. The final product was overwhelming. I will not be able to explain it adequately in words: captured within the glass frame was another world. He said it would change his life; make him rich and famous. I was devastated. I would stay behind in my hovel while he would climb the stairs to a paradisal existence. At home our poverty had reduced us to a dog-eat-dog situation. One day I stole the picture.'

The radio commercials had given way to a news bulletin. I sat with a cold hand pressed to the ear.

'Believe me, I did not do it out of envy,' Omar went on. 'I myself don't know why I did it. Selling the picture was a chastening experience. But it was too late to retrace my steps. I had to sell the picture at a throwaway price. I came home and sat like a spectre.' Omar paused. I kept gazing at him. In a climactic moment in the adda at the next table someone excitedly thumped the table and shouted, 'Mouthing secularist shibboleths while you set up an Islamic state? Disgusting!' And the radio played a nerve-soothing number.

'That night my friend committed suicide,' Omar began again. 'When I got news of my friend's death, shame and a guilty conscience nearly drove me mad. Forgetting everything—like eating and washing regularly—I sat by his grave one whole month. I used to hit my head on the ground. I put up with jokes, jeers, insults from everyone. Many years have passed since then. On the 27th of every month—the date of his death— I sit by his grave all night. Many have described it as madness. Everyone explained it was meaningless and tried to dissuade me from going there. But my heart cannot be swayed.'

As he spoke, Omar's eyes became moist again. He shook his head and declared, 'I am a greedy son of a bitch. This is how I want to do penance. You know, I can stake my life on anything. But what, after all, is the value of this ugly life of mine? I am haunted by a fear. Suppose I steal you, win you by bartering my life, but discover that though I seem to have got all that I wanted, you are not there.'

My fingerprints showed on the cup. I sat still like a deaf mute. The fog settled around us. Omar was back to the subject of his friend. 'His name was Apu. If I ransack *Pather Panchali* will I find that Apu?'

'I am also an artist,' I said calmly. 'There was a time when I would do anything to be able to paint. One day my younger brother found a pair of gold earrings . . .'

'Forget it. You need not tell me. Knowing that you paint makes me fear for myself. You must have observed that I have never expressed any enthusiasm for it.'

'Then should I give it up?' I asked him suddenly, perhaps as a test.

'Oh no, how can you even suggest it?' He seemed genuinely distraught. 'Only, it is best not to entangle a jinx like me with your passion. I am a thick-skinned ignoramus. What do I understand about such subtle things? Have you noticed, I have used this opportunity to start talking like you? Give me half a chance and I will turn into a king of the microphone. That's why people warn against petting monkeys.'

'Stop it!'

After scolding him I sit still for a long time. I am so weary I cannot even move a finger. But Omar's personality has no room for slackness. He gives himself a shake and in a moment assumes his usual, relaxed tone. 'I haven't given you the big news. See how easily I can be distracted. I have found a place for you. Of course it has been a hell of a hassle, Didi. It's a little far, but the bus service is good. There is no running water; you will have to depend on a tube well. That's why the landlord settled for 100 taka.'

I drag my numb body out of there. The two of us walk down the pavement. Father had died in the solitude of midnight. Scanning the vast crowds I seek his face. Everything is hazy. Omar is sporting an oversize jacket, a scarf, and his bristle is back on his cheeks. The sandals are a size too small. His heels protrude. I have grown used to seeing him like this. In fact, on the days he spruces up, the outcome is incongruous. Suddenly thrusting his hands into his pockets, he puckers up his nose and asks, 'So, are you coming tomorrow to see the house?'

'Yes. Pick me up in the morning. We will travel through the fog.'

Then come the narrow alleys, drains, heaps of refuse, rotting cotton husks, ruffianly youths puffing on bidis, bloody sanitary napkins in the middle of the road, the prolonged coition of two dogs. At last Omar drops me home. I enter, stepping over a suicide, an exquisite nightingale—a martyr for love that calmly sacrificed its blood to produce a red rose—and the unbearable inner torment of another person.

I cannot sleep because of restlessness. I am torn by the perennial conflict that sucks me dry and raises me into the void, then flings me into the depths of a divided world. When my breath gets stuck I sit up in bed. My pillow has burst, scattering the cotton all over the bed. It is stuffy and airless. A cockroach scuttles across the floor. I gulp down some water. I turn on the light with unsteady fingers and set up the easel. I wipe it clean. I feel tired. I step out the door. The world is shrouded in dense darkness. I notice that a sliver of light from a lamp post has fallen on the veranda. How extraordinary is its spread. Where it has fallen, its brilliance has diluted the surrounding darkness. The fog is gathering. Nature is turning white. A cold wind. Gradually, I grow calm. I draw the shawl around my body, keeping my head erect. With curious eyes, as if I were seeing it for the first time, I keep gazing at the scene.